Millie McDine

by

Margaret Scrowther

Millie McDine

Chapter One

T he long row of terraced houses were shrouded in darkness, lit only slightly from the dull yellow glow of a street lamp. A young man with straggly, dark hair was sat in his parked van; his fingers were still wrapped around the steering wheel, his knuckles white from the force of his grip. His face creased as he lowered his head to peer at the child that lay on the seat beside him, then further still as she yawned and pushed her chubby fists into her flickering eyelids. He turned his head and focused his gaze on a building bearing the name: Beeches Guesthouse, which was situated at the end of the street.

The steering wheel was damp and clammy by the time he drew his hands away, and with his trembling fingers, he opened the clasp on the gold chain that hung around his neck and shoved it inside his jeans pocket. Opening the door, he stood for a moment, held a hand to his heaving chest and blew the stale air from between his lips. He opened the passenger-side door and lowered himself to the child, scooping her up in his arms. She tucked her head into his neck as he turned on his heel and stepped towards the guesthouse. It was a place that her head was supposed to rest forever, but chances were it would never rest there again.

Lifting his arm, he pressed his forefinger on the doorbell and stood swaying the child in his arms while he waited. The door opened and a stout woman took its place, her arms were folded and she had her hair in rollers – sign enough that she was not happy to see him here at this time of night. Maybe she wasn't happy to see him at all. Her sharp eyes narrowed behind horn-ribbed glasses and her eyebrows lowered as she peered at him.

I know you'll not be glad to see me, but please tell me Sadie is here,' he begged.

'She's not. I haven't seen her for years,' she said, clamping her lips together and lifting her hand to close the door.

He kicked his leg out and stood with his thick boot between the door and the frame, then said, 'She left us weeks ago and I thought she had come here.'

She studied him with her piercing eyes, and said, 'I remember you now. You're the gypsy that my daughter ran off with years ago, and never once wrote to me or her father to let us know how she was doing. It killed him, the stress of it all – do you know that? Look, there's no place for you here, so what are you doing standing on my doorstep with a baby?'

'She's your granddaughter, her name is Mildred.'

The colour drained from her face as she clutched her hand to her chest. With a sharp look at the child, she inclined her head and beckoned him inside the porch. He stepped inside and waited as she closed the door. As she turned around to face him, her expression was stern. 'I'll see you in the guestroom,' she said. Then she wheeled around and strode ahead.

He followed her past the reception area and walked into the guestroom, which was situated near the passageway and opposite the dining room. She lifted her hand and beckoned him to sit down. He slumped down onto a leather chair, noticing the child's eyelids flickering as she snuggled close to him.

'She left this letter,' he faltered, as he fumbled inside his trouser pocket and drew out an envelope. He passed it to Sadie's mother.

She pursed her lips as she pulled the letter out of his hand and heaved another weary sigh as she glanced at Mildred. 'It's late, no wonder the child is tired,' she said.

'I don't know what I'm going to do now,' he replied. 'Would it be possible for her to stay here until I can get something sorted?'

'What? Don't be so ridiculous. It's out of the question. The child doesn't even know me, she'll fret and I'm fifty years old. I don't have the

2

patience nor the time, not to mention the resources,' she said.

Kitty got to her feet and paced the floor, then swung around and pointed her forefinger at him. 'Sadie was a good Catholic girl, and you changed her with your sultry looks and your swagger.

She was a fool to leave, and now you don't even know where she is, what sort of relationship is that?' she asked.

The young man shook his head and said, 'My family never accepted her, plus she couldn't adjust to our way of living. It was hard in the winter, without any heating in the wooden shack. Sadie hated skinning the rabbits and washing was a problem too, we had no running water. I had to bring it from the stream and put it into a large container and boil it outside. She thought it sounded romantic, but soon realised she didn't fit in with the other women. That's why I'm begging you to help us,' he said, as he wrung his hands together.

'There's nobody else to help me, I don't have any family. This breaks my heart, have you any idea how I feel? We've been dumped and now you won't help – no wonder your daughter turned out the way she did,' he said under his breath.

Kitty faced him with her chin lifted, nostrils flared and eyes ablaze. 'Well, it looks like I've no other option, but it can only be a temporary measure. And if Sadie ever shows her face around here I will take my hand back and clash it over both her cheeks. Now, go and get Mildred's belongings – I take it you have brought them with you.'

The young man's taut face relaxed and he nodded.

'Then hurry up and go, before she wakes. What I'm going to do I don't know, but I suppose we have to get through it somehow,' she said, as she watched the sleeping baby upon him leaving the room.

On his return, he bent over and placed the bags and cases stuffed with clothes and dolls onto the floor, then he stood over his daughter, lowered himself to his knees, put his hand inside his pocket and pulled out the chain and attached the locket to it before laying it beside Mildred. 'I'll look for your mammy and we'll be back to get you,' he said, as he sniffed and swiped his brimming eyes with his hand.

'You better had,' Kitty said.

Moments later, they were headed towards the front door, the seeds of a newly-discovered life sewn and watered, the usual comforts and freedoms gone in the breeze.

As she shut the door, Kitty stood with her back to it and closed her eyes. She stood for a moment before moving away to peer once more at the child. 'Poor little soul,' she whispered, as she sunk to her knees and put her hands inside the bag. She pulled out nappies and baby clothes and then she looked inside the larger bag and heaved a sigh of relief to see that there were boxes of baby milk and plenty of bottles.

Resting her hand on the mahogany rail, she climbed the first set of winding and red carpeted stairs which lead towards the guestrooms. As she stepped along a passage towards the second staircase, she stepped through a door leading to her private apartment where she placed Mildred's belongings down onto the sitting room carpet.

Yawning, she headed back down to the guest area and hovered over the child. She drew her up into her arms and noticed a damp patch on the settee. After a quick change and a little back and forth rocking to send her back to sleep, she laid the baby down onto the settee and wiped her forehead with the back of her hand. It was definitely time for a drink.

With her finger and thumb pressed to her brow, she stepped into the lounge and crossed to the drinks cabinet. Pouring a strong drink into a glass tumbler, she slumped down onto the sofa. She took out a cigarette from a packet of Capstan Full Strength, swiped a match against the hearth, then lit the cigarette and inhaled deeply. She lowered her head to peer at the letter that she had pulled out of her pinafore pocket.

Her hand shook and her eyes filled with tears as she began to read Sadie's letter, but partway through her expression hardened to a look of fury. 'Bitch,' she hissed, as she tore the note in two and threw the two pieces of paper onto the grey ashes that lay in the grate.

She turned her attention to the other document in her lap, and unfolded the paper to discover that it was Mildred's birth certificate. She had been born on 28th of October, 1944. Kitty looked over to the sleeping child, who she could still see through the half-open doorway, and thought she looked rather old for barely being one year old.

She laid the paper on the table and sat with her arms folded, as she read that her father was called Joseph Riley. Why had this certificate been passed on to her? But there was only one reason – her daughter had no intention of returning for her baby, and now, neither did Joseph Riley. Kitty realised her mistakes almost instantly. She had been stitched up, burdened with a child, birth certificates and all, and left to her own devices, to bring up a child in a world of growing insaneness and catastrophe. Isn't that life? She thought. Isn't that just a wonderful life?

She hauled herself up and poured another stiff drink into her glass and sat smoking until her eyes became heavy. When life gives you lemons – or in this case a stranger in the form of a sleeping baby – you make lemonade, and then proceed to use that lemonade as a mixer for your liquor.

The shrill and sudden screech from Mildred woke her. Kitty jolted to her feet and ran across the hall, making it to the baby's side in ten seconds flat. As she peered at the red-faced child, kicking her legs and waving her fists, she lowered her head into her hands. 'I'm in no mood for you today madam,' she said. 'I was sound asleep.'

She unhooked her dressing gown from the door, wrapped it around herself and leaned over the child. 'Shush,' she whispered, as she swept her up to soothe her, but Mildred stiffened and turned her face away. 'I see how it is,' she said, as she put the baby down again and shook her head. She didn't have enough alcohol in her entire house to be dealing with this.

The phone in the kitchen was in her hands only a matter of seconds later, and she stood listening to the ringing sound as the line summoned a connection. There was only so much one woman could take before she needed to vent to her friends, and even at this early stage, Kitty was close enough to the edge to consider cracking out the whiskey – that was never a sign of anything good.

Hearing the sound of feet shuffling up the back stairs, Kitty turned in her seat to face a small woman with a loose permed hairstyle and a six-year-old chubby boy with dark hair. As they made their way into the room Kitty said, 'Nora, there you are, I was just trying to ring you. Can you believe what Sadie has done? I didn't even know that she had had a child. That pikey Joseph Riley came in dire straits and asked me to keep the bairn until he can get something sorted. I just can't cope with this situation, it's driving me crazy already and it's only been a matter of hours,' she moaned. Then holding up the chain and locket she said, 'He left this too.'

Nora sat with her arms folded to her chest for a moment, then holding out her hands, she snatched hold of the chain when Kitty slung it towards to her. 'Open the locket. You'll see a photograph of my daughter and her gypsy boy,' retorted Kitty lowering her eyes to the ground.

'Eh, she's his double,' announced Nora as the two women held their gaze on the two photographs.

Kevin smirked and cast a furtive glance at Kitty when she scowled and swiped the necklace from Nora's hand. 'It's going inside my wardrobe and staying in my jewellery box. I don't want to look at it or ever let Mildred know of its existence,' she spat.

Nora sat with a solemn look. 'Yes, just put it away and leave it there,' she announced as she got to her feet and walked out into the corridor. Kevin slinked behind them, his eyes following Kitty as she stepped inside her bedroom with the chain and locket in her hand. Moments later, she stepped back out and went back in the room where Mildred was fast asleep and almost looked as if she had never wailed in her life.

'She looks strange,' said Nora. 'Her eyes are wide, as though she's had a shock. You need to see the health visitor because the child looks traumatised to me.'

Kitty wrung her hands together and debated the facts. Kevin stood with his eyes raised to the ceiling. Leaning his fat body against the door-frame, he opened his mouth wide, yawning. Kitty found herself wondering what her life was coming to when she noticed his blank bored expression. He didn't have to worry about a borderline stray child she thought, suddenly finding herself jealous of a six-year-old boy.

'How can I possibly cope with her when I've been an absolute wreck since Sadie left and never returned? It's going to be impossible. It's a good job I don't have any guests staying at the moment, what with all this going on. I could murder Sadie for putting this on to me,' she whimpered, as tears sprung again to her reddened eyes.

'I don't blame you Kitty, but you have to pull yourself together. That bairn is relying on you, and I think once you have gotten over the shock of what has happened you'll be able to cope. You've got me to run this place too when things get busy, so you'll always have spare time to tend for the poor thing,' Nora said.

Kitty wiped her eyes as she turned to look at Mildred, who by this point had wriggled off the sofa and was head banging the carpet as she screamed, as if she was trying to tunnel into the basement using nothing but her skull. Kevin grinned and saw this as one big playtime, as six-year-olds always did, so he slammed himself onto the floor beside Mildred and began playing peekaboo. Still the crying persisted; the little devil was having none of it.

Kitty shook her head as she made for the door. It was time to call the doctor to get an opinion on the poor baby's health. The sound of the crying filled her ears all the way along the corridor, making it obvious to her that it was no longer a case of not having enough alcohol in her house to be dealing with this mess; it was more like there wasn't enough alcohol in *the world* to be dealing with this mess.

Chapter Two

Hunched with exhaustion after months of Mildred's behaviour, Kitty's red hair was streaked with grey. The doctor and health visitor both gave their advice after witnessing Mildred's full blown tantrums.

The health visitor was here again today. She was a big-bottomed woman with a long nose and whiskers on her chin, but despite her impressive size, still cowered as Mildred picked up her plate of food and threw it at her. The woman's hair and face were covered in potato, cabbage, meat pie and gravy. She looked like a walking food ad.

Kitty grabbed Mildred by the hand and marched her into a quiet room. Once there, she stood with her finger pointed at her and said, 'You will stay here, until you have calmed down. Do you hear?'

She returned to the kitchen to see the health visitor sat wiping a hankie over her bag and face, scowling like it was some sort of new fashion trend. Once she heard Mildred quieten, Kitty pushed the door open, stood with her hands on her hips and asked her again if she had calmed herself. But Mildred ran out of the door with a pouted mouth and threw herself to the ground once more, banging her head on the floor.

The health visitor shot to her feet and said, 'This child needs a referral to a children's psychiatric hospital.'

Kitty called her angered stance and raised her with a thunderous one. 'Indeed she does not. I'm not having her poked and prodded as though she's retarded,' she snapped. 'Give her until her second birthday which isn't too far off. Sometimes she's okay, she's just confused with her parents deserting her, and can't express herself properly.'

The health visitor's lips clamped together as she swung around and headed for the door. Kitty held her hands to her belly and chuckled for the first time in months as she thought about the health visitor's food-covered face. She looked hilarious when she was stood there with Mildred's dinner tangled in her hair. And when it slid down her face, Kitty nearly split her sides trying not to laugh.

She lowered herself down on the sofa and Mildred raised her big brown eyes towards her and whimpered, 'Mama.'

Kitty's heart melted as she looked at her perfect oval face, her small nose and dark curling lashes. 'How could Sadie turn her back on this innocent little child?' she asked herself.

Leaning over, she drew towards Mildred in a close embrace. The poor baby sighed, clasped her fat little arms around Kitty and fell asleep. As Kitty sat there, watching the sleeping child with a feeling of warmth in her chest, she knew that this little girl would go on to change her life for the better.

Easing herself up, Kitty gently removed the baby's arms aside. She rose to her feet and headed for her bedroom where she pulled open her wardrobe door. Peering at the jewellery box with a sombre look, she bit her bottom lip. Then, plunging her hand inside the wardrobe, she gripped her fingers around the wooden box, no longer able to fight the overwhelming sense of yearning.

She pulled open the lid, took up the chain; clicked open the locket and her eyes brimmed as she peered at her wayward daughter's face. Her already shattered emotions began to build as she stared at the gypsy with the swarthy-skinned, handsome face that mirrored her granddaughters. Her mind recalled how Joseph Riley had stood on her doorstep with a pleading expression in his eyes while he held Mildred in his arms.

'I'll never let you know how you were abandoned by both your mammy and daddy,' she spat as she snapped shut the locket, then flung it inside the jewellery box by the chain. Its very existence was burning her fingers before she slammed the lid closed.

Then, her gaze went to the white envelopes which lay on the shelf. Mildred's name was sprawled in capital letters across the front of them. Each one had been posted from different locations. When the first envelope arrived, Kitty peered at a birthday card, then flung it down granite-faced. Pacing wall-to-wall, emitting fumes from her cigarettes, she imagined the worst. But, time moved on and, after two more envelopes containing a birthday card fell through the letter box, she then began to relax.

With her head in her hands, she slumped down on her bed pondering just what would she say to her granddaughter when she was older and when she began to ask her any awkward questions about her parents. If she ever found out the secret she was hiding, she would never forgive her. It's for her own good, she thought, pushing the uncomfortable image from her mind as she lay back on the bed and closed her tired eyes.

Then she heard the exasperated exhalation of breath. She blinked as she eased up and rubbed hand across her face to see a mop of black corkscrew hair, dark brown sparkly eyes, framed with thick black lashes and, they were gazing intently at her, while chubby fingers clutched pink birthday candles.

Kitty smiled and ruffled her granddaughter's hair as she stood to her feet. Mildred trotted behind her into the kitchen where she pulled out a chair and stood watching Kitty transform a plain cake into a work of art. It was coated in white icing sugar and piped into elaborate shapes. Silver balls and bright red shiny paper wrapped all around it completed the task.

Then she glanced at her watch. Red-faced, she cut and filled assorted sandwiches; whipped up tinned cream for the trifle and melted bars of chocolate for the gateau. By four in the afternoon, everything was ready. The white tablecloth was laid. Bone china crockery had been brought out for the occasion.

Both torn paper and toys littered the lounge as Mildred sat on the floor playing with her friends. They were all absorbed in a game when Kevin's sly pale eyes swept around as he moved stealthily from the room. Nora and Mrs Lowther from next door were in the kitchen helping Kitty with hot and cold drinks. Then, they all bustled back into the lounge, pulled out a chair and sat around the table.

Kitty clapped her hands and raised her eyebrows at Mildred. She looked up then scrambled to the table, where she sat beaming, wearing her new frilly party dress. Kevin sauntered back to the room eyeing the food greedily, licking his lips at the table heaving with trifle, cream cakes of every assortment, as well as the birthday cake and the elaborately piped chocolate gateau.

Kitty began singing, 'Happy birthday dear Mildred,' when everyone else joined in. Mildred eyes shone as she leaned over, puffed out her cheeks and blew out her five candles when Kevin removed his hand from behind his back and grinning like a Cheshire cat, he placed the gold necklace and open locket onto the tablecloth.

Mildred giggled, while the colour faded from Kitty's hot face. She stood mute and held one hand to her heaving chest then held a firm hand onto the nearest chair. There was a collective gasp before the room fell silent. Kevin's eyes glittered with malice.

'Why have you been poking around my bedroom? You nasty little freak,' Kitty shrilled, seeing his feral expression.

Nora pushed her seat back and glared at Kitty. 'Don't you dare call my child a freak,' she hollered.

Mildred's bright eyes rounded then filled with tears as she peered at the startled faces, then she gazed at her grandmother with a quizzical look as Kitty quickly swooped up the jewellery.

'Why are you annoyed Gran? Who are those people in the locket?' asked Mildred with an utterly innocent expression.

'It's my mother and father when they were young,' Kitty lied, her hardened eyes locked on Nora's equally hard and bulging.

Lemonade spewed out of Kevin's mouth and spattered over the tablecloth as he began to laugh hysterically.

'Get him out of my sight Nora,' demanded Kitty as she held her hands to her face.

Nora's fat cheeks were scarlet as she lurched towards her son and hauled him up and away from the table still sniggering and poking his tongue out at the children sat wide-eyed.

11

'That child is evil,' snarled Kitty pointing her finger towards him. 'The sooner you admit you have produced a misfit the better,' she yelled to the huge swaying derriere retreating through the door.

'Does it mean we won't be going to Aunt Nora's to see Kevin's Charlie Chaplin films anymore now?' asked Mildred, sad-faced.

'If he comes to apologise for his behaviour, then I'll think about it,' replied Kitty stiffly.

'Well, you need Nora for the running of the guesthouse,' pointed out Mrs Lowther as she sat peering at Kitty's surly face over the top of her teacup.

Kitty sat tight-lipped with the chain and locket clenched in her hand. Then, standing to her feet, she said, 'I'll telephone Nora tomorrow. I won't let that brass-faced upstart break our friendship.'

Little did she know what lay ahead . . .

Chapter Three

Nearly ten years had passed since the confrontation between Kitty and Nora at Mildred's fifth birthday party. They made-up but Mildred always avoided Kevin whenever she could. Especially after he began tickling her while she watched his films. He would move his hand up her thigh and probe his stubby smelly fingers into her knickers.

But it was difficult lately, especially when he began working at the guesthouse. Nora had begged Kitty to let him work there. Which she did – under sufferance, no-one else would employ him because of his reputation: a thug, bully and a pest with the female staff.

One morning, when Mildred's hands were clasped around the mop and bucket handle, she passed him on her way to the guest bedrooms and gave him a withering smile. Then, pushing open a bedroom door, she stood for long moments, sweeping her eyes all the way along the passage. There was no sign of Kevin, only the dimly lit passageway and the fragrance from the flowers in a vase on the windowsill.

She stepped inside the bedroom and closed the door, when it flew open. She swirled around to gaze at the fat spotty-faced youth with the pale eyelashes and piggy eyes that were glinting as he crept towards her, with a finger pressed to his wet lips.

Mildred jerked her feather duster at him. 'What are you doing in here?' she demanded. 'Don't think of tickling me, 'cos I'll scream the place down and you'll be sacked.'

He lifted his shoulders. 'I'll just deny it,' he scoffed, as he lifted a hand and began twiddling her hair with his fat fingers.

She raised both hands and shoved him away, then stood with her hands on her hips, her face twisted in contempt. 'I wish I had a dad, he would punch you Kevin Jones,' she said.

Kevin's top lip curled into a sneer, as he threw his head back and laughed. 'You have a dad. He came here and left you. You have a mam too, but she didn't want you either,' he sniped.

Mildred's eyes widened. 'I don't believe you, you're lying,' she replied in a quivering voice.

He smirked. 'I remember when you were first brought here your grandmother didn't want you either.'

Mildred's face crumpled as she swung around and stormed towards the door. Kevin lurched towards her and grabbed hold of her arm to pull her back, but she lifted her leg and kicked him in his shins.

'I'm telling Gran what you've said,' she screeched as she ran headlong into their private apartment.

'He said *what*?' demanded Kitty.

Mildred sat with shoulders hunched and face blotchy as she sobbed. 'Tell me it's a lie Gran,' she pleaded. 'You said that my parents were dead. If it's true, then you must be cruel to say that.'

Kitty shot to her feet. 'I know what I could do with that upstart. Sit there, I'm going to look for him and he'll wish he hadn't been born,' she said, as she stormed out of the sitting room.

Mildred paced back and forth as she waited for her grandmother to return. Kitty returned with a contrite look which only confirmed Mildred's suspicion. 'Why did you lie when they are very much alive?' she yelled, as she sunk to the floor on her knees and began wailing with deep shuddering sobs.

Kitty leaned down, clasped hold of her arm, pulled her to her feet and guided her towards her bedroom.

Slumped down on the bed, she gave Mildred a grave solemn look. 'I'm so sorry Mildred, I didn't want to tell you anything until you were older, but since that damn idiot has opened a can of worms, I cannot go on pretending. Can you remember the locket that Kevin showed you on your fifth birthday?' Mildred raised her reddened eyes, and in between sobs, she nodded her head.

Kitty clasped hold of her hand. 'Do you want to look at it again?'

Mildred bit her lip. 'Why?' she asked.

'Because I lied, I said they were my parents. But they are your mother and father,' sighed Kitty as she rose off the bed and pulled open her wardrobe door.

As she took out the jewellery box, she pulled out the necklace and passed it to her granddaughter in silence. Mildred swiped her wet face with her hand as she peered at the handsome young man and the pretty girl with the long fair hair.

'Is that my mam, she's very pretty,' gushed Mildred as she went to look at her reflection. 'But, I look like my father and I'm a wild Romany girl.'

'Don't say that,' snapped Kitty. 'You're not wild.'

You don't know me, thought Mildred as she glanced once again at her parents' photograph.

'Your father was desperate when he came that night, vowing to come and get you once he'd gotten something sorted, but he never did. I often wonder why – because he sent you birthday cards until you reached the age of five – but then no more after that,' she said, clasping her fingers around the envelopes. Removing them from the shelf she passed them towards Mildred with her lips compressed and eyes averted, unable to look at the reproachful face peering at her.

Mildred drew her darkened eyes away, then lowering her head she reached her fingers inside each envelope and pulled out her birthday cards, staring at them wide-eyed. Tears dripped off her chin as she sat open-mouthed as she held them to her chest.

'He never wrote a letter, only a card until I was five,' she sniffed, brushing her tears away, with her fingers. 'It's all a mystery. Something must have happened to him and my mother too, what do you think Gran?' she said.

'I really don't know,' replied Kitty, as her eyes glistened with unshed tears. 'Sadie left at the age of sixteen to be with your father, but she couldn't stand the Romany life. She wrote a letter to me years ago asking for forgiveness.'

'So did you reply to her and let her know about me?' asked Mildred with brightened eyes.

Kitty drew her lips together as though she had just sucked a lemon and said, 'Indeed I did not, I wasn't having her coming here and building your hopes up only to have them dashed down. No way – she's too damn fickle.'

Mildred looked at her grandmother's set face. 'Can I read the letter please?'

Kitty got up, sighed and crossed to the sideboard. Taking the envelope out, she handed it to Mildred.

She sat peering at the document in her hand for long moments, then said, 'She's living in

London, why don't you write back to her and tell her about me?' Mildred asked, with her palms held together as if she was praying.

Kitty reached her hand out and snatched hold of the letter. As she put it back inside the envelope, her face was stern. 'I don't want her name mentioned again,' she shrilled.

Mildred shot up and grabbed hold of her hand, but Kitty held her hands up. 'I've said no, and I mean no,' she said, then stepped out of the room in silence.

Mildred's face crumpled as she sank to the floor, lowered her head and wrapped her arms around herself. She was still no further forward to getting to properly meet her mother, and at this rate, it would probably stay that way forever.

Chapter Four

The sun shone against the curtains and the birds were twittering in the bushes when Mildred's eyes opened. I'm going to get that ugly fat Kevin Jones back for what he said yesterday, she thought to herself as she pushed the bedding back.

Slipping her legs over the bed, she crossed towards the window. Pulling the curtain aside she looked down the back entrance and saw him. Her lips compressed and her eyes glistened with malice. His new motorbike, a red and silver Royal Enfield was stood shining in the back yard. He had a box of vegetables in his hands and he was strutting about, whistling tunes.

She narrowed her eyes and said to herself, 'I'll get even with you mister. You thought it was funny what you told me yesterday, well I'll show you funny.' She turned her gaze away from him and went towards the bathroom. 'You'll be laughing on the wrong side of your face later,' she chuckled.

After her bath, wrapped in a thick white towel, she stepped passed her grandmother's bedroom and saw that her door was ajar. She stopped in her tracks as she peered inside to see that her gran's face was gaunt and yellow, and there was a film of sweat visible on her brow. She lay there shivering against the pillows that were propped against the brass-leavened headboard.

'Gran, what's wrong?'

Kitty lifted her hand to her head and said, 'It must be a bilious attack, that's all. Can you fetch me some aspirin tablets?'

Mildred stepped closer and leant over the bed, but jerked back as she wrinkled her nose. 'I'll just open this window for you before I go. You need some air in here,' she said, as she turned on her heel and stepped back out of the room.

Back in her room, she quickly got herself ready. She slipped on a cool cotton dress over her bra and knickers and ruffled her hair a little. From there she made her way to the kitchen. Pulling open a drawer, she took out a small sharp knife. Scrambling down the back stairs, she crept towards the lower kitchen window and peeked through to see Nora. She had her back to her and was stood next to the cooker with her ample arm moving at great speed.

Further down the yard there were two brick buildings, where the coal and logs were kept. Mildred heard the sound of sawing and crept down to the building, where she put her face beside the crack in the door and saw Kevin stood with his back to her. She grinned as she moved away and stepped towards his motorbike.

Pulling the knife from the sleeve of her dress, she dropped her hankie to the floor. She knelt to her hunkers, moved her hand towards the hankie, then sank the knife into the back tyre, enjoying the blissful sound as the air whizzed out of it. Then, creeping further along, she stuck the knife into the front tyre too. She jerked her head around to see that the coast was clear and then stood up and strode away, heading for the shop.

On her way back, she held her face towards the sun and smiled to hear the birds singing. Reaching the guest house, she lowered her eyes to the deflated tyres and smiled. Striding through the yard, she dashed into the back door and took the stairs two at a time.

'That'll take the smirk off your fat chops,' she whispered.

Humming a tune, she held a glass under the tap and stepped back out of the kitchen to check on her grandmother. 'I'll go and help Nora in the downstairs kitchen, but I'll be back to see how you are Gran,' she said.

Kitty raised glazed sunken eyes and nodded her head as she reached for the pills and water.

'Gran looks terrible,' muttered Mildred, as she slipped on her overall.

Nora swung around to look at her and said, 'I've never known her ever take to her bed, she must be ill.'

Mildred blew out her cheeks, while sweeping strands of hair from her brow as she stepped towards the window to push it open. Kevin was stood beside the motorbike with his fingers raked through his hair and his acne-covered face bright red. He was sat on his hunkers, glowering and peering at the deflated tyres.

He looked around and saw Mildred watching him. She jerked back when she saw his surly face. He stormed into the kitchen, making her heart leap. But she stood beside the sink with a tea towel in her hand and cast him a casual glance.

'Somebody's let me tyres down, I swear I can see a slash in them,' he said, as he threw himself into a chair at the side of the large wooden table.

'No,' Nora barked. 'That motorbike cost me a lot of money. Who would do a thing like that?'

'I don't know, but they're dead when I find out,' he snarled, as his darkened eyes shot towards Mildred.

'I'll just go and start the guest rooms,' Mildred said in a tight voice, while she folded the tea towel over a rail. Twirling around to leave the kitchen, she glanced at Kevin and saw the glowering look he was casting towards her.

'Do you know about this,' he demanded, as he shot off the seat and thrust his ugly, fat face into hers.

'Of course not,' she said, with widened eyes. 'That's a horrible thing to do, they must be jealous – whoever they are,' she said, as she dashed out, and climbed the stairs to the second floor.

If he dares to come up here and touches me I'll hit him with this mop, she thought to herself as she put the bucket inside the storage cupboard. Sweeping her eyes around, she made her way along the passage to the linen cupboard, where she closed the door and began sorting what bedding she needed. With her arms full she turned around, when the door was yanked open and Kevin squashed his big frame inside and slammed the door closed with the heel of his shoe.

His pale blue eyes glistened with a malevolent evil darkness as his right hand shot out and his stubby fingers gripped her throat. His left hand tore at the buttons on her dress exposing her breasts. His eyes clouded while his white coated tongue slicked over puckered lips. He moved his hand away and shoved it down between her thighs then thrust his fingers into her knickers.

'It was you who slashed my tyres, did you think I wouldn't guess?' he snarled, with his lips drawn back over his yellow teeth.

'It wasn't me, I don't know anything,' she squealed. 'I've got to get back to Gran, please let me get out,' she wailed, while her heart thudded wildly against her ribs.

'Oh no, you're not getting away lightly after what you've done, you jumped up little madam,' he hissed, as he drew his hand away and fiddled with the fly buttons on his jeans.

In just one second, he had grabbed her hand and pushed it inside. 'Ooh that's good,' he gasped. 'Move your hand up and down.'

Mildred's face contorted as she squirmed and gagged, but he was too strong. He shoved her to the floor, where eventually he jerked and shuddered. 'Say anything about this to anyone and you're dead bitch,' he rasped, as he pushed her aside and stood to his feet to fasten his jeans.

Mildred lay on the floor, her face white and screwed up in hate.

Kevin curled his lip. 'I'll leave you something to remember me by,' he sneered as he pushed the door open.

She heard his footsteps fading along the passageway as she lowered her eyes to peer at her palm, it was smelly and sticky. Her face twisted as her stomach heaved. With her tongue hanging from her mouth, she gagged as she pulled her torn dress together and burst into noisy, gulping sobs as she staggered out of the cupboard and along the passageway.

Breathing hard, she ran up the flight of stairs and tore through the private apartment and into the bathroom, where she pulled the dress off and slung it to the floor. Leaning over the bath, she turned on the taps then sunk to the floor on her knees with her face crumpling.

Tears streamed down her cheeks while she vowed to get revenge for what he had just done. All she could think about was his horrible smelly penis that had throbbed and jerked like a spitting snake, while he forced her hand around it. 'I'll get you back somehow, you big fat bastard,' she kept repeating to herself.

If Gran knew how I swore she would be shocked, she thought, but I like swearing. I'll never be a good Catholic girl no matter how many times she makes me go to that bloody church. And that stupid Nora would never believe that her wonderful son would be capable of such things, as she's so bloody blinkered. He's so sly and devious, he would deny everything. His portly mother's fat pink cheeks would wobble with contempt and her bright blue eyes would bulge even more than usual, while she strutted about like an angry hen.

The bathroom door handle turned and rattled. She gasped and shot up. 'Who is it?' she asked in a quivering voice, concluding her reverie.

'It's me, Gran, what on earth are you doing? I need to get in.'

Hearing the sharp voice, Mildred heaved a long sigh as she stood up and stepped out of the bath. Unlocking the door, she pulled it open to see her grandmother stood peering at her with lips clamped together, her green eyes sweeping her from head to toe.

'What's going on? You've been crying and why are you having a bath at this time of the day?' Kitty asked.

Mildred's chin quivered and she flung herself towards Kitty. 'I've been upset and worried about you Gran, you looked terrible this morning.'

'Well it's a good job I'm fine now,' she said disentangling herself. 'But I don't believe it's me that has got you in this state. Has that loose cannon been bothering you?' she asked.

Mildred shook her head, averting her steely gaze.

'Why don't I believe you?' hissed Kitty.

Mildred turned away and dashed to her bedroom, where she flung herself down on her bed and thumped the pillows with her fists.

Chapter Five

It was the start of the six-week school holiday and another busy day at the guesthouse. People were stood in the passageway surrounded by cases and bags. Young children ran around the place, chasing one another as they waited for their taxis. Mildred stepped out of their apartment and stood peering over the top banister, surveying the scene.

Turning her head, she saw Kevin's big frame moving around the passage on the second floor. She swung around, went back inside and headed for the kitchen. With her elbows leant on the bench, she gazed out of the back window at the lush green fields and trees swaying in the breeze, and heaved a long sigh.

It was a sunny morning, a day to be out with her friends. To go to the cinema, or to the café bar and listen to the latest records, but her grandmother's illnesses had only grown since that first spell two years ago, which meant that going out was out of the equation.

Moving away from the window, she put the kettle on the Aga stove then put two cups on the bench. Sprinkling tea leaves into the teapot, she poured on the boiling water and waited for the tea to settle as she poured milk into the cups.

Stepping inside her grandmother's bedroom with the tray in her hand, the sun shone through the sash window, highlighting the pink flocked walls, the cream bedroom furniture and a white fluffy wool rug that lay on the floor.

White lace bedding completed a sense of calm in the room, but Kitty lay moaning. Her face was gaunt, her skin matching the whiteness of the pillows that she was propped up against. Then, when she broke into a paroxysm of coughing, the bedding was covered in brown fluid. The stale smell of sweat that mingled with the underlying reek of nicotine made Mildred's stomach churn. But she forced herself to move further towards the bed where she sat on the edge, placed a cool hand on her grandmother's clammy brow and bit her bottom lip to stop the tears that threatened to fall.

Kitty blinked open her weary eyes and watched Mildred pull the soiled bedding back.

'I'll get some fresh bedding and get you a clean nightie,' she suggested. 'And, don't you think it's time you got the doctor here too Gran? This has gone on too long, and I'm worried.'

'No, I don't want any doctor, but I'm fed up of being confined to this damned bed. So pass me my dressing gown and if you could run me a bath, I'll get changed,' she said, as she clicked her finger and thumb together.

Taking up the dressing gown that was draped over a chair, Mildred laid it down on the bed and made her way to the bathroom.

With the bath filling, Mildred recalled how her grandmother had gotten up at the crack of dawn in summer or winter with her arms moving to and fro, she would be seen striding along the two mile route that took her to St. Hilda's church. Then, when she returned to the guesthouse, she would make her way to the kitchen to speak to Nora. They would pull out a chair and sit at the large pine table that dominated the white tiled and spotlessly-clean kitchen, to discuss the daily menu and any other problem that arose. The good old days, Mildred thought, how I miss the good old days.

Stepping back out of the bathroom, she stepped back into Kitty's room to tell her that the bath was ready, but stopped as soon as she entered. Her grandmother had lain back again with her mouth gaping open, her nose pinched and pointed; her eyes closed and sunken. She stepped over to the bed and tapped her on her shoulder. Kitty raised vacant eyes.

'Gran, you've fallen asleep, the bath is ready,' Mildred said.

'Okay, give me a hand up.'

Mildred took a sharp intake of breath as she noticed that her grandmother's skin was now hanging like stretched dough from her arms and legs. It was hard to see her like this. She had always been a big buxom woman, but now, to see her like this Mildred felt physically sick as she led her towards the bathroom.

'Do you want me to help you into the bath and stay in case you fall?' Mildred asked.

'Certainly not,' Kitty snapped, glancing over her shoulder with a scowl.

Mildred stood with her arms folded and shook her head, but the dark look was enough. So instead of offering a response, she simply turned on her heel and went back to her grandmother's bedroom. She dragged the soiled bedding off the bed and pulled it along the floor as she headed along the narrow, dimly-lit passage and stepped down the mahogany staircase and into the reception area.

She faced the new maid, a young girl called Molly. Her fair hair was piled up on top of her head. Thick and black pencil was drawn around her large eyes and her lashes fluttered like spiders legs.

'My grandmother's bedroom needs cleaning and also the dining-room too,' Mildred said, noting Molly's pink lips compress. 'Is there some sort of problem?' Mildred asked, leaning closer to her face.

The girl jerked back and scurried away.

'Stupid bloody cow, standing giving me dirty looks,' she whispered as she swung around to run back up the two flights of stairs to find Kitty shuffling out of the bathroom with her mouth gaping and a hand at her heaving chest. She hooked her arm around her waist and lowered her down on a brown leather sofa in the lounge.

Kneeling down, she lifted her legs up onto the sofa and her stomach lurched to see how thin they were when she covered her with a blanket.

Once Kitty had closed her eyes, Mildred left the room. She headed down to the large white-tiled kitchen, which was set between the dining-room by a dividing wall. A wooden rail hung from the ceiling with colanders and pans and every cooking gadget going. Nora's comfortably-rounded hips sashayed as she placed a tray of eggs near the Kenwood mixer on the wooden table. Kevin was stood next to a sink full of dishes, suds up to his elbows as she stepped inside to speak to Nora.

He turned his head and winked his eye. Mildred cast a sour look as she turned around and stepped towards the back door. Pulling the door open, she stepped into the yard with her hands on her hips. 'That stupid maid hasn't put the dirty bags of bedding out when I told her to,' she whispered to herself, when she spun around.

Up close to her, there was a smell of dankness from sweat. Kevin was there, puckering his lips. Her brown eyes narrowed to slits as he moved nearer. He pressed himself up against her once more, forcing her up against the brick wall between his flat palms.

His sly eyes were burning with desire. 'You shouldn't be so sexy Mildred, with your long corkscrew black hair and big titties, I can't help it,' he whispered, clutching his clammy hands around her.

'You disgust me,' she hissed. 'And you stink. Get your filthy hands off me,' she demanded, as a feeling of revulsion charged through her and had rendered her arms with infection.

'I want to teach you things, things you should know now you're nearly fifteen,' he rasped.

'I do know, thanks to you. Now get back inside before I tell Nora what a slimy piece of shite she has for a son.'

Kevin moved away with bottom lip jutting, shoulders slumped and hands in his pockets, when the kitchen door creaked and Nora stood in the doorway, her frame filling the space. 'What are you doing? Get in here now,' she demanded, swiping her hand across her wet brow.

Mildred chuckled watching Kevin following his mother like a little puppy dog. She walked down the yard, through the large gates, inhaling much needed fresh air. She stepped along the path by the side of the guesthouse then stood at the corner before returning back inside. A large black car emerged further along the street. Her brow creased as she watched the car slowing down, then it stopped by the kerb at the front of the guesthouse.

A smartly dressed woman wearing a navy blue and white spotted full skirted dress, short white lace gloves, white poppet beads and white stiletto shoes and bag, stepped out of the car as though arriving to a glittering occasion. Her hair was shoulder length and blond, she had heavily made up grey eyes that were fixed on Mildred.

She turned her back to the woman and stepped inside the front entrance and headed for the dining room. The round tables were covered in blue and white checked cotton cloths, matching the curtains at the window. A small vase of flowers on each table, added to the cheery atmosphere.

Bending to her hunkers, she picked up a paper napkin and pushed scattered chairs closer towards the tables, when she glanced in the mirror and caught sight of the woman stood behind her. Mildred spun round to face the fancy dressed woman who was giving her a critical gaze.

'Excuse me, can you please tell Mrs McDine that I have arrived – she is expecting me,' she announced.

Mildred lifted her chin and stood with mouth pouting. 'My grandmother is unwell, so can I be of any assistance?'

The woman's eyes widened and red stained lips parted. 'No, she replied, fixing her with a hardened expression. 'Just tell her it's Sadie – she'll want to see me, I know that she's ill.'

Mildred stared at her open-mouthed for long moments with only the metallic ticking from the wall clock puncturing the silence.

'Well, take a seat and I'll tell her you're here,' she replied between gritted teeth as she watched the woman take a hankie out of her bag, wipe it over a chair, before lowering herself down. Then she crossed her legs and sat in silence as her eyes surveyed the dining-room area.

Forcing a smile, Mildred left the room. With her eyebrows gathered, she headed back to find that Kitty was refreshed though still pale and wan. She was lounging in the kitchen with a cigarette in one hand; a cup in the other.

'There's a woman sat in the guest room who wants to see you. She says she's called Sadie.' Mildred paused, studying her grandmother's reaction to her name. 'She's got more edge than a broken piss-pot,' she remarked.

Kitty's eyebrows snapped together while she sucked hard on her cigarette. Blowing out flumes of smoke, she stubbed the cigarette out in the ashtray, pushed her chair back, eased herself up then clutching at her chest, she moaned before collapsing back in her chair.

'It's her, I know who it is. Why is she here now?' shouted Mildred.

'Never mind, you'll find out soon enough,' she replied, raising her hand in dismissal. 'Go on then, stop standing there, tell her to come up – I have plenty to say to her.'

'And so have I,' rasped Mildred, her eyes glistening dark with anguish as she spun around and dashed down the stairs to the guest room to find Sadie stood by the widow with her head lowered; fingers pressed against her brow.

'Grandmother will see you now. Just follow me.' Then to her surprise the woman's chin quivered as she moved towards her. 'I can't do this, I should never have come – it was a mistake, tell your grandmother I'm so sorry.' Her voice wavered as she side-stepped Mildred, but before she could stop herself, Mildred swung around and strode towards the door and stood in front of it, blocking her way.

'Get out of my way,' she demanded, but as she raised her eyes again to meet Mildred's her face crumpled. She sank down on the nearest seat and lowered her head into her hands. Mildred sat staring at her for long moments. Rising to her feet, she headed for the bar, filled a glass with brandy then returned back in the guest room to face Sadie. 'You know who I am, don't you?' she demanded, as she held the glass towards her.

Sadie jerked her lowered head up as Mildred thrust her face near hers. With her eyes narrowed to slits and through her teeth, she hissed, 'I'm the daughter you abandoned, you cruel bitch. You sit there in all your finery, you disgust me.'

Sadie's eyes filled. 'I don't expect you to understand,' she whimpered, as she put the glass to her lips, tilted her head back and drained the brandy in one gulp.

'No, I don't understand! I didn't know how I would feel if I ever met you, but now I know. I feel nothing but contempt. I remember my grandmother weeping and crying every time she looked at the locket my father left, when he brought me here.'

Sadie's lips parted. 'Your father bought you here?'

'Yes, he was desperate, the night he brought me here. Gran said he was crying. He didn't want to leave me, but he had no choice. He couldn't leave me alone while he had to go and look for work. But you did . . . you chose to leave us both. If it hadn't been for my lovely gran, I would have been put into an orphanage,' she snarled with her lip curled. Swiping a tear away with her back of her hand, she jumped up. 'I can't endure to look at you.' She turned to run blindly through the building until she reached her grandmother, where she threw herself down on the sofa in floods of tears.

'Mildred, I would never have asked her here if I hadn't been so ill, but I have no other choice,' uttered Kitty with her hands clasped to her chest. Mildred's hands were clenched as she lifted her tear soaked face twisted with rage. Through deep shuddering sobs, she screeched, 'I hate her, I hate her,' when Sadie appeared in the doorway and emerged into the room.

Kitty's head shot up as she faced her daughter with eyes blazing. Sat with arms folded, she peered at her from head to toe with only the dull metallic sound from the pendulums swinging behind the glass within the grandfather clock. 'See the damage you've done? Well, I hope it was worth it, the way you went off and never looked back,' she scorned.

Sadie opened her mouth to speak, but Kitty put her hand up as she raised hardened eyes. 'I'm too tired for an argument Sadie and don't give me that look of hurt because it won't wash. I'm at the end of my tether with worry. The hospital have told me there's nothing more they can do for me and since you are her mother, then it's time you acted as one.'

Sadie moved towards her mother and slumped down beside her with a contrite look. 'I know that. I would like nothing more, but I can't just come and live here! I work and there's my husband to consider,' she said, as she turned her head to glance at the forlorn figure sat weeping bitter tears.

Mildred raised her flushed crumpled face once more and shot off the sofa. 'Live here? What do you mean – live here? Why have you asked her that Gran?' she cried, waving her arms.

'Because I know I'm not going to get better,' she replied, as she lowered her eyes unable to look at the pleading look in Mildred's.

'You will, we don't need her,' she assured, before turning to glare at Sadie. 'Anyway, don't flatter yourself, I don't want you here; you're the last person I would want to look after me,' she snarled.

'Mildred please calm down,' snapped Kitty, raising her hand to her brow. 'I know this is a shock, but you're going to make yourself ill if you carry on in this way.'

There was a long silence, Mildred's flushed face creased and contorted as she rounded on her grandmother.

'Calm myself!' she repeated. 'How can I calm myself? I have had nothing but lies from you Gran, and now Lady Docker arrives and sits there like butter wouldn't melt, well this is my life you've both wrecked through deceit, so, no, I can't and won't calm down. I hate both of you,' she scorned.

Kitty peered at her daughter with face tightly set as her permed hair before turning to face Mildred. She shot a meaningful look as she grasped hold of her clenched hands. 'I've told you before I had to protect you from knowing the truth. I didn't want you knowing that you were abandoned.'

'I didn't abandon her,' argued Sadie. Turning to face Mildred, she sat wringing her hands. 'I was devastated to have to leave you here – because they didn't believe in modern medicine and Mildred you were a sickly baby. You would never have survived because they made their own concoctions from plants and herbs. There was no electricity either, only candles and it was freezing in winter living like that.'

'Then, you should have left Joseph and come back to live here with Mildred, but no you swanned off without a thought, so stop trying to make yourself out to be a victim or a paragon of virtue – because you will never be either,' sniped Kitty.

Mildred snatched her hands out of her grandmother's grasp; her face was now blanched, her mouth a white line with anguish as her eyes switched wildly from face to face.

'I'm scared Gran, I don't want you to die,' she wailed as she flung herself onto her.

'Neither do I Mildred, but maybe God has other plans,' replied Kitty with a sombre look on her lined face, as she eased herself up. But as she did her mouth twisted and her legs gave way. Mildred fell to her knees beside her on the floor and gasped to look into her glazed and vacant eyes. Kitty's lips moved but she made no sound.

'What's happened to Gran?' she cried, peering up at Sadie who was stood transfixed. Mildred sprang to her feet. 'We need the doctor, don't just stand there,' she cried as she crossed the room and picked up the telephone.

As she placed the telephone down, she swayed around to see that Nora had emerged inside the room and was also stood to the spot with her stubby fingers clasped around her fat pink cheeks and she stared into the room, the same question on her mind as on Mildred's: what had happened to Kitty?

'Help me get her up off the floor,' demanded Mildred.

The two women sprang into action and lifted Kitty to the sofa where she lay ashen faced with unfocused bleary eyes. A loud knock that echoed along the passageway punctured the silence. Mildred swung around, raced through the building and pulled the door open. The doctor shot a quick glance and gave her a curt nod as he stepped over the threshold in a cloud of cologne, and with his fingers clasped around a leather bag he followed Mildred as she led the way to the lounge. He sunk to his hunkers then grabbed Kitty's limp wrist with his thumb and finger and prompted her to speak. 'Kitty, it's Doctor Hartman, is everything alright? Can you hear me?' Her eyes flickered briefly but she then relapsed into an unresponsive state once more.

'This lady needs to be in hospital immediately. Her unresponsiveness is extremely alarming and her brow is as hot as the sun's surface,' he remarked, as he raised his head and glanced around at his mute audience. He then stood to his feet, deciding to take action himself. 'May I use you phone?'

Mildred pointed a finger towards the sideboard. The doctor strode across the room and grabbed the phone to request an ambulance as soon as possible and then placed the phone down. He swung around and inhaled a soothing breath of fresh air. 'The ambulance will be here shortly. There's no doubt in my mind that she'll have to spend a few nights or so in the hospital. Someone should pack her case; prepare some things for her stay.' He then bent to pick up his case and turned to leave when Mildred rushed towards him and clutched his arm, her eyes pleading. 'She will be coming back, won't she?'

He grimaced. 'She's in the best place and they will do their best for her,' he reassured as he stepped through the door.

Mildred followed him to the front entrance. 'Thanks doctor,' she said as she pulled open the door. He stepped over the threshold with a curt nod of his head. 'Good day, Miss McDine,' he replied, then turned to strut down the path and towards his car.

Stepping back, she closed the door. She stared at it for a few moments and then turned around with a sullen look. The longer she was confined, then the longer Sadie would be around and that was intolerable. This was a living nightmare that she was unable to escape from, she thought. Heaving a long and heavy sigh, she made her way back to the lounge when she heard raised voices. She sped in her stride. What was all the fuss about? No one could be arguing at a time like this. She reached the door and her brow furrowed, she paused in the doorway to see Nora stood glowering up at Sadie with her finger pointed. 'You've caused this,' she bellowed.

Sadie snorted, clasped hold of her finger and shoved her backwards. Nora lost her footing and fell to the floor. 'Don't point your finger at me lady, or you'll regret it, I'm warning you,' retorted Sadie, looming over her.

Nora lay on the carpet red faced and breathing heavy. She grabbed the arm of the sofa to haul herself up. 'I bet Kitty's had a stroke with all that you've put her through. Why don't do you go back from where you've come from – you're not welcome and, let's face it, if she hadn't asked you to come, then you wouldn't have,' she snarled. 'If the worst happens then Kevin and I will live here to run the place. I've been running the place for ages now anyway.'

Mildred took a sharp intake of breath and dashed into the room with the rash rising on her face and neck at the thought of Kevin staying there overnight.

'No, that's out of the question, Gran wouldn't want that,' she gushed

'Why not?' demanded Nora, her face flushing and eyes peering at her.

'I'd rather not say,' she said as she looked away with the rash now scarlet on her neck.

Sadie glared at Nora. 'Stop putting Mildred in an awkward position, she's told you Mother wouldn't want that, so just leave it.'

'Huh, lady muck here's taking over, get back to where you belong, you bloody slapper,' snarled Nora, thrusting her face up to Sadie's.

'By, you've got a lot to say for yourself. You need to sort your own son out first before you make any comments about me lard arse.'

'What are you talking about?' snapped Nora.

'That brat of yours has been forcing himself on Mildred.'

'He has not! What do you know what goes on here?'

'When mother wrote to me, she told me what she knew about your son. She knew a lot more than what anyone thought, as nothing escaped her what went on here,' she said, as she turned her face to look at Mildred. 'That was one of the reasons for me coming here – to keep my eyes open and report to her what I saw.'

'What?' spluttered Nora, swaying around to face Kevin who had slouched into the room and was stood with mouth opening and shutting like a floundering fish.

'Is this right?' she spluttered, with her fat fingers splayed on her ample hips.

'Can you both stop arguing,' shouted Mildred, before he could say anything. 'Have you both forgotten Gran is lying there ill, and all you two can do is bicker?'

Everyone turned their head to look at Kitty. She was moaning, moving her head from side to side, while her skinny arms thrashed about. Her eyes were glazed and sunken, while her lips moved, but still there was no sound.

Mildred ventured into her grandmother's bedroom. Her face crumpled and eyes filled with tears as she gazed around her room. Her rosary beads were hanging from the headboard. 'I'm not religious God, like Gran is, but please don't let her die,' she pleaded. 'I'll go to church every morning if you let her live,' she whispered.

Kneeling down and pulling out a small case from underneath the bed, she swiped a tear away as she placed it on a chair and clicked it open. Her eyebrows shot up when she peered at a new pair of slippers, nightdresses, soap, towel and toiletries that Kitty had already put in the case. The only thing missing was a dressing gown which she would need. She moved to the wardrobe stood inside an alcove and reached for the dressing gown. Sadie stepped inside the bedroom regarding her with a steady look, her winged eyebrows drawn together in an ominous frown.

'Mildred, I'm sorry, I really didn't expect this to happen, but I have to get back home. I'll make arrangements for leave from work. But, I will return, there's no way that woman is going to take charge here, especially with that son lurking around. Also, as I work for social services, I'm informing them of the situation here. You've made it very clear that you don't want anything to do with me. I know how you must feel and if I could only turn the clock back I would. I've been so selfish and now I just want to make things right, but you won't allow that to happen. But I'm telling you this Mildred, you will be made Ward of Court and the decision will be made for you. Is that what you want? To either live with foster parents or in an orphanage until you're of age?'

Mildred gave her a sullen look. 'I can't forgive you for abandoning me,' she snapped. 'Or what excuses you have to give, other women have hardship but they don't leave their children,' she replied in a cool manner as she turned her back to Sadie.

'The ambulance is here,' Nora said as she waddled into the room, poking her nose through the door. Mildred stuffed the dressing gown inside the case, dashed out of the room in an instant and hurried through to the front entrance. She pulled open the door to face a dour, portly man with thick grey hair. He was accompanied by a skinny fellow with a bald head and a broad smile, the stretcher clutched tightly by his side.

Mildred beckoned the men inside and they followed her through to the lounge where Kitty lay. Nora was hovered over her and squeezing her hand, telling her not to worry. She would see that everything was fine and that she would take care of the place while she was in hospital. Kitty eyes flickered when she was lifted onto the stretcher. Mildred leaned over, kissed her cheek, put her case beside her and she was whisked away into the waiting ambulance. Stood in the doorway, Mildred watched the ambulance until it was out of sight. She stood there for a brief moment before heading back inside. She entered the room with her chin quivering. Unable to compose herself any longer, she slumped down on the sofa, held her hands to her face and wept noisy gulping tears. Nora was sat stone faced, with her arms folded beneath her ample chest, while Sadie sat snivelling; mopping her dry eyes with a lace hankie.

'You can wipe those crocodile tears too,' snapped Nora. 'Guilt is it?'

'You're a horrible little misfit,' Sadie bellowed as she rose and faced Mildred. 'I'll phone you later to find out what the hospital have said. Okay?' Mildred shot her a cool look and nodded slowly. Sadie turned her head to cast a sour look at Nora, then stepped out of the room with her high heels clattering as she dashed down the passageway.

Nora curled her lip as she got up to go make her way back to the kitchen. 'The room smells better already,' she said with a gleeful glint in her eyes.

Mildred couldn't wait to wipe that smirk off her mouth. 'Sadie is reporting social services about the situation I'm in. Also, she is having Kevin investigated for what he's been doing to me.'

Nora's head jerked back. The grin slid from her fat face at the sound of Mildred's words.

Chapter Six

Kitty returned back from hospital a couple of days later. Mildred was exhausted through lack of sleep. Tossing and turning in bed, she would fling the bedding back, get up, stomp around her bedroom or pummel the pillows with frustration.

Curling her lip up and pulling a face behind the guest's unruly children gave her a twisted pleasure. Sometimes she would stick her tongue out from behind a cupboard door and hold two fingers up at them.

The doctor prescribed tablets after he saw her gaunt and sad face, but the pain was ingrained because now she knew her grandmother was going to die and her life would change forever.

She became rebellious, resentful and insolent by disrupting the class at school. The first morning after the six week break, she slouched into the school yard with her skirt short, skimpy and showing a lot of thigh. Thick black liner was drawn around her eyes, while her lips were glossy with pink lipstick.

Girls were giggling with their hands clasped over their mouths. The boys stood wide-eyed. The headmaster, a small rotund man with bald head and thick rimmed black glasses, breezed into the yard with his briefcase in his hand. He stopped in his tracks as he peered at her with stretched face. She was stood leant against the wall; casting him a piercing stare.

The headmaster lifted up his hand, curled his finger and beckoned her towards him. She moved forward with a sullen expression on her face as he pointed to the hem of her skirt. With eyes rolled, she unfolded the waistband until it reached the acceptable length. He turned away with a sour expression, to make his way into school, but as he glanced over his shoulder, he caught her stood with two fingers raised and her tongue stuck out.

The bell clanged and they all trooped inside the building for assembly. The headmaster's thick eyebrows protruded over the frames of his glasses as his eyes surveyed the children stood looking at him.

He lifted up his hand, curled his finger and beckoned her towards him. 'Go to the front, turn and face the line,' he demanded. She side-stepped, went to the front then, turned around to face the class with her arms by her sides.

He advanced towards her like a raging bull. He snatched hold of her hand, pulled a thick strap out from behind his back and wacked it over her upturned palm. Her face creased and her eyes welled with tears as he lifted his arm back to strike again but, before he could, she took her leg back and thudded her foot between his legs.

A loud gasp and sniggering echoed around the hall as the man groaned. With his face contorted, his legs buckled as he sunk to the ground.

She turned on her heel, strode to her seat, slung her satchel over her shoulder then as she crossed to the door, she took a sweeping glance around to see the pupils grinning like Cheshire cats. She ran out of the room and broke down in tears as she raced out of the school yard and didn't stop running until she reached the local park.

Her chest rose as she gasped for breath. She sat down on an old wooden seat and pulled out a packet of Woodbines from her blazer pocket that her older friend had bought for her.

Striking a match, she lit the cigarette. 'He can expel me, I don't give a shit,' she rasped to herself, as she glanced up at the dark cloud that hovered over her, matching her mood.

Sullen-faced, she dropped the cigarette butt to the floor. A tall woman passing by with a basket of shopping clasped in both hands, stopped to give her a black look.

'Do you want your eyes back?' Mildred spat, as she shot up and sprinted away.

Rain poured from the heavens on her half mile route back to the guesthouse. She burst through the front entrance of the guesthouse with her hair plastered to her brow. Her eye makeup was streaked across her cheeks as she stormed up the flight of stairs and flung her bedroom door open. Gasping and screwing up her face, she screeched with rage while she wrenched off her blouse and skirt and flung them to the bedroom floor. She turned to look at her dressing-table. In two strides, she bent over, swiped her comb, make-up and a box of talcum powder, scattering the powder everywhere.

Throwing herself down on her bed, she lay peering up at the ceiling when she heard a sound from her grandmother's bedroom. She sat up, pulled open her bedroom door and walked into Kitty's room to find she was in a deep asleep, but moaning with pain. Stepping back out, she heard a loud knocking on the front door.

With clenched teeth and hands, she strode down the two flights of stairs, gave a weak smile to a couple of guests who were laughing and joking as she yanked the door open.

Two men were stood facing her. One was a tall thin man with a long hawk nose and beady eyes that were glowering at her behind thick framed glasses. The other man was elderly and dapper, with his white hair pressed into two waves and a thick drooping moustache covering his lips. With a case in his hand, he said he was a doctor and said he had come to visit Mrs McDine.

He lifted his leg to step over the threshold, when the other man with his face beetroot red, pushed him aside, as he pointed a finger at Mildred. 'You are a disgrace,' he hissed. 'I've come to tell your grandmother about your behaviour today and, I'm going to see to it that you are expelled.'

'I don't care, I'll be leaving in a few months anyway,' she snorted.

The doctor lowered his eyes to peer at the man. He was frothing at the mouth with a film of sweat on his brow, which he was swiping with a handkerchief as the doctor told him that Mrs McDine was too ill to see anyone. The man pushed his spectacles ever higher on his long nose and threw a sour look before he swung around and marched down the drive.

'That got rid of the old bastard,' Mildred snorted.

The doctor winced and his eyebrows shot up to his perfectly preened hairline as they made their way along the passage. She caught sight of him as he glanced in the mirror. He was pressing two fingers into the waves while turning his head from side to side to check his profile. An aroma of Cologne filled the stairways as he followed her up to the sitting room.

He stepped over and drew a blanket back to examine Kitty who lay skeletal with a waxen complexion. Lowering himself into a chair, he wrote out a prescription for Mildred to take to the chemist. As he turned to face her, he rubbed a hand over his chin and said he was approaching social services of their situation.

Mildred sat sullen faced. 'My mother in London says she's going to tell them too which means they'll put me in an orphanage. I would rather die than go in one of those, but I don't want to live with her either,' she yelled, waving her arms up in despair.

The doctor sighed as he laid a hand on her arm and squeezed it. 'I know this is an awful time for you Mildred, but you are too young to be alone, I'm sure you must see that's not possible,' he said as he rose to his feet. 'I would like to stay and talk about this, but I have other people to visit, please go for the prescription as soon as you can, your grandmother is in a lot of pain.'

Mildred sat with shoulders lowered and bottom lip jutting when the doctor left the room and dashed downstairs. Once she heard the door close, she asked her grandmother if she needed anything while she was at the chemist.

Kitty opened her sunken, dark rimmed eyes. 'Get two bottles of Lucozade please,' she croaked.

Stepping outside the guesthouse, she gazed up at the clear blue sky and covered her eyes with her hand. The sun was a golden ball of heat and it helped to lift her spirits as she breathed in the scent from the colourful roses growing either side of the path. Stepping away, she turned round the corner and made her way along the road to the chemist shop.

The brightly lit chemist was packed with men and women waiting for their medication. She handed the prescription to a middle-aged lady with bright red hair. After receiving the goods, she stepped outside to go to the corner shop for the Lucozade.

Sauntering by the corner shop, she paused to read a colourful poster in the window advertising a forthcoming fair. She stood for long moments, her mind recalling the first time she had gone to the fair with her friends. They had bought candy floss and stepped inside a tent to look at the bearded lady where big bottles contained the bodies of disfigured babies in liquid. She had twisted her face in disgust and dashed outside, watching the big wheel and other carousels, while music blared and teenagers screeched. But sitting in the dive bomber, was her turn to yell. It jerked and twisted so much, she thought she was going to die.

Smiling at the memory, she moved away from the window and stepped inside the shop. 'Can I help pet?' enquired a woman with wrinkled skin and small black eyes as she emerged from a doorway behind the counter where trays of eggs and a large wooden barrel of butter stood.

Mildred pointed to the bottles behind the counter. The woman narrowed her eyes then tightened her lips as she gave her a sly sideways glance. 'Are you from the guesthouse?' she paused, studying Mildred carefully. 'It's just I've never seen you around here before.'

'Well, I don't know how. I only live ten minutes away from here. My grandmother is very ill. I don't think she's going to get better either,' she said, wringing her hands together.

'Really? I'm sorry to hear that. What terrible news. Tell Kitty I'm asking after her,' she said with a solemn expression as she folded her arms under her flat chest. 'Your grandmother usually keeps me up to date with everything that's going on in her life. But someone said that Sadie had made a return. I was really gobsmacked, she's got a nerve showing her face around here again,' she remarked clamping her thin lips together as she put the two bottles on the counter.

Mildred's eyes glinted as she put her cash in her held out palm, then, as she leant over the counter, she thrust her face at the woman. 'And you're a sour- faced, old, prune. Sadie is my mother. She may not have made the wisest decisions in her time, but that doesn't mean she didn't love me. She was just too young to cope and people like you piss me off – bloody paragon of virtue,' she rasped.

The woman's lined face stretched as Mildred lifted the hatch at the side of the counter. She swooped inside and grabbed a packet of cigarettes from the shelf. Thrusting her face into the woman's again, she pulled her lips over her teeth like a feral cat, threw the money on the floor and stormed out of the shop to make her way to the chemist with her mind in a whirl. What if everyone else felt the same about Sadie, did they look down on her also, because she was illegitimate – a bastard, so Kevin had said one time when he was taunting her.

She stepped inside the chemist staring at her knees. Under her lashes she saw an elderly woman looking down her nose at her, so she moved away to peer at the shelves. Her palms were clammy and heart raced, she wanted to turn around and run out, when a voice shouted, 'Mrs McDine from the beeches guesthouse – anyone?' She stepped closer to the counter where she reached for the medication and rushed out of the chemist.

On the way back home, her heartbeat slowed down and her tense shoulders relaxed, but as she approached the corner she saw Father Black stepping out of his car. He looked around and her heart sank, he was on his way to see her grandmother, and wearing a funny black hat with a tassle attached. His big ears stuck out at the sides giving him a comical look as he peered at her with lowered white eyebrows as he turned on his heel. But he wasn't comical he was an obnoxious man with a pointy face and cold grey eyes that cast scathing dirty looks at the parishioners who didn't attend his church.

Dashing up the path she pushed the front door open, glanced over her shoulder and groaned to see his long skinny legs advancing behind her. She moved aside as he stepped over the threshold with his usual solemn, angular face and air of sanctity, as he removed his hat and hung it on the coat stand.

When they reached the top landing and headed for the sitting room, he lowered his face towards hers, peering at her thick black lined eyes and her pouting mouth, covered in the palest pink lipstick.

'When are you going to grace us with your presence at church?' he asked in his pretentious pseudo-posh voice as he wiped his brow and slumped into the nearest soft leather wing backed chair. Cold eyes glanced around the room as he admired the expensive paintings on the cream walls, the open white marble fireplace and the sturdy pale wooden furniture stood on the thick woollen beige carpet.

'The day that God's existence is proven. So in other words: never,' she spoke cockily.

She swung around to avoid his sour smelling breath which was pouring into the room as he retorted, 'I'm offering the sacraments to your grandmother, you should kneel and pray too,' he barked.

'That's not going to bloody help her though is it?' she replied in a scathing manner. 'Medicine will help her, the doctor will help her; hospital will help her. But God! God is not going to help her,' she snorted as she turned her back to him.

'You're heading for trouble with that attitude young lady. You should be ashamed of yourself, talking about our lord in such a blasphemous manner.'

She stuck out her tongue, waved two fingers up at his retreating back. She ventured into the kitchen and pulled open the scullery door to put the bottles away. Then she sat down at the table, waiting for the priest to sod off.

Tapping her fingers on the kitchen table and biting her nails down to the wick, she thought he would never go, but eventually she heard the door close. Or rather slam.

She stuck her head around the sitting room door to see her grandmother lain back against the pillows. Their eyes met as she handed her a glass of Lucozade. 'Is it okay if I go to Annabelle's for a little while Gran?' Kitty raised her hand and inclined her head.

It was almost a yes. It was good enough for Mildred.

Chapter Seven

The big wheel and a number of carousels were already set up in the middle of the field when Mildred crossed over the road and stood peering through the iron fence, watching the sturdy trailers as they towed the showmen's caravans. Horses and brightly coloured stalls and intricately carved, gilded and painted wooden gypsy's vardos were stood beside the larger shows. She looked beyond them and fixed her gaze on a handsome youth next to the waltzer.

He had the brightest blue eyes, a deep dimple in his chin and dark hair tied back with string. A shirt was tucked into his jeans, a checked handkerchief was tied around his neck, and he was stood with his head cocked to the side; the corners of his mouth turned up to see her appraising him.

He gave her a lingering look with the muscles on his arms flexing, as he lifted up a set of steel steps to attach them to the carousel. He stared at her for a further moment, placed the steps down and began walking in her direction.

'Will you be coming to the fair once we get all this set up?' he asked, smiling the most gentle of smiles.

'I might,' she replied, looping her wild hair around her finger.

'Well I'm Danny. I work on the waltzer. You should definitely come,' he quipped once again, as he winked his eye.

'Okay, I suppose I could, but I care for my grandmother and don't get out much.'

Danny made a sorrowful face. 'Well, that's a shame, a gorgeous girl like you stuck in the house missing all the fun. Try and get away, I'll give you a free turn,' he said, sweeping a hand through his hair. 'I'll be sure to keep an eye out for you. What's your name?'

'Mildred McDine,' she answered. 'And I bet you say that to all the girls?' she asked, as she studied his cheeky face for a split-second. His smile faded as he stepped closer towards her. Looking deeply into her eyes, he stroked her hair. 'Can I call you Millie?'

'If you want,' she said while her heart flipped and her eyes opened wide as she swung around and sashayed away with a smug look across her face. Turning to glance around, she saw him still stood watching her. She waved her arm and smiled as she saw him stood blowing her air kisses. With a spring in her step, she beamed, and floating on a cloud of bliss, made her way to Annabelle's house.

Pressing a finger on the door bell, she stood at the door and waited. Suddenly the door was thrust open and her friend was before her. Her flowing blonde hair shone in the sun, she was all doe–eyed, her deceptive angelic face a work of art.

'I know I take ages, but I've got to look good when I check out the talent,' Annabelle said. She picked up her handbag, strode down the hallway and breezed out of the house. Mildred followed; her brown eyes rolled up heavenwards.

They were now stood near the field where the fair was still in the throes of activity. Men were shouting at one another as they hammered the carousels together, women with olive skin wearing colourful head scarves and large gold hoops in their ears were leaning out of their vardos scolding the ragged children who ran amok.

Annabelle nudged her as they grew nearer. Her big blue eyes were scanning Danny, who waved his arm then moved out of view as he helped to erect the carousel.

'I've clicked,' Annabelle squealed. 'Ooh he's mine! I can't wait for tomorrow night for when the fair opens. Come on, let's go and watch them.'

Mildred shook her head and was about to say no, but before she could, Annabelle clasped her arm and dragged her into the field. She stood smiling and fluttering her long eye-lashes at Danny, until her smile faded when she noticed that the long-lingering gaze he shot was for Mildred and not her. He looked at her just like he had before, only this time more in-depth.

Annabelle turned on her heels and stormed a few yards away from where Mildred was stood. She spoke quickly, the huffiness in her voice incredibly apparent. 'I'll have him by tomorrow,' she said as she looked over shoulder, shooting a hardened look at Mildred, who simply lifted her shoulders and held her outstretched hands up in the air.

'It's not my fault he thinks I'm fit.'

Chapter Eight

The following day she met Annabelle as planned. As they walked into the fair, they encountered the sound of generators, mixed with the smell of diesel, the sugar sweetness of candy floss, toffee apple kiosks; the vinegar overtones of the chip wagons and the fried onions of the hot dog vendors. Music blared from the dodgems and the walzter.

Danny was spinning a seat around as they climbed up the creaking wooden steps. Glancing towards them, he smiled broadly and held out his hand to help Mildred into a seat. Annabelle struggled to step into the seat herself, noticing his eyes were still aimed at her friend.

Coloured bulbs flashed and the spinning seat eventually slowed down when the carousel came to a stop. Mildred's eyes were closed and face blanched. Annabelle nudged her to get up, but she was unable to move because everything was still spinning. Danny leant over, pulled her up and guided her down the steps.

'Come on, get up,' hissed Annabelle. 'You're holding up the ride and everyone is looking at us.'

Mildred turned her pinched face and raised her eyes to see Annabelle stood with her arms folded. Her eyes were glistening with spite. 'I suppose I'll just have to go on the rides on my own then,' she spat, as she swung around and flounced away.

Danny shook his head and swept his hand through his hair that was now hanging long and loose. 'What a spoilt little madam,' he said, turning to glance over his shoulder at his boss who was waving his hands back and forth like a malfunctioning clock. 'I have to get back to work, but I can meet you tomorrow in the Copper Kettle café. You better go home and have a rest, you look ill.'

'I'll survive. What time tomorrow?' she asked with a cool expression on her face, while holding her churning stomach.

He held up four fingers as he stumbled away, back on the spinning ride. Annabelle caught up with her and turned to her stone-faced when she said she was meeting him the next day in the café.

'Thanks, I know when I'm not wanted, you would've been going with me, but now you just want him,' she rasped, as she threw her head back, stamped her foot in the grass then stormed away pouting.

Mildred lifted her shoulders and made a face at her while she swung around. Her cheeks were flushed by now, and butterflies fluttered in her chest. She threw her arms up in the air and twirled around, humming a tune as she made her way back home. There was no chance of her getting to sleep tonight, not now that she had plans with the gorgeous Danny the following day.

Chapter Nine

The heat and smoke hit her face as she pushed the café door open, where inside the aroma of expresso coffee and cigarettes mingled. Walls were painted bright orange and covered in black and white posters of Elvis Presley and all the latest heart throbs. A record blasted from the juke box in the corner; teenagers were stood bent over and peering at the list of songs available. The Formica tables were strewed with cups and tin ashtrays overflowed with cigarette butts. The place was like a hipster's dream.

Wearing a low cut black dress with white polka dots, fitted at the waist and full skirted, Mildred looked as though she had just stepped out of Vogue, with her smooth olive skin, large brown eyes and full red lips. She spotted Danny only moments after walking in, sat with his head to one side, smiling broadly.

Waving his arm, he beckoned her to sit beside him. He jumped up, scraped his chair back and pulled out a chair for her. She lowered herself down onto the seat with her heart skipping. He pointed at the coffee machine on the counter across the room. She was unable to draw her eyes away as she watched him saunter over to the counter. He was wearing a black leather jacket and blue jeans, and his hair was tied in a ponytail at the nape of his neck.

To the right of him she saw a group of young men with their hair fixed into quiffs that flopped over their eyes. They jeered at Danny with an expression of derision, but a group of girls were stood giggling at each other and fluttering their lashes as they gawped at him.

She sat feeling self-conscious with herself now, because her hair was a cascade of cork-screws while theirs were either in a beehive style or back-combed in a bouffant style. She panicked now too. What if he preferred those girls to her? She was no match for that sort of girl.

She watched Danny walk back with the drinks. He lowered himself down onto the chair and then leant his elbows onto the table. He sunk his head into his hands and gazed at her.

His eyes were twinkling, and it made her hand shake as she picked up her coffee. 'You must have a great time going to different places, meeting new people,' she said, as the red rash crept up her neck and face.

Danny shook his head and leant towards her. 'Not really. I sometimes wish I could just stay somewhere, you know? I just begin get comfortable someplace and then we've got to pack everything up and move on. It must be good to have a stable home, instead of living this way – from one place to another. I left mine when I was fourteen, my father was a brute and he often beat me and my mother. When she became ill and died, I couldn't bear to be near him, so one day I just packed a few things and walked away. I began working with the fair and the showmen not long after, and the rest is history.'

Her eyes clouded over and her smile faded. Danny reached over the table, entwining his fingers round hers. 'Penny for them?' he asked, as he leant back in the chair.

'I'm sorry, I didn't realise you had suffered such a hard life,' she muttered.

He shrugged his shoulders. 'If I hadn't been working with the fair I wouldn't have met you, would I? Things aren't all that bad. Especially now that I have this wonderful view ahead of me.' He stroked her cheek gently, his hands a soothing elixir amongst all of the world's chaos.

She was on fire, blushing and gushing as if the colour red was heavily in fashion. But all of the colour drained from her face just as fast, when the door was flung open and an all-too-familiar face wandered through. It was the last person she wanted to see. Not Annabelle, no, it was much worse.

Sly pale blue eyes flicked around behind lowered eye-lashes, while the acne-covered fat and bloated face flushed scarlet. He slouched towards the counter, wiping his runny nose with his hand, and then wiped it onto his jeans.

The heavenly cloud Mildred was on evaporated in seconds. Red blotches appeared on her neck and her hands shook while her mind raced. Knowing how sly he was, she knew he could ruin things for her, by telling Danny what he did to her. And worse, lying about it and saying she enjoyed it.

As soon as he spotted them, he turned from the counter and advanced towards their table. 'What are doing sitting with a pikey?' he snarled.

'Get away and leave me alone.' Mildred hissed, feeling the blood in her veins beginning to heat up.

Kevin fell into the seat opposite Danny, glowering and pointing a stubby finger at his face. 'I'll warn you now pikey. This is my girlfriend and there'll be trouble if you get too friendly – get my drift?'

Danny rose to his feet and squared up to Kevin. 'I get your drift you fat fuck. And I'm no pikey either.'

Kevin's eyes glazed over and his nostrils flared, as he clenched his hands into fists. Lifting his arm, he thudded his fist into Danny's face. Danny stood motionless for a few seconds before turning his back. Kevin glanced about and smirked, but Danny spun around and thudded both fists into his fat gut, sending him sprawling to the ground. Lads were pointing their fingers and chortling as they watched Kevin moaning and holding a hand to his belly.

Mildred pushed her chair back and rose to her feet. With her hands on her hips, she lowered herself over him. 'I hate you with a passion Kevin Jones, you're the last person I would ever want to go out with. Your mother and my grandmother may be friends, but you and I will never be.'

Wheeling around, she stormed out of the café, leaving Kevin still on the floor groaning. Danny rose to his feet and followed her out to see what all the fuss was about. He clutched hold of her hand, pulled her away from the café. 'I'll take you home,' he suggested. 'I don't know what's going on, but he clearly thinks you are his girlfriend.'

Mildred stamped her foot. 'I'm not his girlfriend, he's the most disgusting person you could ever meet,' she wailed with her face creasing and tears filling her eyes. 'I'm really scared of what he will do to me,' she blurted out.

Danny's eyes were cold as ice. He stood with his arm wrapped around her waist. 'What do you mean?' he asked.

Mildred grimaced. 'It's complicated.'

Danny stood peering at her with a quizzical look for a little while, then shrugged his shoulders. 'Okay, just forget him and enjoy the rest of the time together. I'm famished, there's someone selling hot-dogs over there,' he said pointing his hand towards a mobile food stand. He held her hand and guided her towards a woman wearing a cap. Her head was lowered as she stood behind the counter with the delicious aroma of fried onions lingering around her.

'We'll eat them in my caravan,' he suggested, as he took money out of his jeans pocket.

They sauntered towards the caravan. She stepped inside; her eyes gleamed as she swept them around. He waved his hand for her to sit on a faded seat. They ate their hot dogs and drank lemonade in comfortable silence.

Once they had finished, Danny broke the silence with a question that had clearly been on his mind. 'So, are you going to tell me why you're so scared of that thug Mildred?'

Mildred shot him a sharp look. 'He's my grandmother's housekeeper's son. He makes me do things that I really don't want to think about.'

'Like what?' he asked with a dark expression.

'He won't leave me alone, he has put his hands where he shouldn't, and worse of all, he forces my hand inside his jeans until he comes,' she whimpered, as the bright red rash crept up her neck. 'He's twisted. My granny is dying and I will be going into an orphanage, I can't stand it, I feel like running away. I thought my parents were dead, but I've just been told that my father is a Romany gypsy, he's called Joseph Riley. My birth mother lives in London. But I'm not going there, I hate her. She buggered off and left me when I was a baby,' she gabbled.

'Calm down Millie,' urged Danny as he leant over, kissed her tenderly on her closed lips, and then pulled her close towards him.

It was a gentle sort of kiss, quite chaste and proper. She leaned against him savouring every second as his long hair fell against her cheek. Melting in his arms, she was unable to resist him as she ran her fingers through his hair. She kissed him long and hard, instinctively pressing against him, powerless to stop as he manoeuvred her so that she was underneath him.

Panting, she put her hands on his chest and pushed him off her. She snapped to a sitting position and pulled her crumpled dress down and sat primly, biting her bottom lip. 'What must you think? I'm complaining about Kevin and I'm behaving like a tart.'

'You're not a tart, we just got carried away. Someone had to be sensible,' he sighed playfully as he pulled her to her feet.

It was getting late. It was time to head home.

'Shall I walk you?' he asked with a caring expression on his face.

She nodded her head, pecked him gently on the cheek, and said, 'I'm afraid you have no choice in the matter.'

Walking along the path at the rear of the guesthouse, their arms were entwined around each other. He pulled her into the neighbours' darkened enclosure and kissed her until her chin was sore from his stubble.

Gasping for breath, she pulled away as she checked her watch. 'I have to get back, my gran needs her medication, but I can't wait to see you tomorrow – that's if you want me to?'

'You bet, I can't wait either,' he whispered, as he bid her goodnight with one final peck. Then he headed off back to his caravan.

Mildred almost skipped down the pathway and into the yard door. Even despite Kevin's interference, her date with Danny couldn't have gone any better.

She was so deep in happy thoughts, so engrossed in the magic of the day, that she didn't even see the pair of narrow, pale blue eyes peering at her from behind the lower kitchen window.

As soon as she stepped inside the back door, she turned the key in the lock and turned to climb up the backstairs. Hearing the kitchen door creak, she turned her head and held her breath when a figure lurched towards her and wrapped a pair of hands around her mouth. With a muffled scream she struggled hard, but the arms were too strong and she was pushed forward, falling onto the stairs. Her clothes were hauled up from behind and she could do nothing about it. Her knickers were ripped off and someone was rubbing themselves against her in a frenzy of desire.

'I know what you've been up to, so are you going to be a good girl and do the same for me?' Kevin hissed, as he fumbled with the buttons on his jeans.

Her heart thudded, she could barely breathe, only shake her head from side to side as she attempted another muffled cry, but his smelly, fat hand was pressed firmly over her mouth.

He groaned and shuddered, howling like a banshee. He jumped back and released Mildred. She scrambled to her feet, pulling her crumpled skirt down and pressed herself to the side of the wall, as Sadie scrambled down the stairs with savage eyes, her fingers splayed like talons.

She hauled herself at him, digging her long nails into his face. He screeched as she moved her fingers away, dragging his hair out by the roots. 'How did you get in here you filthy rotten beast?' she hollered. 'I'm telling the police that you've raped my daughter,' she gasped, her breathing erratic.

'He was waiting for me. We never use the back entrance, so I don't know how he got in, but he did,' wailed Mildred, her cheeks streaked with tears as she glared at him.

'I was not, you rotten liar, you asked me in here,' he muttered, his pale eyes now dark with malice. 'You think she's sweetness and light, well, she's not. She's seeing a gypsy and going into his caravan too,' he snarled.

Sadie cast Mildred a sharp look at that comment, and in doing so didn't see Kevin's finger slide over his neck in a cutting action. He unlocked the door, yanked it open and sprinted down the yard.

Chapter Ten

A loud hammering on the internal door that separated the McDine's quarters from the staff and guests' area caused Mildred's eyes to jolt open. She had been awake all night, tossing and turning over what Kevin had done to her. Eventually she'd fallen into a fitful sleep, just as the darkened sky had transformed into the pink and golden shade of dawn.

Mildred sat bolt upright, blinked her eyes, pushed her bedding back and leapt out of bed. As she dashed to unlock the door, it flew open and revealed an angered Nora Jones, who was stood there with a face like a thunderstorm. Her lashes were blinking like crazy as she prodded her fat finger in Mildred's face.

'I had the police at my door last night,' she boomed. 'They took Kevin away. Where's Kitty? I want to see her now.' Her hands were pressed on her ample hips. She pushed past Mildred and stormed into Kitty's bedroom.

'Well I heard you before I saw you Nora, and stop shouting at Mildred,' croaked Kitty, raising her head off the pillow to glare at her. 'Don't stand there trying to protect him. You don't know what he's done, but I do. If Sadie hadn't returned from London when she did, Mildred would have been raped. Your son is a disgusting animal and deserves to be locked up. Tell him not to show his face here again.'

'I don't believe you. I'm not going to stand here and listen to this,' Nora hollered. 'If he's not welcome here, then I'm not staying either.'

'Suit yourself,' Kitty mumbled, as she laid her head back against the pillows and shut her eyes.

Nora swung around with a snort as she stormed back to the lounge. Mildred was stood with clenched fists as Nora lurched towards her. Screeching, she dug her nails into her cheeks, then wrapped both hands around Mildred's neck, just as her son had the previous night.

Sadie stepped out of her bedroom just in time to witness the altercation. She strode towards Nora, dragged her off Mildred, slapped her across the cheek and flung her aside.

'How dare you lay a finger on Mildred! It wasn't my mother who informed the police either. I informed them, it was me you deluded woman,' she hissed, prodding her finger into Nora's sneering fat face. 'You should be ashamed of yourself, the way you've behaved. If I catch you laying a hand on Mildred again, I assure you it'll be more than a slap that you get from me.'

Nora sat upright, holding her cheek. 'When did you arrive? I might have known you'd be at the back of this. You think you're a paragon of virtue don't you, with your swanky clothes and newly-found posh voice? But you can't hide the fact that you spawned a half gypsy – just look at her,' she snarled, pointing at Mildred, before she swung around and stormed out.

Mildred lifted her foot and kicked the door shut. She moved over to the wall and stood in front of the mirror above the fireplace, scrutinising the scratch marks and spots of blood on her reddened cheeks.

'That bitch wants locking up too,' she said as she moved away, her eyes blazing with anger. 'That was assault. My face is a mess now and I was meant to be going to the fairground later,' she complained, as if it was the most important thing on planet earth.

'There's something I need to say while I'm here,' said Sadie, as she moved into the kitchen and picked up the kettle. 'Now I know he's a swine, but he also said that you had been in someone's caravan. You're not even fifteen yet and you're hanging around with show lads? You're too young to be going into a stranger's caravan. You'll get yourself into trouble.'

Mildred shot her a harsh look as she sat with her arms folded. 'You can talk! You weren't much older when you got pregnant with me,' she said.

'My point exactly. That's why I don't want you making the same mistake. I don't want you ruining your life too.'

'My life? My bloody life?' repeated Mildred, rounding on Sadie. 'My life has been one fat lie and now, to top it all off, my gran is dying. What sort of life will that be? I can only see nothing but misery for me. I was only having a bit of fun for once. I'm like an old woman, cleaning and making beds all the time. The fairground is the most fun I've had in ages.'

'Well you won't be anymore, because while I'm here I'm taking charge of everything. You know there's no getting better for your gran and last night's drama has brought everything to a head. I'm cancelling all the next guests that are due. I must act today as soon as we've given them their breakfast. I'm telling them that due to illness, we're closing. So come on, let's get moving,' she ordered, while clapping her hands together. 'It's no good sitting there looking like a wet weekend.'

Mildred shot to her feet, turned on her heel and stormed into the bathroom.

'Who does she think she is? Not been here two minutes and she's already ordering me about,' she whispered to herself, as she turned on the shower.

With a towel wrapped around her, she went into her bedroom, dried her wild hair and dressed in the coolest cotton shift she could find. She dashed downstairs to the guest kitchen to see that Sadie was already pulling open cupboard doors and peering into the large fridge.

Somehow, they muddled through the breakfast routine. Sadie ran around the kitchen mopping her brow, totally flustered and unaware of the silent glares that Mildred was casting over her shoulder.

Stood at the sink, up to her elbows in suds, Mildred washed the never-ending pile of dishes while Sadie was in the dining room, strutting around wearing a tight-fitting skimpy top and a small, frilly pinafore that barely covered her pencil skirt. Stood all dolled up with eyebrows preened and arms waving, she tried explaining the situation to the guests.

As she sashayed back into the kitchen, she flopped down on the nearest seat and removed her stiletto shoes. Mildred looked at the strands of hair that straggled from the intricate arrangement that she had combed her mop into. 'Are you just going to stand all done up and chatting, while I slave away in here?' she asked.

'No, I was just explaining things to them,' she replied in a contrite manner.

'We've also got a problem. Kevin used to do anything manual, he brought the commodities here. Also, he hauled bedding and towels back and forward to the cleaners. We'll have to take on someone else,' said Mildred, as she began drying the dishes with a tea towel.

'I'll be writing letters and making a few calls before I go into town on business, so you'll have to stay in with Gran till I get back,' said Sadie.

Mildred gritted her teeth as she walked beside her in silence, while carrying a mug of tea and a slice of toast for her grandmother. When she stepped inside Kitty's bedroom, she stopped in her tracks, holding her breath she peered at Kitty's complexion. Her eyes were sunken and her skin the colour of wax.

'Gran, wake up,' she said, but there was no response.

Still frozen to the spot, she yelled, 'Wake up. Please Gran, wake up!'

Kitty's chest rose and she stirred. Heaving a long sigh of relief, she placed the tea and toast on a tray beside her chair. Bending over, she supported her grandmother's back as she lifted her gently up and held the cup to her lips. Kitty's chest was wheezing and rattling, but she drank a small amount before her head flopped against the pillow and her eyes closed.

Now Mildred was back in her bedroom, pacing back and forth and chewing her nails. She kept peering at her watch, wondering how much longer Sadie would be with those phone calls and letters before she went out.

It was now midday and the fairground opened at two. She was itching to see Danny for half an hour. I'll have to warn him that Kevin will be out for revenge, especially after being locked up by the police, she thought, as she hopped from one foot to the other.

Hearing the sound of clattering heels behind her bedroom door, she rushed towards it and yanked it open to face Sadie reeking of perfume, rolling her perfectly made-up eyes and arching her eyebrow. 'Don't forget, no going anywhere until I get back,' she gushed, as she swayed around, and her heels clattered down the back staircases.

'Bloody drama queen,' muttered Mildred as she flew to the window above the back kitchen.

Sadie was dashing down the yard. She yanked her car door open and zoomed away. Mildred blew out her cheeks, stepped away and headed towards Kitty's bedroom. The door was left ajar and she was still flat out. Biting her bottom lip; wringing her hands together and wrinkling her brow, she was torn in two. But when she thought of the handsome face of Danny and the feel of his hot kisses, she was on fire and unable to stop herself.

She pulled open the front door. It was an Indian summer and the sun dazzled her eyes, but felt soothing on her bare shoulders and arms. She wore a low black top, a flared skirt and elegant, multi-coloured raffia mules. Butterflies began fluttering in her tummy and a tingling feeling of anticipation swept over her at the thought of meeting Danny again. But the scene of her granny lying prone and barely breathing was foremost in her mind too as she glanced left and right.

Closing her mind to that thought, she ran over the road and made her way past the carousels, trucks and sideshows and towards his caravan. She tapped on the door and stood there dry-mouthed with her heart a flutter.

The door opened and her face beamed, because the moment he saw her, he crushed her tightly in his arms. She was so thrilled that she could barely breathe, but she pulled herself away. 'Danny, I need to get this out. When you walked me home yesterday, Kevin waited for me in the kitchen. And when I entered through the door, he overpowered me and tried to do things to me that that I didn't want him to do. Sadie was demented, scratching his face and attacking him, then she phoned police. He's been arrested, but he'll be back out and he'll be after you now that he knows about us.'

The smile on Danny's face vanished. He stood for several seconds staring at her, then his eyes darkened, hooded and narrowed. Consumed with a surge of bitter rage, he balled his hands into fists and whispered, 'I'll kill him,'

Mildred realised her mistake instantly and there was only one thing she could do to correct it. She took the initiative to bring about a happy state of affairs and began kissing him long and hard, pressing herself against him. She reached for his hands and put them to her breasts. Danny's tense shoulders relaxed as his long hair brushed against her cheeks.

She was overwhelmed with the sensation, feeling a tightening in her belly, as he stroked her nipples with his finger. She gasped with pleasure and was astonished with the sensation. She couldn't remember anything feeling like this, a wanted need that had to be sated. As she unbuttoned his shirt, he pushed his knee between her legs, his hands kneading her buttocks.

Unable to stop Danny's heated passion, she gritted her teeth and took it. This was hurting her more than she expected, and she was glad when he gave a strange sort of shudder and collapsed on top of her.

As she lay beneath him, she grimaced, feeling slightly cheated. Was this what all her friends had been telling her about with feverish excitement? Well, if it was, she wasn't very impressed. She was sore, messy and now wished she hadn't done it.

Danny moved aside and lay whispering sweet nothings in her ear. She sat up and swept her fingers through her hair.

'Come away with me,' he suddenly blurted. 'I'm eighteen and I can look after you. You wouldn't have to go into an orphanage, plus you would be free of that creep forcing himself on you.'

She sat open-mouthed, her eyes wide and twinkling. Then she slumped forward and sat glum-faced, her chin in her hands. 'I would love to Danny, but how can I leave while my granny is dying. I would never forgive myself. Why has this happened too soon?'

He clasped hold of her hand and gripped it tight. 'I'll write to you at the guesthouse when I move on. We will keep in touch that way, and a year will soon pass – come on,' he urged. 'Don't get all upset.'

She forced her lips into a smile but felt broken-hearted at the thought of him being out of her life for a year. The thought was interrupted when a loud banging on the side of the caravan made them both jump. They both shot up and scrambled to their feet. She straightened her skirt, while he grabbed his jeans and pulled them up, then slung on his shirt. The banging continued.

As Danny opened the door, he was met by a stocky built man who was stood with a bull neck, curly black hair and swarthy skin. He was stood with his arms folded, his expression hard. He cast Mildred a surly look, seeing her stood behind Danny. She felt her face hot with guilt at the way he was staring at her crumpled clothes.

She looked down at her skirt to see it was streaked with blood and to her horror, out the corner of her eyes, she saw her bra and knickers lying on the floor where she had dropped them. The man's eyes widened to see them too. He dragged his eyes away from the articles to run them over her skimpy top. A shiver of distain ran down Mildred's spine, seeing his lustful eyes leering at her voluptuous breasts. She let out a moan, sunk to her knees and keeled over, lying beside her bra and knickers.

'I need a doctor, quick,' she gasped, lying with her eyes closed and face contorted.

Danny and the man stood with gaping mouths as she rolled around on the ground. The man turned around and hurried out of the caravan to go and fetch some help. Once she heard the sound of his heavy footsteps leaving, she opened her eyes to look up at Danny's taut face. She sat up and began giggling. 'Well, I had to do something to get my knickers and bra, I couldn't just bend over and pick them off the floor when he was leering at me,' she laughed.

Danny sat wide-eyed while raking his fingers through his hair. 'Millie McDine, you are the wildest girl I've ever known.'

'That's me,' she sniggered, twisting her finger around a wild curl. Then suddenly, remembering her grandmother, she pulled him towards her, clasped her arms around his neck and kissed his lips, his face, his ears and neck.

'I'll see you tomorrow,' she shouted as she dashed out of the caravan.

Racing through the field, she dashed over the road, flew into the yard and ran up the stairs. Reaching the top landing, she stopped and tiptoed towards the lounge with her fingers crossed behind her back. Peeking through, she heaved a sigh. There was only the gentle sound of the radio playing an old ballad and no sign of the drama queen.

Stepping back she dashed into her bedroom, where she yanked the bloodied knickers and skirt off, hurried to the bathroom and got washed, then pulled on clean knickers and a pair of jeans. Bracing her shoulders, she headed towards Kitty's room. As she got nearer to her door, she stopped and pressed her finger and thumb against her nose. There was an offensive smell emanating from the room, and the door would not open.

She shouted her grandmother's name, but was met with silence. With her heart thudding like a drum, she lifted her leg and kicked in the door. Kitty was slumped behind the door making guttural sounds, while thick reddish-brown gunge seeped from her gaping mouth. Her eyes were fixed and blank.

Mildred keeled over, as though punched in the stomach, and stumbled backwards out of the room, her whole body trembling.

Her legs and arms were numb, as though she was wading through water, as she stepped into the lounge to telephone for help. The receptionist answered and told her an ambulance would be there soon. She clutched hold of a chair as she moved in a dreamlike state, her mind in a spin, when she remembered the elderly lady from next door whom Kitty went to church with. She put her hand against the wall for support as she staggered through the building. The ground kept coming up to meet her eyes and the walls swayed from side to side.

Somehow, she reached Mrs Lowther next door, and thumped on her window with her fist. The old lady appeared at the window with a scowl on her face, but seeing tears streaming down Mildred's cheeks she dropped the curtain and hurried for the door. The door was wrenched open, and Mrs Lowther reached forward to grab hold of Mildred as her legs gave way and she collapsed to the floor.

The old woman clapped her hands to her mouth, as her eyes peered around to see if anyone could help her. She turned around and shuffled through to her kitchen, where she brought out a glass of water. When she returned, Mildred had stirred. She rose to her feet and grabbed hold of a bracket for support as she begged for her help. 'Please! It's my grandmother, she's behind the door and won't wake up,' she wailed.

Her world was crashing down around her. Her lovely old Gran, that had rocked Mildred on her knee and who had kissed away the scratches and scrapes of life, was now dying. Tears shuddered from her as the woman shuffled behind her, puffing and panting as they went through to the back of the guesthouse.

Seeing Kitty lying in a terrible state, she jerked back at the sight before her. Taking a deep breath, she pressed her fingers to the side of Kitty's neck to check her pulse. Then, turning around, her eyes sought Mildred's. She shook her head as their eyes finally met. Mildred let out a loud wail as she bent over and flung herself onto her grandmother.

'She'll need the last rites,' whispered Mrs Lowther, as she hooked an arm around Mildred's shoulders and pulled her close in a comforting hug. 'The doctor will have to be informed too. I'll have to get her cleaned up before anyone arrives. I'm terribly sorry,' she spoke softly.

But Mildred was too consumed with guilt and sorrow to notice the odour and mess. If I hadn't gone to see Danny, I would have been there to help you in your time of need, she thought as she lay down beside her grandmother, rubbing a hand over her paper thin cheeks. 'I'll never forgive myself for being so selfish and leaving you so long. I'm so sorry granny. I wish I was a quiet and gentle granddaughter, but I'm not. I'm wild and reckless. Please forgive me,' she whispered, as her tattered emotions flowed through her.

There was the sound of feet approaching, and muffled voices, but she still lay beside her grandmother with her eyes closed. She didn't want to open them, and thought that maybe if she didn't, somehow she would stay in the dark forever, and never return to the terrible light of this bitter reality.

Sensing she was being watched, she quickly turned her head and pulled her brows together to see Father Black. He was stood with his customary pious face, cold hawk eyes peering at her with a look of distain. Mrs Lowther was standing wiping her eyes with a hankie, while another couple of neighbours were clutching each other and peering at Kitty's skeletal, sunken face.

'Can someone please cover this lady with something while I give her the last rites?' he asked, while pulling out a handkerchief to cover his beaky nose. Then, with his other hand, he clicked open a case, where he took out a set of rosary beads, a small bottle of holy water and a small silver round tin containing ointment, which he dipped his finger in, then made the sign of the cross with it on Kitty's brow. He began to pray.

'Well, don't just stand there gawping, get down on your knees and pray with me,' he barked at Mildred, as the old women hovered over the other side of the room. Clenching her teeth, Mildred sank to the floor and cast him a sideways look of malice. Hysteria was building inside her and before she could stop herself, she leapt to her feet.

'I've just lost my grandmother and you're looking down your long beaky nose at me, trying to preach your religion. You've not one bit of Christianity in your old bones. Go fuck yourself,' she screeched, as she lurched herself at him and whacked him hard across his face with the back of her hand.

There were shrieks and gasps from the women who were stood cowering, as Mildred's blazing eyes swung round to glower at them. She raced out of the room, down the back stairs and out of the door, where she stood in the heat with tears streaming down her cheeks.

Her eyes darted over the road as she watched the carousels, heard the laughter and blearing music. She abruptly spurted across the road and ran into the field, mingling with the crowd. She past gaudy stalls with candy rock, fluffy toys and goldfish swimming in bags of water, all of which were there to entice children as they peered up at them with a look of glee.

The waltzer was in full swing, crammed with teenagers stood all around it. They watched the carousel whizzing about while loud music blared. People were jumping on and off and Danny was collecting fares. All she wanted was his muscular arms wrapped around her, while he smoothed her shattered nerves. Everything would be alright then, everything would feel bright again, and she would be able to cope with the nightmare that was taking place in the guesthouse behind her.

Unable to speak to him, she turned around sullen-faced. Barging her way past happy and joyful people, she headed towards the stream nearby. This always soothed her, whenever she listened to the trickling sound. She sunk down and sat wondering how could life carry on as normal, when hers was falling apart? She laid herself back in the grass, with the heat from the sun and fatigue, her eyes flickered and she fell asleep.

Drops of rain wet her face and woke her. The sun was sinking and it was chilly. She shivered as she sat up, peering at her watch. Jumping to her feet, she raced through the fields and back to the guesthouse, where she saw the stationary police car.

She stopped in her tracks when she noticed that the policeman sat in the passenger seat was peering out of the window and giving her a quizzical expression. Dropping her eyes, she looked away, but raised them again to see the car doors open. The policemen stepped out and were making their way up the drive, advancing towards her.

'Mildred McDine?' the tubby policeman asked, with his uniform stretched over his big belly. He was looking at her with a solemn expression on his ruddy face, as the younger fellow stood giving her an appraising glance. 'Can we come in?' he enquired.

Mildred nodded her head and her stomach rose. She pushed the front door open, wondering what could be wrong. Had the man phoned the police about her in the caravan? Did he know she was underage and had been having sex? With her mind in a whirl, her knuckles whitened, as she clutched her hands at her sides.

She stood aside and beckoned them in, and raised scared eyes at them as they stood in the passageway peering at her. She turned her back to close the door and the silence was deafening. She quietly led the way to the guests' lounge, where she found that she hadn't just slipped into an ending nightmare at all. The nightmare had in fact only just begun.

Chapter Eleven

'No! I don't need to be examined,' she screeched, as she swung around to run out of the door, but the large officer lurched towards her and clasped her in a tight grip.

Father Black came thundering down the stairs and advanced towards the policeman with his finger pointed at Mildred. 'Take that spawn of the devil away, she attacked me,' he gasped, as her arms and legs flailed in an attempt to free herself from the policeman's grip.

'Please, I need to see my granny. What's happening? ' she shouted.

'I've been here all this time,' boomed Father Black. 'You disappeared, and I've had to stay, since there was nobody else. The doctor had to write a death certificate before the undertakers could take your grandmother's body. So, where have you been? Up to no good I suppose,' he rasped.

Beads of sweat stood on the policeman's brow as she wriggled and broke free, scrambling up the stairs. Puffing and panting, the policeman staggered up after her, but had to stop to wipe his clammy brow when he reached the first landing. He leaned over the banister with a beetroot fat face and hissed at Father Black. 'I don't know what's going on, but we're here on a matter of much importance.'

'A matter of importance!' he spat. 'Mrs McDine's body is being removed from her home, you should have more respect for her.' Pulling his lips to a fine line, he swung around to wrench the front door open.

A tall angular woman wearing horn-rimmed glasses was stood with her hand raised to knock on the door, when he pushed past her, knocking her aside.

She pulled a long face as she stepped into the passageway. 'That man is ignorant,' she snapped, as she inclined her head and acknowledged the younger policeman who was stood with his lips twitching. His portly boss was dashing down the stairs, still wiping his scarlet face and furrowed brow as he slumped down on the bottom stair.

Craning their neck and tilting their head, they all peered up to the top landing, where Mildred's deep and shuddering sobs could be heard. Behind her, there was the sound of scuffling feet. Two men with a solemn expression and dressed in black from head to shoes were removing Kitty's body, which was stretchered and covered with a blanket. The younger policeman leapt to open the door as one of the undertakers turned to Mildred and said her grandmother would be in the chapel of rest until the funeral.

She wiped her tear soaked face and nodded her head. Closing the door, she stood for long moments before she could turn around.

'I'm not going to the police station,' she announced, with her arms crossed, as she lifted her bowed head and red-rimmed eyes. Seeing the woman stood wearing brown brogue shoes, a tweed pleated skirt; cameo brooch pinned in the collar of her cream blouse, she gave her a quizzical look.

The woman's thin lips with a faint shadow of a moustache compressed together. 'Mildred. My name is Miss Small. I'm a social worker, and I've been appointed to accompany you for an examination at the police station,' she said in a gentle manner.

Mildred's eyebrows drew together. 'Why? I don't need an examination?' she snorted.

'Your mother accused Kevin Jones of rape, so we have to examine you to prove whether he was innocent or not, as it is a serious charge,' the portly policeman explained. Turning to face the woman, he said, 'Miss Small here will be supporting you.'

Mildred's face stretched. 'I told you I'm not having an examination and you didn't listen to me when you arrived. I don't need any support either, my mother is here. She'll be back soon.'

Miss Small gave her a grave look and heaved a sigh. 'I'm sorry Mildred, I have yet more bad news for you. Your mother contacted social services this morning and explained your circumstances. She was very upset, but said she had to return to London.'

Mildred's mouth dropped open as she stared at the woman for long seconds. Then, turning on her heel, she ran up the flights of stairs, leaving Miss Small to hurry behind her as she moved through the building and strode into Sadie's bedroom, where she pulled open the wardrobe doors and stood with her mouth ajar.

'She's gone when I need her most, just like she did when I was a baby,' she burst out. 'Why am I'm not surprised? She's a disgrace, do you know that? She knew how ill my gran was, and said she would sort everything out. So, that's what she was sorting out was she? Well she can fuck right off.'

Miss Small winced at the bad language as she stood surveying Mildred's malevolent expression, but understood her bitter rage. 'I'm so sorry Mildred. It seems she's married to a controlling man and has to dance to his tune. I will have to ring her and let her know about your grandmother. She's going to have to face you at the funeral, and if this goes to court, which I know it will, then she'll have to see you again to give evidence. I know it's easy for me to say it, but put her out of your mind for now. Go in your bedroom and put some clothes in a couple of cases, as well as anything sentimental. We have to go.'

Mildred was stone faced as she got up and went towards her room. 'What about the guesthouse?' she asked, turning to face the woman once more. 'We can't just leave everything. There's food in the kitchens and nobody is going in my granny's room to poke around,' she hissed, as she strode to Kitty's room.

Kitty's black bag was left on the floor, she bent over and picked it up, hugging it to herself with tears spilling down her cheeks. 'What will happen to me now?' she wailed. 'Will this examination hurt?'

'It's a bit uncomfortable,' said the social worker. 'Afterwards I'm taking you to a home for young girls. It's not too far from here; it's in the country and is very nice.'

'I'm past caring where it is. Nothing can be worse than not having my granny to take care of me,' she replied with anguished eyes, gazing at the empty bed before turning on her heel and scowling, wishing the woman would just disappear.

Miss Small followed her to her bedroom, where she lowered herself onto a chair and watched as Mildred dragged drawers out and yanked wardrobe drawers open, hauling her belongings out and slinging them onto the bed. How am I going to see Danny now? I was meant to meet him tomorrow for the last time, but she's hanging about like a bloody bad smell, I wish she would piss off, Mildred thought, as she pulled out her cases from underneath her bed.

'Times pushing on Mildred,' said Miss Small, pushing her blouse sleeve aside and checking her watch.

Mildred's mind was a whirling pool of madness, and her stomach was churning. They were going to examine her, and once they did, they would discover she had had sex. There was only one thing to do, and that was to lie and tell them that Kevin did rape her. There was no way Danny was getting into trouble. He was eighteen and would go to prison, and she couldn't allow that. Kevin deserves all that he gets.

Her heart began racing in her chest. She gulped for air as beads of sweat appeared on her brow. Somehow she had to see Danny to tell him what had happened.

'I'm just getting my stuff from the bathroom,' she said to Miss Small, as she moved away.

Stepping into the bathroom, she looked at the dirty washing basket, put her hand in and snatched her blood stained clothes. Bracing her shoulders, she tip-toed to the landing, raced down the back stairs, into the yard and pulled the bin lid off. Dumping the bloodied clothes inside, she raced towards the field.

'Where's Danny?' she yelled at a young lad, as she shoved past the crowds that still crammed the space around the waltzer. He shrugged his shoulders nonchalantly, clearly not interested. She turned around and dashed down the steps, racing towards his caravan. She halted instantly, as she saw him sauntering towards her with a wide grin on his face.

She threw herself at him in hysterics, as she told him what had occurred and that now there was a social worker waiting to take her to a care home. Danny's smile faded; his eyes were like steel as he held her quivering body. 'Take me with you,' she beseeched, clutching at his arm.

Danny swallowed hard and was blurry-eyed when he told her it was impossible. She collapsed to her knees, pummelling the grass and wailing.

People pointed and sniggered as he glanced around, pulling her to feet. Feeling her heart breaking in two, she stood for long moments, searching his handsome stony face. When she realised she was beaten, she swiped her hand across her wet cheeks, tilted her chin, swung around and raced through the field with Danny calling after her.

The world as she knew it had come to an end, a bitter, non-sparing end.

She reached the guesthouse to see Miss Small putting her belongings inside the boot of her car. She glanced up to face the broken child as she shut the boot and then handed her Kitty's bag. Mildred's eyes were dry and as cold as steel as she grabbed it. There were no more tears left to spill, now that her heart had turned to stone.

She sat in silence with the black bag on her knee while Miss Small drove the car away. Away from her home, away from Danny; away from everything that once was.

'I know you don't want to talk about it, but what Kevin Jones did to you, he'll get his just deserts,' said Miss Small, with an indignant look on her face.

Mildred turned to face her with soulless, empty eyes, and poured out her blinded, empty soul.

Chapter Twelve

Kevin Jones had been detained in a police cell further in town. For all it was summer, the cells were situated where no sun ever penetrated the thick walls to warm the place, and he was lying shivering on a narrow bed that stank of sweat and the thin blanket that covered him was also reeking.

His chin quivered as he raised his eyes and peered up at the bare light bulb attached to wire. 'That bastard, Kerrigan has had it in for me for years, while I've ducked and dived, but, now am friggin' banged up, I wish now I had had me end away, it would have been worth it. And, if it hadn't been for that stuck up bitch Sadie Carr catching me with Mildred, I wouldn't be stuck in this shit hole. I don't know why I bothered she's locked at the friggin' knees. It's just that pikey she's got the hot's for – stinking bastard,' he snarled.

Slinging the blanket off, he sat up and got to his feet. They must be letting me out, since I've done nowt anyway, he thought, as he heard the key scraping in the lock. The door was pushed open and a burly police officer faced him with cold grey eyes and thick hairy eyebrows. 'The girl has been examined. I have to take you to the interview room. Kerrigan is waiting to see you.'

Kevin's head jerked back. 'What do you mean? She's been examined? I didn't even touch her,' he yelled, as he stepped towards the policeman. 'I'm innocent. I'm not getting blamed for something I haven't done, you've got to believe me,' he implored. The PC shook his head. With clamped lips, he rolled his eyes, grabbed his arms and held them at his sides while he marched him out of the cell, whimpering like a baby. Yawning, the PC turned the key in the lock and turned around to see Kevin stood with scared eyes and quivering chin, as he escorted him to the interview room.

A lean man with wavy corn coloured hair was sat with his elbows leant on a desk, hands clasped together as he surveyed the surly acne faced youth advancing towards him. He raised an outstretched hand and beckoned him to take the seat facing him. Kevin slumped down with lower lip jutting; glowering at Kerrigan,

'Well, you've shit in your nest now laddie!' he remarked. 'That young lass you forced yourself on has been examined and guess what? She's lost her cherry. Have you got anything to say about it?'

Kevin's hands were shaking as he raked his fingers through his hair, his pale eyes wide with fear. 'It wasn't me, she's been visiting that pikey at the fairground, he's been at her,' he spluttered.

'Hey, don't insult my intelligence. How many times have I caught you red handed and you've wormed your way out of it, well, not this time mate. Kevin Jones, you are to be detained in custody and whatever you say shall be taken down and used in evidence when you appear in Court.'

Kevin's face twisted as he leapt to his feet. Kerrigan clicked his fingers and told the PC to take him back to his cell until he was to be transported to Durham jail.

Kevin collected phlegm in his mouth and spat it into Kerrigan face. Kerrigan's eyes narrowed then bulged, blazing as the green gunge slid down his cheek. He pressed his hands on the desk, scraped his chair back and rose to his feet. Circling Kevin, he swiped his hands across his face and wiped it off. With his lips pulled tight over his teeth, he squashed the slime into Kevin's fat cheeks while lifting his foot. Booting him in the stomach, Kevin groaned, keeled over as his legs gave way and he crumpled to the floor. Kerrigan bent over, thrust his big face into his. 'Get the fuck out of my office laddie, because your cards are well and truly marked now,' he growled as he swung round with a reproving glare, then stood with his back to him. The PC hauled him up and dragged him back to the cell howling and shouting his innocence.

Chapter Thirteen

Cutting the car engine, Miss Small pointed towards a Victorian building, where ivy crept along the brick walls and against the leaded windows. It was set behind a high stone wall and set in the depths of the country. Mildred could smell cows and green grass, before the social worker turned a small handle on the car door to wind the window up.

'This place is run by the Methodists, and it's called The Willows,' she remarked, as she turned to face Mildred's sullen countenance. 'It's no good, looking at me like that, you know you can't stay on your own, so come along, the Matron is expecting you.'

Mildred got out of the car and stood peering at the place with tears glazing her eyes. She had a sinking feeling in her stomach wondering how long would she be kept here. Swiping her hand across her brow, she swung around, her eyes darting everywhere. She surveyed the area, intending to get away from there as soon as she could, but wondered how she would manage for money, then, remembered, her grandmother's black bag. She held it closer to herself when Miss Small tapped her on the shoulder making her leap with fright.

'Come along, there's no good standing in a dream,' she retorted. Mildred slouched behind the social worker and stood waiting as Miss Small lifted her hand and rattled the handle attached to the letter box. The door opened. A stooped woman wearing a drab grey dress with her white hair pulled up into a bun stood aside, her watery eyes peered at

Mildred with a disapproving expression.

'This is the housekeeper and this is Mildred,' said Miss Small as she introduced them both. Mildred acknowledged her with a grimace. The woman merely turned away and asked them to follow her along a passage. It had a shiny wooden floor that smelled of beeswax and it held a still, dismal atmosphere, which reminded Mildred of the convent that the Catholic school sent them for a retreat. Silence was expected, except when they were chanting prayers –which was most of the time. With her heart sinking at the memory of it, she watched the woman stop outside a door and push it open.

The room was basic. No pictures or ornaments were to be seen. The walls were painted cream and natural light filled the room at best. A single bed, with a bale of bedding stood with a metal bedframe; a set of plain wooden drawers and a wardrobe, stood on either side of an alcove. Her belongings were put down on the bed by Miss Small, who gave Mildred a brief smile.

'I'll be back to take you to your grandmother's funeral, when I find out when the date is,' she said. Then, turning, she left Mildred and the housekeeper facing each other in the cold and hostile atmosphere. She pointed a bone thin finger at a sheet of paper attached to the closing door, before twisting her face and looking Mildred up and down. 'Those are the rules of the home. I expect you to adhere to them wholeheartedly. If you fail to do so, you shall find yourself in serious trouble, is that understood?'

Mildred reluctantly nodded her head and retracted her gaze. The housekeeper snarled, yanked the door open, and then glanced over her shoulder. 'I'll be back soon, that bed had better be made upon my return. 'When I do, it's off to see the mistress.' She gave a wry smile and then closed the door firmly.

Mildred moved towards the window and turned the handle to open it. To her surprise, it opened, and when she gazed down, there was an outer building attached that faced a large well-kept, walled garden. Her eyes narrowed, would it be possible to get onto the roof and then slide down the drain pipe? If so, then freedom. But, with freedom came the need for cash. She clicked open Kitty's bag and peered inside to see an old purse, rosary beads and a bank book.

She lifted the rosary beads out and thought back to the days when she sat next to her grandmother in church watching her lips move in silent prayer, as the beads slipped through her fingers. Opening the purse, she stared at a wad of notes and her eyes lit up. Then, turning the pages of the bank book, her eyes widened and brightened to the point that the cold dark room actually felt bright and warm. There was a zipped compartment, containing a brown envelope, and her name was written on it. Curious, she pulled the folded envelope open and took out a sheet of paper and read the content.

My darling Mildred, You are my only benefactor. Your mother will not be pleased, but she doesn't deserve a penny after how she left you. My solicitor has the copy of my will. You know the one, based in Percy Street, Newcastle. Take the bank book to him and he will deal with everything for you. I wish you a happy and safe life, your devoted gran.

She sat with the letter in her hand with her lips trembling, and the writing blurred, as hot tears filled her eyes, and ran down her cheeks. Totally absorbed in what she was reading, she didn't hear the door pushed open. The housekeeper stepped inside the room with a stern look on her face.

'I expected the bed made and your things put away, what on earth have you been doing?' she scolded.

Mildred's head shot up as she shoved the letter and bank book inside the zipped compartment and clicked the bag shut. She leaped off the bed and advanced towards the housekeeper, where she followed her to face a diminutive, attractive woman with short hair. She was sat in an armchair, the heat from the burning flame of the fireplace which stood next to her, apparent on her reddened cheeks. She inclined her head and smiled as she held her hand out, beckoning Mildred to sit in the chair opposite her, while the housekeeper stepped out of the room.

'I'm Dolly-Belle,' she said. 'I hope you will be happy here. We try to make the transition a happy one – especially after what you've endured. I know it's all very strange for you, but we will try our best to make you feel welcome, and if you don't cause any trouble, then we will get along just fine,' she said, as her eyebrows met as she glanced at the papers on her knee. 'I see your fifteenth birthday is next week and you would have been leaving school.'

She raised her eyes and drew in breath. 'This report from your school doesn't put you in a good light. Nevertheless, if you prove to me that I can trust you, I'll allow you to work for my friends who own a café down the seafront. But, you'll need to know the rules I have set out and I demand they are carried out by each child that resides here. Each day a bell is rang for any activity. We start the morning with prayers and breakfast. All domestic duties will be carried out under strict supervision from your housemother. We also have teachers who come in for a few hours a day. At bath time you are not allowed dressing gowns as they get wet when you take your place in the queue. If you are shy, then wrap the towel around yourself, while you wait your turn. When you reach sixteen, you will leave here, but by then, you will have learned a trade and be able to get employment, go back to your room and dinner is at six,' she said, then leant her head back and sat with her eyes closed, becoming totally relaxed.

Mildred stood for a few moments gazing at her, then realised that she was being dismissed. She stepped across to the door in silence and made her way back to her room. After making her bed and putting her belongings away, she slumped down the bed and buried her head into her hands while hot tears flowed once more.

Swiping her eyes, she glanced at her watch as her stomach rumbled, and was glad it was meal time, she was starving. Pulling the door open, she glanced along the passageway in both directions but there was no sign of anyone. All the other doors were closed. Why hadn't anyone come out yet?

She turned on her heel and followed the lingering aroma of freshly cooked food, looking to locate the deliciousness. She stopped and glanced through the dining room glass panelled doors, to see a pine panelled room with a black and white tiled floor. Bright red and yellow coloured flower paintings were hung around the walls, while vases of fresh flowers were dotted about on the windowsills, giving the room a cheery atmosphere. At the back of the room was a counter with an assortment of food. Girls of every size and height were waiting to be served by a stout woman wearing a wrap - around pinafore. Taking a deep breath, she pulled the door open, stepped inside and advanced towards the counter where she gazed around, watching the rest of the room in silence. But as she did, she wanted to retreat. She realised that as she stared, they were all staring back at her. All eyes were focused in her direction. Even people in front of her in the queue had turned to observe her. She smiled. 'Hallo, I'm Millie,' she whispered to the girl in front of her. 'I feel lost here and don't know anyone.' The girl smiled as she leaned towards her, right on close and said she could sit beside her and whispered what was good on the menu and what was not. 'Keep away from the broth, unless you want to spend hours on the loo,' she laughed.

Soon, she was sat chatting and wolfing down the wholesome food, her worries all completely behind her. She told them about her grandmother dying and that her mother didn't want her. Which was met by a chorus of sympathy. Already, she was beginning to feel she was part of a family, even though it was dysfunctional.

Once the meal was over, she followed her new friends to another part of the home. It was a cosy room where pink velvet curtains were draped at the windows. Soft squashy settees and chairs were placed around the room. Shelves were stacked with books and a TV stood in the corner. She was sat chatting, when a housemother emerged into the room and called her name. She got up and was told to follow her. She stepped inside a white tiled kitchen, similar to the one at the guesthouse and groaned to see dirty dishes; pans and large containers piled high. A young girl was stood behind the sink up to her elbows in soapy water.

'You can go, now,' she said to the girl. 'Mildred you can take over.'

After two hours, Mildred eyes were hanging off her face. She dragged her feet as she crawled to her bedroom, slumped down on the bed, hauled the covers over herself and slept.

A tap on her door awoke her and she turned her head to see Miss Small breezing inside her room. 'Mildred, what are you doing still in bed? It's nearly midday.'

Mildred sat up and squinted as she yawned and ran her fingers through her wild curls.

'I'm surprised you haven't been told to get up?' she remarked as she lowered herself down onto a chair, the bristles on her chin more prominent than normal. 'I've come to tell you the funeral is tomorrow, so have you something appropriate to wear?'

'I can't face it,' Mildred replied, dropping her creased face into her hands.

'Now Mildred, you have to be strong.'

'Well, I'm not and I'll never be,' she shouted. 'Have you any idea what this is like? Yes, everyone here is lovely, but I just want my gran,' she wailed.

Miss Small paced the room and gazed out of the window with her lips clamped. Eventually, Mildred slipped out of bed and told her what she had discovered in her grandmother's bag and asked if she would take her to Newcastle, to inform the solicitor what had happened to Kitty.

'I've already informed him about your grandmother's demise,' she remarked in a clipped voice.

'But, I need to see him, and get his advice about Grans bank book,' she persisted.

'Well, you'll need an appointment for that. In the meantime, I can take care of it for you, as we have a safe in the office at work, which is there specifically for emergencies such as this.'

'No. I'd rather see the solicitor, so please make an appointment for me while we are in Newcastle for the clothes.'

Miss Small threw her a dark look as she picked up Kitty's bag and marched out to the car.

Mildred had a restless night before the funeral, every time she closed her eyes, the vision of her grandmother appeared, then Kevin forcing himself on her, but worst of all was the expression on Danny's face that she couldn't get out of her mind. She realised he was right, he couldn't take her away with him, but why did he have to be so unfeeling?

As she awoke, she pushed her bedding back; sat up with a sullen face listening to the rain drumming against the window. Typical funeral weather, she thought as she swung her legs over the side of the bed and stepped to the window. She heaved back the curtains and stood in silence watching the rainfall. The droplets were just like her thoughts: numbersome and falling out of the sky, crashing onto the ground at an unfathomably fast rate. Pressing her hot brow against the cool window, she already wished that the day was over before it had even begun.

Miss Small arrived at The Willows dressed in a long black coat and a hat covered in black net that concealed most of her face as she stepped out of the car. Mildred was stood in the doorway; her face was pinched, with dark circles underneath her eyes. Miss Small stepped towards her, clutched her arm. 'It was your grandmother's wish that she would be taken from the guesthouse.'

Mildred gave her a sharp look. 'Have you seen anything of Sadie?'

'No. I suppose she would feel very uncomfortable if she did appear – after what happened.'

'Well, I'll not hold my tongue between my teeth when I see her – if she appears that is,' she retorted as she stepped into the car.

'Mrs Lowther and a couple of women have done everything that your grandmother organised. There's a glass of whisky or sherry available before the service and a lovely spread for afterwards,' said Miss Small.

'Trust Granny!' she remarked. 'Right to the very end, she had to be organised. OK, let's get this ordeal over with,' she announced with a tremor in her voice, then, turned and strode through to the front of The Willows. Her friends were stood in silence and head lowered as she stepped by them.

'I hope Sadie doesn't appear,' she snapped, as the social worker turned the car out of the drive, then sat grim faced and silent as she sank into the seat. Approaching the guesthouse, Mildred peered towards the field where the fair had been held. In her mind's eye, she saw Danny. He was stood with his long hair flowing, a small scarf tied around his neck; his shirt sleeves pulled up and he was stood balancing himself, while the carousel whizzed around. Blinking teary eyes she looked again. There was only a green field and an elderly man shuffling along, leaning on his walking stick, while his dog ran around.

The front door of the guesthouse was ajar. Mildred's stomach was churning, hearing the buzz of voices from the guest lounge as she forced her shaking legs to move inside the passageway. Walking slowly, but also with purpose, she turned her head and gazed at the dining room, where Nora's homely meals were relished by everyone. There was only silence, no tempting aroma of food, just a vacuous atmosphere. Then, she turned towards the guest lounge, where once, people gathered, laughing, chatting or just listening to someone sat at the piano. Maybe a bit too merry, with a sing-song after too many drinks, or just someone stood round the bar. It was always the hub she contemplated as she moved further, until she was inside the room. People were sat around the soft grey and blue seating. Women held a glass of sherry in their hands, po-faced and stiff backed. The men stood smoking a pipe or cigarette, clutching a glass of whisky. Everything was still the same. The brasses, and plates around the walls, the crystal chandeliers, the heavy deep blue brocade curtains draped at the window, but where the piano once stood, now a coffin was in its place, stood on a sturdy wooden plinth.

The place fell silent. Everyone turned their head to stare at the girl with the swarthy features and wild black hair, whilst she slowly sobbed at the sight of her grandmother's coffin. They spoke in hushed tones as they cast her sympathetic; feeble smiles, while they sat clutching flowers and wreathes. The front door clashed open with an echoing thud.

Sadie Carr stepped in, elegant as usual, wearing a black smart trouser suit, a neat black hat with net, styled to conceal her eyes. She turned her head towards Mildred, the bright red glossed lips smiled tentatively. Mildred gave a cursory nod when two women sashayed in behind Sadie, their bulk blocking out the light.

A silence descended in the room once more as people stared with jaws dropping and eyes widening. A chorus of whispers filled the room. The women were six foot tall, half-caste, they had bleached-blonde plaited hair and a pair of ample breasts that hung out over their blouses which were both too tight and low. Their outfits were hardly suitable for a funeral: bright red mini-skirts, legs, thick and fleshy, squeezed into black fishnet tights.

Women sat giving each other contemptuous looks or averted their eyes while pulling their skirts over their knees. The men's eyes gleamed and bulged out of their sockets as they observed the trio sashay over to a table and grab two glasses each. Sadie broke the silence, brazenly gazing around the room. 'These are my friends, twin sisters, Crystal and Pandora. Also, I know what you're all thinking, but Kitty was my mother and I have every right to be here – and so do these two.'

You could hear a pin drop, except for a slight snigger from a woman. She took one glance at the affronted faces and covered her mouth with her hand. The sisters looked at each other with a perfectly-plucked, raised eyebrow. Crystal turned round and glared at the woman, who quickly averted her eyes, and stared, with a fixed expression at the carpet.

Crystal lit up a cigarette, inhaling deeply, as she bent over the woman. 'What's so funny? Do you want your eyes back, eh?' The woman's eyes widened as Crystal loomed closer. 'I'll ask you once again, what's so funny?' The woman's face creased up as she covered her eyes. The atmosphere was now tense. Crystal turned to Pandora. 'That bitch is askin' for trouble.'

Sadie pulled the netting further down her face. 'Take no notice of that ignorant woman, you two are as much welcome as anyone,' she said curling her lips. 'Anyway, I want to introduce my daughter Mildred.' She beamed a bright smile over towards her. The sisters turned their head, peering hard at Mildred.

'My God, you are your father's daughter alright, your hair and skin, you're the very double of gypsy Joe,' Cooed Crystal.

Mildred grimaced, wondering what the woman knew about him, and under her lashes, she swept her eyes around the room, while Sadie gave Crystal a poisonous look. 'This isn't the time and place if you don't mind,' she snapped.

Mildred leaning her head towards her mother lowered her voice, 'I don't know how you dare come here bold as brass Sadie. Did you know I found Gran dying on the floor after you left, and I had no one for support. If it hadn't been for Mrs Lowther next door to sort everything out for me, then I don't know what would have happened. You said you were going to sort things out. Huh you did that alright!'

Sadie sat sniffing her nose and wiping a hankie over her dry eyes. 'I didn't expect her to die so soon, did I? It's taken a lot of guts for me to come here today.'

Mildred cast a fierce look, her eyes cold as steel. 'Well, why did you?' she snarled. Swaying around, she turned her back. 'I'll wait in the kitchen till the hearse arrives,' she said, as hysteria rose in her belly; her voice tight with emotion. Sadie pushed the net up over her hat, still dabbing at her dry eyes. 'I'm so really sorry,' she whimpered as the door closed.

One of the mourners strode into the lounge and told them the hearse was outside. Four men wearing black suits and ties stepped inside the room. They tipped their heads and gave everyone an acknowledgement, before lowering themselves over the coffin. Lifting it onto their shoulders, they went out of the room. Everyone stood to their feet and trooped slowly out the house and towards the cars in silence.

Mildred tugged at Sadie's jacket just as she was about to step into the large black car, parked behind the hearse. 'I don't think so!'

Sadie stood with her fingers spread on her hips. 'I'm her daughter,' she whined.

'Yes, when you want to be' snarled Mildred as she swung round tight-lipped. Sadie scowled, pulled her hat further down over her face when someone pointed to a taxi arriving to take some mourners to the church. She stepped in, wriggled in the seat and ignored the way the man gave her a disapproving look as he moved himself further away in the seat, squashing himself in the process.

Mildred peered at the sea of faces stood waiting for them to arrive. The church was packed, she watched the on-looking guests as they followed in behind the coffin. It was a requiem Mass. Prayers were said, hymns sung and the priest blessed the coffin with burning incense which wafted flumes of smoke. Eventually, people trooped slowly out the church.

Mildred looked up then averted her eyes as she stepped out of the church. Father Black was stood at the back shaking hands and nodding. The tall, sour-faced man gave her a knowing look and placed his hands behind his back.

'I'm sorry about your grandmother,' he said, before his cold eyes hardened. 'But I have still noticed your lack of absence from church lately.'

'I can hardly get to church when I don't even live here anymore can I? – even if I did, I still wouldn't come,' she cast him a sullen look as she walked away for the committal. People were stood with their head lowered, while the priest began to pray and swing the censer as the coffin was placed into the ground. Mildred's face crumpled as her legs gave way. Miss Small clutched her by her shoulders. She breathed deep, then kissed a single red rose, lingered a moment to whisper goodbye, while she dropped the rose onto the coffin. When she raised her reddened eyes, she gaped to watch her mother's performance: she was knelt over the grave with face creased, weeping and wailing as she kissed and dropped six red roses.

'Guilt getting to you?' hissed Mildred, as she turned around and walked to the waiting funeral car.

The women were sitting in small groups chatting beside the nice spread in the sitting-room when they returned. Tea bone china was ready, complete with milk jug and sugar bowl. A wall cabinet was packed with bottles of alcohol. Sadie breezed in and made straight for the drinks cabinet, where she poured herself a large whisky, tilted her head back and swallowed deeply. Pouring another large drink, she did the same again. Then, as she turned around, sweeping her eyes around the room, her mouth dropped open to see Nora Jones waddling in wearing a large brimmed brown hat, trimmed with lace and a smart skirt and jacket. She gave a smile and nodded at the women who were sat with their back rigid, mouth tight and eyebrows raised.

'I hope there won't be any trouble today?' commented one of the women as she surveyed the sour look that Sadie was throwing at Nora.

Nora cast a caustic look back when her eyes reddened and filled up with tears. 'Sadie, you don't know how I wish I had never fallen out with Kitty, because we never made it up before she died,' she sobbed.

'And whose fault was it that you did fall out?' Sadie snarled, thrusting her face in hers, as the women remained silent, glancing at each other with a nervous look. Nora ignored the remark, turned her back to Sadie and walked over to the drinks cabinet, where she filled a large glass of vodka and also threw her head back and swallowed it whole as other mourners sauntered into the room, unaware of the tense atmosphere between the two women. Mildred sat baleful faced and shoulders slumped, while Miss Small stepped towards the table, filled her plate and sat munching sandwiches, pies and cakes.

The door was pushed open and Sadie's minders strode in linking arms. Sadie stepped unsteady on her feet as she approached towards them, then, pointed her forefinger towards Nora.

'See that women sat there bold as brass, well, she was my mother's friend for years – until I caught her son forcing himself on Mildred,' she slurred. 'She refused to believe me or mother and now he's locked up.' There was a collective gasp, while others sat with hands clasped to their face watching with bated breath as the room fell silent.

Nora advanced towards Sadie with her bulging eyes blazing. 'Well, at least I didn't abandon him when he was a baby and now your daughter's been taken in care because you still don't want her.'

Sadie's eyes flashed with fury, she took her hand back and swiped Nora hard across her face. Nora staggered against a table, sending ash trays, bottles of wine and glasses of alcohol flying. She lay sprawled on the floor, her face covered with ash and cigarette ends stuck in her hair, while her new hat was battered and clothes soaked with drink.

Pandora fell to her knees and pulled her to her feet, but she still staggered about too intoxicated to stand still. Pandora tried to pick the tobacco out of her hair, and taking a hankie out of her bag, she spat on it to clean her filthy face, much to the annoyance of Nora as she twisted and squirmed.

Mildred's head was lowered, then she leaped up and exploded. 'Well, you've really made a show of yourself and me into the bargain. Do you think I want my private life discussed to all and sundry – you've done it now! I never want set eyes on you again,' she yelled.

Miss Small sat with her back ram-rod stiff, but carried on taking a bite out of a cream cake. Bending over, Crystal began picking up glasses and bottles off the floor to put them back on the table. 'I thought us lot were bad, but she puts us in the shade,' she said tilting her head at Nora who was still sat with glazed and blank eyes. While Mildred sat with her eyes downcast, knowing she hadn't lit the fire. But by accusing Kevin of rape, she had ignited a much bigger furnace and now had the burden of guilt hidden deep inside her.

Crystal gave her a long lingering look with clamped lips as she poured a drink and handed Pandora a glass. 'I didn't know her son had done that? God kid, as if you didn't have enough going on having to stay in care while burying your granny.' Then, turning to gaze at Sadie, she remarked. 'So, why did you not say anything about this then? And, as a mother, why didn't you step in and take Mildred back with you?'

A look of pain crossed Sadie's face.

'I couldn't, you know what a bully I'm married to, he wouldn't let me,' she whined before she dropped her head and began sobbing. Crystal pursed her fat lips together and lifted her shoulders. 'You thought you were on a good thing when you met him, but remember what he was like, entertain the punters' or you would be back on the street.'

The room fell silent, only punctuated by the sound of gasps from the women, their faces stretched and mouths dropped open. Unable to blink, they sat glued to their seats, while their husbands cast Sadie lewd looks. She leapt at Crystal, shoving her hand over her mouth and darting coy eyes around at them all. 'Shut up, nobody needs to hear this.'

Crystal pulled her hand away and sneered. 'We might be rough and ready, but we would never have deserted a daughter; leaving her in care like you have – you disgust me.'

Mildred stood with her eyebrows raised as she turned to leave with Miss Small.

'She left me with my grandmother when I was a baby to go off with gypsy Joe as you call him – some people never change,' she said with a reproachful look. Pandora leant towards Nora, hooked her huge arm around her and pulled her to her feet. 'I think you better get away home.

The show's over.'

Nora raised glazed eyes up at her as she swayed. Then, picking up her battered hat, she shoved it on her head, staggered crab style and barged into Mildred and Miss Small as they headed towards the front door.

'Shift,' she growled, lifting her elbow near Mildred's side. But, Crystal following behind loomed over her, and as she yanked the door open, she pushed the portly woman out of the house. Nora sprawled onto the ground and fell to her knees, which dragged her skirt up, exposing her huge backside. Crystal stood holding her belly in hysterics when she saw Nora was wearing huge pink silk knickers; they were down to her knees, stretched tight, with her big fat thighs encased. Mildred and Miss Small spluttered. Nora was dragging herself up and staggering away as though pulled through a hedge backwards. Crystal slipped an arm round Mildred's shoulder and gave her an assuring squeeze as she said goodbye.

Chapter Fourteen

L ife went on as normal in the home, but for Mildred McDine, life would never be the same again.

She ached for her grandmother and Danny, but seethed whenever she thought of Kevin. A cold shiver would course through her every time she thought back to that night. Often, her hands clenched and mouth set when she thought of what he would do when he was released from prison. He would catch up with her and she would pay for stitching him up, so she knew she would have to leave the area as soon as she could.

But in the meantime she was held back having to stay in the home until she reached sixteen. Her main tasks were to go to the laundry room once a week and take clean sheets and pillowcases to each bedroom and once a month, she delivered a packet of Dr White's sanitary towels to each room. But this only increased her anxiety and the size of the black cloud she was under. Because, whenever she opened her wardrobe door, she peered at three unopened packets, which sat on the shelf staring back at her.

It was now late October and her birthday. She should've been happy, but she hadn't had a period since she lost her virginity in the summer. Pacing back and forth in her bedroom, her stomach rose. She wished the day was over. No sooner had she thought about it when her door burst open, and her friends charged in the room with cards and gifts wrapped up in colourful paper.

'Well go on then, open them,' demanded Margaret. A large, bulky girl, whose teeth protruded; her black hair always greasy.

Her other friend, Vicky clasped her arms around her and planted a kiss on her cheek. Mildred forced a wide smile on her pale drawn face and thanked them as she pulled the paper off the presents.

As she opened her cards, she was unable to hold back her tears any longer. Margaret and Vicky's smile vanished as she sat with her head lowered in her hands. 'Usually I would have had a card from my granny, I'm sorry, I still miss her so much,' she apologised, sniffing and wiping her eyes.

'It's okay, we'll leave you and see you later,' said Vicky, and they turned around and headed for the door.

After they left the door was pushed open again, and a thin housemother with grey hair poked her head into the room. 'You've to go to Miss Dolly-Belle's room.'

Mildred wiped her eyes, nipped her cheeks and took a deep breath. Heading along the corridor, she dragged her feet and her expression was downcast as she made her way to Dolly-Belle's office. Standing outside, she gave a light tap on the door and stood back waiting.

It opened, and the trim diminutive woman looked up at her with a broad smile on her face. She raised her hand and beckoned her to enter. 'I am very pleased to tell you that you will be starting work in a café near the coast tomorrow. You have been here three months now, and I have had nothing but good reports about your behaviour and that you have done your chores without any complaints. Do you have any questions?'

Mildred shook her head.

'Well, be ready for eight sharp. It will only be light duties, like peeling potatoes, chopping vegetables at first, and when they think you're able, they will have you taking orders from customers. I will see you later, in the dining room, where everyone will be gathering for your birthday.'

Mildred thanked her and left the room beaming, just to get away from the confines of the home and to feel free would be heaven. She put her problem to the back of her mind and decided to live in the moment and enjoy her day. It was her birthday after all.

Blinking open her eyes, she moved her arm along the bed covers and turned the shrill alarm clock off. She peered at the clock to see, it was seven in the morning. Yawning, she slipped her legs over the bed and caught her reflection in the mirror opposite. The face that peered back was drawn and pale. She held a hand to her stomach and slumped back down on the bed and tucked her head beneath her until the queasy feeling went away.

'This is the second morning, I'm feeling ill,' she whispered to herself. 'Please God, don't let me be pregnant.'

Standing to her feet, she went to the window, pushed it open and gulped in the fresh air, before she stepped back and hurried to get washed and changed. On opening her bedroom door, she put her hand over her nose, stopped, bent over and retched, the smell of grease making her ill. Wiping a hand over her clammy brow, she stepped inside the dining room and ordered a sweet tea, hoping it would clear the feeling of sickness.

Some of the girls were sat in there already, eating their breakfast over some hushed gossip. They were waiting to be picked up by the bus to take them to their various working locations. A thick-built man wearing a cap and badge walked into the room, he gave them a nod of his head and then stepped back out. Chairs were scraped back as they trooped out to the waiting mini bus.

Mildred sat chewing her nails as she peered out of the window, feeling buoyant, though scared in equal measure, wondering what the women would be like, and if she would be able to do the job to their satisfaction.

As she stepped out of the bus and onto the pavement, she waved to the other girls as the vehicle moved away. With her shoulders back and head held high, attempting to seem confident despite her looming nerves, she made her way into the small café.

The walls were painted cream and brasses and ornaments hung from beams on the ceiling. Four men who wore overalls were tucking into full English breakfasts at one table, and a tall lean man wearing a suit and tie was sat reading a newspaper at another. A gang of manual workers who wore caps, jackets and haversacks came strolling in and slumped down, scraping their chairs back.

Mildred sniffed the strong aroma of coffee as a tall, thin woman approached her from the far end of the room. She wore a shirt and a pair of slacks, and was sporting a crew cut hair style. Her black, piercing eyes scrutinized Mildred's every move as Mildred held out her hand. 'Pleased to meet you, I'm Mildred McDine.'

Ignoring her held out hand, she took her into a room at the back of the café, pulled out a chair and pointed to one opposite. Mildred lowered herself down into the chair and watched her take a cigarette out of a pack on the table. She lit it as she leaned back in her seat, inhaled deeply and then squinted as she introduced herself. 'My name is Miss Atkinson, my partner will be along in a while. She's run off her feet at the moment; you must've noticed how busy we were when you arrived.'

A short, podgy woman with tightly curled permed hair strode inside the room, breathing heavily. She drew out a chair, wiped a hand over her clammy brow and sat beside the tall woman as she asked, 'Do you have any experience working in a café?'

'Yes, my grandmother had a family run guesthouse,' she replied, in a calm voice.

The larger woman curled her lip and nodded slowly. 'So what exactly did you do?'

'Everything, from cleaning the rooms and changing beds to helping out in the kitchen when it was required.'

The women raised their eyebrows as they turned to look at each other. 'We've decided to give you a month's trial,' said the masculine Miss Atkinson, after long moments of whispered debate.

'But, I thought the housemother said the job was mine?' asked Mildred with furrowed brow.

'It's not up to her I'm afraid, we've had to be careful as we've had girls in the past that have let us down badly. Another thing, what on earth can you do with that unruly hair of yours? It'll have to be tied up. We don't want any hairs in anyone's meal.'

Mildred's lips stiffened, but she smiled between gritted teeth. 'I'll tie it back and keep it pinned up.'

The plump one waddled back to the front of the café while the masculine woman got up and pulled a cupboard door open. Then, pushing an overall into her hand, she said, 'There's a sink full of dishes to wash in the kitchen next door, but there'll be an even bigger rush at noon, so you have plenty to keep you busy.'

Well wasn't that an exaggeration? As Mildred stepped into the kitchen, she groaned instantly as soon as her eyes locked on to the amount of dirty dishes that were piled high on the floor as well as in the sink.

It took a long time to work her way through the heap. And to make matters worse, as soon as she'd finished, slips of paper with orders started to pour through the hatch, leaving her and the cook running ragged. There was no offer of help from the two owners.

Prawn jacket potatoes were a nightmare as she was not allowed to defrost them till an order was taken. Welsh rarebit orders were a challenge too, as she had to whip the eggs up, add the cheese and then watch it under the grill as she's dashed around, wiping sweat from her brow.

Miss Atkinson came in to the kitchen halfway through an order, clapping her hands like an excited seal. 'Come on, come on girl, you must hurry with these orders, people are waiting,' she said.

Mildred's eyes brimmed. She was worn down and felt like walking out. It was a slave they wanted, not a kitchen assistant. Thankfully though, once everyone had been fed, she was allowed an hour-long break.

She had a snack then slipped her overall off and went outside, where she slumped down onto the nearest seat and leaned back, breathing in the fresh sea air. Once rested, she stood up and walked along the promenade, enjoying the respite and the late October sun on her face, wondering if it was worth the back-breaking job, knowing at the same time that there was no choice. If she didn't do it, she would be back trapped in the home, and she definitely didn't want that. Not now. Not ever.

Chapter Fifteen

After six weeks of this toil, her eyes were sunken so far into her skull that if she looked to her left she'd probably see her brain.

As she hauled herself out of her bed on one rainy morning, the queasy feeling got the better of her as soon as she pushed her feet into her slippers. She had to step towards the window and inhale the fresh air until the queasiness subsided. By now, another pack of Doctor White towels had been stored in her wardrobe, and she knew that it was time to face reality. She was pregnant and in deep trouble – in more ways than just one.

Stumbling into the bathroom with a hand held to her mouth, she sunk to her knees and clasped the toilet bowl as she retched. Someone was banging on the bathroom door, but the vomiting would not abate.

Eventually, she stood up and opened the door. Her face was ashen and dark circles were prominent under her eyes. Crawling back into her room, she slumped back on her bed and lay there until the feeling subsided, but in doing so, missed the vehicle that took her to work. The housemother didn't help her, so she had to wait until the next bus came and took her there to face Miss Atkinson checking her watch.

'You're late again Mildred, this will not do. If this carries on, I'll have to have a word with Dolly-Belle and we will have to let you go and get another young lady who we can rely on for timekeeping. We're expecting a busy day today, so come on chop, chop!' she briskly told her. 'You are to learn how to stocktake today too.'

Sullen faced, she made her way into the back room to change into her overall. The plump Miss Boyle was stood behind a mirror patting her permed hair. Her eyes widened and cheeks flushed like pink marshmallows, as she observed Mildred's expanding belly. She turned away from the mirror to gaze fixedly at her as she struggled with the buttons on the overall in silence.

'Mildred, I need to have a talk with you,' she said as she cleared her throat. 'There's something delicate I have to ask you. Well, it's just that Miss Atkinson and I have noticed how peaky you look and we have taken note of how you're always feeling sick. You're not, well, I just can't bring myself to say it ... '

Mildred lowered her gaze and bit her lip as she continued.

'You know you would have to leave, if you were expecting. We have a good reputation in this café and we intend to keep it that way. And we can't with that,' she said as she lowered her voice, peering at her swollen belly once more. 'Well, especially if it's what we think.'

Mildred looked down at the dumpy woman, studying her serious face. 'Yes. I'm pregnant,' she uttered with her chin quivering.

'What?' The dumpy woman's hands shot up to her face. With a gaping mouth, she leant against the wall for support. Shaking her head, her cheeks wobbled like jelly as she picked up a paper napkin and waved in front of her face.

Mildred ignored Miss Boyle's stricken look. 'If you're worried about me being an embarrassment to you then I'll just go now.'

'I really don't know what to say,' she replied, becoming flustered.

Mildred lifted her shoulders and sighed. 'What is there to say,' she replied as she pulled her overall off and hung it up. 'If you'll just pay me what I'm due, I'll leave now.'

Miss Atkinson appeared in the back room. Her sharp eyes searched Mildred's wretched white face and then switched to peer at Miss Boyle, who was stood with her hands clasped around her flushed cheeks. 'What's going on? We've got a queue waiting out here,' she snapped.

'Mildred's told me she is having baby,' said Miss Boyle, while flapping her hand over her hot face.

'Go and see to the customers and then have a sit down before you fall down, she won't be the first and she won't be the last.'

Miss Boyle turned on her heel with a vacant look as Miss Atkinson beckoned Mildred to her office and pointed to a seat. She took out a cigarette and blew flumes everywhere. 'Well, I thought myself that you were, but I was hoping you weren't. How will you manage? You've told us your mother's never bothered with you.'

Tears filled Mildred's eyes as she sunk her head into her hands, and then her screams filled the room as she began to wail loudly. The colour drained from Miss Atkinson's face, she clutched hold of her, and pulled her towards the rear door and out of ear-shot, when the small plump woman came rushing towards them with a scathing look.

'Everyone can hear what going on,' she snorted, throwing Mildred a withering look.

Mildred's face creased, and she groaned as she sunk down on an old rickety seat by the door, gripping her hands to her belly. 'Oh I'm in agony,' she wailed as she rocked with pain.

The two women stood speechless, peering at one another, when Miss Atkinson said, 'Mildred, you need to see a doctor.'

Mildred's face creased as huge tears filled her eyes. 'I can't,' she replied in a tight voice. 'They'll tell Dolly-Belle.'

The woman leant over and thrust her face in hers. 'Don't be so stupid, you look ill, I think you have something else wrong with you, you're in so much pain.'

'I don't know what to do,' wailed Mildred. 'Please don't tell Dolly-Belle.'

The woman took a deep intake of breath. 'She'll have to be told,' she said. 'You can't deal with this alone. Yes, it'll be a shock but she'll do her best for you.' Then, giving her a hardened look, she asked, 'Does the father know of your predicament?'

'I was raped and he's in prison,' she squeaked as another pain gripped her.

'You poor girl, this is not your fault. Can you manage to stand up?' She nodded her head. 'Right, as soon as I get you back, I'm seeing Dolly-

Belle.'

'No. Please no,' Mildred pleaded.

Miss Atkinson watched as Mildred shuddered and spluttered. The thought alone was enough to send her whole world crashing down. She did as any desperate and terrified girl would, and splayed herself over the table with her head in her arms and loudly cried into the woodgrain.

'Can you manage to walk?' asked Miss Atkinson. Mildred nodded her head as the woman turned to her partner. 'You see to the café and I'll take her to the home.' She pulled Mildred to her feet and Miss Boyle whirled around and stomped back inside with a face like fury.

Taking Mildred by the arm, she was about to do something that would make this living nightmare even worse. A thing Mildred never thought possible. But that was the thing about nightmares, when the darkness swarms, they only multiply.

Miss Atkinson braked and cut the car engine. Pulling open the passenger door, she leaned in and helped Mildred out. When they limped into the entrance, where a few girls were gathered glancing at each other, they turned to watch Mildred being supported to her bedroom.

Gasping, and unable to stand the pain, she pulled up her skirt and dragged the girdle down that hid her secret, then flopped back and lay on her bed, rubbing her hand over her swollen belly. With baleful sunken eyes, she lifted her head and looked up at Miss Atkinson, who stood with her face stretched; eyes bulging, as she picked up the girdle and marched out of the room.

A housemother pushed the door open and stepped inside Mildred's room with a bowl in her hand. 'I've been told you've got a bug, so stay away from anyone until you feel better,' she said, then stood mute and stilled with shock, her face stretched as she observed the swollen belly too.

Swaying round, she walked from the room and ran along the corridor to Dolly-Belle's where she was sat with her elbows placed on the desk, her expression solemn. 'Do you know that Mildred McDine is having a child?'

'I'm aware of her predicament,' she stated. 'I've phoned for the doctor, so please close your mouth and get back to your duties.'

The woman's lips stiffened as she dropped her eyes and stepped back out in silence.

Chapter Sixteen

S adie Carr stood on her toes and lifted the case from the shelf above her head. Pulling the carriage door open, she stood in the corridor and looked over to the left of the Tyne to see coal trains and pit heaps. As the train chugged slowly to the right and then left again, it crossed the railway bridge then moved to the immediate right, where the Swing Bridge and Tyne Bridge came into view.

Her stomach churned as she stepped onto the platform and shivered as she pulled her cream duster coat closer, wishing she could go straight back to London instead of having to appear at the Magistrates Court in Market Street, Newcastle, to face Kevin Jones at his trial.

Her mind recalled the telephone call she had received from Miss Small before she left for her journey to Newcastle. Mildred was pregnant and ill in the Royal Victoria Hospital with anaemia and also had to have her appendix removed. Could anything else go wrong? She wondered. Her bully of a husband would never accept Mildred and a child.

But if she didn't stand by her she would never be able to fill the void that lay between them. And now that she had met her daughter, she really wanted to fix what she had broken all those years ago.

She joined the throng of people and walked over the bridge that connected the two platforms, making her way to the other side. She glanced to see a public house situated inside the station, next to it was a well-known newsagent. She stepped inside the shop, clicked open her bag and handed her money over the counter to a smiling young man

95

as she asked for cigarettes and matches. Stepping out of the shop, she then headed through one of the arched columns and past a newspaper vendor where a barrow boy was yelling at the top of his voice about the impending court case.

Taxis were stood near the pavement. She waved her arm and smiled at a taxi driver who jumped out and opened the door for her. She slumped into the seat. 'The Douglas Hotel please,' she said as she sat chewing her lip and clasping her gloved hands together, going over the situation in her head. What should she do? She didn't know if she could visit Mildred or not, and if she could get over the mental aspect of it, how would she physically go about it? If only she could tell her the truth about what her life in London was like she thought when the taxi stopped.

She faced a stone built building with a sign above the doorway. The main door opened and as a man stepped outside she could see a wooden interior door with small glass panels. She paid the cabbie and collected her case.

She stepped through the doors and headed for the reception. A young girl with bouffant hair and equally styled lashes that were thick with mascara fluttered as Sadie advanced towards the counter. 'I've already booked a room, it's under Mrs Carr,' she said, as her eyes darted around at the plush red velvet and brass interior. The girl flicked through a ledger, then handed her a key with the room number on it.

She gave a weak smile, turned and moved briskly along a wooden-panelled passage, up a flight of stairs with a rich patterned carpet and along the landing, checking the door numbers on each side closely, looking for her room. Seeing the door at last, she smiled and heaved a sigh as she pushed the key into the lock and stepped inside.

The room was small, but cosy, with a single dark wooden wardrobe and a matching dressing table. A single bed stood with pink padded headboard, floral pillows and bed cover.

Opening the wardrobe door, she put her clothes inside then stood in front of the mirror. Taking out her lipstick, she slicked it over her mouth. Once she had fixed her wind-battered appearance, she stepped out of the room and decided she would go to the hospital and face Mildred, because after all, she was giving evidence in her defence.

And more importantly, it was her daughter and just because things had been rough, that didn't mean she didn't totally regret what she had done when she was a baby. If only I had the chance to go back, she thought, I would have left with Mildred, instead of just leaving her with Joseph.

As she passed Charlotte Square, she walked further up Low Friar Street, where people were milling around the newly-opened Mayfair ballroom. She was choking for a cigarette and could have done with a strong drink to settle her nerves too, so she decided she would do just that. She stepped inside the building and made her way down the stairs. As soon as she did, it was almost as if she was thrown into a time machine and transported back to the past.

It perfectly mirrored the night club where she once worked as a hostess for her one-time pimp and now husband, who kept her with his endless amounts of cash. They lived in a mansion, with an ornate, gabled porch and grand stone entrance hall, where marble statues stood facing one another. Then you crossed to a decadent lounge where logs burned in the grate inside an open stone fireplace. Carved Italian furniture adorned the room, where a winding staircase led up to a hand painted panelled landing. This gilded cage was her prison and husband Mikey was her jailer.

Just thinking of his hairy, fat belly that wobbled when he demanded sex gave her goose pimples. She shuddered at the thought as she stepped towards the nearest bar, wondering how much more she could take of him.

The bar was packed three deep with people. She stood on her toes and ordered two large vodkas. Sashaying to a seat, she pulled out a packet of cigarettes from of her bag, lit up and inhaled deeply, watching a group of men as they sang in harmony, gliding about the stage.

Four hours later, ten empty glasses were stood on the table and the ashtray was overflowing. She scraped her chair back and stood to her feet. With her hand gripping the rail, she stepped slowly up the stairs to make her way back to the hotel.

Chapter Seventeen

Holding a hand to her head, Sadie groaned when she woke to see the room lit-up. She moved her arm from beneath the covers and squinted. 'God, I've slept in,' she gasped, as she shuffled towards the bathroom and peered into the mirror to gaze at her tatty hair. She ran a bath and sank back, wishing she had never drunk so much. Wishing she hadn't drank at all.

Bathing quickly, she dried herself, opened the wardrobe, and took out a red mini shift dress, black polo neck jumper, boots and a bag. Combing her hair into a French pleat, she applied her false eyelashes and makeup then went downstairs to telephone for a lift to the court.

When Sadie arrived, Miss Small was already there. She was accompanied by an advocate who had had been selected to represent Mildred by social services. The advocate was a portly woman with a stern look on her face. She and Miss Small sat with their heads close together in deep conversation.

Wearing the latest London look, Sadie sashayed towards them. Miss Small and the advocate jerked their faces up and sat with their thin lips clamped shut. Their eyebrows shot up as they looked her up and down.

The court usher shouted, 'Mrs Carr.'

Taking a deep breath, she tilted her chin, pushed her shoulders back and stepped inside the court room, where her eyes swept around the sombre room. The elderly Judge was sat high up at the front of the room, below him were the prosecution and the defence barristers.

The jury were sat at the side of the court, only their heads were visible behind a tall wooden fixture. Kevin Jones was stood in the dock, flanked between two burly looking prison officers, his mouth in a sneer of hatred and his eyes like dagger points. He glared at Sadie as she stepped towards the stand.

Sadie moistened her lips with her tongue and swallowed as she waited for the prosecution barrister to begin his cross-examination. She laid her hand on the Bible and swore to tell the truth. After half an hour of questioning, he thanked her and returned to his seat. But it was when the defence barrister – a sour-faced man wearing a wig and black gown – approached her that her heart thudded in her chest and sweat trickled down her spine.

'Mrs Carr,' he said, a condescending smile crossing his lips. 'Is Mrs your actual title or just a false one, when you're actually living over the brush so to speak.'

Sadie's large lashes fluttered as she listened to the sniggers following his remark. 'I am not living under the brush and I take offence at your attitude towards me. I have a mansion in London with a gated lodge, so do not speak to me in that manner,' she retorted, her eyes burning with anger.

Several more titters could be heard in the spectator gallery. The defence barrister ignored her contempt. 'Can you repeat what you saw on the night Mildred McDine was allegedly attacked by this young man,' he said as he pointed to Kevin. 'Because, my client denies the rape charge as he stipulates that your daughter was seen going into a showman's caravan on the night in question.'

Sadie crossed her legs, feeling her bladder about to give way with fear, as all eyes in the court and the spectator gallery were fixed on her. She gazed into cold, pale eyes, while she told him what she saw. 'I came to the top of the backstairs to see Mildred pinned face down on the staircase. Her clothes were crumpled and her face a picture of terror. He was on top of her, thrusting, jerking and moaning. He only stopped when I shrieked as I raced down the stairs and mauled him.'

The man's cold eyes darted to and fro and his thin lips pursed as he smirked. He turned to the Jury with a sly look, and said, 'This woman has come today in the defence of the daughter that she abandoned as a baby, running off with a rogue gypsy. After that she ran away from him too, sold her body, took drugs and is alcohol-dependant. Now, when the girl needs her again, she has the audacity to stand here like a paragon of virtue, while her daughter is left in the care of social services. Ask yourselves now: can you take the word of a person with the morals of an alley cat?'

Several more titters were starting to form, but the judge cut them off early as he barked, 'Objection. I fail to understand what Mrs Carr's reputation has to do with this case.'

'I'm merely trying to point out that this woman is nothing more than an unreliable witness and a fantasist,' he remarked coolly.

'Objection,' shouted her solicitor as the court erupted.

The Judge brought down his gavel with a crack and the room was filled with silence again. 'May I remind the court that it is Kevin Jones on trial here, and not this lady. Please stand down Mrs Carr.'

Sadie's chin quivered, and as she stepped down and glanced up at the gallery, she saw Nora Jones sat with her arms folded, still like an oil painting. She was casting her a venomous look. Smartly-dressed women sat with their eyebrows raised as they threw a steely look, while the men nudged each other, casting her frank looks.

She stumbled from the court room with as much dignity as she could muster and dashed past Miss Small with her head lowered. Miss Small leapt to her feet and grabbed her arm to pull her back. 'Has the verdict been reached yet?' she asked.

Sadie's face crumpled as she disentangled herself from the social worker, turned on her heel and ran. And she would keep running until she passed out and died, or until the corruption of her twisted past could no longer keep up with her.

Chapter Eighteen

Social workers had been regular visitors at Mildred's bedside to follow her progress. It was now three weeks since the court case. She had recovered from her operation and was ready to move into the mother and baby home that belonged to the Presbyterian Church. Sadie had visited her and had tried to build bridges, but as soon as Mildred saw her walking in with other visitors, she turned her back, pulled the covers over her head, and refused to speak.

Now that she had time to think, she wondered if she had done the right thing, when she turned her head to see Miss Small walking into the ward with a young nurse. Her expression was glum as she rose to her feet and picked up her case.

'Don't look so serious Mildred, you'll be fine,' Miss small assured.

The nurse winked her eye, clasped an arm around her and wished her good luck.

As Miss Small drove past the University and Hancock museum and then out of Newcastle, Mildred peered out of the car window. She watched the world pass her by, head filled with thoughts, belly filled with her soon-to-be baby. She vowed at that very moment never to have sex again.

She watched teenagers sauntering around with not a care in the world knowing she was no longer going to have that luxury. Knowing that soon she would have a baby to care for and responsibilities to adhere to. The closest thing that she would get to freedom would be when her baby slept through the whole night without waking her up. That would be her new definition of freedom in her soon-to-be reality.

As soon as this baby was born, she would get it adopted and once she was seventeen she would be free to go wherever she wanted. She was sick of having to dance to everybody's tune. She wanted out, and the sooner the better as far as she was concerned.

The car slowed down as they drove into a courtyard where a large Victorian building stood. There were tall leaded windows upstairs and down, and window boxes filled with late summer flowers flowing in the breeze were placed on the cream window sills. White stone pots were stood on either side of an arched wooden door.

Miss Small turned to her with a tight smile as she cut the engine. With a long, drawn out sigh, Mildred pushed the car door open and stood peering at the entrance to the building, wondering what lay behind it.

The door opened and a woman with flowing red hair stepped out carrying a baby wrapped in a shawl and an elderly man with a bald head followed behind her. The man clasped the woman's hand and they embraced as they stepped towards a car. Mildred drew her eyes away and raised them up to a window where she saw a young girl who was stood peering at the couple, her face was contorted and she was weeping.

Mildred forced one foot in front of the other as she stepped over the threshold. She saw passages leading left and right; facing her was a large staircase. A couple of prams were stood in the passage and two heavily pregnant girls were dusting and sweeping the place. They stood and gave Mildred a long lingering look as she and Miss Small moved further along the passageway until she stopped outside a door.

Miss Small tapped her knuckle on the door and they were told to enter. An elderly woman with a toad-shaped mouth, wearing spectacles perched on the end of her pug nose, was sat behind a desk peering up at them as they moved towards her.

'Who have we here then?' she asked in a clipped voice, her sharp eyes casting a contemptuous look at Mildred, while her social worker lowered herself into a seat.

'Mildred McDine,' she answered. Lifting her chin, she gave the matron a steady look, while she thought that she didn't like the look of her ugly hatchet face.

'You'll address me as Matron when I speak to you,' she snapped. 'Have you brought the baby's clothes with you?'

Mildred's jaw dropped. 'I didn't realise I had to bring any.'

'Well, did you think we were going to supply them?' she asked.

'I haven't had a baby before so how was I to know,' she replied as her hands clenched into a fist. Then, turning to cast a venomous look at Miss Small for not telling her about this, she leant towards her and whispered in her ear. 'I don't like it here, I want to go back to the home on the coast.'

'What's that you said?' demanded the Matron, her expression stern. After long moments of scrutinising Mildred, she slowly rose to her feet. Stepping around to the front of her desk, she thrust her face into Mildred's. 'I don't think I like your attitude young girl. While you're here you follow my rules. If not, I will make life hard for you. So you'll keep quiet and talk when you're addressed, do I make myself clear?'

'Yes,' replied Mildred through gritted teeth.

'Take the girl to room twenty-two on the second floor,' she said, as she waved her hand in a dismissive manner at Miss Small.

Miss Small rose out of her seat and gave the matron a cold look. Mildred followed her to the door, trying her very hardest to resist the urge to scream.

Once in the passageway, Mildred's face creased and she broke down weeping. 'I hate that woman,' she sniffed while stomping behind the social worker onto the first step of the staircase.

'Well, don't get on the wrong side of her and you'll be okay,' Miss Small whispered, as she turned her head to see door twenty-two.

'A good fuck is what she needs. But then, who would? With a face like a smacked arse, nobody would touch that,' Mildred snarled as she stepped inside her room.

Miss Small turned to face her with a grin on her face as wide as the English Channel. She pointed her forefinger at Mildred and through a smile said, 'Please try to behave – if that's possible. You heard what the matron said, so take heed. I'll be back in a few days with the baby clothes.'

Mildred cast a cold look at Miss Small when she pulled open the door, then closed it behind her. 'Yes, go back to your perfect bloody life. Just leave me here at the mercy of that old cow,' she said to the closed door.

She crossed to the window to peer at a busy main road. It was tree-lined and in the distance she saw the town moor, where every year, the field was turned into a dazzling fair with music, flashing lights, exciting rides, booths and sideshows.

'Could Danny be there where all the pretty girls will flirt with him?' she pondered, scowling at the thought.

Placing her hand over her swollen belly, she felt his baby kicking. She stood for long moments watching the fair. Her mind went back to a time when she had been allowed to go there at the age of thirteen with her friends.

She was drawn to a gypsy woman who was stood outside her caravan with gold hoops in her ears; wearing a red satin, low-cut dress. Her dark eyes were focused on Mildred too. The woman drew her hand up and inclined her head towards her caravan. Mildred's friends gathered around her giggling, but she pushed them aside and stepped inside the gypsy's bow-top and brightly decorated caravan, then stood gazing around at the stained wood, painted in gold and floral motives, the cut glass mirrors and embellished cupboard doors.

The woman smiled at her as she lowered herself down on a stool beside a small round table covered in a white cloth, where she peered at a pack of black and gold cards and an assortment of crystals. Clasping hold of her hand, the woman turned it over to peer at her palm and her smile disappeared. 'Your rebellious nature will bring you sorrow, and there will be lies and deceit, which will impact on your life. Things will improve, but not until later, then you will be a very wealthy lady.'

Turning away from with the window, she pondered on the gypsy's warning, knowing the terrible lie she had told about Kevin, when she heard a light tap on her door. She crossed the room, and opened her door to face a girl who looked to be twelve years old. She had a pitiful look on her young face, a bobble in her tatty fair hair, skinny arms and legs and was in late stage of pregnancy. 'Do you mind if I come in? I'm so scared; I only came here and don't know anyone,' she squeaked.

Mildred sighed, realizing it wouldn't do any good avoiding everyone. 'Me neither, come in, I'm new too,' she replied in a low tone.

'I'm Mary Kelly and I'm only fourteen. My father beat me and put me in here, he think it's from a one night stand, but it's the lodger who is the father,' she whimpered, as she continued. 'They depend on his rent, so I couldn't tell the truth,' she wailed, as her scared eyes searched her face.

'I'll tell my social worker and she'll help you,' Mildred told her. 'You can't be allowed to go back there.'

The girl shook her head. 'I've got no other choice,' she replied wringing her hands together. 'It's that or run away.

Mildred clasped the girl's hand. 'Look, we've both put in here through unfortunate circumstances, both our lives are rotten. I'm heart broken. I've just lost my grandmother. I'm scared to have this baby alone and I can't get in touch with the baby's father to tell him I'm pregnant, or where I am, so let's make a pact: we stick together the time we're here.'

Mary's fraught face softened and she nodded with the excitement of a Labrador, as her eyes welled up with tears of happiness.

But even with Mary's company, the days dragged by in the home. The day started at six thirty, with floors to wash and toilets to clean. A lot of the girls didn't like getting up early, but it's what she'd been used to when she lived with her grandmother. But then, she had plenty to do: first school, and then her many chores later.

Sighing and dwelling about the past, she whirled around to see Miss Small. She stepped inside the room, with both hands clutching bulging bags. Mildred gave her a wan smile. 'I'm sorry, I was in a foul mood, but there's just too much happened too soon, I can't deal with it all,' she said, when the colour drained from her face and she slumped against the bed.

Miss Small clasped her hands around her shoulders to steady her.

'I'll be alright?' she replied, rubbing her hand over her eyes, 'I'm just exhausted and drained, I'll be okay in a minute.'

Miss Small helped her to a chair.

'I've met many people in my job, but you always seem to be fraught, full of anger too, is there something you're hiding?

'No,' she snapped. 'Why would you think that?'

'I don't know, there's just something not quite right,' she said rubbing her chin with her finger and thumb. 'Well, I know your birth mother hasn't helped matters by abandoning you when you were born and that carry-on at your grandmother's wake didn't help matters either.'

'She came to see me when I was ill in hospital, but I was horrible to her too. I didn't want to speak to her, but when she left I wished I had – oh I'm so mixed up,' she said turning her back and crossing to her bed. 'There's something I want to show you.'

The social worker's brow furrowed as she watched Mildred pull out her grandmother's bag from underneath her pillow. Opening the bag, she took the letter and documents out and gave them to Miss Small for her to read.

'This is going to make a big difference to your life Mildred, once all the legalities are sorted out, you're going to be very comfortable, but you'll still need our support as you are so young,' pointed out the social worker peering at Mildred's face draining of colour. 'Are you okay?'

'I don't feel so good,' she gasped as she sunk to her knees.

'I think you need to be admitted for observation, there must be something causing this pain. I'm having a word with the matron.'

Mildred clutched her arm in an attempt to stop her, but the room began swirling around. Her legs gave way as darkness evolved and advanced around her.

Chapter Nineteen

In the maternity unit a doctor stood with his stethoscope around his neck, his face was craggy and his brow wrinkled as he moved his hands over her swollen belly. He turned to a younger doctor and beckoned for him to do the same. The two men stood peering at her and as he turned his head towards the younger fellow, she heard him speak in a lowered tone and couldn't catch what it was, but their faces were solemn. 'We will keep you here overnight and if your temperature drops, you should be okay to leave,' he said, patting her hand. 'But it's bed rest until then.'

'I feel much better, I would rather go back to the home,' she suggested, planting a bright smile on her face. But, seeing the stern expression, she closed her mouth. After the doctors had left the ward, Mildred lifted up her arm and waved her hand in a beckoning manner towards a young nurse. 'I need to telephone someone. The doctor says bed rest but it's important, I must speak to my social worker,' she pleaded. The nurse gave her an inquisitive look but suggested she could bring the telephone on a trolley for her. Mildred's taut face relaxed as she watched her step inside the ward pushing the trolley with a large black telephone balanced on it. But, when she rang social services Miss Small was not available. Mildred clashed the telephone back down and sat scowling, wondering if she could just go, get up and sneak out without anyone knowing. As her eyes swept around, she looked at the row of beds opposite to see patients lying prone and on either side of her; they were too old and too ill to bother. But, there was a nurse sat at a desk near the door. She gritted her teeth, why hadn't she brought Kitty's bag with her, she thought, but then she decided it should be okay, she had hid it well between the mattress and the bed springs. Now she wasn't so sure.

'When are those bloody doctors coming,' she whispered to herself as she sat peering towards the door, hoping to see them step inside. By dinner time they trooped in, stopping at each bed and peering over the person and discussing everything as they slowly moved about the ward. Mildred sat with her teeth munching her finger nails by the time they reached her bed. She raised her head and beamed up at the doctor with her fingers crossed behind her back, hoping he would let her get out.

'Mildred's temperature is back to normal,' said the nurse, stood next to him. The doctor's face was stern. 'You can go back home, but you have to rest as much as possible. Nurse, ring the mother and baby home please,' he said, as he turned his back and peered at the wrinkled faced woman lying with her mouth gaping in the next bed.

She leapt out of bed, pulled the curtain around and got ready. Sat on her bed, she wrung her hands, by now the nails were bitten to the wick before a housemother stepped inside the ward.

On her return back to the home, she leaped out of the car and stood pacing back and forth while waiting for the door to open. Dashing past a housemother, she hurried towards her room, pushed the door open and stood transfixed. Marlene Potts, a surly slovenly girl was sat on her bed feeding a baby.

'Why are you in here? This is my room,' she spat with her arms folded.

Marlene glanced up. 'The matron gave me this room, so you'll have to sort it out with her.'

Mildred's face was blazing. 'Get off that bed now,' she demanded.

'No I will not,' replied Marlene.

'You bloody well will,' she ranted as she pushed her aside. Marlene sat glaring at her as she pointed her forefinger. 'Get out NOW.' she snorted.

Mildred swung round, her face creased as she stepped along the corridor then towards the Matron's room without stopping to knock. 'Why is Marlene Potts in my room?' she demanded to know, as she pushed the door open.

The Matrons head jerked up. 'I beg your pardon. You knock before you enter this room.'

'I've only been away for a while and she's in my room, why?' she cried with arms raised,

The Matron glowered. 'Did the door have your name on it?'

'No, but I had all my things in there. I want her to get off the bed. I hid my bag underneath the mattress and bed. The bag has important documents and a bank book, and she won't let me check it, so you have to make her,' she wailed, her eyes brimming as she thumped her fist on the desk.

'Excuse me young lady, DO NOT demand I do anything, I won't be spoken in that manner.'

'But, Marlene Potts has a bad name in here. You don't know it, but she's a thief.'

The matron merely sniffed, pressed her lips together; waved her hand in a dismissal gesture.

Mildred's face crumpled up into a ball and she began to cry. 'I'm phoning the police,' she screeched. The matron's face resembled a beetroot while her eyes were cold as ice. 'You will do nothing of the sort; I'm warning you do that at your peril.'

'If my bag isn't found, I couldn't give a shit about peril,' she snarled as she spun around and stormed to Mary's room, panic stricken. 'I need to get in my old room to check for my bag. I hid it, but I've got a feeling Marlene Potts has found it and that old harridan won't do anything,' she seethed, clenching her fingers to a fist.

Mary gave her a pleading look. 'Her door was slightly open, so I peeked in and she was sitting going through your bag but I didn't have the guts to do anything!'

'What? The bitch won't know what's hit her. I'm going to kill her,' she stormed.

Mary jumped up and grabbed her arm. 'You've just been ill in hospital; you'll just make yourself ill again.'

'I don't give a flying fuck,' she ranted as she flung the door open.

Stamping along with her lips pulled back over her teeth, she stormed past two girls. They looked at her face of frenzy, gasped and shrunk back against the wall, watching as she lifted her leg and kicked the door in.

Marlene shot off the bed as Mildred crashed into the room.

'You've got my bag and I want it back now,' she demanded.

Marlene raised her eyes up to look at her, her mouth twisted into a smirk.

'And how do you know, has little Mary been telling fibs?'

Mildred bent down, thrust her face into Marlene's with her chest rising and as she stood there for a split- second, her eyes were on fire – lit up with angry heated flames. She grabbed hold of Marlene's hair and hauled her up and off the bed, dropped her shoulder and reclined her arm, before swinging her fist forwards, crashing it into Marlene's smug face. She was flung backwards and landed in a heap on the floor, where she lay flat moaning and groaning. The rumpus woke the sleeping baby in the cot in the corner as a housemother raced inside the room and stopped in her tracks watching Mildred hauling the mattress up and pushing it over onto the floor. Her blazing eyes clouded as she gazed at her bag. She snatched it up, stuffed it under her arm, just as the door was pushed open and a nurse dashed over to tend to Marlene when Mildred's face creased and she let out a loud moan. Her legs buckled, and she sunk to her knees, holding a hand over her belly, when blood began to trickle down her legs.

The nurse ran out of the room shouting for assistance. Mildred's eyes were wide with panic as she collapsed to the floor, her clothes now soaked with blood, but the bag still firmly clutched in her hand. Marlene Potts snatched her baby out of the cot and scrambled out of the room, with the colour draining from her face.

The housemother was leant over Mildred, clasping her hand and speaking in a soothing manner when eventually, two ambulance men strode into the room carrying a bag and a stretcher. Mildred was screeching with fear. 'We'll take over now,' he reassured the woman.

She stood up, white faced and shaking as she put Mildred's belongings in a small case. They lifted Mildred up onto the stretcher. Mary was stood quivering with her hands clasped to her face as they hurried past a sea of faces all standing wide-eyed as she was lifted into the back of the ambulance. The siren rang out as it raced past traffic, driving through red lights, then the Hancock Museum; Newcastle University and zoomed into the grounds of the RVI hospital. The doors were flung open, she was lifted out and they raced inside the hospital, making their way to accident and emergency department where the handover was given to the nurse on duty.

She was wheeled straight to the operating theatre. A nurse clasped hold of her hand, told her to keep calm, but she could feel she was passing something out of her as she gazed up at a huge round light above her and steel instruments in trays.

'It's the baby,' she screeched, it's coming.'

A doctor examined her. 'It's not the baby, but you are losing too much blood, we will have to operate now.'

She lay with her creased face pale, and bottom lip trembling. Placenta Previa was mentioned. The doctor turned to the young nurse beside him and spoke in a lowered tone. The nurse stepped over the room and came back with a syringe. She inserted the needle in Mildred's leg and clamped a rubber mask over her mouth. Mildred struggled, but soon everything was hazy as her eyes closed.

Distant voices were heard and the sound of metal wheels trudging along the ward awoke Mildred from the effects of the anaesthetic. It must be the tea trolley she thought as she croaked, 'Nurse, nurse.' But no-one heard her feeble cries. She laid her head back against the pillow and moved her hand over the large strip of bandage that covered her belly and traced the clips underneath with her forefinger.

Putting the discomfort and queasy feeling aside, she pressed her hands down on the mattress and pushed herself up to a sitting position. Young girls and woman were sat up in bed with their babies suckling at their breasts or waddling about in their dressing gowns.

At each bed, a baby cot was stood. Most patients had cards and flowers in vases and were sat chatting to a visitor. Biting her lip, she slipped her legs out of bed, when a nurse advanced towards her and made her get back in bed. 'I need to see my baby, I had a section so I don't know what I had,' she pleaded. The nurse gave her a searching look and lowered her eyes to the front of her bed. Picking up the file attached, she read though the documentation then placed it back, hooking it to the bed. 'It seems you had a baby boy,' she smiled. 'He's in special care, as he was very small.'

Mildred's eyes sparkled and she smiled broadly. 'Can you take me to see him? I'm dying to meet him.' The nurse shook her head and said she had too much to do. Mildred's face fell, but settled back waiting for someone else to take her there. But, each time, she asked, there was one excuse after another.

Wincing as the clips from the operation nipped her skin, she slipped out the bed, wrapped her dressing gown round herself; walked through the ward and along the corridor. A young auxiliary nurse rushed towards her. 'You need to get back into bed,' she gushed, but she shook her head. 'I've been asking to see my baby for two days, please take me to see him,' she begged the nurse.

The nurse brought a wheelchair, and she was wheeled out of the maternity wing. Through silent white tiled corridors where a strong aroma of antiseptic lingered as they advanced towards the special care wing. They were handed a gown and blue plastic protectors to put over their footwear for infection. She was wheeled towards the incubators, where she gazed at the babies and read the labels tied on the side of their glass incubators. And then she read it, the one that she had been looking for: 'Baby McDine.'

Holding her hands up to her face, she gazed in awe at her baby boy. His hair was jet black; he was the double of Danny. Unable to control the overpowering feeling of love for him, her face twisted with grief and despair as she broke down sobbing. Seeing her distress, the young nurse grabbed hold of the chair and was just about to begin pushing her out of the ward when Mildred grabbed the nurse's arm and reassured her. 'Please, I'm okay. I'm just overwhelmed at the sight of him.'

The nurse relented and Mildred simply sat in awe, gazing in disbelief at her baby. 'I'm going to call him Daniel James,' she said. 'I think he'll suit that name, he'll make up for all the awful things that have happened and I'll love him and protect him, and maybe one day he'll see his dad,' she cooed as she smiled once more at her child when suddenly, her head fell heavy – like a wrecking ball – and fell forward onto her chest.

Why is everything so woozy? Thought Mildred a she blinked her eyes and attempted to focus, when a young woman with ginger hair, a freckled nose and glasses came into view. She was stood looking down at her with a worried look on her face.

'What's happened? Where am I? Where's my baby?' she gasped.

The young woman leant over the bed and clasped her arm. 'Calm down, you've been ill, you had a relapse and lost a lot of blood, we thought you were going to die.'

Her eyes widened with shock. 'But where's the baby?' she asked once more

'I can't tell you that?' she whispered, lowering her eyes.

'What do you mean you can't tell me,' she whimpered, with desperate thoughts racing through her mind.

'The matron from the home made arrangements for your baby to be adopted. She thought you wouldn't be able to look after him as you had no means of supporting yourself. It was in his best interest that he was adopted, in the meantime you have to stay in the home till they find you a place to stay.'

'What?' she bawled at the top of her voice, as she began trembling. 'I showed Miss Small the letter my grandmother left me after she died, she knew I would be able to manage once everything was sorted out, why didn't she do something?' she screeched.

'Miss Small had a stroke while you were in hospital; she's too ill to help you. So, I've been asked to cover for her until she's well. My name is Sandy.'

'I don't believe it,' she yelled in horror. 'I'm jinxed, bad things happen to people who get close to me.'

Sandy put her hands on her shoulders and looked her square in the face. 'Mildred listen to me, the matron doesn't care about anyone's feelings.' She looked over her shoulder towards the door. 'I don't know how people in her position get away with the things they do.'

Staring mutely with tears streaming down her face, Mildred clung to the woman. 'You must be able to do something for me, please, please I beg you.'

Sandy gently pulled her hands away. Stepping back from Mildred, she began to pace the room with a hand held to her forehead. 'I can't it's out my hands, I'm so sorry, I never thought this would happen.'

'Where's my bloody bag now then?' yelled Mildred. 'They've taken my baby, but if all my documents have been taken I'm going to take a load of tablets, then they'll regret it,' she warned.

Sandy bent down and picked up a large bag. She stuck her hand in and took out her precious black bag which she'd kept safe for her.

Mildred balled her hands into fists with fury, when the door was pushed open, and a sturdy nurse stepped inside. Her shoes squeaked with every heavy footstep she took. Mildred's veins throbbed at her temples.

'She's been told,' Sandy said glumly as the nurse walked over to the bed stared at Mildred's white face and red swollen eyes.

The nurse reached for her wrist and, pressing her finger and thumb against it, she checked her pulse. She then placed a thermometer in her mouth as Sandy left the room. Mildred yanked the thermometer out of her mouth and slung it across the room, shattering the glass everywhere. When the nurse stepped back into the room, she peered at the shattered glass and gasped to see Mildred.

She lay with glazed vacant eyes, her wrists were slashed and the blood spread over the white sheets, down the side of the bed and onto the floor. The nurse pressed the emergency bell. Medics raced inside the room and applied firm pressure on both wrists then rushed her to the operating theatre.

The convalescence and treatment eventually brought her back from the brink. She had a room to herself and spent most of the time alone, not needing or wanting anyone's company. Sandy was her only visitor.

On one of her visits, she clasped hold of her hand. 'You may not want to go back to the mother and baby home. Especially after what the matron did, but it's that or an orphanage until you are sixteen.' Mildred's face creased at the thought of the pug nosed harridan, but she decided she would face her again – in fact she couldn't wait to face her again. The weakness in her legs began to strengthen and her wan face had a semblance of colour.

With her chin tilted and shoulders back, she stepped back inside the Presbyterian home. The girls circled around her. She smiled thinly back at them and stood for a while, before heading towards her room.

Once inside, she blew her cheeks out, thinking this was a big mistake. Everything came flooding back as she put her case down and taking her jacket off, she slung it on the bed. She opened her bag and peered at the blue and white label and kissed it as she tucked it away inside the bag. Daniel's name and the date he was born had been written on the label. But that was the only thing she had to remind her of him.

Placing the bag in her locker and securing the lock, she slipped the key inside her bra as she strode across the room. Then, stepping along the corridor, her heart thudded against her ribs.

The Matron was sat behind her desk as she slammed the door open. Her glasses fell off her nose as she jerked her head up and her toad mouth fell open as Mildred advanced towards the desk, looming over her. The woman gasped and shrank back in her seat as she spread out her hands, clutching and sweeping the desk in an effort to find her glasses.

'What are you doing, standing staring at me like that? Get out of my office, before I have you slung out.'

Mildred clasped her hands on the desk as she leant over, hissing through gritted teeth. 'Why did you take it upon yourself to have my baby adopted?' she snarled.

Matron's face was rigid. 'Don't you remember? You sighed to have your baby adopted?'

'What? No way,' she yelled. 'I was given something to make me calm down. I never signed anything, so you better get my baby back.'

The Matron smouldered. 'You signed a document when you had the section; obviously you didn't read it correctly.'

'I'm sure there was nothing about adoption in it. I know I was terrified and grieving with my granny dying,' she yelled as she stuck a forefinger finger in the matron's face. 'You're going to regret this, I'm going to the police and they are going to know what you're really like, because behind that matron's uniform you are a wicked and evil woman.'

Matron laughed nastily. 'You better not be threatening *me* young lady. I did it because you have no means of supporting yourself or the child. Surely you can see it was for the best? You have no legal guardians now your grandmother has gone. Your father is a wondering gypsy; your mother's a raging alcoholic – and you, well, you'll never be anything but trouble. Look at you, you're the product of two misfits,' she remarked with a sniff. 'Now go. And close the door as you leave, I have work to do.'

Mildred's hand swiped all her papers off her desk; her voice was now dangerously low. 'Repeat that again,' she said, as she walked around the desk, thrusting her face into hers.

The matron jerked back, but her eyes were steely. 'You're an ugly and bitter old hag,' she hissed, like a spitting cat. 'You're consumed with spite and jealousy because no man would want to come near that dried up, stinking old fanny of yours.'

The matron's eyes clouded over as she leapt up. Mildred lifted her hand back and struck her with a resounding crack on her cheek. Mildred's fingers tugged at her hair as she hauled her to the ground, where she dived on top of her. Pulling clumps of her hair out, she lifted her arm back and thudded her clenched fist into her face. Blood spurted from her nose and her false teeth shot out of her mouth. She lay moaning and a gurgling noise ignited in her throat.

The door was pushed open after a nurse had heard the commotion. Her hands flew to her face as she gazed at Mildred. She was stood glowering, her chest heaving, and hands covered in blood. The nurse pressed the bell and then sunk to her hunkers to check the matron. Both her eyes resembled plums: swollen, purple and black. Her gaping mouth was bloodied and toothless, and she was comatose.

Standing to her feet, the nurse dashed out of the room and returned with a silver kidney-shaped tray containing a syringe. She turned to peer at Mildred, now sat impassive, her eyes vacant and unseeing. The nurse stuck the injection through her cotton sleeve and watched as she slumped over.

Chapter Twenty

U nable to move or focus, Mildred felt someone prodding her shoulder. She turned her head to look around, and through a haze it seemed a woman wearing a thin nightdress covered in stains with tatty hair and a toothless, gaping mouth, was tugging at her hair with smelly fingers as she cackled and screeched.

'Get off me,' Mildred slurred as she attempted to pull the woman's hand away, but her arms were pinned down in a straightjacket.

With her heart thudding against her ribs, she gagged watching saliva dribbling down the woman's pointed chin and turned her head away, as her stomach rose. 'Where is this place?' she moaned, sweeping scared eyes around to see that she was in a room that resembled a prison cell. The walls were painted white, there were two single beds with a metal frame, and raising her head towards the window, her heart sunk to see it was fixed behind metal bars.

I must be in prison and they've shackled me in this straightjacket. I must've killed her. Well, the fat ugly bitch asked for it, she thought, when she took a sideways glance at the woman shuffling around her bed. Her wild glazed eyes peered at Mildred while she shoved a crooked finger up her nose and pulled a big green snot out and wiped it on Mildred's bed sheet.

'Where's the bell? I want the nurse,' slurred Mildred, twisting her face, when the sound of a key turning in the lock filled the room.

A stern-faced woman with a formidable manner appeared. Her black beady eyes darted towards her. 'The doctor said we had to lower your medication, so no funny business.'

Mildred cast a menacing look at the blurred vision of a nurse. 'I can't do anything, never mind any funny business, I want this straightjacket removed.'

'Oh, do you now? Well you won't get that off till the manager thinks fit. By all accounts you've got the devil in you. You've been meddling with things you shouldn't.'

'I've meddled with nothing,' she whimpered as her eyes filled with tears. 'Why am I'm in a straightjacket and where am I?'

'You are in an asylum for insane people. People like you have to be restrained,' she snarled.

'I'm not insane, so there's no need to truss me up like an animal, and if you don't take me to the toilet, I'll wee all over these sheets, I'm bursting,' she moaned

'I'm just doing my job,' she snapped as she leaned over, hooked her arms around her waist and dragged her up to a sitting position. As she swung around, she brought a wheelchair towards her bed then dragged her into it, before unlocking the door and wheeling her along a corridor to the sound of people wailing and crying, menacing sounds from behind the thick concrete walls.

She sat with her hands over her ears quivering as the nurse wheeled her towards a block of smelly toilets. They were freezing inside, a temperature similar to Antarctica. Mildred was hauled up out of the chair, her nightdress dragged up over her bare backside and then she was pushed down onto the toilet. The nurse stood with her arms folded and mouth drawn tight.

'I need to see my social worker, she'll get me out of this place,' she moaned as her head began to clear.

'She's got no say in here,' the nurse snapped. 'Are you quite finished?'

She nodded, and then she was hauled back into the chair, wheeled along to her room and shoved back into the metal bed. The prick of an injection caused her arm to tingle as though she had been lying on it for far too long, then the air started ringing in her ears as the nurse left the room. Mildred lay there paralysed, wondering if her social worker knew that she was in this dreadful place. And if she did, why was she not doing something about this living nightmare? She was halted in her thoughts, her eyes began to get heavy and soon she drifted off into a deep sleep.

Each day, she endured the same routine, only now without the straightjacket. Though the conditions in the asylum were a burden enough as it was. The place was awful, barely even fit to house rats, let alone actual human beings.

Alice – the creepy, stinky woman that she shared the room with – began to worsen. She wandered around at night, tried to get in her bed, called for her mother. It was easier just to let her get inside with her, at least that way it was warmer. Even if she did stink, it was better than being cold.

If only there was a magazine or a book, maybe that would have made things bearable. But there were no such things and no television to watch either. Mildred's rebellious spirit disappeared through time. She became morose and lost weight, then became distant, detached and passive. She was always exhausted through lack of food. Or rather, because the food that was served was unpalatable. Cold porridge made with water was a luxury in this place.

There was a calendar on the wall and each day she would put a cross through it and ponder about how long she would have to stay in this terrible room. She often lay dreaming about her baby, wondering what he was doing.

She lay with her eyes closed as hot tears trickled down her pale, sunken cheeks and was unaware that the door had opened. Someone tapped her on her shoulder and her eyes blinked open. She brushed the tears away with the back of her hand and peered up at a young man with a strong jaw.

He had a mop of light-brown hair that was cut neat in a short style, and he was stood with a furrowed brow as he peered at her. 'Mildred, I am the manager of this hospital. You will be pleased to know that we have informed your social worker that your condition has improved, and we are thinking of letting you on to one of the wards.'

She sat up and clasped her hands around her knees as she took a long intake of breath. 'I should never have been put here with this mad woman, chained up like some sort of animal. It's inhuman to be treated that way,' she retorted.

The manager gave her a stern look. 'You came here kicking and screaming. We had the report from the home, from the Matron. She assured us that you were unbalanced, demented and psychopathic to anyone around you, so you were treated accordingly. But we have seen for ourselves that you are suffering from deep reactive depression, which is being dealt with. Also, someone has been making enquiries on your behalf.' He held a letter in his hand. 'You are now able to receive visitors, but you have to stay here at the present time, we have to give you intense therapy until your mental health improves.'

Mildred lifted her shoulders and shrugged. 'It's going to take more than that to fix me. All I want is my baby back. When I do get out of here, I will be going to the police to report the Matron who caused this.'

The manager sighed and ran a hand through his hair. 'You will be wasting your time Mildred. I have known this happen to a lot of young women, their babies are snatched from them or they are forced to give them away.'

She cast a defiant look as the manager held out his hand. 'Come along and see the ward for yourself, I'm sure you'll agree it's much better than being in a lock-up. A nurse can bring your belongings,' he said.

She slipped her legs out of the bed and followed behind him. They walked along the long corridor, where the sound of screeching and wailing were heard, but as they stepped further, the sound subsided, and she found herself stepping into a brighter ward, filled with a lot of warmth and way more colour.

A row of beds faced one another on each side of the ward. Patients were sat in chairs, casually reading a book or in conversation with other patients. There was a nurse stood with a vase of flowers in her hand; she smiled at the manager when he spoke to her in a lowered voice and pointed towards an empty bed.

He turned and stepped away, leaving Mildred with the nurse. She was a portly woman, with a friendly face. Her eyes disappeared into her chubby cheeks as she smiled and put a hand on Mildred's shoulder. 'I'm sure you will be happy in this ward. You are allowed to leave and go into the canteen or television room, but you have to inform me or any other nurse before doing so.' She pointed towards a cubicle. 'That's our station there,' she said as she stepped away.

Mildred smiled and sat on her bed. She opened the envelope that the manager had given her, and as she scanned the contents, her eyes glistened.

Chapter Twenty-One

O nce Mildred received visitors, she began to flourish. She gained weight, the sunken cheeks filled out and there was even a sparkle back in her eyes. She would be seventeen on her next birthday and she was well enough to leave the institution. No longer needing to be monitored by social services, though she would miss Sandy her social worker, who had visited her on a regular basis and who had looked after her black bag and belongings.

Butterflies were fluttering in her tummy as she made her way towards the manager's office. She stood for a while, took a deep breath and then lifted her hand and tapped on the door. He pulled the door open and inclined his head for her to take a seat. She sat down and studied his serious face, wondering if this is what he did with all his patients.

'We are pleased that you have made a full recovery and can now look forward to a happy life. It won't be easy, because you'll never forget what that woman did. The gut-wrenching hurt will never go. It's not right and not fair, you young girls are treated badly these days. But I hope that one day things work out for you, and I hope you find your child.'

Mildred shrugged her shoulders. 'I doubt it, the Matron saw to that. I suppose I might get over it one day.'

The manager massaged his creased brow. 'You're not the first and you won't be the last. It stinks the way they get away with it, but time is a good healer. You have your whole life ahead, so live it well,' he said with a smile as he cocked his head to the side. Then, pausing he asked,

'Have you made any plans?'

She heaved a long drawn out sigh. 'I've had time in here to reflect on everything and the letter was from my birth mother. Hopefully we can build bridges because I need to move away from here, there are too many bad memories for me to stay. There'll always be narrow-minded people pointing their fingers, thinking I'm possessed or something and I can't be dealing with that. In the meantime, my friend Mary has offered me a place at her house until I can get something sorted out,' she said as she gave a tight smile.

He leant over his desk and placed his hand on hers gently. She got up and nodded her head towards him. 'Thank you,' she said. 'Thank you for everything.'

As she walked out of the office, along the eerie corridor and finally out into the fresh air for the first time in what felt like forever, she hoped with every millimetre of being that she would never have to go back there again.

It was a cold September morning. As she stepped outside, she gazed for the last time at the cherry tree that she had watched through her window. She noted how the leaves had changed colour through the seasons, it had been one of her ways of passing the time. It was the only taste of the outdoors that she had ever gotten during her stay, though it was nothing in comparison to the flavour of the air as it hit the back of her throat.

Now the leaves were withered and brown and they fluttered across the grass as she walked by them. She caught sight of a silhouette at the entrance of the grounds, between the huge, wrought iron gates. She bolted towards Mary as soon as she realised it was her, who wrapped her arms around her and held her in a warm embrace.

Mildred glanced over her shoulder and saw a young lad stood next to a battered old car. Her heart leapt in her chest when she caught sight of him. Mary released Mildred and placed a reassuring hand on her midback, spinning her around and leading her towards the young man. 'This is my brother Sam,' she said, with a twinkle in her eye.

He gave her a wide smile and she noticed how he reminded her of

Danny, but his hair was short and curly, and he was stockier. Mildred greeted him, wishing she had met him anywhere other than at a mental asylum.

'Our Mary has told me how you've been treated. You're welcome to stay until you get somewhere else. Not that we have much ourselves, but I guess it's home,' he said, as he stepped back and opened the rear door of the car.

Mildred sat peering out of the window and heaved a huge sigh of relief when Sam drove away from the asylum grounds. It was a short journey to Mary's house, but as they drew nearer, Mildred noticed how shabby the area looked. They drove past a public house with cracked windows, and as they did, a man with straggly hair and a woman with a darkened stain down the inside of her jeans staggered out through the doors.

Mildred's eyes widened. 'Have you seen that couple, her jeans are soaking wet.'

'Oh that's Gwen. She's always wetting herself when she drinks too much, we're used to it,' Mary laughed.

'God, I would be ashamed,' remarked Mildred as they drove past a school then turned down a back lane where there were two rows of terraced flats.

The car slowed down as Sam cut the engine and Mildred gazed out at a neglected building. Ivy was clinging to the outer walls and the net which hung behind the windows was grey. Mildred stepped out of the car and held her breath as she followed Mary. When they reached the entrance Mildred was faced with a door that was patched up with hardboard and covered in dirt.

She stepped inside the house which had been converted from flats to a simple upstairs-downstairs, three bedroom house. The smell of stale grease and cheap perfume lingered. The lino on the kitchen floor was scuffed and torn, the cooker covered in streaks of grease and the front room smelled purely of poverty. The fireplace tiles were either broken or missing, while piles of ironing were heaped on the top of an old cupboard. The armchair and sofa were worn and shabby.

Mary's dad was sat near the fire. He was a craggy-faced man with a bald head, thick ginger eyebrows and a beard. Mildred wasn't sure if that greasy stench was coming from the kitchen or from her dad. Maybe it was from both. He was smoking a cigarette and his huge belly made a guest appearance, hanging over greasy trousers.

'By you're a big lassie,' he remarked as his watery blue eyes leered at her voluptuous breasts.

'Dad, behave,' scolded tiny, mouse like Mary. He threw his head back and laughed. Mildred peered at the only two teeth he possessed: they were stained yellow and brown.

Mary threw a dark look at him as she crossed the room, Mildred following behind. She pushed open a door that led towards a passageway, the stairs and bedrooms. They stepped along the passage that was crammed with bags, boxes and an old bike.

As she climbed the stairs and reached the landing, Mildred took a peek at the first bedroom they passed, and noticed a slim figure lying on top of the bed. She clenched her finger and thumb to her nose, preventing the strong odour of stale sweat from entering it. A woman with lank black hair and sallow skin sat up and moved off the bed to step towards the doorway. She leant against the door frame with a sullen look on her face.

'Mam, this is Mildred, she's very grateful for you letting her stay – aren't you?' she gushed, turning to smile and nod at Mildred.

'Yes, very,' answered Mildred, with a bright smile, but noticed Mary's mother's thin lips press together and her eyes harden before she dropped them to gaze at her chipped, red-polished nails.

The thudding sound of heavy footsteps was heard advancing up the stairs and then Sam appeared on the landing. His mother's eyes switched between him and Mildred with an unspoken threat. He ignored the look and stepped into his room. 'I'm having a nap before I leave for the night shift at the pit,' he announced and closed his door.

Mildred sensed the look in the woman's eyes and knew what she was thinking: that she was either insane or possessed. She realised no matter where she lived locally, she would always have to put up with that stigma and must get away before it became too much.

She stepped into Mary's bedroom and her eyebrows shot up to see it was quite acceptable, with a double bed, a cream wardrobe and a matching dressing table with a sunken oval mirror in the centre. Mary was sat on the bed, her sparkling eyes beaming at Mildred. But Mildred's face was sullen as she set her case down on the floor. 'Mary, I saw the look on your mother's face, she doesn't like me and I know she doesn't want me here.'

Mary's mouth hung slack. 'Oh take no notice,' she remarked. 'She's a bit of a crosspatch, that's all.'

Mildred shook her head and held her hand up. 'Hey, I've gone through hell-and-high water. So I'm not prepared to stay here just to have her giving me looks to kill,' she snapped.

Mary shot to her feet and dashed out of the room leaving Mildred stood peering at the closing door. Then just as fast, the door was flung open again. Mary stepped back inside and behind her was her mother. 'Tell her Mam, tell her she's welcome here,' she urged.

The woman slowly raised her cold eyes towards Mildred. 'I'm a friend of Nora Jones. Talk of the town is that you accused her son of rape when he didn't do it, and he's had to leave the area because of you, so this puts me in an awkward position. If she finds out you're here, we'll fall out through it.'

Mildred took a deep breath to give herself time to think. 'Kevin Jones interfered with me from the age of four years old. He is a danger to any lass with a pulse. You can believe what you like, personally I'm past caring. I've been through hell, and just want to get on with my life, so I'll go now to save you the bother of having to tell me to leave,' she said. She bent over, picked up her case and brushed past Mary's mother.

The woman's eyes widened at her forthrightness as she stood with arms folded under her skinny chest. 'Well, when you put it that way, I'm seeing things differently. I didn't know he had done that to you when you were a child,' she muttered, raising her hand in an impatient manner. 'Put your case down and unpack. And from this point on we'll not mention his name again.'

'I don't want to think of him, never mind mentioning his name. And, I'm not possessed either, I've been suffering from deep reactive depression

– and in the circumstances, anyone else would do too,' she remarked.

Mrs Kelly gave her a quizzical look before turning around. 'I'll pop to the fish shop and when I get back we'll have a chat – you intrigue me Mildred.'

Mildred frowned. Talking about what had occurred would open old wounds, but if she said nothing, then she would always be seen as a troublemaker and a liar. She slumped heavily onto the bed, knowing she had told terrible lies, but it was either Kevin or her. She had no other choice but to lie for the rest of her life if it came to that.

Mary clasped hold of her hand and squeezed it as she winked her eye. 'Come on, put your things away and have a chat to mother, if anyone can put your reputation right, she can.'

Mildred grimaced then she unzipped her case and began to put her clothes in the wardrobe. Mary pulled out a box of records from underneath her bed, blew the dust off and stood peering at them, deciding what to choose to put on her Dansette player for later. She turned to Mildred and said, 'You won't have heard the latest Elvis song yet have you?'

Mildred twisted her face. 'No not really, it wasn't exactly a place of joy, Mary.'

They stood chuckling and then headed downstairs, where the smell of fish and chips wafted along the passage. When they stepped into the sitting room, Mary's father was sat with cheeks fit to burst, as he hummed a tune while shovelling the food into his mouth with his stubby fingers.

'Yours is in the oven,' said Mrs Kelly, sat by the fire, her spidery fingers holding a cigarette in her hand. Mildred pulled out a seat and sat at the table wide-eyed, as Mr Kelly swiped his hand over his greasy mouth, belched and lifting his fat backside, broke wind. He stood to his feet before waddling to the door that led to the staircase. 'Get your lazy arse up now,' he hollered to Sam. 'We're going to be late for work.'

Mildred clasped a hand to her mouth, having to stifle a laugh. There was the sound of thudding feet on the stairs. Sam slammed into the room, rubbing his hands into his eyes, just as Mary hurried in from the kitchen with two plates of fish and chips in her hand and passed one to Mildred.

'Where's mine then?' he asked, pulling a huffy face.

Mary lifted her thumb and jerked it towards the kitchen. He swaggered through and slumped down, sitting opposite Mildred, where he kept raising those come-to-bed blue eyes and arching his brow. Mildred kept her eyes on her plate, appearing to be cool, but her heart was aflutter and her nether regions were heating up.

Both girls were tired after the men had left. They had sat chatting to Mrs Kelly who kept asking awkward questions, but it was a different story when Mildred brought up the subject of the lodger who was staying with them too. 'I could pay double whatever he's paying,' she suggested.

There was an odd look in Mrs Kelly eyes, as though she was startled and flustered. Her gaunt cheeks flushed and her hands flapped as she laughed it off. 'No, it's quite alright,' she gushed.

Mildred cast her a quizzical look under her lashes as she rose up to go into the kitchen. 'What a shit-tip,' she uttered under her breath. Dirty dishes were piled up and not washed from goodness knows when. 'Do you want these dishes done?' she asked, popping her head through the door.

Mrs Kelly was sat by the fire still, her legs the colour of corned beef. 'Yes, if you want. I'm hardly going to say no,' she answered, as she sucked on her cigarette.

As she put her hands in the greasy grey cold water, she turned her head and twisted her face up, when she looked through the open bathroom door. The walls and ceiling were blackened from rising damp and the lino was torn and smeared. She put off from going to the toilet which was down the yard. It was smelly, with a brown-stained bowl, and no seat to sit on. Newspaper was used instead of a toilet roll. It was cold too, so she couldn't blame Mary for having a pail in her bedroom during the night.

The purpose of the pail was made obvious with what occurred the following morning, when Mildred heard the sound of trickling water that came from the corner of the bedroom. She sat up, and once her eyes were accustomed to the darkness, she realised it was Mary. She was sat on the pail, peeing like her life depended on it. 'I've got to get to bloody work,' she moaned as she got up and unhooked her dressing gown off a nail in the door.

Mildred shivered, pushed the heel of her hands into her eyes and yawned as she stepped out onto a cold wooden floor, then grabbed her dressing gown and slung it on as they walked downstairs and stepped into the front room. A small electric fire was placed in the middle of the floor and Sam was sat huddled around it with a plate of toast on his knee.

He glanced up and smiled at the girls as they slouched past him. Mary went into the kitchen to make toast and hot drinks as Mildred yanked open the back door and stepped outside into the cold yard and towards the smelly toilet. Wrinkling her nose, she hovered over the brown-stained toilet bowl. Shivering, she dashed back into the kitchen and through to the small cramped bathroom, where a rim of dirt was still visible around the inside of the bath, the enamel worn down to the metal.

She twisted her face as she quickly washed. More than ever, living in this situation forced her to make her decision. She must write a letter to her mother and hopefully get away from this stinking place.

Chapter Twenty-Two

A portly solicitor was sat behind his desk with his glasses perched on top of his bald head and was appraising her as she stepped inside his room. He scraped his chair back as he stood up and leaned across a desk that was cluttered with files. Clasping her hand in his, he proceeded to pump it up and down. 'It's good to see you Mildred, how are you? Take a pew.'

She pulled out a seat and lowered herself down. 'I'm still missing Gran so much and I'll never come to terms with what that matron did, by taking my child and then accusing me of being possessed or unhinged and forced into an asylum.'

The solicitor gave her a searching look. 'Well, first, let me deal with your finance and then we can discuss the rest shortly. Kitty was a very astute lady, what with all her investments. She gave me power of attorney, which means I could deal with all her finances. The guesthouse was sold, but you will have to wait until you are twenty-one before you get the full settlement. There's quite a large amount of capital that I have invested for you, so in the meantime you can have an interim payment from that and also the cash from the bank book will have to be transferred to your name. I will get my secretary to write a letter for you to take to the bank. The money invested will help you to live in comfort. It has been held in a high interest account, so I will write to them to let them know the situation. You should be able to draw the interest each month. In the meantime, you can go along to the bank, show them the book and the letter.'

'Thank you so much for your help. I'm staying with a friend at the minute, since I've only just gotten out of the asylum. I'm not a snob, but their place is manky. When I first went there her mother was very cold towards me, because she had heard all sorts of rumours. I don't want to live around here any longer than I have to, everyone thinks I'm crazy.'

The solicitor gave her a look of sympathy before clearing his throat. 'You've certainly had a lot to contend with. It will please you to know that the matron from the home is being investigated. It seems she wasn't having the babies adopted, but selling them.'

Mildred's mouth dropped open. 'So, that means my child was . . . sold?'

'Yes, I'm afraid so,'

Her head hung. She sat for long moments before she looked up with eyes of ice. 'It wouldn't pay for me and her to ever meet, or I would kill her with my bare hands,' she hissed, between gritted teeth, as she abruptly stood up and held his gaze.

Holding out her hand, she clasped his and headed for the door, so didn't see the wide-eyed solicitor peering at her over his specs as she pulled the door open. Stepping out of the room, she made her way towards the waiting room. She didn't have long to wait. The prim woman with her hair swept into a bun walked into the room and gave her a cool look down her nose. She handed her the letter and without a word, swung back around and walked out.

Mildred pulled a face. Stuck up cow, she thought as she went past her office to see her sat behind her typewriter. The woman's lowered eyes glanced up and gave her another cold gaze as she walked past. Mildred tilted her chin and stuck out her boobs as she pushed the outer door open. 'You sit there looking down your nose at me bitch, as if you're some kind of queen. Well you can fuck right off,' she whispered, curling her lip.

Stepping by a shop window, she caught sight of her reflection and saw her sullen face. She stopped and shook her head. What the hell am I doing, letting that stupid cow get to me, especially when I've got everything to look forward to from now on, she thought as she headed towards Northumberland Street, where she stood gazing at the latest fashions in Bainbridge's, Fenwick's and C and A's, before stepping inside Carrick's café.

Inside a young, willowy waitress appeared at her table, wearing a white apron over her brown uniform. Mildred glanced at the menu then placed her order, which the woman scribbled down on a small notepad.

Mildred sat looking around the busy café. People were sat facing one another over the tables, eating and chatting, but her mind was in whirl and she couldn't focus on anything other than the spinning sound of its overworked cogs. She had a whole new chapter in front of her and she was going to do it right.

The waitress stepped towards her table with a smile on her face and a tray in her hands. She devoured the tasty snack, then pushed her chair back and stepped towards a matronly, big-breasted woman who was sat behind a desk wearing a pale pink woollen twinset, and handed her the chit and money.

Lifting her sleeve, she checked the time on her watch and then turned her head to see Hancock's Museum. She stepped past students that were strolling around and climbed the steps into the entrance, where she spent the next two hours intrigued at all the unusual objects and animals that were inside, before she eventually strolled back to the bus depot at the Haymarket.

As she sat looking out of the bus window, a feeling of elation and excitement dealt a punch deep in the pit of her stomach. It made her want to leap for sheer joy. She was free after being confined inside the asylum for so long. Finally, she was truly free.

But, it would take a very long time to recover from the ordeal of having her baby snatched from her and then being labelled as possessed or insane through that vicious woman who was called a matron – more like a monster, she thought, just because she was a dried-up, frigid spinster.

The bus pulled away and she clicked open her bag. With her eyes peering at the blue book tucked inside the bag, her mind ticked with thoughts of all the things she was going to do. First, she would pay a decent board to that weird mother of Mary's with her spidery fingers and skinny shoulders. Then, tomorrow, which was a Saturday, Mary would be off work for the weekend. That meant they could go out and buy the latest clothes, bags and shoes. Treat themselves a little bit. Splash the cash, feel positive and forget the misery they had both endured through other people's actions.

With her long checked coat swamping her slight figure and her wild curls, she cut a strange figure as she got off the bus and made her way to the local bank. She swept her eyes around and saw two elderly women sat behind the counter, protected by a metal guard. She stood in the queue until it was her turn, then stepped towards the counter, took out her book and slipped it through a gap in the bottom of the mesh.

The woman opened the book and her grey eyebrows rose to her hairline as she read the letter that the solicitor had written. Raising her startled eyes up, she peered at Mildred. 'How much do you want to withdraw?'

Mildred raised her shoulders. 'I don't know, enough for a new life I suppose? A thousand pounds should cover it.'

The woman's hand flew to her chest. 'I'll see to this, take a seat while I deal with it.'

Mildred stepped back and lowered herself down onto a chair at the back of the room with a smile on her face. The woman's startled expression reminded her of the birds that fluttered in the front guesthouse garden.

The woman returned to the counter with her mouth gaping, as she peered at the pages of the book. Mildred stood up, collected her book and cash, and headed for the main door.

The women rose off their seats and stood leaning over the counter, watching her stride out of the building with a book full of cash, but dressed in dowdy attire. She stood outside the bank and glanced once more at her watch. She had half an hour before the shops closed and she kept looking down at her dated shoes that were scuffed at the toes.

A new boutique had opened near to where Mary's house was. It was lit up and mannequins were stood in the window wearing the latest clothes. She dashed towards it and pulled open the door to step inside.

Her face beamed, to see the array of modern skirts, shoes and bags. She went towards the rails, picked out the shortest shift dress then dragged off her old scuffed shoes when her eyes glistened to see black patent boots. She pulled them on. They fit perfectly, so she kept them on as she pulled out cash from her purse. Pressing the money into the owner's hands, she stepped outside with her arms bulging with bags, and headed for Mary's.

But, as she advanced towards the place, her face dropped. I've been here for two bloody months, but now that I've got money, I can move on, she thought as she stepped inside and was assailed with the usual rank smell.

Mary's mother was stood in the kitchen behind an old-fashioned washing machine that had a mangle attached. Piles of wet clothes were heaped onto the draining board. Mildred let her eyes drift about the place and analysed the many things that made it so dirty, as the back door was pushed open.

Mildred turned around to see a tall man with brown, sleeked hair in the doorframe. He was wearing a gold medallion which hung on a chain round his thick neck. His cold eyes glinted as he looked her up and down and his thin lips drew into a sneer, rather than a smile. Mildred tilted her chin and acknowledged him with a nod of her head. Out the corner of her eye, she caught an intimate look pass between him and Mrs Kelly.

It was a strange sort of look, one that she couldn't really explain. He suddenly turned away and swaggered into the front room. Mildred followed him. The lodger was sat reading a newspaper, and she stepped past by him as she pulled open the door leading to upstairs. Sensing she was being watched, she turned her head and caught the furtive look he was casting towards her from behind his newspaper.

Mildred curled her lip up as she climbed the stairs as she headed for Mary's bedroom, where she placed the bags down on the carpet. She cast off her old clothes and was stood in front of the mirror wearing a snazzy black and white checked outfit, with a black polo neck jumper and the black patent leather boots, when Mary sauntered into the room. Mary's smile faded when she saw the new clothes that Mildred was wearing as she twirled around.

'I know what you're thinking, so tomorrow we are going to get you glammed up too,' Mildred said.

Mary gave a wan smile as she raised her hands up in protest. Mildred stood with her hands on her hips, eyebrows raised. 'Stop pretending that you're not bothered, 'cos you are.' Clasping her by her shoulders, her eyes darkened. 'I've met that bloody lodger. If he comes near me I'll kick his cock off,' she spat. Mary gave her a sideways glance and smirked, before bursting into a fit of laughter.

Chapter Twenty-Three

The girls hunched their shoulders against the wind as they walked along the lane and then towards the main street, making for the bus stop. Mary's hair was pulled into bunches at each side of her head which she had tied with an elastic band. Her coat was thin, short and worn at the cuffs and collar.

Mildred's cork-screw hair was wild and her coat flapping. Mary's boots were ancient, zipped up and gaping at the toe. They scrambled onto the bus and hurried up the metal stairs to the top.

'Eh Mary, I never imagined I would be doing this a few months ago when I was stuck in that asylum,' gushed Mildred in a loud voice, when she turned around in her seat to see the conductor: a tall woman wearing a cap with the ticket machine in her arms, stood at the top of the stairs and peering at her with a frown on her face.

Mildred exploded with laughter as she dug Mary in the ribs. Mary clasped her hand to her mouth and her shoulders shook, seeing the conductor giving Mildred a long perplexed look before she moved along the bus.

An hour later, they arrived in Newcastle where they made their way down Northumberland Street to the sound of carols being sung by the Salvation Army and the sound of clanging as people dropped money into their red charity tins.

Further down, a large Christmas tree stood tall with a busker stood by it, entertaining the passing crowd with his flute. Dashing into the warmth of C and A's, Mildred bought two warm but modern coats, one for each of them. She also bought two shift style dresses for Mary.

Then it was to the shoe shop, where pointed toe and high stiletto shoes and boots were packed into boxes. Lastly it was the hairdressers: a fancy salon where the windows were draped in cream voile, walls were painted amethyst and gilt mirrors adorned the walls.

Women were sat in a line, waiting while their set hair was cooked under dome-like hairdryers. A snooty girl with her long nose stuck in the air advanced towards them and simmered, as her cool and immaculate made-up eyes swept over their hairstyles. 'Would you like to follow me please,' she said as she turned around and sashayed through a beaded curtain and into another room.

They removed their coats and handed them to her. She took them as though they were a couple of stray cats. Another skinny girl with her hair cut in a Mary Quant hairstyle appeared. Mildred noticed her gaping at her wild hair through the reflection in the mirror. She swung her mass of corkscrews around to throw a menacing look at the girl. 'Have you got a problem?' she spat, glaring at her with eyes of ice.

'No,' the girl gasped as the scissors made an appearance. Piles of dark, curly and blonde straw hairs were left on the floor as they stepped out of the salon now totally transformed. But the most important items were the bottles of cider, sherry and cigarettes.

They sat in Mary's bedroom mixing the cider and sherry and swilled that back as records blared from Mary's Dansette player. Once the makeup had been applied and a fine-handled metal comb tweaked into their hair, they stepped out of the bedroom laughing and giggling. They made their way down the stairs and burst into the front room.

Sam was sat on the sofa and as he turned his head to glance up at them, his eyebrows shot up while his jaw fell in the opposite direction. Both looked stunning, wearing black and white striped blouses but with a different coloured sleeveless, shift dress and tight-fitting black patent leather boots. A jacket was slung over each arm as they teetered out of the house in a fit of giggles and jolliness.

The local dance hall was only a short distance away. They stepped inside and handed their jackets to a woman in the cloakroom. She gave them a ticket to keep. They swung around, with black pencilled eyes glistening, and watched couples jiving and twisting on the dance floor.

A glitter ball on the ceiling twirled around, casting beams around the walls and floor. The crowd seemed to part and a good looking lad with long side-burns at the side of each cheek appeared and began swaggering towards them.

He wore a drape jacket, skinny jeans and beetle crushers. He looked at Mildred directly and said, 'Hey pretty thing, want to dance?'

She shook her head and said, 'I can't dance.'

He leant forward, grabbed hold of her hand, led her onto the floor and, guiding her through the fast dance moves, twirled her around with absolute ease.

When the music stopped, she inhaled deeply and smiled as she walked towards Mary, who was stood gazing into some young man's eyes. The lad she had danced with followed behind Mildred; his eyes held an eager expression, his full mouth in a wide grin as he clasped an arm around her waist. She swung about, pulled his arm aside and turned her back to him. But he was persistent.

He grabbed her again and drew her against him. Mary turned towards the cloakroom attendant to get her coat. Mildred dashed after her and stood with her arms folded glaring at her. 'We've just got here, are you mad?' she snapped, seeing her staggering about, her eyes glassy and wide.

'I'm only going further along to the pub for an alcoholic drink, you can't get any in here,' she slurred. 'I'll meet you back in here later.'

Mildred's face tightened. She gave Mary a blazing look and turned to face the lad. 'I'm sorry, I'm not interested,' she said, tilting her chin and handing the woman her ticket for her coat. The lad slouched away with his esteem shot and shoulders stooped, as she turned on her heels and followed Mary.

She was staggering about and giggling while the young lad bent her over and covered her mouth with his, before they swayed into the local public house. It was smoky inside, loud music resounded off the walls from a juke box. Men were stood leaning over the bar and every seat was taken. The tables were heaving with glasses.

The women raised their eyes and swept a furtive gaze over her, while the men at the bar leaned up, turned their head and she saw their eyes light up in appreciation. 'You can all piss off too, arseholes,' she whispered underneath her breath.

Hours later, Mildred dragged Mary out of the lads clutches. She staggered and stumbled as Mildred supported her, shivering and unable to feel her toes.

The lights in the house were out as she guided Mary into the yard. The back door was locked too. She bent down and picked up pebbles from the ground and slung them up at Sam's bedroom window. The sash window was pushed up and he stuck his head out, peering into the darkness. 'Where've you two slags been till this time in the morning?' he shouted.

'Charming. Open the bloody door we're freezing,' slurred Mary.

Eventually the door was opened and he stood glowering at his bedraggled sister who was stood grinning and swaying. 'I've been to work all afternoon and just got in after twelve, so I'm knackered and all you can do is stand grinning,' he snarled as he swung round and stormed away.

Mildred shut and locked the door then wrapped her arms around Mary, hauled her upstairs and dropped her onto her bed.

Stepping back downstairs, Mildred switched on the kettle and poured herself a hot drink. Shivering, she sat huddled on the settee, sipping her drink and enjoying the warmth of the fire. When the heat finally hit and the warmth of the drink sank into her chilled bones, she drifted off into a pleasant sleep.

She didn't hear the living room door creak open or see the lodger slink into the room. She was blissfully unaware. Until she felt the sofa dip and knew someone was sat next to her. She turned her head and seeing who it was, she moved aside and rose to her feet, but he clutched at her arm and pulled her back down next to him.

His sly eyes moved constantly from side-to-side as he smirked, before thrusting his face into hers. 'I've noticed the way Sam looks at you. I think he is sweet on you. Come here, I'll give him something to be jealous of,' he rasped, with his tongue hanging loosely.

Lunging at her, he covered her mouth with his, while grasping at her breast. Mildred squirmed and struggled. 'Get off me you dirty bastard. Your breath stinks, and I know what you did to Mary,' she screeched.

She didn't see Sam step inside the room and stop in his tracks, glowering at the lodger. 'What did you just say?' he barked, as he advanced towards him with eyes cold as steel and teeth clenched. He leant over and hauled him up off the settee, prodding a finger into his chest. 'What did you do to our Mary?' he thundered.

The lodger grabbed his finger and yanked it away sneering. 'Your sister's a little tease,' he laughed nastily.

Sam's voice lowered to a harsh whisper. 'Wait until my mother hears your lies, you'll be kicked out and good riddance, I've never trusted you. '

The man's eyes glistened as he threw his head back and snorted. 'You don't know your mother like I do,' he replied, raising one eyebrow and chortling.

Sam's eyes bulged. He gripped his fingers around the guy's throat and squeezed until his knuckles whitened. 'Don't you dare imply anything about you and my mother,' he rasped as he released his hand and flung him down to the floor.

Holding his hand to his chest, the lodger heaved. 'It's time you knew the truth about me and her.'

The colour drained from Sam's face as he lurched forward as though pushed from behind. 'Ask her for yourself,' the lodger said. Lifting his shoulders, he shrugged, and chuckling to himself, he pulled open the door leading to upstairs.

Sam's fingers clenched and unclenched as he stood with a savage expression on his face. He lurched towards him and hauled him down to the floor. Lifting his arm back, he thudded his fist into his face. The man keeled back and a crack was heard as his head hit the hearth. He lay groaning, but Sam lifted his leg and stamped on him, again and again, ignoring the screams from Mildred. She fell to the floor, dragged Sam off him and knelt down beside the man, pressing her fingers into his neck for a pulse.

With a deep sigh of relief, she looked up at Sam who was redder than hell. She laid a soft hand on his arm. 'It's not worth you getting yourself into trouble over him,' she whispered as she got to her feet.

'You're right,' growled Sam as he slumped down on the sofa with his head in his hands. 'But the bastard needed to be taught a lesson.'

Mildred shivered as she knelt beside the dying embers in the grate. She listened intently as Sam said, 'I'm having this out with my mother – about her and him. Plus, our Mary would never have a one night stand, she's too timid.'

'Mary will kill me for telling you this Sam, but what he did do was rape your sister and she had to say that it was from a one night stand, knowing your family needed the money he provides.'

Sam's eyes were vacant for a long moment. Shaking with emotion, his chin quivered as he jammed his hands over his face. Mildred moved towards him, put her hand under his chin and lifted up his head. She saw the hurtful look in his eyes as he gazed deep into hers.

She encircled his neck with both hands as her heart thudded in her chest. Sam did what he had wanted to do since he had first met her in the mental asylum car park. He kissed her, long and hard. Panting, she responded eagerly, before pain crossed her face. The thought of being pregnant again filled her with dread. Dragging herself out of his embrace, she leapt up off the sofa and strode towards the door that led upstairs.

Climbing upstairs and into Mary's bedroom, Mildred groaned to see that Mary was still sprawled and fully clothed, fast asleep on top of the bed. She shook her, but there was no response. She got undressed and pulled the bedding back. As she slipped underneath the sheets, she lay there recalling Sam's kiss and how she had felt. She had wanted him so much.

What's the matter with me? She thought. Am I a wicked girl who can't help herself? It seems the only way forward was to spend the rest of her life avoiding any contact with him or any other man, because she couldn't go through the trauma of having yet another baby snatched from her clutches. Life is so unfair, she thought as her eyes became heavy.

She woke before Mary the following morning. As she turned her head to look at her friend lying asleep, her stomach lurched knowing she would go crazy when she told her that Sam knew the truth.

Sensing she was being watched, Mary turned around in the bed and saw Mildred's tense expression. 'What's the matter, you look worried?' she asked, as she sat up, sunk her face into her hand and leant up on her elbow.

'There's no other way to tell you this Mary, but Sam knows the truth,' she said.

Mary's face stretched. 'What?' she slurred.

'After you went to bed I fell asleep on the sofa and that bastard lodger got up and tried it on with me. I lost my temper, told him I knew what he had done to you and didn't know Sam was in the doorway and he heard. He said you were gagging for it, so I blurted the truth out. I'm sorry Mary, but there's more. He says him and your mam are lovers.'

Mary leapt up out of the bed and sat on her bucket with a sullen face as Mildred wrapped her thick dressing gown around herself and went down to the front room to see the door stood open. She crept inside and swept her eyes around. The room was empty but freezing cold. Shivering, she pulled out the small electric fire, before bracing herself for the ordeal of the outside lav.

Mary was sat by the fire raking ashes out when she returned. She walked back into the front room to see that Mrs Kelly was sat hunched over, her long hair straggly and the usual wan expression across her face.

Mr Kelly was sat hacking and coughing as he leant over the fireplace and spewed phlegm onto the grey ashes. Mildred screwed her face up as she cast a sideways glance at Mary who dropped the phlegm and ashes into a pail.

Mr Kelly lit a cigarette while peering up at Mildred's tense face. 'What's wrong with you this morning, I can sense an atmosphere as cold as the bloody weather outside. What's going on?'

Mary avoided her father's eyes. 'I don't know what you mean dad.'

Mr Kelly bellowed, making Mildred jump. 'Don't take me for a bloody fool, I know when there's something wrong. You two went out last night and weren't in when I went to bed, so what's happened?'

'We had a good night and forgot the time, so we got back rather late, that's all,' answered Mary.

Mr Kelly's eyes narrowed. 'I hope you weren't messing about with lads again,' he rasped, wagging his finger in her face. 'I won't forget what happened when you messed about the last time, and then ended up with a belly full of arms and legs.'

'Mr Kelly, Mary didn't have a baby through a one night stand – it was that filthy lodger you have living here that did it. He came on to me too last night and if Sam hadn't come into the room, he would have done the same thing to me,' said Mildred.

The colour drained from Mr Kelly's face as he turned to see Mary running out of the room. He lurched out of his chair and crossed the room, yanking the door open. 'Sam, get down these frigging stairs,' he bellowed.

Sam thudded down the stairs and walked through the door, brushing his fingers through his hair. With a furrowed brow, he peered at his father's white face and bulging eyes. 'Tell me what you know about Mary and that baby of hers? I want the truth. Now!'

'It's true dad, Mary did fall pregnant because the lodger raped her. It wasn't her fault.' He took a sideways glance at his mother's tight-lipped expression, but said nothing more because his father's fists already pounded the table. He sent plates, cups, and cutlery flying everywhere, while Mrs Kelly sunk further into the seat.

'If I find out he's been anywhere near you, I'll blow his balls to kingdom come,' he hollered at her.

She averted her eyes and sat dragging on a cigarette as her husband strode across the room and flung open the door leading to the passageway, where he stormed up the stairs with Sam clutching at his arm.

'Dad, I gave him a bloody good hiding last night. He's probably away. He will be if he knows what's good for him.'

Mr Kelly shrugged Sam off him. When he burst into the lodger's room, he prowled about, and then growled as he thudded back down the stairs. 'Get out of my way. I'm going to get my gun back off Archie, and if you have any sense you won't stop me. He took my bairns innocence, and I did nothing. If I had known all along that it was him he would be dead now,' he rasped, as he stormed out the house yelling and cursing. He marched down the yard with intent. Sam rushed behind him, pleading for him to see sense.

Mary's mother turned on Mildred with her forefinger pointed at her. 'Why the hell did you have to say he got Mary pregnant when it's not true, go and tell her I want to see her now,' she hollered.

Mildred's mouth gaped. 'I said it because it's true. It is true, I'm telling you.'

She prodded Mildred in her chest. 'You have too much to say for yourself, lady.'

Mildred ignored the remark and stormed from the room, hurrying to Mary's room where she lay on her bed, her face creased and sobbing. 'Your mother wants to know if it's true about you and the lodger,' said Mildred.

'You had no right repeating what I said, you've betrayed me,' she screeched, her face scarlet with anger.

'Mary, you can screech and scream as much as you like because it needs to be sorted out what that low life did, if he's not sent packing he will do it again, he's an animal,' replied Mildred.

'But mother will slap my face if I go down there,' she wailed.

'I'll stop her if she tries,' assured Mildred when the bedroom door was flung open and Mrs Kelly came charging in and lurched herself at Mary, grabbing her hair. As she lifted her hand back to strike her, Mildred caught her wrist and pulled her aside. 'Get off me,' she hissed as she turned her venomous face towards hers. Mildred shook her head and tightened her grip when the sound of feet thudding up the stairs flooded the house.

'Is that you dad?' cried Mary.

'No, it's me, Sam,' he replied. He stopped in his tracks when he saw his mother and Mildred tussling. 'What the hell's going on?' he demanded.

Mildred released her grip and threw her hands into the air. 'Your mother refuses to believe what that lodger has done,' she said.

Mrs Kelly glowered at her before turning her attention to Sam. 'Have you found your father yet?'

Sam opened his mouth to speak when a movement was heard from down below. They all flinched. Then, as they moved towards the landing, they crept downstairs and Sam pushed open the living door. He stepped inside. Mildred and Mrs Kelly followed behind with bated breath.

The lodger gave Mrs Kelly a pitiful look as he pointed to his face. His eyes were swollen and blackened, and a dried up trail of blood was crushed to right the side of his face. 'Have you seen what he's done,' he rasped as he pointed to Sam.

Sam lurched at him. 'Have you got a death wish? I told you to get away and not come back. Dad's found out and he's out looking for you. He's bringing a gun back, so get upstairs, get your belongings and sling your hook before he gets back.'

The lodger's bloodshot eyes peered at Mrs Kelly as he leapt to his feet. 'Are you just going to stand by and let me get thrown out?' he whined. 'You said if we were found out, you would leave with me.'

Mrs Kelly dropped her eyes, seeing Sam's darkened, glowering expression and shook her head. She looked past him to see her husband. His eyes were bulging and spittle oozed at the sides of his mouth as he staggered into the living room. Swaying against the doorpost, he raised the gun up and aimed it towards the lodger. 'You filthy rotten bastard,' he slurred, thrusting his eyes into the lodger's white face.

'She came onto me, honest, she was gagging for it,' he wailed.

Mr Kelly swiped a hand over his mouth. 'You took my bairns innocence and let her take the blame for a one-nighter. If that wasn't enough, she got pregnant and had to go through that ordeal. Well mate, you're going to pay . . . and you're going to pay well, 'cos I'm going to teach you a lesson you'll not forget. I'm going to fucking kill you,' he snarled as he lowered his voice. 'You better move it, before I blow your balls to kingdom come.'

The lodger's fear-filled eyes turned to give Mrs Kelly a pleading look, but she stood quivering. 'Are you going to allow this Shelley?' he pleaded.

She shrieked, 'Shit Jack. For God's sake! Don't be so stupid.'

Jack mocked her, thrusting his face into hers. 'Stupid?' he growled through his teeth. 'Is that all you can say after what this piece of shite has done to our Mary?' Grabbing her arm, he hauled her aside.

'Are you going to tell him the truth?' asked the lodger, quivering in his shoes.

She shook her head again. Mr Kelly growled as he glared at her and asked, 'What's he talking about?' Then, seeing the lingering look they gave each other, his glazed eyes narrowed and his face stretched.

Jack saw red and that was all it took. The first blow connected to the lodger's face, sending him reeling. Lights exploded in the lodger's head as another blow split his mouth and nose open. Teeth and blood were projected everywhere, in every direction. Jack Kelly's face and hands were covered in blood after only a few seconds. He bent down and picked up the shovel that was on the hearth. He held it above his head almost in slow motion and then slammed it down on the man.

Sam dragged the shovel out of his father's hand as Mrs Kelly fell to her knees caressing her lover's face. 'You big bully, you've nearly killed him,' she whimpered. Then as she turned her head, she glared at her husband. 'I'm reporting you to the police; they'll lock you up for this.' With a guttural sound from Jack Kelly's throat, he hauled himself at his wife and began punching her repeatedly. Then he began to beat her, really beat her, enjoying the yielding of her body beneath his fists.

Sam flung himself over his mother and whimpered, 'Dad, have you lost your mind, you've nearly killed her,' he screamed.

Her head hung like a ragdoll. Sam lifted her up and put her down on the settee. Mr Kelly swayed and slurred as he came to his senses. With his face distorted, he stared at his blood-soaked hands and fell to his knees, when the sound of frantic thudding penetrated the eerie silence.

The noise galvanised Sam. He crossed to the window, pulled the curtain aside and gasped.

'What is it?' asked Mildred.

'It's the police,' he replied, fixed to the spot with a look of terror in his eyes.

The loud knocking continued and still no-one moved. Mildred went to the back door and pulled it aside to face two policemen. 'We've had a phone call about a disturbance,' said a stout police officer. 'Can we come inside please?'

Mildred stepped aside and they walked in, straight through to the front room, where they were greeted with the disturbing scene. The walls were splattered with blood and the lodger lay motionless on the floor, his features distorted while Mrs Kelly lay unresponsive.

'Some domestic,' remarked the smaller of the two officers as he surveyed the beaten figures and broken furniture. 'Did you do this?' he asked, turning to look at Jack Kelly, who was sat with his bloodied hands clasped around his lowered head. He lifted red eyes and nodded his head.

The officer peered at the prone bodies as he rubbed his finger over his jutting chin. 'Well I've got no other choice but to arrest you,' he said, as he whipped out his handcuffs and fastened them onto Jacks wrists, marching him out the room.

Chapter Twenty-Four

C hristmas was cancelled in the Kelly household.

The lodger recovered but was never seen again. Once Mrs Kelly was better she sent a friend to collect her belongings so that she could set up home with the lodger, away from prying eyes and loose tongues. Jack was let off with a caution. His wife and her lover just wanted the whole thing to be forgotten so that they could go on without any further hassle. But Jack's drinking spiralled out of control. He was a mess, snapping and snarling at anyone who spoke to him.

He was a broken man, and had retreated into a world of his own. Mary was worried about his health. He hardly uttered a word to anyone, except to curse his wife and the lodger. People began to ignore him in the street, especially when he was mortal drunk and had wet himself. Which happened on more occasions that Mary would care to admit.

Sam went to Newcastle to sign up to join the army. He was leaving soon and it was for the better as he was carrying a lot of animosity around. It took nothing for him to explode and lift an arm in a threatening manner. His anger would be better off being put to some sort of good use. At least with the physical activity and tough nature of the army he would have some form of release.

As for Mary, she felt she was unable to leave her father. Whenever she went out people either averted their eyes or stared at her while she shuffled along, her face level with the ground.

'Do you want a bloody photograph?' Mildred would holler while squaring up to anyone who had staring problems. Most made a hasty retreat seeing the venomous look on her face.

As time went by, Mildred had had enough of Jack Kelly. He always stunk of stale beer and his attitude towards her and Mary was terrible. It was time he pulled himself together she thought. She looked at Mary's sullen face after he had thrown his dinner plate which was full of food at the wall and refused to clean it up. Mildred stood with her arms folded, surveying her downcast face.

'Look at you, you're so miserable, this isn't right. You have to get away from here. I'm past caring what they think of me after Nora trashed my reputation, but you are so miserable with your father. It just can't go on,' she said, the truth echoing out of her like a warning siren.

Mary leapt up off the bed with her arms in the air. 'I know what you say is right, but I just can't leave dad, can I? He needs me,' she replied, lowering her head in her hands.

Mildred stood with her hands on her hips. She heaved a long sigh. 'If you feel like that Mary, then there's nothing I can say that will make you feel any better. But, I've had enough of the small-minded people in this town. The ones who give you darkened looks and whisper behind your back. I've stayed longer than I intended, so I'm going to leave for a new start in London. I've been in touch with Crystal and Pandora, whom I met at my grandmother's funeral. I've asked if I can stay with them and I intend to see Sadie when I get there. I want to see if we can build bridges. I'll write to you when I get my own place and I'll be hoping that you do change your mind. You're just young and you've got your whole life ahead, I think you're mad not to leave with me.'

Mary's face creased as tears filled her eyes. 'So when are you going then?' she asked in a flat tone.

Mildred lifted her shoulders. 'As soon as I get word from the sisters,' she replied. An air of tension filled the room. Some bridges would be built. As for others, they were going to burn in the fiery depths of hell.

Chapter Twenty-Five

As the taxi arrived at Newcastle Central Station, Mildred's heart thudded in her chest and her mouth was parched, but her brown eyes shone in contrast with the rest of the city. She stepped out of the car and waited, whilst the man opened the boot and pulled out her cases. Clutching her bag, she pulled out her purse and handed him a hefty tip. The plump fellow's eyes widened as he peered at the cash she gave him. Bending down and picking up a case in each hand, she made her way towards the large arches. Struggling with her cases, she stepped through the arches and stood sweeping her eyes around.

There was noise and commotion everywhere. People rushed back and forth maniacally and a voice echoed throughout the entire building over the intercom. She made her way to the ticket office. 'One ticket to Kings Cross please,' she said, with her smooth brow creased.

The bald-headed man behind a glass partition smiled. 'Don't look so worried,' he said, as he pushed a ticket through the partition towards her. 'That will be ten pounds, the train leaves from platform five.'

She raised her eyes at the clock, noting she had nearly an hour to wait, which with the chilliness of the morning would seem more like two. She moved away and glanced around, finally seeing a public house that was situated inside the station. Picking up her luggage, she slouched towards the bar.

As she opened the door the heat hit her hard. The place was packed and noisy as hell, but she expected nothing less. Moving towards the bar, she put her cases down and in the struggle to reach her purse, she dropped her bag and her purse spilled open. Coins rolled around on the floor, scattering everywhere. Her cheeks were scarlet as she reached down on her hunkers to collect them.

Right before her face she saw a pair of hands fly out, the money disappearing into them. 'That's my money,' she hissed as she straightened up and looked into the brightest blue eyes she had ever seen. They were twinkling at her as a young man with a broad smile held the coins in the palm of his outstretched hand. Mildred gave him a contrite look. 'I'm sorry, I thought you were going to pinch my cash,' she said, her cheeks burning redder. 'Let me get you a drink for helping me,' she flustered. 'I'm usually a confident person but since I've walked into the station I'm a mass of nerves.'

The young man brushed his fingers through his tousled hair as he introduced himself. 'I'm Gavin, pleased to meet you,' he said as he stuck out his hand to shake her hers. 'I work in a hospital in London, but I've been home for a short break.'

'Millie,' she replied, taking his hand in hers. 'I'm travelling to London too.'

'Well you can relax now as we're both going the same place, just follow me when the train arrives.'

Mildred smiled thinly, then turned to face the bar attendant where she bought a vodka for herself and a pint for Gavin. 'Thank you, but you didn't need to do this,' he said with a broad smile on his handsome face as she past him the glass. 'Bottoms up,' he grinned, then as he watched her turn around and step away, his smile faded and was replaced with a frown.

Placing her belongings on the floor, she put her drink down on the table, then settled herself down and opened her handbag. Taking out her compact, she slicked pale lipstick on her dry lips. Her eyes appraised Gavin through the compact mirror and found his full lips and the deep dimple in his chin very enticing. He's certainly attractive, she thought, but he must belong to somebody with that handsome face. She let out a sigh, twiddled her thumbs and gazed about, wishing it was time for the train. She hated waiting around.

Remembering her book, she opened her bag again and took it out. She spent the time with her head lowered, absorbed in the story. But the tale was interrupted when she felt a tap on her shoulder. She gasped and glanced up. Gavin pointed towards the open door and said, 'The train will be leaving in ten minutes Millie.'

She closed her book, shoved it in her bag and stood up. She collected her belongings and followed him out of the pub and over the bridge to the other side of the platform. They watched as the train arrived. He had a first class ticket too, so they made their way to the front of the train. He lifted her case for her and pushed it in a rack, while she sunk down onto the allotted seat. As he slumped into a seat further along, the aroma of his aftershave wafted through the enclosed compartment.

Peering out of the carriage window, butterflies fluttered in her stomach and her heartbeat increased with excitement and fear in equal measure. She watched the tall metal bridges and buildings of Newcastle disappearing as the steam train chugged south bound. There was no turning back now. She was on her way to the bright lights and places of interest in London.

Glancing over the seat in front, she looked at the back of Gavin's head and felt a pang of guilt. She had been rather off-hand she thought. Standing up, she went towards his seat. He turned his face to see her peering at the seat next to him. 'Is this seat reserved?' she asked.

His eyebrows rose and eyes twinkled. 'No, you can sit here.'

She lowered herself down in the seat when a fat man came into the compartment wearing a uniform; he was pushing a trolley full of refreshments. 'Two small bottles of wine and two packets of sandwiches please,' said Gavin. She clicked open her bag, wrapped her fingers around her purse, but he placed a hand over hers and shook his head.

He pulled the trays down that were attached to the seats in front, placed the bottles on top and unscrewed the tops. She held the small glass as the sparkling wine was poured into it and then another. She had no appetite for the sandwich, but soon began to relax through the wine, feeling light-headed and buoyant, enjoying his company. After another bottle of wine, her eyelids kept closing, plus the rhythm of the carriage moving from side to side made her drift off to sleep until the train jolted.

When she woke, she found her head resting on Gavin's shoulder. She quickly sat up and peered at Gavin's bemused face. 'This is our stop, can I give you my telephone number and meet up in London when you get yourself settled?' he asked as he lifted her case from the rack.

'Yes, yes of course,' she gushed, rubbing her tired eyes and clasping her case as he pushed his hand inside his jacket and handed her the slip of paper. She put the note inside her jacket pocket, wishing she hadn't drunk so much wine.

Her head throbbed and she felt giddy as she stepped down on to the platform once the train stopped. The guard was walking back and forth with a flag in his hand as the throng of people strode away to their various destinations. Bending to pick up her case, Mildred swept her eyes around, suddenly feeling apprehensive. 'My friend is picking me up, he'll be waiting outside the station,' said Gavin. 'Don't forget to ring me,' he said as they stepped towards the exit.

The platform which had hummed with life a little while ago now wore a deserted look, while the train station stood in an eerie silence. Shivering, she bit her bottom lip. Gavin leaned towards her and gave her a hug, then dashed towards a waiting car.

She turned away and made her way towards the bus depot. Double decker and single buses were stood parked in various stands. Her heart sank now that she was alone once more. She was apprehensive as she stepped onto the bus and told the driver where she was going and asked if he would tell her when they arrived at her destination.

After settling in her seat, she began to relax as she gazed out of the window but her mind was on Gavin. She thought about how she was attracted to his easy-going, caring way and his sunny smile. Soon, her eyes began to feel heavy once more and she fell asleep, until she felt someone pat her on the shoulder.

Her eyes blinked open as she sat bolt upright to look at the woman sat next to her with a smile on her face. She told her that the driver had called out to tell her that she had arrived at her destination. Peering out of the window, she saw only her own reflection and the interior of the bus as it was pitch black outside.

Clasping her hand to her face, she apologised, 'I'm so sorry,' she said to the woman as she rose to her feet and squeezed past her noticing everyone peering up at her with a darkened look. Apologising to the driver, she collected her cases and alighted from the bus.

She looked about and stood rooted to the spot. The bus station was large and noisy. She glanced up hearing a clattering noise. Rain was drumming on the corrugated roof, while music resounded about the depot. Two bedraggled young men where stood with a guitar and saxophone. She felt sorry for them and threw coins into a filthy cap that was placed on the floor. Heaving a sigh, she saw a line of seats. She made her way towards them and sat listening to the music.

After waiting for thirty minutes, she made her way towards a public telephone and picked up the receiver. There was no answer. Tight lipped she put down the receiver. She turned around to gaze about once more, her face taut. Then, she spotted the two huge black women gazing around with puzzled looks on their faces.

Shouting their names and waving her arms in the air, she screeched at the top of her voice. Their eyes were covered in bright-blue eye shadow and they were dressed in their usual tight and garish outfits. They waddled towards her, their faces beaming. Soon, she was squashed tightly between four huge bosoms.

'It's great to see you looking so much better and so grown up, we hardly recognized you,' boomed Crystal as each took hold of her cases. Linking Mildred between them, they made their way towards a parked car.

Pandora opened the boot and slung the cases inside. Mildred opened the passenger door and slid into the back seat. Crystal sat in the front with her head turned so she was peering at her. 'We know you've been through hell, so we're going to make up for all that crap kid.'

Mildred's mouth dropped open. 'How did you know?' she asked, as Pandora climbed into the car.

'Sadie told us,' said Pandora, giving her a sorrowful look before turning around and starting up the engine.

'Well she didn't come and help me did she?'

'She did write and wanted to visit you in the hospital but they wouldn't allow it because of your instability,' she replied.

'Really?' she gasped. 'I don't remember much to be honest. But anyway, I would rather not think of it,' she replied, screwing her face up at the thought. 'I want to know what you two have been up to since I last saw you,' Mildred asked, changing the subject.

'Us?' boomed Pandora. 'We never have a dull minute. You'll find out for yourself when you get settled in. We will take you to see the bright lights of London and everything else of interest too.'

'I don't know if I will get on with Sadie. I can't forget what she did, abandoning me when I was just a baby,' Mildred said, her face serious. She clasped her fingers around the locket that her father had left her and sat peering out the window at the tall buildings and the fast-moving traffic.

'We know she feels guilty,' said Crystal. 'She was young, wild and headstrong.'

'Sounds a bit like me,' laughed Mildred as they turned into a wide, leafy suburban area.

Mildred bit her thumb nail as they approached a set of large, wrought iron gates that drew apart allowing the car to pull into the drive. They faced a large Georgian stone-built mansion with a huge square of grass in front of the property. The windows were designed with small panes of glass, while white pillars supported a canopy over the door. At each side of the grey, slated roof were towering chimneys. Mildred stepped out of the car and stood back as the twins sashayed towards the door.

Pandora knocked twice, and then as she glanced over her shoulder, she lifted her arm in a beckoning manner. Mildred's legs were shaking as the door opened. As if by magic, there she was. Sadie stood in the doorway, facing her with a broad smile.

Mildred looked at the woman who had caused her so much anguish, but who also had gone to court in her defence too, and she didn't quite know what to feel. Was it anger or sadness, desperation or forgiveness?

Perhaps it was a shade of each, all balled into one.

Taking a deep breath, she forced her legs to move. She headed towards her mother who leant towards her and wrapped her arms around her in a warm embrace. Then she stood back for the girls to enter.

They stepped into an ornate, gabled porch and through to a grand entrance hall. They walked through the hall and stepped through into a spacious lounge with a beamed ceiling. Brass ornaments adorned the walls whilst the brown eyes of a large stag's head, which was hung over an open fireplace, stared at them intensely.

'You must be tired after all that journey Mildred,' Sadie said, as she inclined her head and held her hand out for her to sit.

'Well, a bit, but it felt good to get away from the small-minded people who were everywhere back up north. Especially after Nora Jones started to spread rumours about me,' Mildred said.

Realising she had said too much, Mildred dropped her eyes while lowering herself down onto a leather sofa. The twins slumped into matching chairs at either side of the fireside. An oval mahogany table held a silver tray with four fluted glasses and a bottle of champagne.

'Oh her,' laughed Sadie. 'It was hilarious when she was sprawled on the floor, covered in drinks and tab ends at mother's funeral.'

'Not as funny as when I pushed her out the door and she fell on her face, with her big arse in the air and her pink knickers down to her knees on show,' spluttered Crystal.

Mildred's tense expression softened with the vision of Nora's knickers in her mind. Everyone sat laughing at the memory.

'This calls for a celebration,' quipped Sadie as she held a cloth over the bottle top and uncorked it. She leant over and filled each glass. Lowering herself next to Mildred, she lifted her glass to hers and winked an eye. 'I never thought this would be possible,' she said as she tipped her head back.

'Well, it wouldn't have been if he was still here,' snapped Pandora. 'No one was allowed here when the almighty lord was at home.'

Mildred turned her head towards Sadie. 'So, where is your husband?' she asked. 'I remember you saying it would make things awkward if I came here.'

Sadie lowered her eyes. 'That was if you were going to stay on a permanent basis. He's confined in a nursing home now as he's had massive stroke. They wanted me to have him here with nursing staff, but there's no chance of that. He was a pig – and still is, he'd be even bloody worse if he was bedbound all day, left to rot and to get even more grouchy than usual.'

'Yes, but you thought he was lovely when he changed the life you were living,' stated Pandora, before she clasped her fat hand over her thick fleshy lips. She took a quick sideways glance at Mildred, seeing the thunderous look that Sadie was shooting at her. 'I didn't mean to blurt that out,' she said, dragging her eyes away.

'Well, now that you have, Mildred will be curious as to what life I was leading, won't you?' she asked with a tight smile. 'Well, to put it simply, we were all hostesses, working in a nightclub. We were expected to be very attentive at all times with men that for the most part made our flesh creep. Especially if they suffered from bad breath and body odour, which was more common than it should have been. They would drool and drape themselves all over you, and you had to put up with it. It was awful, but it was that or starve, there wasn't much choice in the matter.'

Mildred twisted her face and quivered. 'So, you were taken from all that and now live in luxury? But what about you two?' she asked, turning her attention to the twins. 'Are we going to your place after this?'

Sadie interrupted with a glum look. 'I thought you would want to stay here for a while?'

Mildred's eyes widened. 'If that's alright, I will, but what about you two?' she asked twisting herself around to face them.

'I think it would be better if you two could spend some time together rather than stay with us,' suggested Crystal. 'We can all meet up in London, you have our telephone number, so just give us a ring and we'll meet up to show you around the city.'

'That sounds wonderful, I can't wait,' gushed Mildred. 'I still can't believe that I'm actually free to go anywhere I want. I feel sorry for the people I met when I was in the asylum. Some had been there all their life and knew nothing more. They were institutionalised and accepted what they had.'

Everyone nodded their head in sympathy, until Sadie mentioned Kevin's name. 'I wish that Kevin Jones had been put in an asylum for life. God knows where he is.'

Mildred's face darkened at the mention of his name. 'I hate that fat, horrible freak,' she said.

Crystal waved her fat hand. 'Forget him honey. Looking back only gives you a stiff neck.'

She turned to her sister. 'We better get going. I can see Mildred's eyes are nearly closing.'

Pandora raised herself up and gave Mildred another breath- taking squeeze between two cushion sized breasts. The sisters sashayed towards the door. With their loud voices booming and backsides swaying in slow motion, they clashed the door shut.

Mildred stood watching them from behind the window and stifled a laugh. Their bums swayed like enormous balloons enclosed in a bag. Dragging her eyes away, she glanced up at a rowan tree, and sighed with pleasure. The buds had appeared.

It was now spring, a new beginning for nature, and a new beginning for her too. She hoped that through time, she and her mother would mend the void that hung over them like an invisible cloak.

Chapter Twenty-Six

Mildred gazed around her bedroom bright eyed and beaming. It was light, airy and spacious. A cream wardrobe and a matching set of drawers were stood between a chimney-breast. In the open brick fireplace stood a large pink and cream jug, filled with dried hydrangea. Her headboard was brass leavened. Floral lace bedding and matching curtains completed the calm atmosphere.

She took off her shoes and wriggled her toes in the sheepskin rug by the side of her bed. Once her clothes had been put away, she went downstairs to see Sadie sat in the large, white-tiled kitchen.

'Make yourself at home, come on, take a seat, I've made a steak pie and mash,' said Sadie.

Mildred's stomach rumbled. She lowered herself down and drooled as Sadie brought out a huge pie from the oven and a terrine of mashed potato and vegetables.

'This is lovely, I didn't know you were such a good cook,' said Mildred as she took the third slice of pie and wolfed it down.

Sadie smiled. 'I'm not just a pretty face you know,' she said. Her smile faded and she looked up at Mildred. 'I hope you'll be happy here, I just want to make up for everything I've done. I'm so sorry. I was such a terrible mother, and I still am technically.'

Mildred lifted her shoulders and raised her eyebrows. 'We'll not talk about that eh? I think a new beginning would be best. And to start properly with a new beginning, we need to forget about the previous chapters.'

Later, they were sat around the open fire sipping milky coffee, when Mildred asked about her father.

The smile on Sadie's face vanished. 'I walked away still in love with him. I never wanted to leave him, but I was never accepted by the Romany people. We were different cultures,' she said with a sigh. 'So I don't know what became of him.'

'There must be some way we could find out where he is? What about Appleby horse fair. It's on every year, so we could go and ask around. Someone may know his whereabouts.'

Sadie curled her lip, dropped her eyes and made no comment. Mildred realised she had hit a nerve seeing the tight expression, so decided to change the subject. 'I know this is asking a lot, but I suppose I probably am owed a few favours. I have a friend living in awful conditions back home, as her father is always drunk and shouting at her. So, would she be able to stay here until I find her somewhere to rent?'

'Of course she would be welcome here,' replied Sadie, peering at her tense face.

'You wouldn't mind then?' Mildred asked in an astonished voice.

Sadie shook her head. 'Write to her or give her a phone call.'

Mildred sat and peered at her mother. She was so calm and relaxed compared to the other times she had met her.

'I think we need to get to bed, before we fall asleep here by the fire,' suggested Sadie.

Mildred rose to her feet. Yawning, she glanced around at the opulent décor that she was lounging in. She sunk her feet into the thick, cream carpet as she followed Sadie up the oak staircase.

They walked long the landing, where glass wall lights twinkled and exquisite paintings hung. Sadie brushed her cheek, pulled open her bedroom door and stepped inside. Mildred went inside her bedroom and sat down on the cream velvet stool in front of the kidney shaped dressing table. Her eyes lowered to the note that Gavin had written his telephone number on. Shaking her head, she picked it up and threw it into a wicker rubbish basket.

Clicking open her beg, she took out a pen and a writing set. She laid it on the dressing table and leaning over, she began to write to Mary.

Chapter Twenty-Seven

An envelope dropped through the letter box a week later. She pulled out a drawer and slit the envelope open. Her eyes widened. 'It's from Mary, she's coming down tomorrow,' she cried.

Pacing back and forth on the platform at Kings Cross Station, Mildred checked her watch once more. The train was late. She passed her hand across her tense face, then glanced again along the line and saw the train advancing. She peered along the carriages as the train came to a halt and saw the doors open. Hearing her name, she whirled around and saw Mary dragging her cases towards her. She flew towards her excitedly, but noticed how gaunt and pale she looked when she hugged her tightly.

'Sadie's waiting in the car park,' she gushed as she grabbed hold of one of the cases. 'Wait until you've seen Sadie's home, it's fabulous.'

'Are you sure she doesn't mind me staying?'

'She wouldn't say yes if she didn't want you to. Anyway I don't intend on staying much longer, I want a place for us both.' She turned to Mary with a creased brow. 'You do intend on staying here, don't you? In London I mean.'

'Hopefully,' Mary replied.

Beaming from ear to ear, she followed Mildred towards a large car where Sadie was sat watching the pair as they chatted to each other on their walk over. She gave Mary a broad smile. 'I'm Sadie,' she said, thrusting her hand out as she stepped out of the vehicle. 'I've been hearing all about you from Mildred. I'm sure you'll be very happy here.'

'I hope so,' replied Mary. 'Thanks so much for letting me stay.'

Once the luggage was put into the car boot, they zoomed away with Mildred telling her about Gavin and that she had thrown his phone number away.

'She's a fool,' quipped Sadie. 'He's a good mannered lad and you don't get many of those.' Mildred rolled her eyes while Mary clasped a hand over her mouth as she sniggered.

Soon they approached Sadie's home and Mary's eyes widened as she stepped from the car. She stood gazing around at the lush surrounding and the grand house. It was a royal palace compared to the dismal dingy place that she called home.

Removing their shoes, they walked through the front entrance, towards the large staircase and along the landing. Mary's eyes swept over the décor and when she stepped into Mildred's bedroom, the thick pile of carpet felt blissful on her bare feet. She wriggled her toes, enjoying the sensation.

'Like it?' asked Mildred as she lowered herself down onto a pine chair near the window and pointed to the other one gesturing for Mary to sit too. But she stood there gazing dumbly out of the window at the lush grass, shrubs and the colourful array of spring flowers that grew annually inside the walled garden.

She snapped out of her trance and then addressed Mildred. 'Is everything alright with you and Sadie then?'

'Yes, I've been here for three months and she can't do enough for me. It's since she's been on her own that she's changed. I've been meeting Crystal and Pandora and we've had a laugh. I think she's had quite a colourful past but doesn't want to be reminded of it,' she whispered.

'Really? How?' asked Mary, wide-eyed.

'Well, I discovered that she had been a hostess working in a nightclub and had to entertain men or starve. The man she married was the owner and he took her away from all that, but she was treated like a puppet. And since I've been down here I've seen for myself how different it is compared to where we lived, so when we go out you have to be careful,' warned Mildred.

'I will,' she assured.

'What's things like up north?' asked Mildred, twisting her face. 'Were you still getting black looks of people?'

'I saw Nora Jones, and she gave me looks fit to kill.'

'We've been having a laugh about her lying in the street with her big bloomers on show, when Crystal pushed her over after Grans funeral.'

'I wish I had seen that,' laughed Mary.

'I've been looking in the estate agents offices while I've been here too, and the rents are high in the city. But we can't stay here forever, so tomorrow we'll go and see what's on offer around here. I know I've got an allowance each month but that won't be enough, we've both got to get work too, so we'll sort that out as well,' she said, as she rose to her feet and headed towards her bedroom door.

'Something smell's nice from downstairs. I'm starving, how about you?'

Mary jumped up as soon as the words left Mildred's mouth. They scrambled downstairs; into the well-equipped kitchen where Sadie was stood behind an Inglenook fireplace, her back facing them. She swept around with large bowl of curry in one hand and a bowl of rice in the other. She put it down on the table.

'I've been warning Mary to watch herself,' said Mildred, scooping a large spoonful of rice out of the bowl.

Sadie took a sideways glance at Mary with her plain face and mousy-coloured, tatty hair. 'In the city especially, not so much round here. There are drug dealers and pimps on the look-out, especially when they see a young girl lost and alone after too many drinks. So be very careful,' she warned. 'I don't mean to scare you of course, but that's just the way they are around here.'

Mary's eyebrows drew together. 'I don't know if I want to go out now, if it's so dangerous.'

'As long as we stick together we should be fine,' Mildred assured her.

'I'm not stupid. I'll not go wandering off.'

Mildred raised one eyebrow and rolled her eyes. 'Yeah sure, I've learnt first-hand that that's absolute bullshit,' she said. They collapsed in a fit of laughter.

After their meal, Mildred suggested taking Mary for a walk and a look around the village. They strolled along the quiet road and sauntered into the cemetery where an ancient church was stood. Further along the road, they stepped by a public house.

'We'll go in there and have a cool drink,' suggested Mildred.

Inside it was a typical bar: stale beer intermingled with cigarette smoke, wooden flooring and worn red leather seating. Elderly men were sat with their pints of beer on the tables and playing cards. A dart board and notices were pinned on the wall. A brassy blonde woman was stood behind the bar, all Max Factor and dangly ear-rings. She smiled and asked what they wanted.

They sat down on stools facing the bar and ordered lemonade. The place was quiet. The barmaid heard their accent and soon they were sat chatting to her about Newcastle. She stood with her elbows leant on the bar, her ample bosoms spilling out of her tight blouse, but she was a good laugh with her tales from years ago at Newcastle.

It was dusk by the time they left the pub. Vodka doubles had been added to the lemonade drinks. They were celebrating and swaying with arms clasped around each other, as they arrived back at Sadie's.

Their eyes were sunken and glazed when they woke. It was dinnertime before they were able to function properly and they sat with their head in their hands drinking strong black coffee. Sadie was stood behind the cooker frying sausages while they held their stomachs. She gave them a glass each of a concoction that she swore helped a hangover.

Later, they were bright-eyed and ready to face the shops. Sadie gave them a lift and dropped them off in the city. They strolled around, window shopping at first. Then they headed for the Labour Exchange and found there were plenty of vacancies. Mary pointed to the notice board where there was a card advertising for staff in a new nightclub. Mildred gave her a disapproving look, but still raised her eyes anyway to look at the vacancy.

'Well, we can always go and find out. If it's bar staff, that's fine but I'm not doing what mother did when she was a hostess – even if she did get wealthy a husband out of it.'

They turned round and waited in the queue until it was their turn to get advice. They headed towards a desk, pulled out a seat and sat facing a dour young man. 'There's a new nightclub opening, if you're interested in bar work,' he said, yawning wide.

The girls looked at each other and nodded, then turned to face him again beaming. He sat writing on a card then handed it to Mildred. 'The nightclub is half a mile from here,' he said.

They pushed their chairs back and headed for the door, setting off on their journey towards the nightclub.

The entrance was trendy with smoked mirrors and glowing art on the walls. They faced a large masculine woman who was sat in a cubicle. Her face was heavily made up with huge eyelashes that fluttered as she peered at them. Loud music blared from speakers around the walls.

Mildred stepped towards her and handed her the card from the Labour Exchange. The woman dipped her eyes then rose to her feet. 'Follow me please,' she said in a clipped voice. They followed the woman through a doorway and into an office.

Inside there was a pleasant smell of aftershave which was coupled with the scent of freshly-brewed coffee. They faced a man with cunning deep-set eyes, olive skin and black straggly hair, who was sat behind a desk. He held out a hand and gestured for them to take a seat.

Mildred slid her eyes to glance at Mary. She was sat in a trance-like state as he spoke. 'The bar vacancies are now filled but there is other work available. I'm looking for girls who can keep people entertained. They must be able to dance provocatively,' he said, his dark eyes glistening. 'I'll show you around, if you're interested.'

'Yes, we are,' gushed Mary.

He rose to his feet and they followed behind him, stepping back into the main room of the dimly-lit nightclub. Gazing around, they noticed a stage elevated at the back of the room, where voile and silk curtains were draped. A set of drums, two organs and a guitar stood next to the microphone. A long bar filled the entire area on one side of the room and tables and chairs were placed at random.

A tall willowy woman wearing a long flimsy sapphire dress emerged from the shadows. Her features were concealed by a face mask that was sparkling with sequins. The feathers on her small satin headpiece fluttered as she began to dance, gyrating provocatively while arching her back. Peeling off her dress like a silk stocking, she then removed her bra.

Mildred and Mary stood wide-eyed, watching her cavort around in a pair of pink frilly knickers. Slowly snaking around Mildred, she pulled her towards her. Gazing deeply into her eyes, her hands softly caressed her body. Mildred stood transfixed, her eyes unblinking.

The manager smirked in satisfaction, clapping his hands together. She curtsied, removed her mask and, lowering her dark eyes, returned into the shadows.

'Well, are you still interested?'

'No,' snapped Mildred, pulling herself together.

'Yes,' Mary said. 'I can do that too.'

Mildred's eyebrows shot up as she turned to face her. She slid her hand towards Mary's thigh and nipped hard. Mary winced, but began strutting about, gliding around the stage like a swan. She also arched her back, then lowering herself slowly down, she lay on the floor with her legs wide apart as she loosened her bra and slung it across the stage. Mildred's jaw dropped as the manager clapped his hands and told Mary there was a flat above the nightclub that went with the job.

'I'll take it if, I can keep the mask on.'

He gave her a quizzical look. 'Why is that? You don't seem the shy retiring sort.'

'It's my brother. He would be furious with me for parading myself in front of everyone.'

He stood rubbing his finger and thumb against his chin. 'Well, okay, if it means that much, I suppose you can' he said as he gave his attention to Mildred. 'What about you, are you interested too?'

Mildred gave him a tight smile. 'No thanks mate,' she snorted.

Striding from the room with her chin tilted, she headed back outside and stood sullen-faced as she waited for Mary to appear in the doorway.

'Have you lost your bloody mind?' she demanded, grabbing her by the shoulders and glaring her. 'He's a complete creep. You will regret it if you take this job. He's shady as hell,' Mildred said.

Mary disentangled herself from Mildred's grasp. 'It's alright for you, you've got money. I haven't. I don't have a damn penny. He's told me there'll be more opportunities in the near future.'

'I can just imagine what those are too,' Mildred said as she marched away, leaving Mary straggling behind. Slumping down on a bench, she sat with her arms folded. 'That woman had big tits, what have you got?'

'Some men like small tits,' she said in a contrite manner.

Mildred sat scowling, wondering if she had done the right thing, by asking her to come to London. Mary was too gullible for her own good.

Mildred stepped inside Sadie's house tight-lipped and bristling. Sadie glanced at her tense face and asked what was wrong. Mary stepped in behind her.

'Ask her. She's lost her bloody mind. She's going to work in the nightclub, dancing around with nothing on.'

'No I'm not, I'll have my knickers on,' Mary said.

'What?' gasped Sadie. 'Why would you want to do this? It's far too dangerous.'

'I need a place to stay and he says there's a flat with the job,' she whined, her voice rising with temper.

'Who owns this place, do you know?' Sadie asked.

'Someone called Jonah,' Mildred sneered. 'But it was a greasy and long-haired man called Mario who gave her the job, he's the manager.'

'Well Mary, it has nothing to do with me but really think before you go and put yourself in danger like this. I've known young impressionable girls like you who think they are embarking on an exciting life. Then they are never seen again,' Sadie said.

Mary's face crumpled. She sunk her head into her hand as tears welled up in her eyes. She began sobbing her eyes out and wailing. 'You're just saying that to put me off, but it won't, my mind is made up,' she snorted.

Mildred and Sadie watched as she strode towards the stairs and listened as her shoes squeaked and her feet thudded up towards the landing.

Mildred wiped a hand over her face. She's come here and has the frigging nerve to act the drama queen, I'm going to kill her, she thought as she turned to Sadie. 'I'm sorry about that,' she said.

'If her mind is made up then it won't make any difference,' warned Sadie, as Mildred shot to her feet and stood with a sour look.

'It's no good falling out either,' she said, glancing at Mildred pacing the floor. 'It's going to make things very uncomfortable here and I can't be doing with the drama,' she warned.

'It won't happen again,' Mildred said as she stopped in her tracks and headed for the stairs.

Mary was face down on the bed when she stepped inside the bedroom. Mildred heard the sound of sniffing as she sunk down onto the bed. Mary lifted her head and turned to see who it was. She sat up to face Mildred with a petulant look on her face.

'First of all, I want you to apologise to Sadie,' Mildred said in a cool manner. 'She didn't have to let you stay here, so just be grateful that she did. I expect no more dramas. If this job is what you want, then go ahead. So, get some wine down your neck and we'll go and see what the bright lights have to offer.'

Mary gave a feeble smile. 'I'm sorry, I was out of order. It won't happen again, and I'll apologise to Sadie.'

The icy atmosphere was fixed – for now.

Chapter Twenty-Eight

They caught a train into the City.
Noticing a cream-painted tavern with small leaded windows and flowers trailing out of large pots near the doorway, they glanced at one another and raised their eyebrows. The heat hit their faces as they pulled the door open. Raucous laughter, loud music and plumes of smoke greeted them as they stepped inside. Groups of men stood facing the bar and it was packed full. Tiny Mary stood back to let Mildred stand waving her arm at the bar tender as she pushed her way through.

A young man glanced around and gave Mary an appraising look then nudged his friend in the side with his elbow. Mary beamed at him then flicked her hand through her hair, giving him a coy look.

'What's a nice girl like you doing here?'

'Same as you,' she giggled.

'Let me introduce myself,' he said. 'I'm Alan and that's my mate stood there,' he said tilting his head in the direction of a tall, slim lad stood with dark sleeked back hair. Alan nudged his friend. 'Get these ladies a drink, they'll square you up,' Alan shouted at the barman and pointed a forefinger at Mildred. The barman nodded his head and she asked for two large vodkas.

'Thank you very much. I would've been there all night, if you hadn't shouted for me.'

'Fancy taking a seat?' he asked.

Mildred shrugged her shoulders and they headed towards a quieter area of the bar.

'I hear by your accent that you're from the north east,' Alan said.

'Yes. Can you show us where the best bars are?' Mary gushed. Mildred nipped her and threw her a warning look and raised one eyebrow. Mary glanced away.

'Stay with us and we'll show you,' suggested Alan.

They headed into all the noisiest and brightest pubs there was. Two hours later, Mary's eyes were glazed and she was staggering about, drawing attention to herself.

'Mary, you've had enough, we need to get back,' suggested Mildred, tapping her on her drooped shoulders.

With her face taut, she swept her eyes around the room. I wish these two would bugger off she thought, as she glanced about and looked for the nearest exit. Much to her surprise, she saw Gavin who was stood at the bar. She got up and headed towards him with a broad smile on her face. She tapped him on the shoulder as she reached him. He swung around and beamed to see her. 'Millie, I thought you weren't going to get back in touch. I've not heard from you.'

'I know I lost your number. Sorry,' she said, turning her flushed face away, then clasping her hands to her hot face, she swept her eyes around. 'I have to go and look for my friend she's had too much to drink and has no idea how dangerous it is down here compared to home.'

Gavin's face dropped. 'I'll help you find her,' he suggested.

Mildred dashed into the toilets to see the doors all closed. She knelt down hoping no one came into the toilets while she crawled along on all fours peeping through the bottom of the doors like some sort of pervert. She was greeted with the sight of knickers pulled down to the knees and legs splayed. Finally, she saw a familiar pair of shoes and a skinny bum slumped on the toilet floor.

She stood to her feet and thumped her hand on the door and shouted, but there was no response. With her hands clenched to her sides and eyes blazing, she stormed out of the toilets to see Gavin stood outside.

'She's slumped in the bloody toilet, I'll have to get some help,' she shouted above the noisy music. She marched away and returned with a beefy doorman who strode inside the toilets. He thudded on the door with his fist first, getting no response either. As he lifted his leg back, he kicked the door with such force that it broke the lock, almost tearing it off its hinges.

Mildred squeezed inside and sunk to her hunkers. Then, hauling the white-faced, floppy Mary to her feet, she gave the man a withering look. 'I'm sorry about this,' she said.

He stood glaring with his big arms folded and mouth set in a fine line. 'Get her away,' he growled. 'I can't be doing with shit like this. Not tonight.'

'I will, and I'll pay for the door,' she assured him as he hauled Mary to her feet and dragged her out of the hall with Gavin following.

'Now, what am I going to do?' wailed Mildred as she slung her arms around Mary's waist just as her legs gave way. 'I'll never get her onto the tube in her state,' she gasped.

'I'll hail a taxi and you can come to my place, we'll sort her out there,' he suggested.

Mildred face twisted. Heaving Mary's dead weight against her had left her exhausted. She felt as though there was no other choice. She just wanted to be out of these mean streets and into the safety of the indoors. Anywhere was better than staying out here, especially with Mary in such a vulnerable state.

Black cab's whizzed back and forth, crammed full with people. Mildred sullen face relaxed to see a taxi coming towards them. It slowed down and eventually came to a stop by the kerb. They dragged her inside. She sat with her head slumped against Mildred's shoulder on the way to Gavin's student accommodation in the hospital grounds.

They dragged Mary into Gavin's place, which was meagre and minimal. There was only one stained easy chair. The carpet was worn and the antiquated cupboard was scratched with paint peeling off. Mildred cast Mary a menacing look as she stood with a stupid grin on her face. Mary dropped into the shabby chair and let her head fall backwards into the cushion.

Mildred eased herself up and gazed into Gavin's kind face. 'I can't thank you enough. Once she's sobered, we'll get away to the tube.'

He pushed his shirt sleeve up and looked at his watch. 'You'll be lucky, the last tube leaves in half an hour and she'll not sober up in that time. There's only one thing you can do, and that is stay here.'

Mildred shook her head as she glanced around at the bed-sit. There was only one single bed. Gavin raised one eyebrow as his eyes shone. She didn't fancy walking the streets; hauling Mary about like an idiot. 'Well, I'll lie at the bottom and you can lie at the top and that way we won't be tempted into doing something we regret,' Mildred said.

'Who said anything about regrets?' asked Gavin as he reached towards her and drew her towards him. Mildred squirmed and wriggled at first but as his kisses became more urgent, she wrapped her arms around his neck as he guided her towards the bed.

'I don't want to get pregnant,' she whispered as he hitched her clothes up and began caressing the inside of her thigh.

'You won't. I'll be careful,' he assured her as his hand went further and she moaned with pleasure, all her reserve now gone; lost in lust as he grinded himself against her. Visions of the trauma she went through flashed through her mind.

She blinked open her eyes and put her hands on his chest and pushed him off her. 'I can't do this, I'm sorry,' she gasped. 'Not without protection.'

Gavin groaned. He sat up and ran his fingers through his hair. 'It's okay, I understand,' he whispered. 'Do you want a drink?'

She nodded and watched as he heaved himself and opened the cupboard door. Dust floated in the air as he pursed his lips and blew into two glasses. Pulling a cork out of a wine bottle, he poured the wine and brought the drinks to bed.

Mildred sat looking at him and wondered why there wasn't a spark. He was a lovely lad, but it just wasn't enough. They sat chatting and sipping their wine before eventually falling asleep, just as the sun rose and seeped through the bottom of the curtain and along the windowsill.

Upon waking, Mildred eased herself up and glanced over at Mary, who was already awake and looking strangely alert considering how early it was. 'Well, have you sobered up?' Mildred asked.

Mary sunk her head into her hands and began to sniffle.

'What the bloody hell is wrong with you now?' demanded Mildred.

'I've had an accident,' she whimpered.

Mildred shot off the bed and saw the stain down the side of the chair.

'Get up,' she hissed as Gavin slung his legs out of the bed and strode towards the bathroom. Mary was hunched up and whimpering as she moved off the seat to see the look of horror on Mildred's face.

'You stupid bitch,' Mildred barked.

'What will Gavin do?' Mary snivelled and wiped her hand across her wet face as he stepped back into the room to see what she had done.

His smile faded to see the soaked chair. 'Thanks Mary, that was the only seat I had,' he groaned. Mary ran from the room and went into the bathroom where she locked the door and refused to come out.

Mildred sat with her head in her hands as she apologised to Gavin once more and said she would clean the seat for him. He smiled thinly as he clasped an arm around her and said just to forget it as he headed for the door and told her to put the key on string and push it through the letter box on her way out.

'I'll ring you later when I get finished from work,' he said as he breezed out with a sullen look.

Mildred got to her feet and thudded her fist on the bathroom door. 'Get out here and clean the seat while I try and get some clothes for you from over the road,' she barked.

Mary unlocked the door and stepped out. Mildred thrust her face in hers, then taking her hand back, she whacked Mary across the face. Mary gasped as she collapsed in a flood of tears, holding her hand to her hot cheek.

'I'm sorry,' she whimpered. 'It won't happen again.'

'You're right it won't,' Mildred hollered, thrusting her face in hers once more before spinning around and storming out.

After a while she returned with second hand clothes and threw them at Mary. The atmosphere between the two friends was icy on the journey back to Sadie's. Mildred sat silent and sullen peering out of the window, while Mary cast sideways glances the entire time.

As they stepped inside the house, Sadie was stood with her arms folded. She peered at Mildred's set face. 'You could've rung me. I've been worried that something had happened.'

Mildred prodded a finger at Mary who was stood with her head lowered. 'Oh yes, something happened alright. She got legless and we had to take her to Gavin's, where she pissed on his only chair.'

Mary gaped at Mildred. She spun around and ran out of the door, down the path and headed for the park over the road.

'Go after her,' demanded Sadie.

Mildred slumped down. Flinging her right leg over her left knee, she sat with her mouth pursed. 'No. I'll not. I wish I hadn't asked her to come here. She's more bother than enough.'

Sadie stood with an eyebrow raised and sighed inwardly, thinking exactly the same.

Chapter Twenty-Nine

The sun was sinking fast in the west and still there was no sign of Mary.

Mildred had searched everywhere. There was no one whom they could contact except the police. Sadie drove the car out of the drive and took Mildred to the police station. A sullen faced man sat behind a desk in the reception as Mildred advanced towards him.

He raised watery eyes, yawned and raked his fingers through his thinning hair. 'If I had a pound for every lassie that goes missing, I would be well off,' he sighed. 'If she isn't back by next week we'll put out a missing persons notice.'

'Next week? That's not good enough,' snapped Mildred. 'Anything could've happened to her and you're not interested.'

'Like I say, she's just one of many,' he replied. 'Now is there anything else?'

Mildred swung around and marched out. As Sadie drove the car away, she took a sideways glance at Mildred's darkened expression. 'I'm going to call at my friend Roxy. She might be working tonight, but I'll take a chance anyway,' suggested Sadie, as she drove through the streets of London and headed towards Soho.

'What does she do?' asked Mildred, peering around at the darkened area, where almost every doorway had red-lit doorbells. Her eyes rounded at the sex shops and strip clubs advertising scantily clad girls.

'She's a high class prostitute. She's been doing it for years and has made a fortune, so she can pick and choose when she wants to entertain.'

Mildred's head swung around to peer at her mother, her eyes rounded. 'She's a hooker? Does it not shock you what she does?'

'Not really. Well, it did at first, but I'm just so used to her now it's like water off a ducks back, so put your eyes back in their sockets.'

Mildred gazed out the window to see they had driven down one of the dark alleys and were now parked outside a row of terraced buildings. 'I don't know who this Roxy is but it's certainly dodgy round here,' she whispered as she watched Sadie heading towards a doorway.

She lifted her hand and pressed the red-lit doorbell. A haze of red light was visible behind lace curtains at the window.

She must be into bloody red, Mildred thought to herself, seeing the net pulled aside. She stretched her neck further to see an elderly woman peering out the window. She had a long nose and a pointy chin. She resembled a wizened gnome as she peered at Sadie.

God, she's too bloody old to be a prossy though, she thought as she watched the door open.

The old woman stood talking to Sadie and then closed the door. Sadie turned around and walked back to the car. 'She's at home in Mayfair,' she said as she turned the key and drove away again.

'Who was that at the window?'

'She's an old prostitute who works for her,' she replied in a flat tone.

Mildred shook her head, wondering what to expect when they got to Roxy's. Plus Mary's disappearance was on her mind too.

Sadie brought the car to a halt outside a flamboyant and elaborate Edwardian townhouse. Carved woodwork adorned the balcony, veranda and porch. Floral curtains were draped behind the bay windows.

Mildred stood with her jaw dropped as they approached the large door. Sadie lifted her hand and pressed the doorbell. The door was pulled open and Roxy stood in the doorway. She was middle-aged with blonde hair that was shoulder length and wavy. Mildred thought she was very attractive, with high cheek bones, rose-bud shaped lips and wearing a thick cream dressing-gown. Her green eyes lit up to see Sadie. She gestured for her and Mildred to enter.

'This is my daughter that I've told you about over the years,' said Sadie.

Roxy leant towards Mildred and wrapped her arms around her in an embrace. 'You are a picture aren't you? So very unusual. You would make a great model with your skin colour too.'

'From her father,' announced Sadie in a blasé manner as she slumped down and gestured for Mildred to do the same.

Roxy peered at Mildred's tense face. 'Is there something wrong? Do I upset you or something – I suppose Sadie has told you what my profession is,' she said, teetering over to a long wooden sideboard, where she lifted up a bottle of whisky and glasses.

'No, I'm not bothered what you do. I'm worried about my friend who has gone missing since this morning. She's a skinny little thing and since coming down here she's changed so much. She's going to dance in a cage in that Ruby's nightclub. You can see where that's going to lead. Then, last night she was so mortal drunk, we had to stay at someone's bedsit and didn't she go and wet herself all over his chair,' gabbled Mildred.

Roxy reached out her hand and squeezed Mildred's arm. 'Shush. You are getting into a right state. I was going to suggest a drink,' she said, turning her head to gaze at the bottle and glasses. 'Give me ten minutes and I'll get my slap on and we'll go to that Ruby's, I've heard the owner is a right shit anyway.'

Walking down a flight of stairs, they removed their coats and passed them to a cloak attendant. As they stepped inside the lower level, they headed for the opulent and sophisticated gaming room with subdued lighting. As she headed to the dance area, Mildred appraised the glass floor now lit with concealed coloured lights beneath it. Smoke billowed from the stage. A resident band played a Dean Martin number.

They mingled around the bar and scoured the dance floor in vain. Next, they climbed the wrought iron staircase that led onto the upper level. The area also had subdued lighting but was more intimate, with candles flickering, casting a glint in wine bottles as couples canoodled and smooched around the tables.

'Well, she's not going to be up here with this lot slopping on,' remarked

Roxy. 'We'll go back downstairs. I need a drink before we look one more time,' she said, as they turned around and walked back down. 'Find a table and I'll get the drinks,' she suggested, as she sashayed over to the bar.

'I just want water,' shouted Sadie as she held a hand to her head and flopped into a chair.

Mildred noticed men sat around the table next to hers. They were all dressed as though they were going to a funeral, but she noticed they wore bow ties and a champagne bucket was placed on the table. The skinny man called Mario that had interviewed Mary was sat beside a suave, well-built man with sleeked hair. Mildred raised her eyes and got to her feet.

'Mario. Have you seen my friend that came for an interview and gave you a demonstration of her exotic dancing?'

The man frowned, then threw his head back and laughed. 'Oh yes, the little skinny one – no sorry,' he smirked, curling his lip up in a smarmy gesture.

Mildred pressed her lips together. Glancing towards the suave man smoking a large cigar she noticed he was sat with his head cocked to the side and appraising her. She gave him a weak smile, before turning away.

She looked at Sadie who was slumped down in the chair, hunched over the table. 'I'll go and tell Roxy to forget the drinks, you're clearly not well,' Mildred said.

Too late. Roxy was advancing towards them carrying a tray full of drinks in her hands when she noticed the suave man. 'Ooh, just the man. Do you know who owns this place?'

'Me,' he grinned. 'Why?'

'We're looking for a young girl called Mary Kelly. She's going to be working in that area that is being put up,' she said as she pointed her finger in the direction, when a fat-faced man with small beady eyes looked her up and down.

'Still on the bash Roxy eh?' he sniggered.

Roxy cast him a menacing look. 'I don't go on the bash. Those lean days are long gone – you know better than to say that. Your wife would have something to say, if she knew what you were like,' she quipped.

His smirk faded and his fat face turned the colour of beetroot as she pursed her lips and flashed green menacing eyes in his direction.

'I can't be bothered with your sarcasm, we need to locate a young girl,' she said once more.

'Aren't we all,' the fat man sniggered as he drew on a fat cigar and sent clouds of smoke everywhere.

'Shut up, you ugly fat ponce. We are being serious, she is staying with my friend Sadie and her daughter Mildred,' she said, inclining her head in their direction, when she noticed the nightclub owner's lips stiffen and his smile fade. But, it was soon replaced with a smarmy smile once more, which didn't reach his pale eyes.

'I remember that girl now,' announced Mario. 'She's not been in here today.'

Mildred's face fell.

'Roxy, are you staying or what? We're going straight home. I don't feel well at all,' said Sadie grimacing as she got to her feet.

'I'll make my way around the Soho area and see if any of the girls on the bash have seen her. Do you have a photo?'

Mildred opened her bag and pulled out a small photograph that was taken while she had been staying with Mary's family. 'Thanks Roxy,' said Mildred as she handed the photograph to her.

Mildred glanced at the clock on the mantelpiece and noticed it was midnight when they got back. Sadie threw her car keys in the drawer and headed towards the sofa. She flopped down with her eyes closed and face twisted. Mildred went into the kitchen to boil the kettle. 'Where do you keep your tablets?' she shouted.

'The bathroom,' groaned Sadie.

'If you drink some hot water with the tablets, it should help your pain,' Mildred said, as she pulled open a door, peering into the small cabinet on the wall, when a dazzling beam of light lit up and swept around the bathroom walls.

Dashing out of the bathroom, she hurried to the front window and peered through the lace curtain to see Mary in an embrace with some man. Then he got back into the car and reversed out of the drive. Mary was staggering about before her legs buckled and she fell to the ground.

Mildred stepped back from the window and swung around, her eyes blazing. She stormed to the door and yanked it open. In a few strides, she was leant over Mary, hauling her to her feet.

'Where the bloody hell have you been?' she spat.

Mary raised glazed eyes and squinted up at her. 'I don't know.'

'What do you mean you don't know?' she snarled.

'I don't know the places round here. I went to a café and got talking to a nice man,' she giggled.

'Never mind giggling, anything could have happened to you. We've been to the police and that new nightclub to see if you were there. And who was that man that bought you home then?' she demanded, grabbing hold of her arm and shaking her like a ragdoll. 'Do you realise how much we've been worried about you? We thought someone had gotten you in their clutches.'

Mary stood rocking as she raised glassy eyes towards Mildred. 'Oh shut up. You think the worst of everyone don't you?'

'Don't you dare tell me to shut up lady,' she bellowed. 'You better tighten on and tighten on fast.'

Mary's reddened and glazed eyes widened as Mildred grabbed hold of her and pushed her up against the wall. 'You're high as a kite, what have you taken?' she demanded.

'Leave me alone, I want to go to sleep,' she slurred as she fell back against the sofa heavy eyed.

Mildred was determined that she wasn't going to have a repeat performance of Gavin's chair, so she dragged her upstairs and left her on the floor, covered with blankets. Stepping out of the room, she peeped through the gap in Sadie's bedroom door. She was lying with her long hair draped over her delicate shoulders, underneath the silk bedding with a pink mask covering her eyes.

The following morning, the atmosphere was strained once more. Mildred was sat behind the large pine table in the kitchen with a cup in her hand. Mary wandered aimlessly through, her hair tatty and make-up smeared. She pulled out a seat and sat opposite Mildred. 'I'm sorry about going off and not returning until late,' she whined. Mildred dropped her eyes and ignored Mary. 'Did you hear? I'm sorry and I'm leaving to go and live above the nightclub.'

Mildred sat with her arms folded and mouth clamped. Mary screeched and swung around, tearing up the upstairs. Mildred pushed her chair back and stood to her feet. She opened the back door to go into the garden and flopped down on a lounger. There wasn't a cloud in the sky.

She laid her head back and closed her eyes, enjoying the rays from the sun. That was, until she head Mary shout from the doorway, 'I don't want to leave on bad terms. Can we at least make up before I go?'

Mildred opened her eyes and sat up. She gave Mary a scathing look. 'Mary, I care very much for you, but at the moment I don't even like you.'

A long lingering silence prevailed. Mary stepped back inside the house and not long afterwards, Mildred heard a car draw up at the front and the sound of a horn tooting.

Chapter Thirty

The days grew cooler and shorter. Leaves withered and fell from the trees, covering the garden like a carpet. Still there was no contact between Mildred and Mary, but Roxy had someone who kept her informed.

'I've been told Mary is dancing around topless. They say she seems cocky and brazen,' she announced to Mildred and Sadie, as they sat around the lounge one late summer evening.

'She looked a skinny, pale-faced, mousy girl on the photograph you gave me when you were looking for her. But she'll have to wear thick Pan-stick, heavily made-up eyes and bleach that mousy hair.'

Mildred sighed deeply. 'I don't want to see her like that, but at the same time, something is drawing me to go,' she announced.

'Well, if you want to, we can get ready and you can see her, but please do not show yourself up,' warned Sadie.

'I won't, I promise.'

They dressed themselves in the latest mini dresses and took a taxi to the nightclub.

People were milling around outside, cars and taxis were dropping couples off. Laughing and dressed in their finery, the three stepped towards the opulent entrance.

The sign above the doorway was lit up with crimson flashing light bulbs. Doormen stood dressed in suits with a bowtie at the neck of their shirts. They stepped inside the mirror-lined walls, before heading for the smoky and noisy interior. Mildred found her eyes sweeping around, hoping to see Jonah, the nightclub owner, whom she had met when she had been searching for Mary.

Since that night, she found she couldn't get him out of her mind, especially at night when she was in bed. In her dreams, he would advance towards her with his arms held out, clasp hold of her hands and put them to his lips, with hungry eyes.

What's the matter with me? She thought as she raised her eyes up the winding staircase, when she swallowed and her heart flipped. There he was, sat at a table facing a very attractive woman. She was sat with a cigarette holder in her hand, her hair flowing down her shoulders, and she was wearing a low-cut red dress. They were both laughing and raising their glasses.

Mildred's belly clenched with jealousy as she stood watching them both at ease with one another. Was he seeing her she wondered, and what did she do for him?

'Penny for them?' asked Sadie seeing her sullen look. Then her eyes followed Mildred's. She looked at her with one eyebrow raised before she pushed her way through the crowd and climbed up the stairs. Mildred followed, and when she reached the top, Jonah dragged his eyes away from the lady. He turned his head and gave her a long-lingering look while holding her gaze. Mildred gave a cool smile, hoping to conceal her racing heart. He glanced at her once again and, pushing his seat back, he leant towards the woman, held her hand to his lips. Then, releasing the woman's hand he turned towards Mildred with a beguiling smile.

'How lovely to see you once again,' he gushed. Then, when he dragged his eyes away and acknowledged Sadie, his smile faded. Mildred turned her face towards her mother to see the darkened look she cast him.

'What are you drinking Mildred?' Sadie snapped.

Mildred frowned. What's her problem, she thought, when she felt Jonah's hand slip around her waist.

'Double vodka and tonic,' she replied.

Sadie's eyes gave a piercing look once more at Jonah, before she strode away towards the bar. 'What's her problem?' he asked.

'Oh, she's being protective of me,' she answered in a blasé manner.
'Why is that?'

'I came to see Mary Kelly. She's an exotic dancer here. We fell out and I want to make up with her,' she replied ignoring his question.

Jonah's brow creased. 'I believe she left here last week.'

'So where is she?' He shrugged his shoulders. 'Can you ask the man who employed her for me?'

'Well, not tonight. It's his night off.' Mildred shoulders slumped. 'I hear from your accent that you're not from around here,' he remarked.

'No, I'm from a place called Ashwood.'

'Really? I've never heard of that place,' Jonah said.

'It's near Newcastle,' she replied, when Sadie returned back from the bar.

He got to his feet. 'Well, I'll leave you ladies to enjoy your night,' he said as he stepped away and went down the spiral staircase.

Mildred gave Sadie a sharp look. 'You were very cold with him. What's he done wrong?'

Sadie pursed her mouth. 'I don't trust him. For God's sake, keep a wide berth.'

Mildred pouted her mouth. 'I'm going downstairs to watch when those exotic dancers come on and I'm going to ask if they know where Mary is.'

'Look, just enjoy your night, Mary's made her bed and now she'll have to lie in it. Concentrate on your own life. You said you were interested to work for my old friend Jonty. Do you still want me to tell him you'll go down and meet him in Sussex?'

'I'm not sure,' Mildred replied, getting to her feet. If I go away to Sussex, then I won't see Jonah, she thought.

'Where are you going?'

'I told you, I'm going to ask if any of those dancers know where Mary has gone,' Mildred said.

Sadie got to her feet too and followed her downstairs to see that Jonah was advancing towards her with the look of a blackbird about to devour a juicy worm.

Sadie lifted her hands to push a drunken man out of her way. He smirked and staggered, lurching himself towards her. 'Get out of my way, you creep,' she yelled, as her eyes scanned the place. Mildred had disappeared amongst the throng of people.

Chapter Thirty-One

Peace Terrace sounded appealing and tranquil – if you weren't accustomed to the area. But behind that sign on the wall, was a dwelling where unfortunate women found themselves, after being promised they would be living in the lap of luxury.

In reality, it couldn't be any further from the truth.

The entrance passage was narrow, dark and dingy. Worn carpets were on the creaking stairs, black mould was all around the ceiling and there was only a bare bulb to lighten the landing. There were two doors on the landing. One was Mary Kelly's, the other one belonged to an old brass. Both women *entertained* with their bondage or fetish sessions.

She opened her purse and peered at the meagre amount. It would buy a few groceries, but she needed a fix, not a ham sandwich. She was sat by the one-bar gas fire, where the walls exposed dark green distemper behind the torn and peeling woodchip.

Mice scampered from holes in the rotting skirting boards. Their tiny black bulging eyes peered at her while she sat huddled over the fire. Her complexion was sallow, pale and drawn. Her mind recalled how just one year ago, life had been wonderful. When she first came to London, it was a new start for a naïve, skinny, tatty-haired girl, who had dreams of bettering herself. If only she listened to Mildred, when she had told her to never touch drugs, no matter what people told you, that they would ruin your life, maybe then she wouldn't be in this mess.

She lit a cigarette and stared at the marks on her arms, all the little red dots where the needles had been. What a fool to believe Mario, for falling under his spell. He persuaded her to try drugs. She found they relaxed her and made her centre of attention with her wit and funny stories. Then, she tried stronger ones, and this progressed until she was hooked on speed and crack cocaine. Now she was a mother with a baby, a little boy called Dean, suffering from withdrawal symptoms through her drug habit.

Wiping beads of perspiration from her brow with the back of her hand, she stood up and glanced at her reflection in the mirror above the tiled fireplace. Her eyes no longer sparkled. They were dull and sunken with dark shadows underneath. Her teeth were stained and unclean, their once gleaming shine never to be seen again.

Her posh gent was coming tonight, and he always paid well. Wonder what he wants tonight? Hope it's not a rough session, she thought as she strode into a red-painted room. She took off her clothes and put on her fishnet stockings that she had attached to suspenders on her lace Basque. Black and white paintings of women entangled in chains were hung around the walls. A leather spanking bench and whipping post dominated the room, while steel handcuffs, shackles and whips were also draped around to accommodate her punters' fetishes.

'Just as well Jean's got the bairn for the night. I can't have him waking up in the middle of a session. She'll get her fix for doing this, but I wish there was someone else, I don't trust that bitch,' she whispered to herself when the buzzer rang. She stepped out of the dungeon to answer it.

'Are you alone? It's Ted.'

'Yes, it's fine. Come up.'

Ted is one of her latest punters: a man in his late fifties. Handsome with a chiselled chin, his body firm and toned, his hair, white and cropped. Wealthy, married and a respected member of the public, he would be horrified if his patients and clients discovered his secret.

As they walked into her dungeon, he kissed her neck. 'You seem on edge tonight Mary.' She shook her head and smiled as he peered at her. 'What is it?' he asked.

She waved her hand trying to appear casual. His eyes lit up as he watched her take her clothes off until she was stood in nothing but her knickers. His eyes darkened with desire as he asked her for a golden shower. He removed all his clothes and lay down on her spanking bench. She straddled him, then lying over him, she emptied her bladder, watching his face contort. He moaned and groaned with pleasure as he climaxed. She got up and went into the bathroom, where she brought out a bowl of scented water and a towel.

She began rubbing her hands all over him, cleaning the smell of urine away, and watched as he began to harden once more. She picked up a whip, thrashing it wildly. 'You are a bad man. Get up. Bend over,' she demanded.

He did as she asked. She advanced holding a paddle, and gave him a good beating as he cried out again with more pleasure. Soon it was over. She smiled not giving away how she felt inside. As she looked at him, she wondered how much longer she could go on doing this. Then, as he draped himself all over her body trying to kiss her, she turned her face away. She refused to kiss; that was part of the deal. Her flesh crept, but she still kept on smiling as he pulled her towards him. 'Mary, I can't imagine what it would be like without my secret visits here. My life wouldn't be worthwhile. I love my wife but she is cold and frigid.'

She shrugged her shoulders. 'Yes, we all have a cross to bear. Life's a bitch,' she said.

'Do you know someone called Mario?' he asked, while he began to get ready.

'Yes, why?' she answered, and noticed his lips press together and his smile fade. Mary's brow creased as she gave Ted a hardened look. 'Why do you ask?'

'Someone told me that Mario is your pimp. Is it true?' he asked, while stepping towards the door to leave.

'He is my son's father and the most ruthlessly cruel person you could ever meet. As soon as I can I am leaving London. I have to protect my child,' she said.

Ted's eyebrows shot up. 'I didn't realize you have a child.'

Mary smile disappeared. 'Yes, and he won't turn out like him, that's for sure' she replied fiercely, her eyes narrowed. A film of sweat was visible on her face as she turned to Ted and forced a smile. 'Have you brought the drugs I asked for?'

Ted's face was taut. He had other thoughts on his mind. 'Yes, yes, I managed to get what you asked. But, Mary I don't know if it is safe to come back, I didn't realize that you were linked to Mario. If he discovers that I come here my wife may find out.'

Mary was quick to assure him as she thought of the drugs and money he gave her. 'He won't be bothered who you are silly,' she soothed. 'All he's interested in is the money I make for him. Look, this set up suits us both. You get your satisfaction and I get mine. So for God's sake give me my fix.'

Ted's face was glum, he was still unsure. Mary was now frantic. The sweat poured from her as she greedily snatched bags of powder out of his hands. She wet her finger and rubbed the powder furiously round her teeth and gums. Once it hit, her shoulders relaxed, and she got a rush of good feelings and happiness, all her troubles faded.

She lowered herself down onto the sofa and closing her eyes in a dream-like state, felt as though she was covered in a thick warm blanket.

He shook his head as he stood peering at her. 'I'll be here the same time next week.'

'Yeah sure, whatever,' she sighed.

As Ted rushed downstairs, he opened the main door to leave, when a skinny man with straggly black hair brushed past him. Swaying around, the man lurched at him and clutched his arm to stop him in his tracks. 'What did you pay her?' he demanded thrusting his face into Ted's in a surly manner.

'Fifty pounds,' answered Ted in a quivering voice.

The man loosened his grip. Growling, he pushed him away and turned to climb up the creaking stairs. Ted stood frowning in the doorway. Pulling up his collar, he strode away with his head lowered.

'Hand the cash over,' snarled Mario, his black eyes glistening with malice as he leaned over Mary with his hand held out. 'I've just seen a punter leave and I know what he paid you.'

Mary sighed and turned over.

He loomed over her and pulled her to her feet. 'Where's the money?' he snarled.

Mary stood swaying, then her legs buckled and she fell back onto the sofa. He snatched hold of her hair and pulled her up. The fist hit her with force as his knuckles connected with her cheekbones. She slammed down onto the ground lifelessly and just lay in a crumpled heap on the floor. 'You've taken that shit again when I told you what would happen the next time you did,' he bellowed, as he rained blows to her body.

A woman with a wrinkled face that was caked in smeared makeup dashed into the room. She flung her huge frame on top of him and hauled him off Mary. 'Leave her alone, you can see she's high as a kite, you'll not get any sense out of her,' she screeched.

Mario's eyes were manic as he stood facing the woman. 'I expect her to make money and not get slaughtered with drugs,' he snarled.

'What you need to do is be a man. Get Mary and your child away from this shitty life. It's your fault, because you got her into this,' she retorted, curling her lip.

'Listen here old brass. You just mind your own business,' he warned, pointing his finger in her face. He swung around and walked out of the room.

The woman stood with her arms folded, peering at Mary, who was now on her knees, tears streaming down her battered face. 'I can't take this anymore,' she sobbed. 'I need to get away with the bairn. Will you help me, I'm desperate?'

The woman gave her a sharp look. 'I know someone who might be able to help you, but she will want money. Plus it'll be dangerous. I felt the same way when I was young like you, but I never succeeded.'

Mary's shoulders slumped as she peered at the woman. Her hair was dyed yellow and it was stiff with sugar and water, a concoction that she used instead of hairspray. Her shoes were white and scuffed, with black stockings that were clicked and torn spiralled in a pattern away from them. Her fourteen stone frame was wrapped in a low cut top and a skimpy skirt stretched over her protruding belly.

'Come on, I'll get you cleaned up,' she suggested while heaving a long sigh.

Mary held her hand up. 'Thanks, but I just need to be alone.'

The woman stood in the doorway with a sorrowful look, before turning around and going towards the door.

'That's the last time, I take a beating' Mary hissed, as she stood to her feet and peered into the mirror. Her eyes were barely open, swollen to twice their usual size, purple bruises were apparent on her swollen face.

Swiping the blood away from her mouth, an ice-cold shiver crept down her spine and she shuddered. 'Flogging me fanny and handing nearly all me money to that ponce while he struts about with a façade about him. Huh, one time he melted me heart and kissed me so passionately. Well mate, no more,' she rasped.

Her mind was made up. She had her child to think of too. She was going cold turkey, even if it killed her. Dean deserved better.

She stood to her feet and went to the bathroom where she ran cold water on cotton wool and dabbed it on her throbbing face. She heard the clatter of feet coming up the stairs. Her heart began thudding as the footsteps grew louder. She snatched the bag from inside her Basque and pushed it between her legs, shoving it where the sun didn't shine.

The bathroom door was pulled open. Mario was stood in the doorway, peering at Mary's bloodied and swollen face. His face crumpled as he stepped towards her and pulled her around to face him. 'I'm sorry Mary. If you didn't get me so riled, I wouldn't lose it. Come here,' he soothed.

He cradled her to him like a child and whispered soft words into her ears as he kissed her hair. Mary winced. She let herself be caressed, but unknown to Mario, she was going to get her revenge – against him, against the lodger and against other bastard that had used and abused her. 'I can't go out looking like this. Will you get Dean?' she asked, playing along with it.

'Yes, I'll do anything for you,' he said, grimacing at the sight of Mary.

'I'll fix us drink first,' she soothed, leaning over to kiss his cheek. He made a face as she turned around and headed into the kitchen.

Putting her fingers up inside herself, she pulled the bag out. In a flash, she untied it and sprinkled half the powder into a glass, visualising herself throwing boiling water all over him and scarring him for life, but this way would be better. A nice overdose would do the trick.

She quickly tied the small bag. Shoving it inside her handbag, she squeezed it behind an opening in the satin lining then clicked her bag shut. Hanging it by the strap on a door handle, she then stepped out the kitchen and into the room, where she cast a sweet smile at Mario as she gave him the glass. 'I've made us both a strong drink, I think we both need it to calm us down,' she suggested.

His eyes were full of remorse as he took the glass. While her pulse raced, she kept on smiling and praying, hoping it would work. In silence, he tilted his head back, gulping the whisky in one go.

'I'm shattered,' he slurred, feeling his eyes becoming heavy.

Then, when he lifted his hands to rub his eyes, he found he was unable to move. His mouth formed words but nothing came out. His dark eyes showed fear as he tried to focus. Everything was blurred. He began frothing at the mouth. Stiffening and moaning, his legs kicked wildly as his arms flailed, sending him crashing to the floor in a seizure.

Mary sat transfixed, watching him eagerly as he squirmed for his life. She stood up with her hands clasped to her face. Forcing her shaky legs to move, she began pacing the room. 'Hope the old brass doesn't hear all this commotion,' she whispered. Mario's voice rose louder as his body shuddered.

The door was pushed open and the woman stood with her jaw dropped. Blinking, she galvanised herself into action and flew out of the room and clattered down the stairs. 'I'm phoning for a doctor,' she yelled.

Mary groaned. She didn't want a doctor. The bastard could die as far as she was concerned. She dashed into her bedroom and hauled her drawers and wardrobe open. Dragging a chair over to the wardrobe, she stood on it, pulled her case down and shoved everything inside. Lastly, she slung on her coat, when her heart sunk. She heard the sound of footsteps approaching up the stairs.

Swiping her hand across her brow, she realised her plans were disappearing like dust. Forcing her scowling countenance into a look of concern, she stepped back into the room. The woman was knelt on the floor beside Mario who had stopped thrashing around and lay unconscious.

'The doctor won't be long,' she said, when they heard footsteps.

The door opened and a doctor walked into the room. He stopped in his tracks and peered at Mary resembling a battered ragdoll, before he knelt to his hunkers. He lifted Mario's eyelids to see that his eyes were fixed and his swarthy skin the colour of parchment, a film of sweat over his face. 'Has he taken anything?' he asked, lifting his head to give Mary a quizzical look.

'I just found him like this,' she lied, wringing her hands together.

'Well, the police will have to be informed,' he announced as he clasped his finger and thumb around Mario's wrist. 'He's in a bad way and may die if he isn't taken to hospital.'

He turned his attention to the old woman. 'Can you go and ring for an ambulance?'

The old woman nodded her head. Glancing towards Mary, her eyes narrowed as she pulled open the door and clattered down the stairs again.

Mary paced the floor, chewing her nails. She thought she had got rid of her problem, but now she was in more bother than ever. If Mario's mob found out she had anything to do with this she was a dead woman walking. The sound of a baby howling was heard and a diminutive skinny woman with small, beady eyes that moved constantly, walked into the room. She frowned at the scene before her.

Mary dashed to hold Dean, who held his chubby arms towards her. 'Jean you couldn't keep Dean a bit longer, could you?' she pleaded.

Jean shook her head. 'No, he wants feeding and I don't have anything in my gaff for him,' she said as she swayed around and dashed downstairs.

Mary hurried after her. She stood in the front doorway pleading with her, when a siren was heard and an ambulance zoomed into the street, swiftly followed by a police car. She clutched hold of Jean's arm while rocking the baby. 'Wait, I'm in trouble. Please, please . . . Have this.' She took out the money that Ted had given her, which she had tucked inside her Basque. Jean's expression softened. She took Dean and scuttled away.

The ambulance doors were flung open. One of the men dashed to open the back doors, while the other brought out a stretcher. They brushed past Mary in their haste.

She was still stood in the doorway, watching Jean disappear with her baby. Then, her gaze went to the two policemen stepping out of their car and advancing towards her with a furtive look on their faces. 'I have to keep calm,' she kept repeating underneath her breath.

The elder of the two gave her a brief nod as he stepped towards her followed by a younger chap.

Her mouth was dry and head throbbing. She looked from side to side, all along the street, to see faces in the doorways, all peering in her direction. She visualised herself racing past all the faces, but instead, she shut the door, turned around, and kept up her mantra, 'keep calm, keep calm,' she whispered as she stepped back into the flat. Mario was receiving treatment, but then they stretchered him and left with a curt nod at the police.

The older policeman with the bulbous red nose and pock-marked skin was speaking to Ginny, the old brass. The younger, skinny one was poking about in the kitchen. He gazed towards her handbag with grey eyes shrewd and sharp as he unhooked the bag and clicked it open. Mary stood with her legs crossed watching him rooting around it with his fingers. He shook it and squashed it, then turned the bag inside out, peering at the bulge behind the satin lining.

He turned his head around and cast a contemptuous look of contempt as he ripped apart the lining. The small bag of white powder tumbled out and fell to the floor.

'Know anything about this?' he asked, as he bent over and held the bag up between his thumb and finger.

Mary's eyes were wide. 'I don't know what you mean?'

Untying the bag, he put his finger into his mouth, then dipped it inside the bag. Sticking out his tongue, he touched the tip with the powder and screwed up his face. 'This is cocaine, my tongue has gone numb and there's something else in there too. You don't fool me one bit, with your wide-eyed look. We will continue this down at the station.'

'Why should I?' she shouted. 'I haven't done anything wrong, so no, I'm not going,' she shrieked, pointing her finger to her face. 'I'm the innocent one here. He did this, planted it inside my bag.'

'You better calm down lady,' the portly one warned. 'And I presume this white powder got inside your bag by the fairies – get going,' he barked.

'I want a solicitor to represent me,' she shrieked as she stormed down the flight of stairs.

Women were still stood around, giving one another meaningful looks as she stepped out of the door. The policeman opened the passenger door and she slid inside. Before they drove away, the women all moved further towards the car, hovering around like a pack of vultures waiting for a tasty morsel.

She glowered at them and then turned to speak to the older policeman. 'You should be taking me to the hospital, not the police station,' she whined. 'If that woman hadn't stopped Mario he would have battered me to death.'

The policeman kept his gaze on the road. Her high pitched voice got more and more vocal the further they went. Beads of sweat had appeared on his wrinkled brow and ran down his cheeks by the time they reached the police station.

The car drove through two tall blue gates that were held back against a wall with barbed wire attached. She was escorted into the building, through corridors, and to an interview room for questioning. A wooden table was carved with various initials and four chairs were placed around it. She wondered how many people had sat there, while the tape recording machine recorded their lies, the very things she was about to produce to save her skin.

The door opened and a young man with black slicked-back hair stepped inside, wearing a smart grey suit. 'Mary Kelly.' It was a statement, rather than a question.

'Yes,' she answered in a low voice.

He took a good look at her facial injuries. 'I'm Henry. I'll be representing you,' he said as he shook her hand. 'Leave me to do the talking, but I need to know what occurred. The police seem to think you spiked Mario's drink – is that right?' Mary bit her lip and hesitated. Henry gave her a searching look, while placing a reassuring hand on her arm. 'I really need the truth.'

Mary glanced to see the machine was switched off. 'Well, if I tell you the truth, can I depend on you?'

'Of course, that's why I am here,' he said. 'Was it Mario who did this to you?' he gestured towards her bloodied face.

'Yes, he did, and for nothing too. He wanted all the money I had, and I wasn't going to give it to him. He's my partner, but my pimp too. I just couldn't take anymore after he beat me up this time. I had some drugs, so I spiked his drink. But I didn't expect this to happen. I just wanted to knock him out with it, but he must have had a bad reaction.'

Henry's lips pressed together, he gave her a dark look as the policeman came in and the interview began.

Mary sat peering around at the yellow walls, hardly listening to what was being said. If that old brass hadn't been there she would have got away, but luck was against her as usual. Hearing Henry speak, she shook herself out of her reverie.

'My client has been subjected to many beatings, which you can see for yourself. She has a young child depending on her too. There's no evidence to suggest that she administered the drug. I'm advising that she be released.'

Mary's head swung around to beam at Henry as the policeman sat back in his seat with his arms folded.

After formal forms for her to sign, she was allowed to leave. Her knees felt weak as she stood up. The interview room door was opened by a young WPC and she escorted her to the front of the police station.

Mary looked up at the grey November sky, but heaved a sigh of relief as she stood in the doorway. She felt someone tap her on the shoulder. She gasped and glanced around. It was Henry, and he was smiling. 'I'll give you a lift,' he suggested.

'It's alright, I'll make my own way home,' she said. 'But, thanks again for your help.'

'There was something I wanted to ask you,' he said, in a compelling manner.

She frowned. 'What is it?'

'Get in the car, and I'll discuss it with you.'

Her tense features mellowed. 'Of course,' she said as she walked beside him to his waiting car.

He opened the passenger door for her. She settled into the seat and peered out of the window at the old police building. Henry started the engine and drove away.

Blowing out her cheeks, she heaved a long sigh. 'What was it you wanted to ask me?'

'How did you become a prostitute?' he asked, straight to the point.

'Through working for Mario,' she sighed. 'He promised me the moon, but it was all lies. The face he shows to the world contradicts the person he really is,' she said.

'That was unfortunate for you then,' replied Henry.

'Yes, it was. And the hovel I live in is only a ten minute drive from here, I'll tell you where to go,' she said. Then, peering out at an unfamiliar scene, she swung her head round to face Henry. 'I think you're going the wrong way. My home is the other way,' she said in a small voice.

Henry sat with his hands on the wheel, staring straight ahead in silence. 'Do you hear me?' she demanded. He still made no reply. Goosebumps appeared on her arms and the hairs on the back of her neck stood up. 'What's wrong with you?' she demanded, tugging at his sleeve.

He swiped her clutching hand off him. 'Shut up,' he snarled.

The colour drained from Mary's face. He was no longer the charming and charismatic man she thought he was. She was shocked into silence while staring at the door handle. If she tried to jump out she would be maimed or killed she thought, but it would be better than what she felt was in store for her.

Her fingers were gripped tight and the knuckles white as her mind raced. They were advancing towards a winding road, with thick trees on either side. There was nothing else but green fields as far as she could see.

'Where are you taking me?' she whimpered, tears now spilling from her fear-filled eyes.

'You'll soon find out,' he quipped as the car came to a halt.

She peered out of the car. They were parked in front of a large red-bricked house. The windows were concealed behind bars. A black door with a large, round handle stood as the main point of entrance.

'I'm not going in there,' she cried.

'You are,' he bellowed. 'You either get out, or I'll drag you out. Your choice.'

With a rigid face, she sat with her arms folded. He opened the car door and stepped out. He walked around to the passenger door and yanked it open. 'Out,' he barked.

She gasped and turned her crumpled face to him. 'What's happening?' she whimpered as she stepped out of the car. He made no reply, but clutched hold of her hand.

She had no other alternative but to follow him up the steps. She held her breath as she waited, whilst he grabbed the knocker and knocked three times. The door opened and a surly-faced woman was stood in its place, staring at her with a churlish look on her face. She beckoned them inside.

Mary followed Henry into a room where an elderly man was sat lounging in a leather-studded chair. He smirked and she stared at small, yellow-stained teeth, which were attempting to hide beneath a drooped white moustache. His dark eyes lingered on her. 'Mary Kelly. Well, well, you're not how I imagined you,' he stated. 'A slip of a lass eh?' Then, his compliant composure faded and his eyes darkened. 'I believe you are responsible for spiking Mario Badialli's drink, leaving his life in the balance.'

Mary stood in silence as her legs shook. Then she spoke in what was barely a whisper. 'It wasn't meant to happen the way it did.'

'So which way did it happen then, Miss Kelly?'

Mary's chin quivered as she lowered her head. 'I can't say,' she said, her voice wavering.

The old man rose and stepped slowly towards her. Without any warning, he took his arm back and thudded his fist into her face. She fell flat on her back, the warmth of the blood spurting down her face causing the room to spin rapidly.

She took to her knees wailing, 'Please let me go, I'm no use to you here.'

'Mario is my son,' he snarled, thrusting his face in hers. 'If he dies, you will wish your father had never spawned you, because I'll hang you up by your fucking flaps,' he bellowed, snapping his fingers together. 'Bella, get her out of my sight,' he growled

A surly woman slouched into the room and inclined her head at Mary. She was stood cowering, white-faced and weeping. The woman grabbed her by the arm and roughly pushed her out of the room, along a narrow and eerily-dark corridor. Opening a door, she lifted her thick leg and booted Mary into the room. She fell to her knees beside a metal bed which had soiled sheets. A bucket, jug and bowl stood on an old cabinet.

'This is kidnap, you can't keep me here,' protested Mary, beginning to wail.

The woman lifted her arm back and slapped her hard. 'Stop the bloody racket, you're giving me a headache,' she said as she stepped out of the room. The key scraped as it turned in the lock.

Mary threw herself down on the bed but the smell was sour from the bedding. She pulled them off to see the mattress was covered in stains and smelled just as bad as it looked. Wailing and screeching was not going to help.

She got up, snivelled and wiped her eyes. Turning towards the window, her shoulders slumped. 'I'll never escape from here,' she groaned, as she peered at the iron bars that were fixed against the brick wall and window-sill.

She stepped back and slumped down onto the bed, deciding that the smell was better than standing. Sweeping her eyes around the room, she looked around the walls and wondered if anyone else had been held here against their will. Did they die? She wondered, now wringing her hands together.

She thought about what Mario's father had said he would do to her if he died. Her face crumpled and she clenched her thighs together at the thought of it. Her eyes became heavy with exhaustion and she fell asleep.

A grating sound woke her. She snapped open her eyes and peered at Bella, who was stood filling the doorway, her arms folded in front of her ample bosom. 'Kelvin wants to see you,' she said.

Chapter Thirty-Two

Just as Mary was being led to face Kelvin again, Mildred's eyes widened as they approached the house she was going to work in. The car drew up outside and she climbed out, following her mother as she advanced towards a bulls-eyed glass-fronted door. As she lifted her hand to ring the bell, a figure approached from behind the glass and the door was wrenched open. An elderly woman stood on the threshold with a sullen expression on her wrinkled face, while Sadie explained the situation.

'I've got my hands full, you'll just have to wait,' she muttered, then closed the door. Sadie and Mildred stood with a look of alarm on their faces, when the sound of a car horn was heard and a sports car came screeching into the drive with the window down and music blaring.

'Hi babe,' Jonty said, winking at Sadie as he turned off the engine.

Mildred swung around to face her mother. 'That isn't who I think it is?'

Sadie nodded her head and smiled as Jonty leapt out of the car and wrapped her in a warm embrace, before standing back with his head to one side while he gave Mildred an appraising glance. 'What are you doing standing there? Have you not rung the bell?'

'I did and this disgruntled old woman took one look at us then shut the door in our faces,' replied Sadie.

Jonty threw his head back and roared with laughter. 'It's a good job Minnie is leaving here. Lately, she's acting as though unhinged.' Taking a set of keys out of his jacket pocket, he walked up the three steps and unlocked the door. He turned around and stepped down towards Sadie's car. 'Give me your key; I'll bring the luggage in. Just make your way inside.'

Mildred stood and gawped as she stepped inside the porch. A scruffy looking Terrier dog came bounding towards them and leapt up, covering her clothes with its mucky paws. She patted its head. 'Good doggie, down now,' she said, as she caught sight of the peeling panelled walls. The place smelled musty. She headed through to the lounge and raised an eyebrow to see a faded sofa and chairs. Ugly black and gold furniture dominating the room.

As she followed Jonty up the winding staircase, she gave a sideways glance at the solemn-faced people peering at her from paintings that hung along the landing. Jonty stopped in his tracks and pointed towards a bedroom. 'That's my mother's room. Like Minnie, she seems to be losing her marbles too. Don't be concerned if you see her wandering around with a blank expression on her face, she's perfectly harmless, and I would feel too guilty if I was to put her in a nursing home,' he said as he turned towards a door and pushed it open. 'This is yours, hope you like it,' he announced, as Mildred stepped inside the room.

'Mmm,' she murmured.

There was a single bed with a brass-leavened headboard. The leaded windows were obscured with the need of a good clean and a stained rug lay on the scuffed wooden floor. Dark, tall, wooden furniture loomed in the room and a strange stench took up the rest of the space. Jonty put down her luggage and headed out of the door. 'I'll see you later,' he replied with a weak smile.

'Mother, what on earth have you brought me to?' she wailed in a lowered tone, as Sadie stepped into the bedroom.

Sadie lifted her shoulders. 'I had no idea. I know his wife and child died in a terrible accident a year ago, but I didn't realise how much the place had deteriorated,' she replied with an arched eyebrow. 'He said he was finding it hard to cope, that he needed a housekeeper. But he's obviously still grieving.'

'I'll hate it here,' blurted Mildred.

Sadie slumped down the bed. 'Don't say you're not going to take the job after I've driven all the way to Sussex.'

Mildred stood with her arms folded. 'Well, would you stay in such an eerie place?'

Sadie blew her cheeks out and lowered her eyes. A tap was heard on the bedroom door. Jonty popped his head around and smiling broadly, he asked her if she would meet him in his study after she had put her belongings away.

Mildred gave him a watery smile. 'I'll come now,' she suggested and followed him downstairs. His desk was cluttered with papers and dirty cups and plates with half eaten food decaying. She held her breath as he inclined his head and beckoned her to sit down on a chair.

She gazed around. A cat was sprawled on a chair. The dog was lying on the floor, it gave her a dismissive look then closed its eyes, but the cat hissed as she perched herself on the edge of the only other chair.

'Quiet Harriet you little bastard,' he rasped. Seeing Mildred's jaw drop, he apologised. 'I'm so sorry darling thing. I can't tell you how marvellous it is, that you've come to my aid. I've been at the end of my tether. The place has gone to wreck and ruin ever since my wife and child died. I took to the drink. Mother was a wonderful help, but lately I feel I'm her father, not her son,' he moaned with a sorrowful look on his face. He swept the fingers of both hands through his thick hair.

Seeing his pained expression, Mildred's heart melted and she didn't have the courage to dampen his spirit. 'I'm only young but I'll try my best to help, I had to take over the guesthouse when my grandmother took ill, so I should be fine here also,' she assured.

Beaming, he got to his feet and pointed to the door. 'Hungry?'

'Yes. I didn't realise how much.'

'Well, come on, hopefully, there's no arsenic in,' he quipped as he pushed his chair back and stepped around his desk. Clasping his hands on Mildred's shoulders, he propelled her out, when frantic thudding noises were heard on the ceiling. He heaved a long sigh while raising his eyes upward. 'It's mother, I know what I would like to do with that stick of hers,' he groaned, as he headed out of the room. 'You and your mother go into the dining room, while I go upstairs to see what on earth she wants now. I'll see if she'll come down to meet you.'

'So you're staying,' said Sadie, as they sat tucking into their meal.

'Yes, but I still feel uneasy. Don't you feel the strange atmosphere here?'

'Like what?'

'Like you're being watched,' Mildred said.

'No. You've got too much imagination.'

'I think that's why he couldn't keep any staff, the place is eerie.'

'It's because it's dark and dingy that's all, with ancient furniture,' Sadie explained.

Mildred raised her darkened eyes and shivered. 'I've always been able to sense bloody spirits.'

Sadie smirked and shook her head when her smile faded. She gazed past Mildred to see that a skinny stooped woman was stood in the doorway. She had black beady eyes and white hair. Jonty was stood behind her with his hand tucked under the woman's elbow as he guided her into the room.

The beady eyes settled on Sadie and she pointed her bony finger at her. 'Who is that woman?' she demanded. 'I don't like the look of her.'

Sadie glowered as Jonty's mother shuffled towards their table and stood appraising Mildred. 'She's alright. What's your name girl?'

Mildred raised her eyes and gave her a steady look. 'I'm Mildred, though some people call me Millie. I'm to be your new housekeeper.'

'Good,' she announced, clapping her hands together, just like a young child. 'I'll call you Millie, it suits you.'

Sadie rolled her eyes while Jonty inclined his head and held his hand towards a table further across the room. The woman shuffled towards it, and sat with her hands clasped together, while casting a sweet smile towards Mildred. But when Sadie turned her head and smiled thinly at her, she dropped her eyes and refused to look at her.

Sadie leaned over the table, her brow creased. 'I don't know what I've done wrong, but you've scored there Mildred.'

'I know, but I'm still not sure about this place,' she whispered. 'At least it will give me time to sort myself out where Jonah is concerned.'

Sadie's face darkened. 'What do you mean?'

'Well, he's been keen on me since I met him. Roxy has warned me to stay away from him, but he's seems so nice.'

'Yes, too nice. I don't trust the man,' she snapped.

Mildred peered underneath her eyelashes, while her mind recalled her last night with Jonah. How he had taken her to his flat and how he had ravaged her. She was left with bruised thighs and her breasts sore from his teeth.

Stood glum-faced in the doorway, Mildred waved Sadie goodbye. What was she thinking of, coming all this way to look after an infirm old woman? Well, it's too late now, she thought as she waited until the car was out of sight, before she turned around and closed the door behind her.

It was early evening, but she was tired. Tired enough to fall asleep and never wake up. Striding along the landing, she averted her eyes as she hurried past the pictures and stepped inside her bedroom. Stood with her arms folded and a frown on her face, she looked at her bedroom door. There was no lock, which she didn't like. Plus the toilet was along the landing, which meant passing those scary pictures. She hoped she wouldn't need to go, when she heard tapping on her door.

She moved towards the door and faced Jonty, whose eyes looked rather glazed as he breezed into her room. He was clutching a bottle of whisky in one hand and two glasses in the other. He perched himself on a chair next to her bed. Mildred's eyebrows shot up and her jaw dropped.

'I had to see to mother, so never had a chance to have a chat, and I would like to know all about you,' he remarked as if it was quite normal to just step inside her room and pour drink into two glasses.

She held a hand up to refuse, but he ignored her protest and pushed a glass towards her. She took a sip and looked at him over the rim. He must be at least forty she thought, staring at his thinning head of hair, but those huge biceps, there was nothing thin about them.

He sat grinning at her, looking as though at any minute he was going to break out into song. 'I know what you're thinking, that this all looks a bit dodgy. But don't worry, I'm going to be a perfect gentleman. I just want some company. It's so bloody rural here, which you can see for yourself,' he said.

Mildred stepped towards the window and peered out to see a thatched white cottage much further along the road. In the distance there was a public house, where a couple of cars stood facing the building. Apart from that, she could see nothing more than green fields and clutches of trees.

'So, are you going to tell me about yourself,' he asked again, taking her out of her reverie. 'Sadie gave a brief description but was rather evasive.'

I bet she was she thought as she took another sip of the strong drink. She wouldn't want you to know she ran off with a gypsy and dumped me. 'Well, my childhood was fine, but my teenage years were bleak. I got pregnant at fifteen and was put in a home. I attacked the Matron because she had my baby adopted without my permission, so she had me confined into an asylum as she thought I was possessed, but I was suffering a nervous breakdown,' she replied in a flat tone, not really bothered if he was shocked.

Jonty sat staring at her for long moments.

'My life is fine now, but I'll always remember my baby's birthday and wonder where he is,' she said with a resigned expression. 'I'm young. I can have other children eventually, when the right one comes along.'

Jonty's face fell. 'Yes. One never gets over the loss of a child,' he replied in a lowered voice.

'Anyway, I don't want to dwell on that,' he said in a lighter tone. 'So, is there anyone special?'

'Not now. He travelled with a fairground group and wanted me to go away with him, but I was too young and Gran was ill. Then I discovered I was pregnant. I did a bad thing, I blamed someone else to protect him,' she replied with a faraway look on her face. 'I don't why I'm telling you all this. I lied. I said I had been raped and the person went to jail. I hope never to meet him again, or my life would be in danger. This is one of the main reasons I had to move away from the North East, plus where I lived, I was the talk of the place.'

Jonty lowered himself down onto the chair. 'God, Mildred, here was me thinking you're just a kid, but you've lived more than me and I'm forty-three.'

She smiled and asked, 'So, what do you do then, apart from looking after your mother?'

'I'm in the entertainment industry,' he replied as he poured more alcohol into her glass. 'I have to promote hopeless acts at different venues and night-clubs.'

'Have you been to the new one called Ruby's in London?'

'No. Not yet.'

Mildred's face dropped. 'I was hoping you knew the owner.'

'Why.'

'I know he's bad news, but that man intrigues me and I wish I could find out more about him.'

'I think I'm going to enjoy having you here, you brighten my very dreary life. Now that you're here, I will be able to get on with my work, so when I'm in the city, I will see what I can find out for you. But you seem very tired, so I will let you get some sleep,' he said as he rose to his feet and sauntered towards the door.

Mildred yawned, smiled and shook her head as the door closed behind him. He needs a nice woman to make him happy she decided, as she pulled her clothes off and slipped into her nightdress.

While she lay in the darkness, Mary's face came into her mind. She wondered where she was and what she was doing. Why was she so stupid to fall for that creep Mario? She wondered as her eyes became heavy. She sighed, pulled the covers around her ears and then she heard her door creak. She felt a presence near her, and something touching her head.

Howling and screeching, she grappled with bony fingers that were pulling her hair out by the roots. She heard Jonty's voice as his feet thudded up the stairs and her bedroom light was clicked on. She peered up at her captor wide-eyed. It was none other than his mother, who was stood with clumps of her hair in her hands.

Jonty's face was thunderous as he dragged his mother away. She lifted her hand and struck him across his face and began whimpering like a child. Jonty was glowering at her with arms folded to his chest. 'Apologise to Mildred at this minute if you want her to help here.'

'I'm so sorry Millie,' she croaked with a contrite look now on her face. 'Please come into my bedroom for a while. I'm scared. Jonty won't believe me when I say the place is haunted.'

'Only if you don't pull the rest of my hair out,' she replied with a tight smile.

'I promise,' she said, as she cast a defiant look at Jonty, before turning on her heel and shuffling away.

Mildred shot Jonty a sideways look of desperation. 'Where's the toilet?'

He pointed a finger towards a door as he leant towards her with a twinkle in his eyes. 'I'll be listening out for the blood curdling screams from you when you enter the lion's den,' he said.

She stood peering at her reflection in the mirror above the sink for long moments while she washed her hands, wondering what she had let herself in for.

With shoulders back she stepped out the toilet and made her way to Jonty's mother's room. She felt as if she had stepped into another decade. It was even more ancient than the rest of the house, with a high four poster bed marking the centre of the room. An ancient, dark wooden wardrobe stood on one wall, whilst a dressing table covered in thick lace and an assortment of perfume bottles took the other.

The old woman was sat on a winged-back chair; her watery eyes stared at Mildred as she patted her hand on the cushion for her to sit next to her. Mildred lowered herself down and turned to face her. The woman grabbed her hand and folded her cold bony fingers around it.

'Jonty doesn't believe me, but this place is haunted with the spirit of his dead wife,' she whispered, as her watery eyes swept around the walls as though the woman was stood listening.

Mildred sat chewing her thumb. 'Why would she want to haunt you?'

'She was a bitch,' she hissed. 'She resented me, because Jonty and I have always been close.'

'It was awful that she died,' said Mildred, not sure of the right response.

'She did it herself. There's a hatch that leads to the loft on the ceiling of the landing. She opened the hatch and tied a rope around a beam in the loft and was found there, hanging on the landing by the paintings.'

'What?' asked Mildred, the colour fading from her face, realising why she felt a cold shiver down her spine each time she past those paintings. 'Why would she do something like that?' she asked.

'Her child died and she couldn't live without him. I miss him too, but I would never do anything like that,' she mumbled.

'Are you sure this isn't your imagination?'

'Of course not,' she snapped, her demeanour now sullen. 'They think I'm losing my mind, but I'm not.'

Mildred felt the hairs on her arms rise, and pulled her dressing gown closer. A shadowy movement on the wall made her gasp. She swung around, but there was nothing to see except for the ancient dark-flocked paper. 'Is there a Spiritualist church around here?' Mildred asked.

'Yes. Are you going to go and see if you can get a message?' the old woman asked, sounding intrigued.

'I thought you would want to come with me and show me where it is. I don't know my way around here.'

Jonty's mother's face lit up and her eyes sparkled. 'That's wonderful. We'll go tomorrow and see what night it's on. I'm so excited now.'

Mildred rose to her feet. 'Goodnight, see you in the morning,' she said as she watched the old woman lower her head to the pillows and close her eyes.

She pulled back the bedroom door. Holding her breath, she ran across the landing and into her room with her heart racing. Too scared to turn her bedside light off, she slid under the sheets and pulled them over her head.

Chapter Thirty-Three

A high pitched clinking noise was heard. It seemed someone was tapping on her window.

She peeked over the bedding to see that the curtains were still drawn together, but the tapping continued from a different part of the bedroom. It had a hollow wooden sound and was coming from the inside the wardrobe.

'Go away,' she yelled. 'Just leave me alone.'

The tapping stopped, but now there was a different sound: a high pitched scratching, on the other side of her bedroom door. The sound had her teeth on edge while her heart thudded like mad, but her fiery temper got the better of her. She leapt out of bed, yanked her door open and hollered, 'I've told you to go away, so fuck right off,' she screeched to nothing except Jonty climbing up the stairs.

He stopped in his tracks and peered at her. His jaw dropped and he gaped at her wild eyes. 'Mildred, what on earth is going on?'

'This place is haunted,' she rasped. 'If I'd known this I would never have agreed to stay here,' she said lowering her tone. 'Your mother's scared witless too, and she told me why. But you won't believe her.'

Jonty's eyes met hers as he drew in a deep sigh. 'So it's true, mother hasn't been imagining things?'

'No, she's not. You'll have to do something about it.'

'Like what?' he asked.

'I don't know. Sell up. Or get the professionals in for this kind of thing. I'm not spending another night here until you do.'

His face fell. 'What about mother? I have to work, and she can't stay here alone.'

'She's slow, but she's still able to get about. Is there anywhere around here that we can stay until we know it's safe to return?'

'Yes. There's a quaint pub further up the road that lets rooms out. But, this just seems so bazaar,' he said.

'Not as bazaar as what's going on here,' she said, as she turned to peer at her bedroom door. 'I'm not staying in there tonight,' she snapped, checking her watch. 'It's still not closing time yet. Can you get me the pub's number? I'm going to stay there.'

'You're not, are you?' he gasped.

'Watch me,' she said with her arms folded, looking intently at his anguished face. 'Come with me to check on your mother, if she's asleep then I'll not disturb her.'

She pushed the old woman's door open and tip-toed inside the room to see her lying in her bed. Her eyes were closed and she was snoring.

'I'll not disturb your mother. I'll just go alone, but tell her I'll enquire about the Spiritualist Church.'

Following close behind Jonty, she went downstairs. Glancing around, she looked up at the landing. A shadowy figure glided along the walls. An icy shiver ran down her spine once more. She rubbed her hands over her goose bumped arms and fell to her knees beside the dying embers in the grate. Jonty pushed a pair of specs onto his nose, and then picked up the telephone to ring the public house. He turned around to face Mildred and stuck his thumb in the air. Her face relaxed while he rang for a taxi to take her there too.

'Will you stand outside my bedroom door again please? While I get changed and fill an overnight bag,' she said.

'Yes, go on then,' he replied.

She turned around and headed for her room. He followed behind her with a pained look, while watching her shoving her belongings into her bag. Hurrying back downstairs, she stood peering behind a curtain until she saw headlights approaching along the driveway.

'Goodnight Jonty, I'll back in the morning,' she gushed as she headed to the door and strode out of it, towards the waiting taxi.

Ten minutes later, she arrived outside the Old Crown. The taxi driver winked as she bade him goodnight. She had tipped him well, just relieved to be away. The pub looked welcoming as she stood facing it: a small lamp cast a cosy glow in each window, beside draped crimson curtains. She stepped on stone flooring in the dark wooden porch, and as she pulled open the door there was a sound of laughter, and a strong smell of stale alcohol.

The room was dimly lit, with an open fire inside a brick recess. The ceiling was beamed with an assortment of horse brasses pinned into them, and there were customers sat appraising her from behind mahogany tables and chairs.

A tiny blonde with back-combed hair and bright pink lipstick was stood behind the bar chatting to a man with a cap on his head. She was a Barbara Windsor look-alike. The man was leant against the bar chatting away when Mildred slid into the gap beside him. In the area behind the bar, the glass shelves were stacked with packets of cigarettes, bottled eggs, nuts and crisps.

The blonde turned her head and cast a broad smile. 'What will it be for you dear? You in need of a stiff one? Perhaps a drink to go with it?' she asked as she chuckled.

'I don't want a drink thanks, and I'll also pass on the other thing,' said Mildred, laughing. She explained that she had booked to stay for the night and asked if it was possible to go straight to her room.

The girl stepped away from behind the bar and opened a door leading towards a dimly lit stairway. Unhooking a key from a rack on the wall, she said, 'Room number one.' She giggled as she passed it to Mildred.

Mildred climbed up the stairs to see the landing was also dimly lit, but had a cosy atmosphere.

She put her key in the lock, stepped inside the room and admired the frilled curtains and bedding. The wardrobe and drawers were antiquated, but at least the place was clean.

She dropped her overnight bag down and threw herself onto the bed, where she lay pondering what to do about her situation. She had agreed to this job and knew it was a relief for Jonty, but she wasn't sure if she could deal with it all.

She sat up sullen faced then, slipping off the bed she yanked her clothes off, pulled on her nightie and cleaned her teeth. Her eyes became so heavy that she had no choice but to put her worries aside. She would face them in the morning, because right now, she was too tired to even think.

As she woke the following morning she felt brighter. She had slept soundly and maybe she had been hasty by thinking of leaving so soon. She would have to conquer her fears and stop imagining that she was being haunted. She would go back to Jonty's, ignore the shadows and the tapping sounds and just get on with it. The peace and contentment of the place was wonderful compared to the fast pace of London, and all that went with it.

Mary popped into her mind once again. She wondered how she was doing, and wondered if they would become friends again.

Ignoring the depressing thoughts of Mary, she washed, dressed and made her way downstairs, where the smell of bacon and frying food made her stomach rumble. She hadn't eaten for a quite a while and she was starving. She stepped towards the hatch and leaned in. 'I would like to order a breakfast,' she said. The young woman turned to face her and smiled as she took her order. 'There's one other thing,' said Mildred. 'Is there a bus service today?'

The girl curled her lip. 'Sorry, we live in the wilds out here, so no there's none on a Sunday. Do you have far to go?'

'Not really, maybe a couple of miles. I'll telephone Jonty, he'll come and collect me,' she announced, and noticed the woman's bright eyes mist over and her smile fade.

'Did you say Jonty?' Mildred nodded her head. 'Rumour has it that the place is haunted,' she said, before inclining her head towards a young man. He had ginger hair and was wearing an open-necked checked shirt. He glanced up from the book he was reading and cast them a broad smile. Mildred noticed he had an open, pleasant face.

'He's a popular medium at the local spiritualist church. He would sense any presence if he went there,' she chuckled.

Heading towards his table, she raised her eyes at the medium while lowering herself into a seat opposite him. 'Excuse me, can I possibly ask you a question?'

Chapter Thirty-Four

Mildred pulled open the front door and smiled at the fresh-faced young medium. He was stood with three other people: an elderly man with a dour face, and two equally dour women, who stood tight-lipped and po-faced.

She beckoned them inside the house. Jonty and his mother Hilly lurked in the background. The medium spoke, 'I'm Scotty, and these are Jim, Belle and Annie.'

Mildred held her hand out to shake theirs, but they acknowledged her with a tight smile. 'Feel free to inspect every room,' she said, but they had already turned their back to her.

Walking about the place while glancing at one another with raised eyebrows, their expressions were furtive. 'I'm sensing a presence,' said Scotty, as he slowly climbed the stairs. On reaching the landing, they all stood rooted to the spot, their heads tipped back, eyes peering at the loft.

Mildred's eyes were wide and her mouth gaped, when Scotty began to whimper in a woman's voice. His breathing became erratic, and he began wailing in an eerie fashion. The rest stood behind him with their hands held up and fingers splayed, seemingly pushing back something that was unseen to her. There was a lot of moaning and weeping from Scotty, while one of the women knelt to her knees as he spoke in a reassuring fashion to the spirit. His face contorted and he collapsed to the floor and lay there for long minutes, his eyes shut and his face ashen.

The ceiling was a blaze of brightness. Mildred's eyes rounded to see swirling vapour drifting around the group, before slowly rising and disappearing through the ceiling. She blinked and breathed a huge sigh. The dark repressive atmosphere faded and a sense of peace and contentment extended over the whole building. It felt as though stardust had been sprinkled everywhere.

Hilly gained a new lease of life. The colour returned to her cheeks and her eyes sparkled, especially when she had a few drinks, which loosened her tongue. Mildred soon learnt that she enjoyed reminiscing about her past.

Christmas was fast approaching, and it really was the most wonderful time of the year. Well, almost.

Mildred gazed out of the window to see that the sky was grey and bleak. The trees were skeletal and the flowers had long gone, withered and died. She turned her face to look at Hilly. She was sat back in her chair with a cup of coffee in her hand. She was watching flames as they licked red tongues around burning logs in the grate.

Mildred bit her lip. 'Hilly, there's something I need to say. I have loved being here, but I do need a break. Mother has phoned me to say that nobody knows where my friend Mary is. She hasn't been seen or heard from in months and I'm concerned about her.'

Hilly's face dropped. 'I hope you'll come back after the Christmas Mildred,' she said with a baleful look on her face. 'It won't be the same without you. You've made me so happy since you've worked for my son. You've made us both happy.'

Mildred laid her hand on her arm. 'Of course I will, but I have to make it my business to visit Mary. There's something fishy about the whole thing and I didn't like the look of that man she was seeing, I had a feeling he was a pimp.'

'Well, you watch yourself. That man called Jonah who you told me about seems a wide-boy.'

'He is. I've tried to forget him while being down here. But it hasn't worked much,' Mildred said, tingling all over at just the thought of him. 'I'll have to see Jonty in his office and tell him I'll be leaving, we need to see what provisions he'll have in store while I'm away.'

Mildred tapped her knuckle on the door before pushing it open. He was sat behind his now very tidy desk with the telephone to his ear. She peered at the cat, lying on the chair. It opened one eye and closed it again, not letting out a single hiss. The dog leapt up and began pawing her, wagging its tail as she stood patting its head.

Jonty put the telephone down and sat with raised brows.

'I need break Jonty. Will this be alright?' she asked, with her fingers crossed behind her back.

He pushed his glasses up on top of his head and sat back in his seat. 'I've just planned a trip to Ireland actually. I've just been speaking to an old relative of mother's. She'll be delighted.'

'When are you going?' Mildred asked.

'In two days.'

'That's great, I'll take her to get some new clothes and anything else she needs,' suggested Mildred as she stepped out of his office to see Hilly's subdued look.

'You've got a holiday to look forward to,' she said clasping her arms around her. 'Jonty has just booked it, so tomorrow we'll go shopping.'

The pitter-patter sound of rain against Mildred's window awoke her. She got up, pulled the curtain back and pulled a face as she raised her eyes. The clouds were gravel-grey. Jonah crossed her mind and her miserable face softened. 'Can't wait to see you again,' she whispered as she closed the curtain, turned around and headed for the bathroom.

Stepping downstairs, she smiled to see Hilly. She was sat in her wheelchair by the fire. Her fur hat was on her head, her coat was draped over her knees and her hands were clasped around her handbag.

'I'll just have a coffee and we'll get away,' said Mildred. 'There's a taxi arriving in ten minutes.'

'There's a large shop that sells good quality clothes where we are going,' shouted Hilly through to the kitchen.

'Mmm . . .' answered Mildred, with a far-away look, her mind still on Jonah.

A loud knock was heard on the front door. Mildred dashed through the passageway and pulled open the door. 'We'll be two minutes,' she said, giving the man a broad smile. Slinging Hilly's coat around her shoulders, she squeezed the wheelchair through the door, closed it behind her and rushed down the path to the waiting taxi.

The wind and rain stung their faces as they got out of the taxi. Mildred pushed Hilly in her wheelchair towards the Salvation Army where carol singers were stood huddled, wearing scarves, hats, jackets and boots.

They dropped money into their boxes and then moved on towards the brightly-lit shops, with Christmas bunting and trees covered in tinsel. The market traders were selling wreaths as well as fruit and vegetables. Mildred pushed Hilly into her favourite shop and hours later, they left with their bags bulging.

The clouds spat out their beads of water and umbrellas all around were opened. The roofs of cars danced with spray while Hilly sat shivering in her chair. Mildred's hair was plastered to her brow as she struggled to push the wheelchair into the bustling café.

An elderly frazzled-looking waitress took their order and they were soon refreshed after a huge plate of fish and chips and a pot of tea. They sat behind the steamy window, watching people dashing by with their umbrellas opened, or with their heads lowered against the wall of rain that persisted.

'I'm going for a taxi. I won't be long,' Mildred said, as she got up and stepped towards the desk and paid for their meal. Pulling open the door, she ran towards a taxi rank. On her return, she folded the chair and helped Hilly into the taxi, where she rested her head against the squab.

Mildred sat gazing out of the window. It was only late afternoon, but already the darkness was rolling in. Her stomach was churning. She would never sleep when she went to bed because she was too excited to get back to London and to see Jonah when she went to the Ruby.

With her thought far away, the taxi stopped.

She took Hilly's hand and helped her out, then put a hefty tip into the cabby's open hand. He beamed and waved jollily at her as he drove away.

She supported Hilly up the staircase and into her bedroom. She put her belongings inside her wardrobe, while the old woman shuffled into the room. 'I'm too tired Millie, I'm having an early night,' she said wearily.

Mildred bade her goodnight and headed downstairs to see Jonty, who was sat lounging on the sofa. 'Grab a glass darling thing, this is your last night before you go back home. I do hope you're coming back.'

'Of course,' she assured, as she held a glass up. He got up and swished the curtains shut, then clicked on the table lamps which gave the room a rosy glow. Mildred poured herself a large glassful of champagne. It would be easy for me to just to stay here and let the world go by, she thought to herself, as she sat with her feet resting on the fender. The sound of Jonty's rock and roll music playing on his radiogram and the vast amount of alcohol he plied her made her feet tap. She grabbed hold of his hand and pulled him up off the settee.

'I can't jive,' he laughed.

But she grabbed hold of him and they jived around the room until they were both out of breath and collapsed down onto the settee in a heap. After another cork was popped, Jonty was sat with his eyes glazed. He flopped back on the sofa, tucked his legs beneath him, and fell asleep.

The melodious sound from the wall clock made her sit up, raise her glassy eyes and see it was midnight. She eased herself up off the sofa and staggered up the stairs, clasping the rail for support.

'Millie, wake up,' someone was saying. She groaned and slid down the bed, pulling the clothes over her ears. 'Millie, your mother is coming to collect you and you're not ready,' the voice persisted.

She pushed her bedding back and yawed wide as she raked her fingers through her corkscrews to peer up at Hilly. 'It's mid-day and you've been asleep all morning,' Hilly said.

Her face creased. She slipped her legs out of bed, vowing never to drink again. 'Thanks Hilly, I'll get bathed and then I'll be okay,' she whispered, rubbing her eyes.

She sunk into the bath and lay back in the hot water. She closed her eyes and Jonah's face appeared in her mind at once. She was on fire as she stood up and stepped out of the bath. 'I'm going to ravage him,' she whispered as she dried herself. After putting on her clothes and slicking on a small amount of makeup, she dashed downstairs.

Sat in the kitchen with a cup of black coffee in her hand, she sighed, feeling sad and happy in equal measure. Soon she would be back to the hustle and bustle of what chapter awaited her and she wasn't sure if she should be excited or nervous. Both seemed to be the best bet.

Turning towards the lounge, she glanced at Hilly. She was sat around the fire with a sombre face. 'It's only for a couple of weeks,' Mildred assured. Stepping towards her, she clasped her arms around her and gave her a warm kiss on her wrinkled cheek. Then, heading for the front entrance, she heard the sound of a car engine. She pulled open the door and saw Sadie's car sweep into the drive.

'Hilly, tell Jonty that mother is here,' she said.

Sadie stepped out of her car with a broad smile as she advanced towards her. 'You look well. It's done you good, living down here,' Sadie announced, as she wrapped her arms around Mildred and held her a warm embrace.

Jonty appeared. His eyes were still glazed but reddened too. 'Hello darling thing, you look wonderful as usual,' he said, giving Sadie an amorous look.

'Can't say the same for you,' laughed Sadie, air-brushing his cheek.

Mildred stooped and picked up her cases while Sadie opened the boot.

'Well, have a good Christmas,' beamed Jonty. 'We'll see you next year then,' he said as he leaned towards her and kissed her cheek.

'You too,' Mildred gushed, as she moved away and sank into the car seat. Turning her head, she gazed towards the house. Hilly was stood behind the window with a solemn look, watching Sadie reverse the car out of the drive. Mildred waved her arm and smiled, but that little voice in her head was telling her that she would in fact not be returning.

'Is there anymore news about Mary?' she asked Sadie.

'I've been asking Roxy, but even she hasn't heard anything,' Sadie said.

'Well she can't have disappeared off the face of the earth. Maybe she's gone back to Ashwood. But I can't see that happening somehow,' she announced, her brow furrowed. 'When I get settled back in London, I'm heading for the Ruby. I intend to find out what's going on.' An image of Jonah's irresistible eyes filled her mind. Throbbing and aching, she clenched her thighs together.

'I hope you're not going to have anything to do with that wide-boy Jonah,' snapped Sadie, as though she had read her thoughts.

Chapter Thirty-Five

The sound of the latest records blared from speakers around the reception area as Mildred sashayed into the Ruby. Men turned their head and raised their eyebrows, giving her a second look. Women stared at her with envious glares.

Her Mary Quant shift dress was thigh high, black and slinky. It clung to her tall and willowy figure like a glove. She had bought it from a trendy boutique in Carnaby Street in London. The bright red poppet necklace, flame red stiletto shoes, bag and bangles complemented the outfit. Her huge false eyelashes fluttered as she swept her brown eyes around at the sea of faces, as she made her way further into the place. Girls were cavorting in cages and smiling brightly.

She pushed her way through the crowd and asked one of the bar staff if she knew where Mary Kelly was. The young girl's fixed smile faded, and she said that she didn't know. Mildred pressed her lips together.

She turned and climbed to the upper level, where she headed for the bar and bought a large whisky. Stepping back, she draped herself over the balcony, watching the hostesses smiling obligingly at elderly men. She curled her lip. 'Dirty old bastards,' she whispered, when a heavy hand was thrust onto her shoulder.

Swaying around, she faced a tall and skinny man. His small, dark eyes glistened. 'Looking for your friend eh?' he asked, his thin lips twitching.

'What friend are you talking about?' she snapped, quickly stepping aside.

'Mary Kelly.'

Mildred's mouth dropped open. 'How do you know Mary?'

'I know her because she used to buy her gear from me,' he replied, puffing his chest out and smirking.

Mildred felt as though she wanted to wipe the smirk off his face but clasped her fingers tight around the handrail. She tilted her chin and held his gaze. 'What did she buy?'

He glanced around briefly, opened his jacket, and then produced a small bag of white powder. 'She drugged Mario and he was left brain-damaged,' he sniggered.

'I don't believe you,' she hissed.

He lifted his shoulders, held his hands out.

Mildred gripped the rail tighter, her knuckles white. He lowered himself down onto a chair and sat with his feet wide apart. 'She was living in a grotty place and Mario took all her hard-earned cash. Prostitutes can make big money you know,' he said, as though discussing a high profile vacancy. 'You're sitting on a fortune,' he sniggered once more. Throwing back his head, he opened his mouth wide and laughed loudly. 'That's what she thought too, but didn't reckon on Mario's father – he's a mad bastard. I've heard he had her done over.'

Mildred gagged to see his yellow coated tongue. Visibly quivering, her mind conjured a vision of Mary being beaten up, or even worse. 'I'm going to tell the police. I need to know if this is true,' she hissed.

He grabbed hold of her arm and pulled her down next to him. 'Get the coppers and you'll never see your friend again. I've known women disappear and never be seen again,' he warned.

Mildred closed her eyes as her chin quivered. 'I can't bare this.'

He leaned closer. 'They say Jonah has something to do with this too, not just Mario's father.'

She twisted her face, feeling her stomach knot. 'Jonah? No, you're wrong. He's not a thug,' she argued.

He laughed again. 'You're right, he's not a thug. He's a gangster, same as Kelvin, Mario's father.'

'Where is he then?' she asked with her arms folded to her chest.

'He was in his office when I came up here.'

She shot to her feet with her face set. 'But he always seems so charismatic and charming,' she said, not wanting to believe any of it.

'It's a front darling. He's a psycho, so be careful,' he warned as he got up and slinked away.

She headed for the bar, bought another large whisky and swallowed it in one gulp. 'Another two large ones please,' she said to the young barman, who was stood with an amorous look on his face. With her head tipped back, she swallowed both drinks.

Her tense shoulders relaxed as she turned away and walked down to the lower level, where she stopped in her tracks. Jonah was strutting about like a cock hen. 'Right, you low life twat,' she whispered to herself. 'I'm coming for you.'

'Mildred,' gushed Jonah. 'How wonderful to see you again,' he said, as she approached him. All her pent-up aggression faded in a second. Her spine tingled and butterflies fluttered in her tummy. He pulled her in close and covered her lips with his. 'Where have you been?' he asked.

'I've been working in Sussex,' she answered in a quivering voice. Feeling the heat from her chest and neck, she was glad the lights were dim in here; her rash always broke out under duress.

'Well, you look wonderful,' he said, as he stepped back, and looked her up and down. 'Who are you here with?'

'Just myself, I thought Mary would be here, but there's no sign of her,' she remarked and watched his smile fade. 'You'll not happen to know where I can find her would you?' she pressed on.

He shook his head. 'Never mind Mary, I want to make up for lost time and buy you a drink,' he said. Snatching hold of her hand, he guided her towards the bar. He forced a smile, but his eyes were like ice.

Chapter Thirty-Six

As she stood at the bar her mind was in a whirl, worrying about how to handle the situation. She glanced around, and saw that Jonah was stood behind her, ordering the best bottle of champagne. 'This calls for a celebration,' he said as he flicked his finger and thumb at a young man wearing a bow tie.

He gestured his head towards a crimson velvet booth. A candle was lit in a bottle with wax dripping down the side, and the table was covered in a lace cloth. 'Take the bottle and two glasses over and I don't want to be disturbed,' he demanded.

Mildred watched the young man carry the tray and glasses above his head as her hand was clutched and she was guided towards the booth. Lowering herself down, she watched the bubbles fizzing as he poured the champagne into the flute.

'To us,' he said as he raised his glass.

'Us?' she queried, as he moved his hand towards hers and caressed her fingers.

'I would like it to be,' he replied, his eyes twinkling. He leaned towards her slowly, causing her to tingle all over.

Forcing herself away, she smiled sweetly as she picked up her glass and tipped her head back. I must not give in to temptation, she kept repeating in her head, but the usual twitch was going to let her down, especially when he slipped his arms around her and caressed her neck softly with his lips.

It became unbearable. She shot up off the seat, but he snatched hold of her hand, pulled her down and covered her mouth with his. Her heart thudded like a drum, feeling scared of the unknown. It was wrong, he was a dangerous man, but she was powerless to stop herself. It felt so right at the same time. She allowed him to guide her through the nightclub, to where his car was parked.

She sunk into the soft leather seat of the plush Jaguar. He sat looking at her with a hungry expression in his eyes before switching on the engine. The car glided along, while a soothing soul song on the radio helped calm her anxiety.

Casting her eyes out of the car window, she looked at the large department stores. The mannequins displaying the latest fashions and groups of people as they sauntered along the brightly-lit streets of London wrapped in thick coats, scarves and boots. The paths were white with frost as Jonah drove towards his apartment in Mayfair.

He cut the engine and parked the car beside an Edwardian townhouse. As she stumbled inside his home, her eyes rounded at the sight. His seating was huge and plush in burgundy and black, the walls were painted white with modern paintings; the accessories chrome and smoked glass. By now, her head was beginning to clear, but she was still at a loss as to how she was going to handle the situation. She hated him and was besotted in equal measure.

She sat on the edge of a soft, squishy chair with scared eyes as he sunk to his knees in front of her. 'You want me as much as I want you,' he whispered. She shook her head, but he got up and pulled her to her feet.

The smell of Brut aftershave and the taste of whisky and cigars on his breath as his tongue probed hers, proved too much. Her body went limp. He lifted her up into his arms and took her to his bedroom.

Writhing and groaning, she reached powerful heights of passion, while time seemed to stand still. Jonah was soaked in sweat as he slumped back against the pillows, closed his eyes and fell asleep. She gazed at him. He was a narcotic and she was now totally addicted. Snuggling close to him, she closed her eyes and sighed in a dream-like state.

Mildred opened her eyes and sat up with a start. It took her a few

227

minutes to realise where she was. Frowning, she raked her fingers through her hair, wondering where Jonah was.

Slipping her legs over the edge of the bed, she sunk her feet into the thick cream carpet. Her clothes were still scattered about where she had flung them off. She bent over and picked them up, feeling a little tense.

Dashing towards the bathroom, she washed and dressed. Sauntering through to his living room she gazed around, but still there was no sign of Jonah. She lifted her shoulders and shrugged as she checked the rest of the house. Her mouth was parched. She decided she would make a coffee and then telephone Roxy and ask her to come and collect her. She couldn't let Sadie know where she had been.

An urgent tapping on the main door echoed through the building. She stepped back out of the kitchen, strode towards the main entrance and pulled the door open. A curtain of snowflakes blew into the passageway. She winced as the freezing cold cut through her thin clothes.

A gaunt-faced young woman was stood hunched at the door, her teeth chattering as she wrung her hands together. 'I need to see Jonah. It wasn't my fault,' she gabbled as her wide eyes filled with tears.

'He's not here, but come in, you must be freezing stood out there,' she said, beckoning her inside.

'He'll kill me,' she whimpered as she stepped over the threshold. Sinking her head into her hands, she began weeping.

'Who will kill you?' asked Mildred.

'Jonah will,' she sniffed. 'He won't believe me . . .' she trailed off as she sat down, pulled out a hankie from her bag and swiped it over her reddened eyes. 'He's given me a place to live as long as I do as he says. So I work for him, but not here. I can't tell you anymore,' she whispered, as she turned to look at the door with a fearful look in her eyes. Then she jumped to her feet. 'I have to go, don't say anything to him. I'll get the money for him somehow.'

Mildred reached for her bag and took out a book and pen, then handed them to her. 'Write your name and telephone number, I will ring you later. Now quick, go before he comes back,' she uttered to the woman, who headed for the front door. Mildred opened the door and the woman dashed away with her head lowered. The snow was still bleaching down.

Closing the door, she pressed her lips together. So he has girls working for him has he, what a total ponce, living off the backs of young girls, she thought to herself while switching on the kettle and spooning coffee into a cup. 'What the hell am I doing with someone like that? I'm no better than Mary and look what happened to her,' she said to the all-white and chrome kitchen as she pulled out a seat and sat down. 'I'm having this and never coming back.'

She heard the front door open and close again. Jonah stepped into the kitchen with a broad smile and headed towards her. Clasping an arm around her shoulders, he bent over and kissed her cheek. He stank of whisky and cigars. 'I thought you would have been still recovering from last night,' he quipped. 'I'm freezing, do you want to warm me up?'

She forced a smile as she pulled herself out of his embrace. 'I need to get home. Sadie will want to know where I've been.'

'I'll take you there,' he suggested. 'The pavements are dangerous; you can't walk in those shoes. Get your bag and your jacket and I'll drop you off at your place. Just tell me where to go.'

She made a face and her heart sank. She went into the bedroom to collect her bag, hoping Sadie would be out running errands when she got back.

Chapter Thirty-Seven

Sadie was wrapped up in a thick fur coat, woollen hat and a pair of sturdy boots. She had a shovel in her hand and was clearing the snow away from the path at the foot of the driveway. She looked to her right at the sound of the running car engine and squinted her eyes to see Mildred stepping out of the Jaguar.

Peering under her eyelashes, Mildred stepped cautiously onto the icy pavement. 'Don't start. I can explain,' she said.

'Don't start?' repeated Sadie. 'I've had Roxy looking for you, but you were nowhere to be seen. Now I know where you were. Well, lady, you're looking for trouble. I've told you he's bad news,' she ranted, with her gloved finger pointed into her face.

As they stepped inside the house Mildred heaved a long sighed and flopped down onto the settee. Rubbing her reddened toes she slipped off her shoes, ignoring the thunderous expression on her mother's face. 'I know how you feel about him, and I agree with you, but I can't just ignore what I feel for him. It's just like you did, when you ran with that gangster you married. Don't say you weren't warned, because I bet you were,' she stated, waiting for the bomb to go off.

But Sadie sat with her eyes closed; fingers pressed to her brow. 'I don't want him here, he's not welcome,' she snapped. 'He gives me the creeps. The way he smirks as if he has something that he knows but we don't. Get rid,' she rasped.

'Don't worry,' she soothed. 'I'm going to get bathed and changed and then I've got things to do. I'll move out and then you won't be affected. I've met a young woman and hopefully she will lead me to Mary.'

Sadie met her gaze then lowered her eyes. 'You don't have to move out for goodness sakes, just be careful.'

'I will mother. I know it's dangerous what I'm doing but I have no other choice. That man said if I went to the police I wouldn't see Mary again.'

'You're a bloody fool,' she sighed. 'A total chancer, just like your father. If he knew what you were doing he would put a stop to it.'

Mildred's head shot up as she peered at her mother. 'Do you know something I don't?' Sadie lowered her eyes and stared at the carpet. 'You do, don't you?' accused Mildred with narrowed eyes.

Sadie clasped her hands together. 'I've heard through the grapevine that he's living in England and doing well, but I don't know anything more. I wonder what he looks like now,' she said, with a dreamy expression. 'I often think about him. If only he hadn't lived that Nomadic way of life, maybe then it would've worked out.'

'One day I'll make it my business to find him, but for now I've got this situation with Mary,' Mildred said, as she clicked open her bag and took out the paper that the woman had written her number on.

She didn't see the glum look her mother cast her as she stepped towards the long sideboard and picked up the telephone to make her arrangements with her.

Mildred arrived at the sex worker's home wearing a headscarf and a pair of heavy-rimmed glasses. Loud music blasted from a public house nearby as a man with a torn jacket and dirty jeans staggered outside, then collided with a lamppost and lay on the ground in a heap.

She stood outside speaking into an intercom. There was a buzzing sound and the door opened. She stepped inside to see the woman huddled in front of a two-bar electric fire. The room was bare except for an old sofa, an armchair and a coffee table. She gestured for Mildred to take a seat. 'I wouldn't have recognised you with that scarf covering that wild hair of yours and those thick specs.'

'You never explained what had happened to you yesterday, when you were in such a state,' said Mildred, removing the scarf and specs.

'A punter assaulted me and took all the money I had made to give to Jonah,' she whined, wringing her hands together.

Mildred's face was dark with anger. 'How much does he expect a week?'

'About one-hundred-and-fifty,' she replied in a flat tone. 'And I have to live on a pittance, which you can tell by the state of this place.'

'How many others are there doing this for him?' She shrugged. 'What a complete bastard. Living off the backs of women while sitting like Lord Fontleroy in his nightclub,' she said, shaking her head.

'So why are you with him then, if you hate him so much?'

Mildred's shoulders slumped, as she shook her head. 'I hate myself too, I really do. It's as though he has put a spell on me. I can't help myself. I first met him last year and found him attractive. My friend worked for him and went missing. I thought that by getting closer to him, I would find out where she was, but he's too sly and crafty. I don't suppose you know the whereabouts of someone called Mary Kelly?'

'No. But I do know someone who everyone goes to when they're troubled. She's an old woman called Rosie. She's usually out selling heather around Camden Market. She also has an old building that she rents near there too, where she reads palms.'

'How will I know that it's her place?' asked Mildred as she put her hand inside her coat pocket to pull out a wad of money.

'There is a gargoyle image beneath the canopy,' she replied. 'His head is lowered, upper arms raised and lower arms facing toward the ground – he's for protection.'

'Well I'll not miss that. Anyway, get yourself something to eat with this. You're all skin and bones. And don't give any of it to Jonah,' she said, as she headed towards the door. 'What's your name by the way?'

'Polly,' she replied.

'Well, bye Polly, it was nice meeting you.'

Striding to the front of the building, she pushed the main door open and pulled her coat closer while she forced her way through the sleeting snow. Surely Rosie won't be out in this weather, she thought to herself as she strode along the snow-covered path, but she maybe in the building she rents.

She headed towards the bus stop and stood there shivering with her collar turned up and her taut face relaxed. A bus was heading her way. She put out her hand and the bus slowed down to stop. 'Can you tell me if this bus goes to Camden Market?'

'Yes,' the fat-bellied conductor replied.

She stepped aboard. The bus was packed, smelly and stuffy too. A young lad gave her an appraising glance. She dropped her eyes, turned her head and peered through the steamy window.

She turned to face a rather haughty looking woman who was sat beside her. 'Excuse me, but have you heard of someone called Rosie? She's very popular with palm readings.'

The woman looked in distain. 'No I have not, I have no truck with the likes of that sort of thing,' she replied, casting a dismissive look down her long nose.

'It might do you good, put a smile on your odious face,' she snapped, as she leapt up and squeezed past the passengers, stepping off the bus.

Walking around, her eyes were darting everywhere, when they were drawn towards a middle-aged, stout woman with a scarf around her head. She was stooped over, inserting a key into the lock of a door, when Mildred dashed towards her and glanced up to see the gargoyle. 'Are you called Rosie?' she asked.

The woman swung her head up, scrutinised her with her eyes narrowed. 'Who's asking?'

'My name is Mildred. I was hoping you would help me.'

'How?' she spat.

'I'll pay you well, if you'll help me. I'm looking for my friend. I've been told you have helped people in need.'

The woman twisted her face. Then, turning the key, which scraped in the rusty lock, she inclined her head. 'Well, come on then, get inside,' she demanded.

The woman headed towards a small round table, slumped down on a stool and pointed her forefinger for Mildred to sit opposite. Heaving a sigh, she snatched hold of her hand and turned it over to peer at her palm for long moments. 'I see a young skinny girl. She's in a hospital bed. You will find her, but you would be wise not too – this friend will betray you. She's jealous and resents you, so be warned.'

Mildred's mouth gaped. 'She would never do that,' she argued, pushing her hand away.

The woman's eyes were dark and hardened as she reached out and snatched hold of her hand again. 'You're dicing with danger lady. I see a suave man hovering around you too. Take my advice and leave it all well alone.' Pushing her hand away, Rosie shivered. 'I can't say anymore. I'm too cold and worn out to concentrate,' she said, hunching her shoulders and rubbing her hands up and down her arms.

Mildred's shoulders slumped, but she put her hand inside her pocket and took out a ten pound note. The woman's eyes glistened. She peered at the amount of money in her held out palm. 'Thank you for your advice,' said Mildred. With a grave expression, she stood up to leave. 'Do you want to share a taxi with me? It's too cold for trudging the streets and waiting for buses.'

'It's okay love. I only live a few streets away.' She clasped hold of Mildred's hand and peered into her eyes. 'Don't ignore my warning,' she said.

'I won't,' replied Mildred, as the woman disappeared into the shadows. She headed for a taxi rank.

Trudging along the pathways, she glanced into houses where festive, brightly-lit Christmas trees and glittery decorations sparkled. Usually she would be excited, that warm, magical feeling that only Christmas time can convey burning brightly in her stomach. But this year, an icy cold hand was gripping her heart, and was growing tighter and tighter with each passing day.

Chapter Thirty-Eight

The ground was covered in a blanket of snow, glistening like sequins. Tree branches hung low with the weight. A festive scene, but Mildred's lips were stretched to a fine line. All she could think about was Rosie's warning, how she had told her to turn her back on Jonah and Mary.

A taxi appeared and she stepped towards it. 'The Ruby nightclub please,' she said to the cabby as she climbed in.

Sat shivering and chewing her nails, she watched as snowflakes fluttered against the taxi window and then slide down, pooling onto the bonnet. The view looked so familiar and yet different as the taxi slowed down outside the Ruby nightclub.

She paid the cabby and headed straight inside the foyer. Removing her coat, she glanced down at herself and groaned. She was wearing jeans and a jumper, not exactly nightclub attire. Luckily, it was always subdued lighting, so she wouldn't be overly exposed. She handed her coat to the woman and got a ticket.

The place was the usual atmosphere: smoky, noisy and crowded. She made her way to Jonah's office. He was lounging on a leather settee, puffing on a cigar. There was a glass of whisky in his hand.

He raised his head and frowned to see her underdressed. 'This is a surprise,' he commented. 'What's up? You look troubled.'

'I am. It's about Mary. I need to know where she is, and don't take me for a fool.'

He pushed his chair back and stood up with his face dark. 'I know nothing about this Mary you keep going on about.'

'I don't believe you,' she snapped. 'I know you're hiding something, my intuition never lets me down,' she retorted, peering at his sullen countenance.

'All I know is she drugged Mario. He's been left brain damaged and Mario's father naturally taught her a lesson,' he snarled.

'Like what?'

'Like something she'll never forget,' he whispered.

'She's in hospital and in a bad way?' Mildred asked.

He peered at her with eyes of ice. 'Who told you this?' he demanded as he got up and stepped from behind the desk. 'You better tell me, or there'll be trouble,' he warned. Lurching towards her, he seized her wrist in a tight grip.

'A gypsy told me,' she answered in a small voice.

His feral features faded and he sniggered. Grabbing hold of her hand, he led her through the club, around the back entrance and towards his Jaguar. 'You're coming with me.'

'No I'm not,' she argued. But he pulled open the passenger door and pushed her inside, then stepping around the driver's door he pulled it open and slid in.

Mildred turned her head and glowered at him, but he leaned towards her. Kissing her lips, while shoving his hand up her jumper, he caressed her breast making her twitch and tingle with longing.

He sniggered again. 'You can't resist me, can you?' he asked, as he removed his hand and turned on the engine.

She sat with her arms folded and mouth pouting. 'I hate you, so please take me home.'

'You're not going home, you're coming to my place,' he said as he drove the car away.

'I'm not. I've been finding things out about you, and I know I have to keep away,' Mildred said, wishing it wasn't actually true that she couldn't resist him.

'But that's what turns you on and don't say it doesn't because I know it does,' he said, smirking and simmering.

Mildred sat in silence. He's right, she thought, he does turn me on because he's so bad, what the hell is wrong with me?

'Have you ever been to a swingers' party?' he asked casually, as he turned the key in the lock and stepped inside the house.

Her brow puckered, but she wasn't going to look stupid. 'Yeah, all the time,' she announced. 'It's one of my favourite ways to have fun.'

He gave her a sharp look as he shut the front door. 'You're a bit young to know all about swinging,' he remarked, as he took the stairs two at a time and headed for his bedroom to change. She followed behind him and stared at his bed. A black full face mask with gaping holes for eyes and mouth lay on the bed, also a whip and a pair of steel cufflinks.

'I don't like the look of those,' she said as she clutched a hand to her chest.

He tucked his finger under her chin, as his eyes glistened with lust. 'Then you haven't lived,' he soothed when the sound of the doorbell rang, tinny and grating.

Jonah left the room and dashed down the stairs. She went towards the items and hovered over them with her lip curled. She heard a woman's high-pitched voice in the passage. 'Is everyone here then?'

'Only Mildred so far, but she doesn't realise what I've got planned,' he whispered.

Mildred heard and her mouth dropped open. She backed out of the room and stepped downstairs whispering under her breath, 'What am I in for?'

Mildred heard a titter. 'You naughty man, here's my keys, put them in the bowl. I better get a good'n tonight. I'm raring to go, if you know what I mean,' the woman said.

Mildred stood in the doorway with her arms crossed, gazing at the woman. She looked like an old porn star, with her wrinkled face caked in foundation and bright red lipstick.

'Ooh, aren't you a looker,' she trilled, as a knock on the door was heard.

Mildred scowled at Jonah as he left to answer the door. The woman stood with glinting green eyes and was puckering her lips at her. Mildred shot to her feet and dashed into the kitchen, where she stood with her mouth dry. He had brought her for a night of sex with this ghastly woman and God knows who else.

The woman stepped into the kitchen and advanced towards her. 'You look terrified dear. Don't be, because we have a great time swinging – swapping partners and that,' she tittered again, rolling her eyes and flicking her hair. 'My partner was unable to attend tonight, so how about a threesome? You, me and Jonah?'

So this is bloody swinging is it, thought Mildred, her face thunderous. 'Look here lady, listen and listen well. I'm not going anywhere your old minge, do you hear? Nowhere close. So fuck right off.'

The woman's smile faded. Then she threw her head back, opened her painted lips wide and screeched with laughter. 'You don't know what you're missing, tell her Jonah,' she cajoled as he stepped inside the kitchen to see Mildred's thunderous expression.

'What's wrong?' he asked.

'She says she wants a threesome with you and me. I bet her fanny is wrinkled as her face. Keep her away from me, she's disgusting,' she ranted

Jonah stepped towards her, wrapped an arm around her shoulder and held her in a tight embrace. 'You don't have to be so nasty to people you know,' he said.

The woman stormed out of the room with her head held high, casting a seething look in Mildred's direction.

'You need a drink,' he soothed with his usual smarmy look as her heart thudded in her chest. She was sure he would sense her fear, but she didn't want to show herself up by standing quivering in front of these weird looking people. So she stepped out of the kitchen and into the living room.

With clammy shaking hands, she gave him another menacing look, as he placed a cut glass tumbler full of whisky into her hand. She tilted her head back and swallowed the lot, while her scared eyes darted around the room. She noticed an elderly man with a drooped moustache. He was peering in a sensuous fashion, and was on his way towards her.

Oh great, another old pervert, she thought as she caught a glimpse of the look in his eyes. She dropped her eyes to step back, but he clutched one of her hands and brought her near. Then he lifted his bony fingers and fiddled with her unruly hair. 'You are an unusual-looking young woman aren't you? With your olive skin and those dark eyes,' he remarked, looking mesmerised.

Before she could stop herself, she wriggled from his clutches and dashed towards the door, praying it wasn't locked. Holding her breath, she yanked it open. People were strolling along outside, the snow covering their footwear while they admired the elaborate Edwardian townhouses with their large panelled doors, gables, dormers and bow windows.

She strode, struggling through the thick snow, past the tall picturesque homes and kept on until she spotted a narrow opening which led along a narrower cobbled street. She stopped, holding a hand to her heaving chest, gulping hard. Bending over, she clutched her hands to her knees, when she heard a rustling sound and sniffed a rancid smell.

She swung around and faced an elderly woman wearing a battered hat and an old torn tweed coat. Her face was filthy, but her eyes were shining. 'Who are you running away from dearie?' she asked.

Mildred glanced to and fro to see that there was nobody around but this tramp. She stinks but that shawl she's wearing will cover my head, she thought, anything is better than being in the clutches of old perverts.

Her teeth chattered. 'I'm running away from some disgusting people. Can I have your shawl to camouflage myself? You can have this,' she gushed as she unclasped the trinket from her wrist.

The woman took off her thick shawl, and lowered gleaming eyes at the bracelet shining in her dirty palm. Mildred wrinkled her nose as she wrapped the shawl around her head and hunched her shoulders. 'Thanks so much, you've saved skin.'

'Good luck dearie,' announced the old woman with a toothless grin as Mildred stepped away.

Keeping her head low, she trudged by cafés and public houses until she spotted a taxi rank. Clasping the shawl closer, she staggered towards the stand. The cabby cast a surly look over her when she opened the door and stepped into the taxi.

'Aldershot please,' she asked. He shut the glass partition behind him and the rear of the taxi. Glowering at her, he turned his head and drove way.

She sat back and shuddered, recalling the old porn star. 'Bah, who the hell would want to touch that,' she whispered, resting her head against the squab. 'And he can piss off as well, the twisted bastard.'

The taxi slowed down and the driver turned his head to peer at her with another dark look. 'I know I stink, but do you have to be so snotty? Drive on and I'll tell you where,' she snapped. 'Frigging arsehole,' she muttered while peering out of the window. Seeing the wrought iron gates and tall chimneys, the glass tinkled as she tapped it with her knuckles.

The taxi halted came to a halt, but the house was in darkness. She held her hand up to the man. 'Wait there.'

'I'm not waiting. You're not getting back in here, you bloody stink,' he growled.

'So would you, if you had the night I've just had, you cheeky shit. Do you want paying or not?' she asked, throwing the shawl aside.

He sat with a sullen face as she lifted her fist and thudded it on the door until she saw a light appear upstairs. Her mother pushed her bedroom window open and peered at her. 'Mother I've got no money and I need to pay the taxi,' she shouted.

The front door flung open. Sadie was stood in her dressing gown, her hair was tied up in rollers and there were a pair of wellingtons on her feet. She stepped towards the taxi with her purse in her hands. 'It's double time after twelve,' he snorted. She took the cash out of her purse and threw it into the open window.

The cabby cast them both a meaningful look as he drove away.

'Cheeky bastard,' Mildred spat while Sadie closed the door.

Mildred disappeared into the bathroom, turned on the taps and sprinkled lavender bath crystals in too. Yanking her reeking jumper off, she pulled down her jeans and then slumped down onto a cane chair while waiting for the bath to fill.

Sadie appeared in the doorway and pulled a face. 'What the hell's going on? You've got the place reeking,' she said as she leaned against the doorframe.

Mildred slowly got to her feet. 'I'm sorry, mother, can I tell you tomorrow? I've had a hell of a day. I just want to get in the bath and go to bed.'

'No, you can't. I'll make us a drink, and then you can tell me what happened,' she said as she moved away.

Chapter Thirty-Nine

The sound of the telephone ringing woke Mildred. She sighed and turned over, pulling the bedding around her head. But the ringing continued. 'Piss off whoever you are, I'm not getting up,' she whispered, feeling all snug as she listened to the sound of hailstones clattering against the window.

Sighing, she turned on her back. 'It'll be him, I'm just ignoring him, he'll eventually give up,' she said. But the ringing continued.

What time is it? She thought as she sat up. Peering at her bedside clock, her eyes rounded. Slinging her legs over the bed, she went to the landing to peer down the open stairs. There was no sign of Sadie.

She stepped towards the bathroom with her eyebrows lowered. I hope that Jonah leaves me alone. I'm in no mood for him after last night, she thought as she pulled open the door and stepped downstairs. Heading towards the front window, she gazed out to see no sign of Sadie's car. The telephone rang again.

Snatching the telephone up, her stance stiffened. 'Just go away Jonah,' she muttered. 'No, don't bother, I'll just ignore you,' she rasped and slammed the receiver down. Stepping back upstairs, she went to her bedroom.

I think I'll go and visit Crystal and Pandora, she contemplated as she looked inside her wardrobe for something smart to wear. She took out a plain black skirt, red jumper and black waistcoat, then sat down on the bed with a hand clasped over her sullen face, wishing she had never got involved with him, and that Mary had never got herself involved with Mario either.

We've both been stupid, she thought as she pulled on her clothes and stepped out of the room. On her way downstairs, she heard the sound of a car horn. 'God, who the hell is making that racket,' she gasped, as she dashed through to the lounge to peer out of the window.

Her jaw dropped. It was Jonah. He was sat in the Jaguar pressing his hand on the horn. She rushed to the front door and yanked it open to see the neighbours stood with solemn faces, pointing and peering at him. Her cheeks were scarlet as she ran towards the car. 'Have you lost your bloody mind?' she shouted above the noise.

Jonah leaned over and opened the door for her. 'Get in because I need to speak to you.'

'I've got nothing more to say to you unless you can tell me something about Mary.'

'Get in,' he repeated. 'I'll tell you what you want to know – but not here.'

She stood peering about to see the neighbours still looking affronted. 'I need my bag,' she said and ran back inside the house.

Hurrying back to the car, she kept her head lowered. Sinking low in the seat, she sat with her arms folded wondering what it was he had to say. He was silent and his expression sombre as he zoomed away.

'Where are we going?' she asked in a tight voice.

He didn't answer, but his chin jutted as he drove on. 'I think you ask too many questions.'

Mildred bit her lip. 'I've only asked one question. Anyway, I'm not happy about what you did last night. You should have told me about those horrible people, especially the old porn star with her ancient fanny. You know some weird folks.'

He sniggered. Then his expression changed to surly.

Her face blanched, as a sudden feeling of fear crept over her. She peered out of the car window and wondered if she could open the door, but then the speed he was going she would be killed. Her hand seemed move on its own accord. Her fingers reached for the door handle and tugged.

'What the hell are you doing you stupid bitch? Do you want to get us killed?' he snarled.

'I want to go back, I've changed my mind,' she squeaked, feeling her throat tighten with fear. 'You're taking me to somewhere dangerous. I can tell,' she whimpered.

'I'm not silly, I'm taking you to my home, so sit back and relax,' he assured, as he moved his hand towards her leg and winked his eye at her. He stroked her leg reassuringly, fondling slowly as she quivered beneath him. It was that feeling again: feeling sick and overwhelmed in equal measure. And she was actually beginning to enjoy it.

She gave a feeble smile back, but still felt uneasy.

Soon they arrived at his home. She gazed around in awe at the decadence, and decided that she would ignore the uneasy feeling. He grabbed her as soon as they got inside. She was pulled to a room where he tossed her down onto a bed. Before she realised what was happening, he produced handcuffs, pulled her arms wide and shackled her to the brass headboard. Her eyes were round with fear.

Chapter Forty

Opening her mouth to scream, Mildred squirmed as she kicked out with her feet. A hysterical bubble was rising in her throat as his eyes darkened with desire. He threw himself down onto the bed beside her.

Sliding his tongue over her lips, he then sunk his mouth into her neck. She felt the deep sucking on her skin and then more pain as he clenched his fingers onto her breasts. Moaning with her eyes shut and face contorted, she turned her head from side to side as he began pulling her legs wide apart.

She moaned with pain which only heightened his pleasure. He sunk his teeth into the flesh above her pubic bone. She screamed. 'Please stop, you're hurting me.' But this only made him wilder.

He bit her again, this time harder, making her bleed as she pleaded for him to stop. But he didn't. He rammed himself inside her and smirked as she screeched. The pain increased with every thrust.

He eventually made a sound like a wounded animal and rolled off. Then to her disbelief, he shifted and began pissing all over her. She lay with her face stretched, watching it trickle down her body and seep into the bedding. His lips were pulled back over his teeth while his eyes smouldered with twisted pleasure. He looked beyond evil as she raised her hate-filled eyes at him.

Grinning and smirking, he untied her hands, as he bent over and softly kissed her bite marks. 'I'm so sorry darling, have I hurt you? Please forgive me,' he said as he rubbed soothing fingers between her thighs and her belly. 'I'll fix us a drink while you get yourself cleaned up,' he whispered, kissing her hair. He got up, headed for the door and stepped out of the room.

White-faced, she lay there soaked with sweat, urine and blood. She slowly moved to a sitting position and sat staring at the reddened bite marks on her body and the red wheals around her wrists. He's more than kinky, he's a psychopath, she thought as she moved her shaking legs over the edge of the bed and staggered towards the bathroom.

Jonah popped his head around the door. 'I've fixed you a drink, so don't be long.'

She gave him a poisonous look. 'I don't want anything to drink I just want to go home. You're an animal.'

He threw his head back and scoffed. 'I'm not an animal, I just happen to be kinky that's all.'

'Did you hear me, I said I want to go home and if you won't let me I'll scream the place down,' she rasped.

He lifted his shoulders and laughed nastily as he tormented her. 'Try it pet, no-one will hear you, this place is soundproofed.'

She screeched at the top of her voice, but realised that he was serious as he stood smirking at her. There was no bluffing here.

'You are going to stay until I decide. I tell you when you leave,' he snarled. With malevolent eyes, he planted a soft kiss on her cheek.

'Why are you doing this to me? I haven't done anything to make you treat me like this,' she whimpered, as she looked down at the bite marks on her body and thighs.

'Oh stop making such a fuss and being a baby,' he snapped as he moved away once more.

She held her hands to her face wondering if other women liked it. Maybe if he didn't lose all control, then she would be able to get used to it. She didn't want to seem like she was a baby, but it was so painful and just plain weird.

She looked in the mirror to examine her neck. The love bite was huge and purple. She twisted her face as she waited for the bath to fill. 'How am I going to hide this?' she asked herself. It was easily the size of a tennis ball. 'Huh, he just got me in the car so he could abuse me and not tell me anything he knew about Mary. Well, I'll not fall for his twisted lies again, the rotten bastard that he is, leaving me in this plight.'

Jonah came back into the bathroom with a broad smile on his face. He leaned towards her, planting a soft kiss on her reddened neck. 'After your bath darling, I'm making you a lovely meal, so hurry up.'

As he went out of the door, she stood with her jaw dropped. He was composed and loving, nothing like the feral creature he changed into when she was in bed.

Sinking back into the bath, she lay with her eyes closed. Was he a psycho? Or was it just because he liked kinky sex? Her mind was a whirl, wondering how she could love and hate him in equal measure. Then she thought about Mary. Why did she have to be so stupid? But she was just as bad now. She remembered the gypsy's warning while she sunk further down into the warmth of the bath, and for the first time in what felt like forever, just let go of it all.

Chapter Forty-One

S adie was sat with a sullen face. When she arrived back home, she discovered that Mildred had gone out without leaving a note to say where she was. She had telephoned Roxy, Pandora and Crystal, but nobody had seen her.

There was only one place she could be: Jonah's house, the stupid little fool, she thought as she stubbed her cigarette out. She got up and went towards the long sideboard, picking the telephone up out of the cradle. 'Have you heard where Mildred is yet?'

Her hands were clenched as she listened to the person at the other end. 'Can you meet me at twelve in the Pineapple?'

Picking up her keys, she crossed to the window and peered out to see that the snow was melting with the pale winter sun. It had emerged between thick, threatening grey snow clouds and the roads were still a sheet of ice. She pulled on her boots, coat and scarf and placed the keys back on a hook inside a cupboard. Lifting the receiver up to her ear, she dialled for a taxi.

As she stepped into the Pineapple pub, Sadie went straight towards the bar and ordered herself a stiff drink. Her hand shook when she stepped back and made her way towards the large stone-built fireplace, where a comforting fire was burning in the grate. Next to the fireplace she noticed a dandy looking man, who tipped his hat at her as she lowered herself down into a seat. She gave a weak smile before tipping her head back and sipping her drink. Roxy entered seconds later. She wore a fur coat that draped over her shoulders, a skimpy dress and knee-length leather boots.

As she bent over to kiss Sadie, she glanced to the left of her and saw the dandy fellow sat grinning at her. 'Hilary, I haven't seen you for ages, how are you?'

The man removed his hat, swept his fingers through his sleek hair and rolled his eyes. 'Well, I have been better,' he replied, folding his arms to his chest.

'Why, what's been wrong?'

'I've lost a vast amount of money through someone I thought was my friend as well as my lover,' he spat, pursing his lips. Roxy and Sadie leant closer towards him as he displayed a feminine manner. 'I'll tell you all about it when I get a drink,' he said, flicking his hair, as he rose and sashayed towards the bar, haughtily admiring himself in the mirror.

Sadie turned to Roxy with a raised eyebrow and a smirk. 'He used to be a drag queen when he was younger,' whispered Roxy.

'Well, he looks like an old queen now,' said Sadie, with her hand at the side of her mouth. She watched him stood at the bar, then he turned around and walked back over with a drink in his hand.

'So, where was I before I went for this? Oh yes, that bloody Jonah. Well, when he first came to London years ago, he had nothing. He wasn't smart like he is now. It was me who got him to where he is. I spent a fortune on him, taking him to the best places and lending him thousands because he said he had the chance of a good business deal, and that I would get my money back.' His face darkened and his voice lowered. 'The business turned out to be a brothel and I didn't have a contract, which was stupid of me yes, but he seemed so sincere, he said he loved me and I felt the same.'

Roxy and Sadie were sat open-mouthed as he carried on, swaying his hands and rolling his eyes up as he lit a cigarette. 'So where did he come from then, before you met him?' asked Sadie, her wide eyes fixed on his.

'Newcastle area, some place near there –Ashburn or Ashwood. Something like that,' he replied casting a withering look at her.

'Ashwood. That's where my mother lived, she had a guesthouse,' Sadie said.

'Well, never mind that,' he said. 'This Jonah is a confident trickster, and a total bastard. He isn't even called Jonah, his real name is Kevin Jones.'

'What?' yelled Sadie. 'Did you just say Kevin Jones?'

Hillary gave her a long sour look. 'You're spoiling my thunder dearie. I'm on about what he did to me, never mind what the hell his bloody name is. I couldn't give a flying fuck what he's called.'

Sadie lips stiffened. 'Did he ever mention what his parents were called?'

'Oh for fucks sake, I know his mother is called Nora. But he hadn't contacted her for years over some bloody issue, he probably fleeced her too.'

Sadie shot to her feet and strode towards the bar. 'Three large glasses of wine,' she demanded.

A tapping noise from her finger nails onto the wooden bar made the barman's face crease. 'Are your nerves bad or something?' he asked.

'Just a tad,' she responded as he filled the glasses and placed them on a tray. She put the money into his outstretched hand and turned around to step back with the drinks. She placed the tray down onto the table. Hilary and Roxy reached for theirs. She sat down, lit up a cigarette and stared into space.

'What's the matter?' asked Roxy.

'Mildred's life is in danger,' she whimpered.

'How so?' asked Roxy, clasping her hand over her mouth.

'That's what I was going to tell you. She thinks Jonah or bloody Kevin, whatever he's called, will lead her to her friend Mary,' Sadie said.

'Yes, it's a right carry on,' said Roxy.

'I'm not bothered about her,' snapped Sadie. 'Mildred has gone off with that Jonah, and I don't know where he has taken her.'

Hilary shook his head, while Roxy laid her hand on her arm. 'I don't have anything to do with a lot of the girls on the bash, but I know he has one of his homes in Mayfair,' Roxy said.

'Right, will you show me where it is? I can't sit here and do nothing,' wailed Sadie with her thoughts growing darker by the minute, as she considered that Mildred may be about to face the same fate as Mary.

Chapter Forty-Two

Sadie and Roxy alighted from the taxi. Pushing a wedge of cash into the man's outstretched hand, she closed his door. Slipping and sliding with their shoulders hunched against the bitter cold, they stepped along the picturesque streets of Mayfair.

'This is it,' said Roxy as she guided Sadie towards the flamboyant and elaborate home. Pulling open the wrought iron gate, they stepped towards the darkened building. Sadie rattled on the door knocker. There was silence. They stepped back and walked around to the window, stuck their faces to it and peered through.

'There's no sign of him or his car anywhere. Now what?' Sadie asked while her eyes rounded in fear.

Roxy grabbed her arm, and dragged her away from the house. 'We'll head to Soho,' she suggested. 'I'll get a taxi's attention.' Opening her fur coat, she hitched up her dress. A diamante and satin black garter at the top of her thigh glittered under the hue from a street light as she kicked her leg out at an advancing taxi. The cab skidded to a stop and reversed back. Roxy winked her eye at Sadie. 'Works every time. Get in.'

'Soho, darling and make it quick,' she quipped as they climbed in.

The man grinned and gave them both a good look as they climbed inside. 'You must be keen going out on freezing night like this,' the man said as the taxi drove away.

Sadie took a photograph of Mildred out of her bag and passed it through to the front. 'We're looking for this girl. Have you seen her by any chance?'

The man dropped his head to take a quick glance. 'Sorry, no I haven't. These young girls come down here and don't realise how easy it is to get involved with unscrupulous people.'

'It's my daughter,' she replied as they passed through the city, which was unusually quiet due to the treacherous conditions.

The taxi stopped at an entrance to a darkened and narrow alley. They faced the rear of tall buildings on either side, where private dwellings and old shops loomed silent and deserted. A young girl passed them with her head hanging low, as though she was looking for something on the ground. She was sniffing and wiping her eyes, then became frantic as the Jaguar pulled up beside her.

The two women stepped back and huddled inside a doorway. They watched the car slow down then stop. The driver door flung open and Jonah strode towards the young girl, who waved her arms around with a pleading look on her face. He stood wagging his finger, before he got back in the car and zoomed off.

They waited until the coast was clear before they stepped towards the girl, and Roxy tapped her on the shoulder. The girl's face was sallow and tear-stained as she gasped and swung around to face them both.

'I'm sorry to stop you, but I need to know something,' said Sadie.

The girl raised her reddened eyes. 'What?' she asked.

'That man who stopped the car, do you know where he's gone?' She shook her head and moved away, but Sadie snatched hold of her arm. 'Is he your pimp?' she asked.

'That's none of your business,' she said, and dragged herself out of Sadie's grasp.

'He has taken my daughter somewhere and I fear her life is in danger, can you please help me? I need to know where he has properties as well as his nightclub.'

The girl pointed towards a black door further along the lane. 'Those are the bedsits he uses and he has other places that I've been to before, where he and his cronies have a good time, with the likes of us to entertain them, if you know what I mean. They are cruel, dangerous and sadistic.

I can't tell you anymore because I'm too scared. Ask someone else,' she said, as she ran away.

Sadie heaved a long sigh and stood with her arms folded, peering at Roxy. She lifted her shoulders and shrugged as another young girl advanced towards them.

She was wearing a short skirt, high boots and a long coat. Her features were taut and sullen as she stepped past them with her eyes lowered. Sadie reached out and clutched her arm. She swung around. 'What?' she spat, her expression hard. 'This is my patch ladies, so piss off.'

'We're not here on the bash, what we need is one of you to help us. Do you know someone called Jonah?'

The girl's eyes clouded as she quickly drew them away. 'Why do you ask that?' she asked.

'He's taken my daughter somewhere and I need to find her, I think her life may be in danger,' gushed Sadie.

The girl frowned. 'He's a sadistic bastard, but I don't think her life will be in danger.'

'They have history and not a good one,' rasped Sadie as she opened her bag and reached for her purse. 'I'll pay you a whole lot more than you'll make tonight hanging around this place if you can tell me where I can find him.'

The girl shook her head. 'I'm sorry, he could be anywhere.'

Sadie's shoulders slumped. 'Thanks anyway,' she muttered, as they turned away. 'There's only one other place, the Ruby,' she suggested.

The red lights from the nightclub flashed and shone, while bouncers stood shivering in the doorway, acting as the only sign of life. Sadie and Roxy stumbled through the doors and into the warmth of the indoor air. 'Thank goodness, I couldn't have stood another ten minutes in that freezing cold,' gasped Roxy, her cheeks the colour of crimson.

'Where were the bloody taxis?' asked Sadie as they dashed to the ladies toilets.

'I don't know, but I was bursting,' yelled Roxy as she rushed to the nearest toilet with Sadie close on her heels.

Stood in front of a long mirror, the two women applied lipstick and brushed a comb through their wind-swept hair. Stepping out of the toilets, Roxy went to the bar, while Sadie walked around, her eyes darting everywhere. There was so sign of Mildred. Climbing the spiral staircase, she gazed around at the couples sat in the subdued area.

She turned around and was stepping back down the stairs when she stopped in her tracks. Jonah was swaggering around, heading for his office. She hurried down the rest of the stairs and strode towards the office door. Her hand shook as she raised it to tap on his door with her knuckle. She took a deep breath, then placed her palms on the door and pushed it open. Jonah was sat at his desk. He looked up at her wide-eyed as she entered.

'What the ....?' he spluttered, as she stepped towards the desk.

'Where's Mildred?' she demanded.

He smirked and rubbed his finger and thumb against his chin. 'Don't you think she's old enough to come and go as she pleases, without you being her bodyguard?' he remarked.

'Yes, she is, but not when she has anything to do with you. You're a cunning, dangerous man and I don't trust you. If I can, I'll do anything to persuade her to have nothing to do with you mate,' she retorted, raising her forefinger towards him.

His pale eyes darkened as he raised them up at her. Placing his palms on his desk, his chair crashed back as he shot up and strode around the desk. In two strides he was stood looming over her, thrusting his face into hers. 'I wouldn't recommend you do that lady. If you have any sense, you'll not interfere between me and her.'

Sadie flinched and stepped back. 'So, where is she?' she asked in a weakened voice.

'I left her wrapped up in a lovely thick robe, sat watching the television with a glass of wine in her hand. She can leave any time she wants. So take yourself out of my office and don't come back in here, throwing your weight around – do I make myself clear?' he threatened.

She pouted her mouth and stood glowering, but swung around and marched out of the room, slamming the door behind her.

Sweeping her eyes around for Roxy as she stormed back, she spotted her watching couples dancing. Yanking a chair out, she sunk down with a thunderous expression. 'I need a drink,' she spat. Snatching up the glass, she tipped her head back and drained it in one gulp.

'Went well then?' asked Roxy as her brows shot up.

Sadie pursed her mouth and sat with her arms folded. 'Huh, he's a total bastard that Jonah. Tried to tell me Mildred's fine, but I don't believe him. I just wish she would get back home, maybe then I could relax.'

Chapter Forty-Three

Mildred breezed into the house. Her swarthy complexion lacked colour and her eyes were heavy with dark shadows underneath. 'Stop giving me that look,' she snapped at Sadie who looked her up and down. 'Jonah's apartment is out of this world,' she announced, as she pulled a chair up to the fireside and rested her feet on the hearth.

'Well, it would be, when you live off the backs of young girls and women like he does.' Mildred glanced at her mother under her lashes, before dropping her gaze. 'Do you still respect yourself then? Being wined and dined with the money that ponce grasps from those poor lasses.'

Mildred shrugged. 'Well that's their fault for being so stupid in the first place,' she argued.

Sadie gave her a sharp look. 'You'll end up in the same position,' she warned.

Mildred shuffled in her seat, while pulling at the polo neck on her jumper. She better not see the state of my neck she thought, seeing Sadie's eyes glistening with fury.

'I went looking for you and I found him at the Ruby. He's a nasty piece of work,' rasped Sadie.

'Why mother?' she shouted. 'You don't know him like I do, you're wrong.'

'I know him a lot better than you think,' Sadie said.

Mildred fixed her widened eyes at Sadie. 'What do you mean?' she asked in a small voice.

'I met someone whom he fleeced when he first came to live in London, and I'll tell you another thing for nothing: he is the same person who abused you when you lived in Ashwood.'

Mildred's jaw dropped. 'What? Don't be so stupid. There's no similarity between him and that Kevin bloody Jones.'

'The man said he had lived in Ashwood before coming to London. He was called Kevin Jones, but changed it to Jonah. If you don't believe me, I'll take you to the man who told me. He said they were lovers. He's even got photographs of them in bed together.'

Mildred shot up and stood with her hands covering her ears. Please God don't let there be any truth in this, I know he's twisted, but surely not that much, she thought as the contents of her stomach threatened to project outwards all over her mother.

Leaping to her feet, she ran blindly up the stairs with tears streaming down her face. Crashing into her bedroom, her face twisted as she removed the damp yellow and red stained bandages. The flesh was swollen and weeping from the bite marks as she pulled off her clothes. 'I need to get a doctor, these are infected, but I can't let anyone know what he's done,' she whispered to herself as she sunk down on her bed.

Her lips quivered as she wept uncontrollably.

A steady even light from the moon beamed through Mildred's bedroom window. She opened her glazed eyes to find that her hair was plastered to her brow and she was soaked in sweat. She eased up and rested her elbow against the pillows as she looked at the clock on her bedside table. Everything was a blur, the walls were spinning. She collapsed back white-faced when her bedroom door opened.

Sadie crossed the room and sat on the edge of her bed. 'I'm getting a doctor, you've been in here since you came back and it's evening time now,' she stated.

Mildred closed her eyes, wishing her mother would stop fussing and leave her alone. But Sadie leaned over her, wiping the beads of sweat from her face and neck with a small towel. 'I'm okay,' Mildred croaked. 'Just give me a moment.'

'Look at the state of your neck Mildred,' gasped Sadie jerking back.

'He's a bloody animal, no wonder you're ill.'

Mildred opened her eyes and groaned as she eased up once again. Moving her legs over to the side of the bed, she gripped the bedpost for support and stood up, but crumpled to the floor with her nightdress hitched up, too weak to move.

Sadie's eyebrows drew together see her thighs covered in bandages. Falling to her knees, she removed one of them and peered at the mess that lay beneath it. The skin was reddened, swollen and the imprint of a bite mark was visible. 'Mildred, what the hell has happened to you,' she whimpered. Lifting aside the rest of the bandages, she scrambled to her feet and dashed downstairs.

'I know it's late, but I need a doctor,' she uttered as she picked up the telephone.

Slamming the receiver down, she ran back upstairs, fell to her knees again and dragged Mildred to her feet to support her into bed. She lay still and lifeless as Sadie dashed from the room and went back downstairs. Picking her cigarettes up, she lit one. Puffing away and filling a glass full of whisky, she paced the floor or crossed to the window, where she stood peering out.

A beam of light appeared in the driveway and a car drew to halt. A tall, slim doctor stepped out of the car. Sadie dashed to the front entrance and pulled the door ajar. The young man stepped over the threshold with his bag in his hand. 'What is the problem?' he asked.

'My daughter has been bitten but not by bugs or a dog or anything like that.'

The doctor's eyelashes blinked sharply and his grey eyes met Sadie's with a solemn expression in them. He followed her to Mildred's bedroom. Mildred turned her head to look up as he stepped inside. 'Mother, I said I didn't need a doctor,' she groaned.

The young man took hold of her wrist, felt her pulse, and pushed a thermometer into her mouth. His face was grave when he shook the thermometer. 'Can I see your tummy please?'

'No, I'm alright,' she whimpered.

'You are a very sick young girl. Your temperature is dangerously high and I believe you have been bitten. If the infection spreads, you could get sepsis, which is a killer. So I'll ask you once again. Can I see your bites?'

Mildred bit her lip and pushed the bedding down. He hitched up her nightdress and pulled the bandage aside to see the swollen bite mark above her pubic bone. Then, as he began removing the others on her thighs, his eyebrows shot up. 'These look like human bites which are badly infected,' he said, shaking his head at Mildred. She shut her eyes and turned her head away.

In silence he took a meaningful glance at Sadie while he opened his case. He brought out a syringe, and sunk it into Mildred's thigh. 'I'm writing a prescription for antibiotics, can you see that these are taken please,' he said in a clipped voice. With a sigh, he clicked his bag shut. 'Whoever did this to you must be unhinged,' he remarked as he turned towards the bedroom door.

'I haven't seen this on anyone before,' the doctor said as he and Sadie walked down the staircase. 'This person is inhuman. If I was you, I would advise your daughter to stop seeing whoever it is,' he snapped, with a look of contempt on his face as he advanced to the front entrance.

'I will doctor, it's a disgrace that someone could do that,' she said. Pursing her mouth, she closed the door behind him. Turning around, she stormed back to the bedroom and slumped down onto Mildred's stool. 'Open your eyes. I know you're not asleep. Was it Jonah who has done this to you?'

Mildred eased herself up to glare at Sadie. 'It was a dog, and you shouldn't have gotten that doctor, I told you not to.'

'Don't insult my intelligence with your lies. It was Jonah. He won't be happy until he's killed you,' she hissed. 'He knows who you are. That you lied and had him put in jail for rape. You've got to put an end to this before he puts an end to you,' she warned, her eyes blazing.

A shrill sound filled the room as the telephone rang. Mildred's rigid face crumpled and she allowed the tears to flow. Her mind was in turmoil going over and over what Sadie had said. Jonah was really Kevin Jones? It can't be true, it must not be true. I don't want this to end, I love him too much. Maybe there was more than one Kevin Jones that lived in

Ashwood, she thought to herself. She didn't know all the people who lived there.

She sat up and punched the bedding with her fists. 'I'm having a bath and then I'm taking a taxi to see him, I've got to know the truth,' she said to herself, as she put her legs over the side of the bed and climbed out. Shuffling slowly along the floor, she went along the landing towards the bathroom and overheard Sadie talking on the phone.

'Well . . . if you must,' she sighed as she placed the telephone down.

Mildred carried on towards the bathroom when she heard footsteps advancing up the stairs. She turned her head around to see Sadie on her way with a glass in her hand. 'Here, get this drink down you, you've been drenched with sweat.'

Mildred swiped her hand across her face. 'I feel a bit better since that injection. I'm going in the bath and then I'm heading for Jonah's.'

'Oh no you're not, you're too ill,' Sadie shrilled.

'Well you shouldn't have said what you did. I'm finding out if it's true what that freak said – if he really is Kevin Jones.'

Sadie lunged towards her and grasped her shoulders. 'Please don't go because your life is in danger.'

Mildred swiped her hands off her and jerked back. Slouching into the bathroom, she slammed the door shut.

Chapter Forty-Four

Sadie pursed her lips and heaved a long sigh as she headed back downstairs. She glanced towards the front window to see Roxy's car advancing into the drive. She stepped out wearing a black velvet turban around her hair and her fur coat collar pulled up.

Flouncing into the passage, the strong heady aroma of Pagan perfume radiated from her. 'So, what's wrong with Mildred then?' she asked, her big eyes peering into Sadie's.

'Jonah has been biting her and they are badly infected,' she croaked.

'What?' she gasped. 'I've had some strange punters over the years, but if they bit me they would regret it,' she said, with her lip curled up in disgust.

'Can you get in touch with Hilary? I need him to speak to her and convince her that he's telling the truth about that bastard Jonah. She doesn't believe me, I can tell by her attitude.'

Roxy's face twisted. 'The only way I'll see him is if he comes into the Pineapple, I don't know where he lives.'

Sadie shot off the seat and began pacing the floor when the telephone rang. When she picked it up, she stood listening then glanced round at Roxy and stood in silence, before slamming the telephone down in the cradle.

'He's got some nerve, says he's coming to see Mildred. Like hell is he!' she rasped.

'What are you going to do?' asked Roxy.

'What can I do? She's eighteen. I can't slap her and ground her. She's in agony but says she's going to see him.'

'The more you tell her not too, the more she'll defy you, to prove you wrong,' Roxy said.

'I told her what I had found out and now I regret it. She wants to know the truth, which is going to put both our lives at risk. This all started with bloody Mary Kelly, I wish she had never come here.'

'Well she did, so we have to think of something to put a stop to this relationship.'

'What do you suggest?' asked Sadie, when she swung her head around.

Mildred was stood with her arms folded, her expression sour. She stepped inside the room. 'You'll do nothing of the sort to put a stop to my relationship with Jonah. I'll decide that for myself,' she shouted, glaring at her mother and Roxy. 'I'm ringing him and I'm leaving here.'

Sadie shot to her feet and grabbed her arm, stopping her in her tracks. Mildred looked over her shoulder with angry eyes. She snatched Sadie's hand away. With surprising strength, she shoved Sadie back. She fell, hitting her head on the onyx coffee table. She lay on the floor with blood seeping onto the carpet.

Roxy sunk to her knees beside her. The colour was fading from Sadie's face as she lay in a heap. Roxy turned her head up and glowered at Mildred. Her hands were clasped to her face when Sadie's eyes flickered.

'Mam, I didn't mean to hurt you,' she gasped as Sadie eased herself up and put a hand to the back of her head. Drawing her hand away, her eyes widened to see the blood. Raising sorrowful eyes up at Mildred, her face crumpled. Mildred's eyes were tear- filled.

'All this for that waster,' said Roxy. 'Mildred, are you really that desperate for a man? Your mother is worried sick for you.'

Mildred cast a pleading look. 'Jonah isn't a nasty man. He won't hurt me.'

'He's been biting you for God's sake; your face is the colour of chalk. Even the doctor was worried for your safety. What does it take for you to wake up and see him for the psychopath that he is?'

Mildred sighed heavily. She turned away and crossed towards the telephone. 'Jonah, come and pick me up in twenty minutes please,' she whispered.

Her hands gripped the stair-rail for support as she climbed up the stairs. As she walked into her bedroom, she dragged her clothes out of her wardrobe and drawers, with her mind recalling how many times she had packed her bags over the months. The day she was torn from the life she had known: the guesthouse, after her gran's death. Then, the wonderful day she left the asylum to live at Mary's hovel. The excitement she felt when she packed her cases to live in this lovely home. And now this, the nervousness she felt upon leaving it.

Breathing a huge sigh, she swept her eyes around her bedroom with a heavy heart. The void that once had existed between herself and Sadie was mended, but now she had to move on. Sadie would never accept Jonah and her love for him was too strong. She just couldn't control it.

As she glanced out of the window, she saw the car approaching. She quickly put her belongings in her case and snapped it shut. Pulling her wardrobe open, she stood gazing at the empty rail. With her coat over her arm and her case in her other hand, she stepped downstairs. She stood for long moments looking at Sadie. 'I'm going Mam, but I'll keep in touch,' she said in a tight voice as she took tentative steps towards Sadie.

She was sat with her lips pressed together and stiff-backed. Mildred leaned over and put her arms around Sadie's shoulders. But, with a surly look, she pulled her arms aside and shrugged her away. Roxy was sat in silence with eyes of ice. Mildred's chin quivered and she swung around. With her sorrowful eyes brimming, she headed towards the front door.

Jonah grinned like a Cheshire cat as he leaned over and opened the car door for her.

Chapter Forty-Five

'Why, the long face?' Jonah asked as she got into the car. 'Sadie is furious with me. She doesn't want me to stay with you after she discovered those bite marks.'

Jonah's eyebrows lowered. 'I'm sorry. I feel ashamed of my actions. I won't do that again. I don't know what happened to me,' he said in a contrite manner, while clasping hold of her hand.

'No, you won't. I've been ill with infection. If I didn't feel so much for you, I would never bother with you again. Even Roxy said she wouldn't put up with being treated that way, and she's had some weird characters over the years. Sadie and I had an argument and I knocked her over. I thought I had killed her. There was a lot of blood when she hit her head on the coffee table. She says I'm a fool for not believing what some man told her.'

'What man?'

'An old man called Hillary. He used to be a drag artist. He actually told her that you two had been in a relationship and even claimed you're not called Jonah, but you're actually some creep I knew years ago called Kevin Jones – as if,' she said with a look of distain on her face. 'He was an ugly fat slob with an acne covered face and he had stinking foul breath too. There's just no comparison,' she laughed when the car lurched forward.

Gasping, she held a hand to her chest, as she turned her head and peered at him with widened eyes. 'What happened there?'

'A burst car tyre on the road,' he lied, with a feral look on his face.

Mildred's eyes were shining with happiness as she stepped once more into Jonah's apartment. She felt the thick carpet beneath her toes as she gazed around at the decadent room. She slumped down and sunk into the sofa, feeling right at home. Jonah picked up her case and headed for the bedroom. When he returned, he sat next to her and began quizzing her about what Sadie had said.

'Don't take any notice of that man,' she soothed, but his face was contorted with anger.

'Where did she see this man?' he insisted.

She lifted her shoulders and said somewhere called the Pineapple. His eyes glazed over as he clenched and unclenched his fingers.

'I have some business to see to,' he suddenly remarked. 'There's plenty of food in here, if I'm delayed just help yourself.'

He picked up a briefcase, blew her a kiss and headed for the door.

She stood at the window and watched him. Jonah was stood beside his car. He swung around and gazed up at her. She waved her hand and smiled. His eyes narrowed to slits as he yanked his car door open. Sliding inside, the door shut and he zoomed away.

Turning away from the window with her brow furrowed, Mildred stepped back. What's wrong with him? She pondered as she stepped along the passage, turning handles to discover many of the doors were locked.

This must be the one she concluded when she turned the handle and the door opened. The room was minimal: one huge wardrobe on one wall and along another, drawers had been fitted. In the middle was a king-size bed with bedside tables on either side. Matching lamps had been placed on top.

She put her clothes inside the wardrobe and stepped towards the drawers. Pulling at the handles, she discovered that some of those were also locked. She tried each one, until a number of drawers slid open. She put her clothes inside. Then pulling out another drawer, she gazed at Jonah's clothes that were folded neatly inside.

She was about to close it, when she caught sight of a tiny key just visible beneath his jumpers. She picked it out and walked around, peering here and there, until she sunk to her hunkers and saw it. She gazed beneath the bed and pulled out a large black jewellery box. With shaking hands, she unlocked the box and gazed at a wallet. Biting her bottom lip, she pulled it out. Then, probing her fingers inside as she opened the wallet, she saw a brown Ministry of Pensions and National Insurance card. On the card was written: Kevin Jones and a national insurance number. Seeing photographs in another compartment, she took them out and peered at them. Smiling back at her was Nora Jones – Kevin Jones's mother.

She held a hand to her heaving chest as her mouth dropped open, before she slung it to the floor as though it had burned her fingers. With her face contorted, she peered at the photograph of him as the uncouth youth she once knew: spotty faced, sly-eyed; heaving fat belly. Her stomach rose, so she stumbled to the bathroom where she emptied its contents. Wiping her mouth, she turned on the tap and sunk her hands into the water to splash her face. The buzzing in her ears got louder and blackness threatened to make her lose consciousness. She clasped hold of the sink, lowered herself on to the toilet and sunk her head between her legs.

Desperate to pull herself together before he got back and saw the card and photographs on the floor, she hauled herself up and staggered through to the bedroom, where she knelt down and put everything back inside the wallet. Her hand shook as she tucked it where it had been. Hauling her clothes back out of the wardrobe and drawers, she was trembling as she slung them onto the bed, when she heard footsteps approaching.

'Fuck, he's back,' she whispered, swiping her hand across her hot face. Snatching up the garments, she slung them into the case, and with heel of her shoe, she kicked it underneath the bed. Holding her breath, she watched the door slowly open. Kevin walked into the bedroom. With her heart thudding, she stood shuffling from one foot to the other.

'You seem on edge,' he quipped as he stepped towards her. He pulled her close, covering her mouth with his.

'I'm desperate for the loo,' she gasped. 'I'm forever putting off,' she said, as she pulled herself out of his arms. Pulling a face and curling her lips, she strode towards the bathroom, where she closed and locked the door. Peering at her ashen and taut face in the mirror, her mind raced. I've got to think of some excuse to get out, I don't care about my clothes, she thought, turning around to pace back and forth, but with no solution whatsoever.

A loud tapping on the door made her gasp and stop in her tracks. She pulled the lock aside and dragged the door open. Kevin was stood there wearing a puzzled expression. 'What's the matter? You were alright when I left.'

'I've got a lot on my mind,' she said as she stepped past him.

'He looked at her with hooded eyes, his face sullen. 'Like what?'

'I just wished I hadn't fallen out with Sadie,' she replied in a flat tone.

'Oh lighten up for God's sake, I thought you were excited about living here?' he asked, as he crossed the room. Opening the drinks cabinet, he poured whisky into two tumblers and held one out to Mildred.

'I don't want one, I'm going out.'

'Out where?' he asked.

'Just out that's all,' she replied in a clipped voice.

'You don't go anywhere without me,' he snapped.

'What? You mean I have to stay in here until you say I can go out, and if I do, I can only with you?' she asked.

'Correct.'

'Well I don't think so Jonah. I'm not a bloody child, I can come and go when I want,' she said, as she bent down to pick up her handbag.

Kevin lurched towards her and as she stood up, he stuck out his splayed hand and grabbed her by the throat. She lifted her arm and stuck her long hard nails into his fingers. 'My women do as they are told, you should know that,' he hissed.

Her eyes were blazing and bulging as he released her and peered at his reddened fingers.

'Well this one doesn't. You should know that too mate,' she replied. 'I'm not one of your bash heads. I'm your girlfriend. You promised there would be no physical violence and you've started already, you just can't help yourself. Everybody has to do what you want, when you want.'

He stood with his head on one side and smirked at her. 'You know me so well,' he sniggered as he held her in a vice like grip, pulling her down to the sofa. With his full weight pinning her down, he hauled her dress up and tore at her knickers, ripping them off.

She released her arm, moving her fingers out towards the coffee table, observing a brass ornament. Grabbing the ornament, she smashed it into his head. His eyes widened then rolled back. He slid to the floor with the colour fading from his face. Blood seeped from beneath his head.

She leaped up, ran to the bedroom and sunk to her knees. Pulling out her case, she eased up and peered through the gap in the door. He still lay sprawled on the floor, his eyes closed.

Holding her breath, she crept past him, when his hand shot out. In a vice like grip, his fingers gripped around her ankle. 'You won't get away from me bitch,' he snarled, but his fingers loosened as his eyes rolled back once again.

She ran out of the room and out of the front door. Her eyes swept around. 'Why are there no telephone boxes round here?' she groaned as she sprinted along.

Turning around a corner with her chest heaving, she saw a police car parked at the roadside. Glancing once more, her tense face relaxed. Two policemen were walking out from the entrance of a police station.

A young officer was sat behind his desk. He looked her up and down as she stepped towards him, collapsing over his desk with snot running down her nose. 'You've got to help me, my life is in danger,' she cried.

Chapter Forty-Six

Mildred sat peering around at the magnolia painted walls in the basic room, tapping her fingers on the scarred table, when the door opened. A skinny man with black slicked-back hair, sharp shrewd eyes and a thin black moustache stepped inside. He slumped down on the seat opposite, leant his elbows on the desk, cupped his chin in his hands and gazed at her in silence. She sat on the edge of her seat biting her lip, when he held his hand out, thrust it into hers and shook it.

'I'm detective inspector Ollie Smith. I believe you have a complaint against a Kevin Jones whom you say calls himself Jonah.'

'Yes, that's correct.'

'And, you're saying this man is a dangerous psychopath. Explain what makes him a psychopath,' he said.

'He's cruel. He tied me up and bit me all over. The doctor had to give me antibiotics for the infection. Look at the state of my thighs.' She lifted her clothes up.

The man's eyebrows drew together. 'Well, it's a nasty and odd thing to do, but this would hardly certify him as a psychopath. Is there anything else?' he asked

'He has brothels and beats the women if they don't make enough money, plus he knows the whereabouts of the prostitute Mary Kelly,' she gushed. 'But he won't say where she is.'

'He does?' he asked, his brows meeting once more.

'Yes, yes,' She gushed.

'So, if this cruel man is dangerous, cunning and a psycho, why are you with him?'

'Because I thought he would lead me to her. She was working for him when she disappeared,' Mildred said.

'Well it hasn't, and now you say your life is in danger. I still don't really see how? He's obviously twisted, but without any evidence, I can't arrest the man. Go home, and keep away from twisted creeps.'

Mildred shot to her feet. 'I can't just go home. I didn't realise I had met him in my past. He doesn't want me to know who he really is. He started interfering with me from the age of four and then as we got older, he would force me down and try to have sex with me.'

The man scratched his thinning hair. 'So he raped you?'

Mildred dropped her eyes. 'No. He didn't, but I hated him so much that I accused him of that. This why my life is in danger because of what I did, I never thought I would see him again.'

The man leaned back in the chair, raised an eyebrow and smirked. 'Sounds like you've been reading too many novels,' he said.

'So you're not taking this seriously?' she asked.

'Well do you really think I would?'

'That's great. I come to you for help and all you do is mock me,' she sniffed. 'I know it's bizarre what I've told you, but I need police protection,' she said, as she thumped her fist on the desk. 'This all started because I thought if I got close to him I would find out where my friend Mary Kelly was. She worked for him, and then disappeared and now there's rumours she's been beaten up and in hospital. Is this true? You should know that.'

'I can't make any comment about Mary Kelly,' he said in a flat tone.

'So are you giving me protection or not?' she demanded.

'I'll have to investigate this matter before I can make any decision.'

Mildred scowled at him. 'Thanks for nothing,' she shouted as she stormed out of the room.

Striding towards the main doors her chin quivered. She wondered if Jonah had come around or if he was still unconscious. If he had recovered, he would find her. He was like a cockroach, creeping everywhere. There was only one solution. It was rather drastic, but necessary. She would have to disguise herself. She would have to disguise herself for the rest of her days.

She stopped in her tracks, pressed herself against the wall and ignored the puzzled glances from the women opposite in the admin office. Sticking her head out of the door, she swept her eyes around looking for a hairdressing shop. Her shoulders slumped. But when she turned her head again, she saw the typists were sat with their head lowered, clattering away behind a glass partition.

The partition was open and an umbrella lay on the counter. She crossed towards the counter, stuck her arm out and snatched the umbrella. Running down the street, hidden beneath the brolly, she retraced the steps that she had taken when she had found the police station. She carried on, turned down the darkened alley, stepped around the corner and beamed to see a row of shops.

Looking to and fro, she ran over the road and pulled open the hairdressers door. An old woman was sat in a chair while a young girl wearing a jumper and mini skirt was tweaking and combing her hair. The young girl turned her head to acknowledge Mildred.

'Do you happen to sell wigs?' she enquired.

'Yes, we have quite a selection she replied. 'I'll be with you shortly.'

The old woman stood up and inclined her head at Mildred as she shuffled towards the counter. She paid, collected her coat and hat, and then stepped slowly towards the door. The girl stepped out from behind the counter and crossed towards a cupboard. She pulled out a large box and placed it on the desk. Mildred pulled out two blonde wigs. One was short and spiked while the other was long and flowing.

'I hope you don't mind, but if you're trying the wigs on, can I suggest that I trim your hair first,' suggested the girl.

Mildred twisted her face at first, but then Jonah's feral face entered her head. She smiled and sat down in the chair. Corkscrew curls lay scattered on the ground as she stood up, pulled on the wig and stood in front of a gilt mirror beaming. Pulling out a scarf from her bag, she swept it around the wig. Placing cash into the girl's hand, she left the shop.

The clouds had cleared, the sky was blue and the sun was shining. Its glint reflected in the spike of Mildred's upturned umbrella. One of her hands clutched her case while the other had a tight grip of the sloped brolly, hoping it concealed her face enough as she sprinted towards a taxi rank.

Sweeping her eyes around as she stepped from the cab, her set face relaxed. She gave the man his fare, picked up her case and hurried down the path. Pushing the door open, she strode through the house and stepped inside the lounge with a wide grin on her face. Sadie was sat on the sofa. She darted to her feet and flew at her. 'What the hell?' Sadie screamed.

'It's me, Mildred,' she said.

'What are you doing looking like that?'

'Never mind, I'll explain everything in a while. I need to get this wig off, it makes my head itchy.'

'This came for you,' Sadie said, as she threw it at her.

Mildred frowned as she opened up the envelope, then her hand flew to her mouth and her eyes widened. 'It's from Sam, Mary's brother.'

'So, what does he have to say for himself then?' she snapped.

'He's in London and he says Mary has been transferred to the Old London hospital. I don't understand what's been happening.'

Sadie glared at her. 'So what do you intend on doing?'

'I'm going to meet him. Oh I can't wait, this is marvellous news,' Mildred said. Sadie threw her hands in the air.

'What's been going on and why the wig?' asked Sadie while Mildred sat beside the fireplace, rubbing her cold feet before dropping her head into her hands.

'Mother, I'm in big trouble. I found his wallet and it confirmed everything you said was true. I felt sick to the stomach and scared for my life. Jonah came back and I hit him with an ornament. He was lying unconscious when I ran out.'

'You left him unconscious. He could be dead. Then, where will you be eh?' ranted Sadie. 'If not, then he knows where you live and he'll not leave it there. God, he could set this place on fire knowing what a loose cannon he is.'

'That's why I went to the police to ask for protection and told them all about him. They were useless. They think I'm some neurotic young girl who has lost her way.'

Sadie's mouth pursed. 'Well, they're not far wrong in that respect. If you had listened and took heed in the first place then you wouldn't be in this situation.'

Mildred scowled. 'I know. Don't rub it in.'

'So, do you intend to spend the rest of your life looking like a punk rock chick?'

Mildred sprung to her feet. 'I'm hoping the police look into his past and everything else that I've told them, about the brothels and everything else,' Mildred said. 'Since getting this letter, everything has changed. I'll ring the police station and let them know where I'm staying when I get booked into a hotel, that's if they can be bothered.'

'What about me?' asked Sadie. 'I'll not sleep in my bed tonight with this carry on,' she snorted. 'In fact, I feel like packing my things and moving away until he's locked up.'

The shrill sound of the telephone made Sadie gasp.

Mildred got up and crossed the room. She picked the telephone up and listened. 'Yes. I'm fine,' she gasped. 'Okay, I'll watch my back.'

She slammed the receiver down and turned around to face Sadie with the colour fading from her face. 'I need to get in touch with Polly.'

Sadie threw her arms in the air. 'Why? What did Roxy say?'

'Never mind that, can you give me a lift into London.'

'You've just gotten back,' shrieked Sadie.

'I know,' replied Mildred as she began pacing the floor. 'But, after that call, I've got to find out where that big bastard is,' she replied as she crossed to the phone, picked it up, dialled a number and stood biting her lip.

The phone was slammed back down. 'No bloody answer,' she moaned.

Picking up her case, she headed inside the hotel entrance which was all fancy, decorated with thick carpets, crystal chandeliers and grey and deep-blue, soft furnishings. Fine voile curtains were draped at the windows, which all added to the intimate atmosphere. She took out some money from her purse, paid the young girl on reception, collected the key and then made her way to the room.

Once her belongings were put away, she took the piece of paper with Polly's telephone number on it out of her bag and went back down to reception.

'Hi it's me, Mildred. Have you got any idea where Jonah is?' she asked, keeping her voice low, while sweeping her eyes around the reception.

Her shoulders slumped before her tone brightened. 'You have that's wonderful. But you can just tell me now, instead of meeting me.' Her face was set as she listened. 'Okay, I didn't realise someone was listening. I'm staying at the Tatler. It's room twenty-four.'

She replaced the receiver.

Holding her breath, she glanced around once more and then went back to her room. The thoughts of Jonah lying on the floor with blood seeping from his head loomed as she clicked open her case. Slumping down onto the bed, she sat with her chin in her hands.

Why was she always getting into one scrape after the other? 'You are a stupid headstrong girl, Mildred McDine,' she said while putting her clothes in the drawers and wardrobe. Taking Sam's letter out of her bag, she sat on the bed and read it before checking the time on her watch. 'Come on Polly, you've had time to get here,' she said crossing to the window.

A light tap on the door gave her stomach an uncomfortable lurch. Clenching her hands and bracing her shoulders, she gripped the door knob. 'Who is it?'

Hearing the high pitched voice answer, she unlocked the door, turned the handle and stepped back to let Polly enter. The woman stood with a frown on her face. 'It's me Mildred. I'm that terrified he's going to maim me or even worse kill me. I've had to go to this bloody extent.'

The woman's lips pressed together as Mildred explained what she had found out about Jonah and didn't know if he was still alive.

'Do you know anything?' she asked.

Polly stood mute and shook her head.

'I've got enough problems of my own, but I have to find out where Mary's baby is, thanks for this you're a diamond,' she said, clasping the paper the woman had given her.

The woman shrugged her shoulders. 'When you rang I had just been giving one of Jonah's cronies a good whipping and he was slavering all over me. Yuk, I wish I could get out of this existence.'

Mildred gave her a sympathetic look. 'I wish you could too,' she replied.

'I can't stay, so good luck finding the child,' she said as she turned and pulled open the door.

As Mildred walked amongst the familiar markets and shops, her mind went back to two years ago, when she and Mary were two excited young and innocent girls. They had plans, both free spirits. Now she was up to her neck, having to look over her shoulder, and her friend was in a critical condition, lying in Intensive Care.

She walked on until she came across the hospital. She stepped inside the entrance and headed for Intensive Care. A sour-faced receptionist faced her on her arrival at the ward. 'Can I help you?' she asked in a clipped voice.

She gave her a cool look. 'I hope so, I believe Mary Kelly is here.'

'Are you a relative?' she asked with a look of contempt on her face.

'Yes, I'm her sister.'

'Well it's taken you long enough to visit her, she's been at death's door. But, what can you expect, leading the life that she was,' she said.

Mildred leaned over the desk and thrust her face into the woman's. 'Don't you dare judge her, you stuck up bitch. You know nothing about her. It's alright for you in your perfect life,' she snarled.

The woman's face blanched as she jerked back. 'You need to wear this,' she replied in a cold manner, as she handed her plastic clothing.

Mildred snatched them out of her hand and tilted her chin as she pulled on the protective clothing. With her heart hammering in her chest, she stepped inside the doorway and swept her eyes around. It was silent, with a sombre atmosphere. A nurse was approaching her with a bed pan in her hand.

'Can you tell me which bed Mary Kelly is in please?' she asked.

The nurse pointed to where a curtain was drawn around a bed.

Her legs began to shake as she stepped towards it. Biting her lip, she pulled the curtain aside. A policeman was sat on a chair; he turned his face to look at her. Sam was sat next to Mary's bed with a solemn look on his face. He looked pale pinched and drawn. He was still stocky with a foreign look about him.

Mildred drew her gaze away and took a tentative step towards where Mary lay. She was attached to wires and her mouth and nose covered with an instrument to help her breathe. She was heavily sedated and embalmed in plaster. As she held her limp hand, the only thing Mildred recognised was the small rose that she had tattooed on her wrist.

Sam's thick eyebrows lowered as he looked at Mildred with a quizzical expression in his eyes.

'It's me Sam – Mildred . . . you remember, Millie McDine which some people call me. I'll explain everything later,' she said while giving him a swift shrewd look.

He switched his eyes towards the policeman then, nodded in response.

A bubble of hysteria erupted from Mildred. She burst into gulping sobs as she gazed at the tiny figure in the bed.

'I'm taking her for some fresh air,' said Sam to the policeman. He raised his hand and inclined his head.

Hooking his arm around Mildred's shoulder, he supported her out of the ward and towards the hospital exit. Her eyes were bloodshot as she stood trying to compose herself in the hospital grounds. They strolled further along the thoroughfare until they saw a public house. The pub was smoky and noisy.

Sam stepped towards the bar. Mildred took the nearest seat. She gazed underneath her eyelashes and heaved a deep sigh of relief. There was no sign of Jonah or any of his cronies.

Sam returned and collapsed into the seat. She picked up her drink. 'I'll tell you what happened when she came to London, it all started so well, until she took that dancing job. She was besotted with Mario and he exploited her,' Mildred said.

CHAPTER FORTY-SIX

Sam ran his fingers through his hair. 'So what happened?'

'She concocted a plan to drug him, just enough to escape, but he had a bad reaction and was left brain damaged. His father is a gangster, he took retribution. Someone is keeping her child from her too.'

'Yes. I've just been told today. When I was in Germany someone said it was on the news about Mary and Mario. So I came back to England and went to the police, but they don't seem to know about a child. Why is that?'

'I think someone is keeping him and there's something fishy going on,' Mildred said.

They both sat quiet, lost in their own thoughts. Mildred gazed at Sam and felt sorry for him. He had dark circles under his eyes and bags down to his cheeks. 'What about your mother? Did you ever get speaking again after she went off with that lodger?' she asked.

He rolled his eyes up. 'Yes, she's my mother after all. I expect you think I'm stupid. Especially after she put that shite first, instead of Mary, when she found out he was the father. She's coming here tomorrow.'

'Really, that's a surprise. She must have some maternal feeling somewhere, eh?'

'I'm a Sergeant Major now Mildred,' he announced with pride on his tense face. 'I bet you never thought that possible after my dysfunctional lifestyle, did you?'

'You were always a good lad. Congratulations Sam. So, is there a lady friend anywhere then?'

'No, I've just concentrated on my career,' he answered proudly before his face darkened. He watched her scared eyes keep sweeping around the pub or glancing over her shoulder. 'I think you need to make a new start, somewhere else, away from all this trouble,' he said.

'I won't go anywhere until I see Mary come out of the coma. We weren't speaking when this happened. I warned her about that Mario, but she changed so much. You know how mousey she was? Well, she began wearing skimpy clothes and her attitude was horrible. I met someone who supplied her with the drugs; he was a low-life. In fact most of them are. That man I was seeing was lovely at first, but then he began tying me up and biting me. I think that's their game. They sweeten you up to high heaven and then send you plummeting to hell.'

'What sort of psycho would do that?' he asked, as his hands shot to his face.

'I told the doctor it was a dog, but he knew.'

'So where is this git then?' Sam asked.

'That's the trouble. He's not been seen, and I'm scared. I lashed out at him with an ornament the last time I saw him, just as he was about to force himself on me. Now I'm a dead girl walking. That's why I've had to disguise myself.'

'He needs sorting.' he growled under hooded eyes.

'He's too dangerous. I was flattered when he began seeing me, then he began acting like a complete psycho,' she said.

'How's that?' Sam asked.

'Because I didn't realise he was the lad I got imprisoned for rape. Can you remember, I told you all about it years ago? It seems he was biding his time. It must have pleased him to see me in pain, he was so twisted. I'm shitting myself, but I've got to get to the bottom of where this baby is for Mary, if it's the last thing I do.'

Sam leaned towards her with narrowed eyes. 'Have you not thought that it *might be* the last bloody thing you do?'

Mildred cast him a hardened look as she sat chewing her thumbnail.

Chapter Forty-Seven

As she stepped out of the taxi at the address Polly gave her, Mildred cast her eyes around the block of tenements. Old broken down cars littered the place and a sulky teenage girl sat puffing on a cigarette. She hurried past the teenage girl and approached a door that was covered in dirt with crude words scribbled on it.

A baby's howl rang through the air as she lifted her hand to knock on the door. It opened an inch and a diminutive woman with small, sharp eyes peered through it. 'What do you want?'

Mildred took a step back and bit her bottom lip. 'Are you a friend of Mary Kelly's?'

'I am and who's asking?' she spat.

'I'm a friend of hers, Mildred McDine. Do you have Mary's baby?'

The woman's small eyes widened. 'You've come to the wrong house,' she said.

'No. This is the right house and that's Mary's child I can hear. Why have you got him?'

'Just go away and leave me alone,' she hissed as she pushed the door to close it.

Mildred jammed her foot between the door and the frame before it could close. 'You're Jean aren't you?' she asked. The woman nodded. 'I'm an old friend of hers. I haven't come here to cause any trouble; I just needed to know where her child was. If social services knew they would step in and take the child.'

'Well they don't and they won't because he's fine here with me,' Jean said.

The door was yanked open all the way and a man with thick, greasy hair and whiskers on his chin was stood glowering at Mildred. 'What do you want?' he slurred. Then before she could reply, he turned to glare at Jean. 'That fucking baby needs feeding and you're standing out here like the useless bitch you are. Get in here now and sort him out. The sooner that kid goes the better.'

'I can take it,' suggested Mildred.

He opened his mouth wide and sniggered, but Jean's narrowed face screwed up in venom at him as he lunged towards Mildred. 'Take the little bleeder away. I've had enough of his squawking.'

She pushed past Jeans hate-filled face, held her breath and wrinkling her nose, she stepped inside the room and headed towards the pram where she lowered her head to look at Dean. His pram was scuffed and a dirty blanket covered him.

She bent further and lifted him out of the pram as Jean walked into the room behind her. Lifting her fist, she slammed it into Mildred's back, causing her to gasp and stumble. Jean snatched him out of her arms and pointed a dirty finger at her. 'Get the fuck out of my house lady.'

Mildred thrust her face into Jeans. 'If I hadn't been holding that bairn I would have floored you, you little poisonous dwarf,' she hissed through her teeth.

The man hauled himself out of his seat. 'If you think I'm fucking putting up with that till Mary is better you can think again,' he mumbled as he shrugged himself into his jacket. 'You don't do anything for nothing either, so why are you so keen to keep it? You can see this lass wants it, so it better not be here when I get back,' he warned as he stormed out of the door.

Jeans' sly eyes were panic stricken as she held the baby tightly to herself. 'I'm not giving him up, I love him and there's nothing going on, I'm doing it out of the goodness of my heart.'

Mildred's face was set. 'Goodness of your heart? Don't make me laugh. I've got your cards marked and I'll be back – this isn't finished.

I don't believe what you say, that you love that child, and I'm going to make it my business to get him off you.'

Jeans small eyes seem to disappear into her cheeks. 'Oh you are? What the fuck has it got to do with you that I'm looking after him?'

'Well I can tell your man doesn't want the baby here,' Mildred said.

Jean snorted. 'I couldn't give a fuck what he thinks. Mary always said that if anything happened I would have him. I was there when these men came and took her away. She handed him to me and asked me to look after him.'

Mildred jerked back. 'What did they look like?'

'Thugs. The usual: broad-shouldered and surly. So don't look down your nose at me, I did her a favour when no one else would.'

Mildred gazed at her with a steely look. 'Well, her brother is here now and he wants to see the child. Her mother is coming from Newcastle too. So I'm going to the telephone box and I'm going to tell him where you live and get this sorted.'

Jeans eyes widened in fear. 'He stays with me and that's final,' she shouted, clashing the door. Mildred swung around and as she stepped through the gate, she saw Jean's husband further up the street, walking back towards his home.

Curious, her eyebrows lowered. She glanced around to see no one, so stepped back and crouched behind an old car. Jean came out of the back door and headed for the washhouse. What is she up to? Mildred thought as she watched Jean step back out with a luggage case in each hand.

'What are you doing with those?' her husband shouted as he walked back into the yard.

Jean stopped in her tracks and her jaw dropped. 'Why are you back already?'

'I forgot my wallet, but what are the cases for?' he asked again as he advanced towards her.

'I'm leaving,' she rasped. 'I've had enough of all this, so don't try to stop me. '

Turning her back, she made for the house. Mildred moved away from the car and crept towards the back gate. She saw him lurch towards her and grab a fistful of her hair. Jean was screeching as he shoved her into the house.

Mildred crept up to the window and peered through. Jean was waving her hand wildly, jabbing scissors at her husband. Mildred stood transfixed, seeing them pierce the side of his neck. Blood oozed through the hand he held to his neck, his legs buckled and he fell heavily to his knees. She stood with her hand clasped to her face watching Jean as she collected spittle in her mouth. Then she leant over him and spat the lot into his blood-streaked face.

Mildred jerked back from the window and crouching low, she scurried out of the yard and ran along the road towards the red telephone box. With a trembling hand, she pushed money into the box. Hearing a dialling tone, she telephoned Sam to tell him what she had seen. 'Get here quick, she's stabbed her husband and I think she's going off with Dean. Hurry,' she squeaked, her throat threatening to close.

Placing the telephone down, she stepped out of the kiosk and began pacing back and forth, swiping a hand across her face.

People passed by her as she waited. Sighing with relief, she saw a black cab approaching. The door was flung open and Sam stepped out with a stern tense expression across his face.

'Hurry, we must get in there before she gets away,' gushed Mildred, grasping his arm.

They raced towards the house. Everything looked the same as it always would, apart from now the back door was ajar. They turned to stare at one another, then Sam pushed the door further. 'Hello,' he called. There was no answer.

'She's gone,' wailed Mildred as they stepped inside.

They crept further into the house and stood transfixed as they saw it. The man lay on the floor, his face the colour of chalk. Around him lay congealed lumps of blood; the walls were spattered in the red stuff. Mildred twisted her face, covering her nose with her hand. The smell was nauseating. Sam's face blanched and his eyes rounded in shock. They moved in slow motion, as though in a trance, as they went from room to room to see the place bare.

Tiptoeing past the body, they stepped into the yard. Sam's hand shook as he swept his fingers through his hair. 'What are we going to do?' he asked as he took out a cigarette, lit it and sucked deeply.

'I can't tell the police what I witnessed. It'll be on the news and in the papers and Jonah will see my name, I can't risk that.'

'Well we can't just leave the poor man lying here. I'll ring them and not leave my name,' suggested Sam, with his face hard and set. 'And then what about that cunning Jean? She's gone off with the baby. Why is life such a bitch?' he snarled as he punched the door and left a gaping hole.

Chapter Forty-Eight

Mildred felt so sorry for Sam, he was beside himself with rage. His handsome face would be dark and the more he drank, he became manic, unable to cope with the fire burning in him He would break down crying to see his little sister so maimed for life. He returned to Germany before Mary recovered from her injuries. It was a long battle.

By this time, Mildred had reached twenty-one and was due her inheritance. She returned to the North East and had seen her grandmother's solicitor who was delighted to tell her she was an affluent young woman now and could do anything she wanted, as she was very comfortable from the sale of the guesthouse and investments. The only thorn in her side was Mary. She would either be silent and withdrawn, or would begin weeping and wailing.

'Mary, I can't take another day of your mood swings. So I'm doing something about it. I'm hiring a private detective. I'll find that bairn if it's the last thing I do.'

Mary stopped her weeping and looked aghast. 'Really?' she asked.

'I'll see to it, just leave it with me.' Mildred took out the telephone book and peered through it. 'Just sit back and relax. Once I get a bigger property lined up and the nursery opened, it'll be bedlam, so I need to do it now,' she said as she prodded her forefinger on an advert. 'Got one here, I shouldn't be long.' She slung on her jacket, picked up her car keys and hurried towards her sparkling new white mini that was stood in the drive.

Mildred stepped into a stuffy and cluttered room. A portly woman with dark hair that was bluntly cut and square was stood with her back to her, gazing out of the window. She wore a twin set and a pair of slacks. She swung around and smiled broadly, thrusting her hand out to shake Mildred's. 'I'm Nancy Bell. What can I do for you?' Mildred opened her mouth to speak when she butted in. 'Don't look so surprised. It's not common for a woman to do this job, but I'm no push over.'

Mildred grinned, she liked her forthright attitude. She reminded her of her grandmother. 'I want you to investigate the disappearance of a child that was abducted a few years ago. I've heard rumours that he was taken to Costa del Sol in Spain,' she said.

'I know where Costa del Sol is,' she said, casting a sour look.

'You'll want names and descriptions. I've written them in this folder,' she said handing her the document. 'Would this be too much to ask?'

'Rubbish,' she barked. 'There's never been a case that I haven't solved. Leave all the information with me and I'll get back to you when I've done some digging.'

'When you do find out something, I want to be there to see they get their just deserts. My friend's body and mind will never be the same again. I've a score to settle with the woman who took him.'

The woman's bushy eyebrows shot up and her lips twitched, as she watched Mildred push her chair back and rise to her feet. 'You'll need my telephone number,' Nancy said, as she leaned over her notepad. She wrote down her telephone number and sat back peering up at her.

'Thanks so much,' said Mildred as she crossed towards the door. Turning around, she asked, 'When will you be going there?'

'When I get a flight booked. I'll be leaving today.'

'Wow, you work fast,' quipped Mildred, smiling broadly.

'Don't be patronising. It's what I do, doll-face,'

Stood outside, Mildred gazed around the shops and buildings. Seeing an estate agent's window over the other side of the road, she crossed over to peer at it. A grey, stone building caught her eye. She read the blurb underneath the photograph to discover that it was in need of repair. Ivy had crept all over the front of the building and the garden was a wilderness. It would need a lot of work done to it, but at least it would keep her busy while she waited to hear from Nancy Bell.

She stepped back from the window and walked through the door. An elderly man with reddened skin and a neat white beard approached her.

'There's an old building for sale in the window, can I have a key to look around it?' she asked.

The man gave her a look of surprise. 'The roof needs replacing and the window frames are rotten, are you sure you still want to see it?'

She beamed. 'Yes, I'm more than sure. It's just what I need for a private nursery when all the repairs and garden are done. I like the way the building is built. One side facing east and the other facing south. The walled garden will be ideal too. The children will be safe in there.'

The man sat back in the seat with his finger and thumb against his chin as she swept out of the room.

Mildred's mind was buzzing with ideas as she drove along. Sweeping her eyes around, she saw it further up the main road. She turned the car down a narrow opening and drove further on until she reached the house. Cutting the car engine, she stepped out and approached the property.

Pulling open the large, wrought iron gate, she stepped through grass and weeds up to her knees. Stood outside the rickety door, she turned the key in the lock. The door creaked and groaned as she pulled it open to step inside. Inside it smelled musty and cobwebs hung like black lace. She stepped into a high-ceilinged passageway, where doors were closed on either side. As she pushed open the one facing her, she entered a large spacious lounge with a stone-built, open fireplace.

She gazed around as she moved further inside. The plaster had come away, but the rooms were spacious. The kitchen will need to be updated, she thought as she turned back and climbed upstairs. There were three bedrooms and a large bathroom. The taps were brass but had blackened with age and the cast iron bath was worn down to the metal. She stood with her arms folded and a smile on her face. She would put an offer on the place and hopefully it would be accepted. She walked downstairs and headed for the front door.

Sweeping through the weeds and grass, she closed the gate and got into her car. She sat there for a while as she planned her future with Mary. She hoped that helping with the children and babies would somehow mend her when she opened the nursery. 'I'll give Nancy Bell a call when I get back,' she said to herself, as she turned on the engine and drove away.

'I'm offering ten-thousand pounds cash for the property,' she said, as she put her hand inside her handbag and brought out a wad of money. 'I may be out of the country for a while, but that should settle the deal.'

The man sat with his jaw dropped and pushed the money back towards her. 'You'll have to sign the contract which takes time. Then you pay, not before.'

Mildred shrugged her shoulders. 'I know, I just thought you could keep it in your safe. Anyhow, you sort it all out and contact me when I need to sign the contract.' She rose to her feet, held out her hand and winked her eye. 'I've got a score to settle with a little chancer over in Spain,' she whispered, leaving the man sat staring open-mouthed at her retreating back.

Pulling off her wig, she slumped down onto the sofa. 'I'm sick of having to wear this wig. In fact, I don't know why I do now; Jonah hasn't been seen for years. If I go to Spain, I'll not wear it, it's boiling over there.'

'There was a telephone call for you when you were out,' said Mary. 'Someone left a message to say they had gotten a cancellation and that they were on their way to Spain.'

Mildred's eyes glistened. 'Things might be moving faster than I thought. Let's hope that woman is as good as she says she is. I've got my passport, and my clothes all washed and ironed.'

'Already?' Mary asked. 'She won't have had time to sort anything yet.'

'Well, just in case she has. There's no time like the present.'

Chapter Forty-Nine

Mildred was stood with the telephone in her hand; her face beamed as she listened. 'You have already? You just got there a week ago.' She peered at her watch. 'There's a flight in an hour. I'll get to Heathrow and meet you at Malaga Airport. See you then.' She slammed the telephone down. 'Mary, that was Nancy Bell and she's positive she's found them, going by the descriptions I gave her. I'm meeting her in a few hours.'

Mary stood there with her mouth gaping as Mildred picked up her case and dashed towards the front door.

Jumping into her car, she zoomed away and headed for the airport. As she stood in the queue, she felt her heart racing. I need a drink, she thought as she stepped forward and placed her case onto the conveyor belt built into the check-in desk.

She sauntered about in the Duty Free section for a little while, and then headed towards a bar where she ordered herself a large vodka.

Eventually it was time to board.

She sat with her fingers clenched as the plane took off, but soon relaxed once she had a few more vodkas. Her eyes felt heavy and she fell asleep. Someone nudged her and she blinked. She turned her head and gazed out of the window to see that the plane was descending, and then it came to a shuddering halt.

The plane doors were opened, the sun shone bright in the clear blue sky. She covered her eyes with her hand as she walked down the steps.

With her heart drumming in her chest, she dashed across the runway and stood in the queue for the passport check. Following the crowd, she breezed into the arrivals area and stood waiting beside the carousel. People were gathered around, peering for their luggage as the carousel whizzed around.

Seeing her case, she leant over, swept it up and then hurried towards the doors. In the other lounge, Nancy Bell was stood wearing a checked shirt and white slacks. Mildred headed towards her beaming from ear to ear. 'Nancy, good to see you again.'

Nancy grabbed her case. 'Good to see you also. There's taxi's every few minutes. It won't take long to reach where I'm staying; I've found a tavern not far from here.'

They stepped out into the bright sunshine to see coaches and taxis stood idle. Drivers were stood around chatting while others held up notices for various destinations. They headed towards the first taxi.

'I've discovered that the woman who you want found is living in Fungarola. I've made enquiries and watched her for the last week and she looks positively fed up – if it's the same woman. When we get in I'll show you her photograph. From what I've gathered, it seems she was paid by someone called Kelvin Badialli to take the child abroad.'

The taxi stopped outside a small white-painted tavern. Mildred stepped out first to see an array of flowers clinging to the wooden trellis on either side of a plain wooden door. Shutters and blinds were closed at the windows. She stood listening to the music that was coming from somewhere in the distance while the sun penetrated her skin, as she waited for Nancy who was struggling to get out of the taxi.

Stepping into the cool tavern, Mildred swept her eyes around. It was basic but clean, just the way it should be. Nancy pointed towards an open doorway and said it was her room.

She stepped inside the small bedroom. A large tapestry took up the wall next to the bed and a floral bedcover draped to the floor from the sides of it. Pine furniture complemented the room. Placing her case on the bed, she stepped out of the room to see Nancy sat at a table with photographs in front of her.

She lowered herself down on a chair and studied them. Jerking her head up and raising her eyes at Nancy, her face beamed. 'That's her alright. What have you found out?'

'First of all, I nearly got myself killed in the process. Secondly, I'll never do again what I did. After my initial investigation I followed her to a café and got talking to her. I told her I was thinking of buying a place out there. She took me to meet someone. From your description I had a hunch this was Badialli.'

Nancy drew in a sharp breath. 'We walked up to him and the man's smile faded when he saw Jean. She told him I was interested in buying property, then she began saying that she was fed up and wanted to go back home. The man got up, pulled her aside with his eyes screwed up. I overheard him say she had the chance of a lifetime with the substantial money he gave her.'

'So what did she do?' asked Mildred, her eyes alight.

'She began raising her voice. She seemed to forget that I was there and so did he, because they began arguing. I heard her mention Mary and her son Dean and that she felt terrible for what she had done.'

'So what happened then?'

'He reminded her she was there as an illegal and that she would get locked up. He would deny everything. She swung round and we went to a pub called Izzy's bar. She ordered drinks and then leant over the bar whispering to Izzy that she had warned Badialli she was going to tell the police that he had paid her to abduct Mary's child. She didn't think I could hear, but I did.'

Mildred gave her a sharp searching look.

'She said she had to get back to England, but didn't have a passport. Then Izzy said she would help her to get away. She could get a day passport from Fuengerola police station, but she had to weep and wail and say she had lost hers. That it was urgent, her mother was dying.'

'So what did she do?'

'She said she would take a chance. But, Izzy got cold feet. She said if Kelvin Badialli knew she was helping her he would think nothing about torching her bar. So, I went with her to the passport office. As we arrived, a big and blonde man stepped out of a car and advanced towards us.'

Mildred drew her widened eyes away and picked up a photograph of Jonah. 'Was that him?' she asked.

'Yes, he had cunning eyes. Little did he know that he was soon to lose that cunning look,' Nancy said.

'What do you mean?' gasped Mildred, her jaw dropped.

'I'll tell you in a minute – be patient.'

'I can't be – go on, quick the suspense is killing me,' Mildred said.

'He peered at Jean's luggage when Badialli stepped out the car, sliced his finger along his throat in a menacing manner. Jean gasped and ran into the office but knew she would be arrested if she said anything. We walked out the office after she got the passport, hoping they had gone as we were ages. I watched the car doors flung open and the two men charged towards us like raging bulls.'

'Ooh this is so exciting, I wish I had been there to see it,' gasped Mildred.

'Thanks. I was terrified,' snapped Nancy. 'We were bundled into a car and taken somewhere remote.'

Mildred clutched Nancy's arm. 'I hope they didn't hurt you?'

'No, they weren't interested in me, but a gun was pointed at me all the same, then at Jean as she was pushed roughly into a house.'

'You must have been terrified, so how did you get away?' Mildred asked with eyes unblinking.

'Jonah's removed the gun away when Badialli lifted his leg and kicked her hard in the stomach. She folded over, moaning when the old man's face contorted. He gripped a hand to his chest and crumbled to the floor. Jonah fell to his knees to help him.'

'I didn't expect that,' said Mildred wringing her hands.

'Neither did I. Jean shot up and ran from the room. Jonah was bent over the old man when he turned his head and attempted to stand up, but she squirted a substance at him. He fell to the floor writhing, holding his hands to his face and howling. Jean was manic and her small eyes were bulging as she screeched that it was sulphuric acid and, that he wouldn't be strutting about like a cock hen anymore.'

'I know it's horrible to say, but I wish I had been there to witness that, after what he's dished out to other people. Karma got him in the end eh!' she said with eyes cold as steel.

'I ran out of the house yelling,' said Nancy. A couple of men were cycling by. They got off their bikes and ran into house. Jonah was screaming with the flesh on his face melting. It was horrendous. One man rushed to kitchen. He strode out with a bowl of water and poured it over Jonah. The other knelt down beside Badialli. He pressed his fingers into his neck, but shook his head and stood up with a grave face. I telephoned for the police and a doctor.'

'So did all this just happen a few days ago?' asked Mildred with a defeated look on her face.

'Yes,' replied Nancy. 'The police arrived and also a doctor. Jonah was taken to hospital and is still there – he's very ill and will be left with life-changing injuries if he survives.'

'Huh, she murmured. 'What happened to Jean?'

'She's seems to have had a breakdown. When she improves, she will be brought back to Britain to face the music.'

Chapter Fifty

B ending over to pick up the letters that had dropped through the letter box, Mildred lowered her head to read them. 'Mary, there's a letter here for you,' she said, her eyes shining. 'It's from Spain, this is what you have pined for and now it's coming true – Dean will be coming home. Nancy Bell was worth her weight in gold, I'll always recommend her if anyone needs a private detective.'

Mary's face was solemn.

What on earth is wrong with her now? Thought Mildred, as Mary's false eye stared wide and glassy at her.

Mary jumped up to peer at her reflection. The face that peered back was a caricature of the face she once had. Her eyebrows had lowered and her shoulders were drooped. 'He won't want anything to do with me. Look at the state of my face,' she wailed. 'I look so ugly now.'

Mildred sighed heavily. I don't know how I would feel in that situation but I'm not letting her get me down. Especially today, I'm signing the contract, and can't wait to see the old building transformed, thought Mildred. She clutched her hands around Mary's arms. 'Now listen, just be glad to see him. You thought you would never clap eyes on him ever again, so lighten up,' she said as she moved away.

'It's from Jonty. He is coming back into this country on some business and wants to introduce us to his new partner. He met him in Ireland. I always suspected Jonty would swing both ways. Isn't it funny how life turns out? I would never have had this opportunity if it hadn't been for his mum and my granny's inheritance. Hilly always appreciated what I did, making her last years the happiest she had. I often think of her, how at the start I was terrified of her, and how we became so close. I never thought she would have left me anything, never mind the amount she gave me,' she said, shaking her head.

'You are the best thing to come into my life. What would have happened to me after I came out of hospital and had the breakdown? I would have been put in a mental hospital. You took me under your wing and looked after me here,' said Mary.

Mildred laid a hand on her arm. 'Oh shut up. Your Sam had to go back to Germany. And your mother . . . well what can I say about her eh?'

Mary sighed heavily. 'I know. She never came, even though she knew I was dying. Well they say a leopard never changes its spots.'

A man was stood outside the front door. Lifting his hand, he rapped the door knocker, which interrupted their thoughts. Mildred headed to the door and as she pulled it open, D.C. Ollie Price was stood standing smiling at her. He stepped over the threshold, brushed his fingers through his sleek-backed hair and straightened his tie as he glanced in the mirror and frowned at his sallow face and dark-ringed eyes. 'I've come to inform you that Kevin Jones and Jean Carter will be getting extradited from Spain in the next few days. Jean will be taken to a sanatorium where she will be looked after.'

'Huh, looked after, after what she did,' said Mildred.

'It'll be Holloway when she's better. Jones's life of crime has come to an end too. He is blind and will need care for the rest of his days. As you know, Dean is still abroad at the moment and with foster parents. His father can't look after him due to his disability. They have contacted social services and someone from that department will bring him for a visit,'

'Visit?' snapped Mary. 'What are you talking about? I am his mother and I'll decide what happens, never mind them.'

'Yes, but you had a bad drug problem the last time you had anything to do with Dean, and all of them knew it. That doesn't look good for you.'

'I did, but that was three years ago. A lot of things have changed since then. I'm clean now, thanks to Mildred,' Mary said.

The D.C. nodded and smiled at Mildred. 'Yes, I believe you have,' he remarked.

Mildred's lips twitched. She was pleased to know that her friend Polly would now be able to walk around freely without him looming over her like a vulture, demanding his pound of flesh.

She blinked her eyes and put all thoughts of Jonah out of her mind as the man spoke to Mary. 'I'll be back tomorrow to tell you what the arrangements will be for a meeting with Dean,' he said as he rose to his feet. Mildred walked to the front door with him.

As she returned to the room, Mary was sat with solemn expression still on her face. 'I'm not happy about arrangements for a visit.'

'Look, I have to meet the solicitor for the contract signing. This place is too small for my nursery and I need to get that building completed as soon as possible before Christmas. We will talk about this later,' Mildred said, peering at her watch.

Chapter Fifty-One

Somehow, Mildred had a feeling that Mary's child would not adjust so easily. He was used to the culture of Spain. He would want to be with Mario – his father and Badialli, his grandfather. He was a baby when he was taken from Mary and now he was being thrust at a strange woman with a huge glass eye. Mildred sighed, pondering how she would be able to cope with Mary if everything backfired. She was bad enough now, if fact she was wondering if Mary's mental health was in decline.

Mildred caught her in her bedroom, going through her wardrobe. When she swung around, she was wearing the gold chain and locket that was given to her by her father, Joseph Riley. Mildred decided that in future she would hide it if she wasn't wearing it. It was her lucky omen and she would wear it when her photograph would be in the newspaper, when she advertised the opening of her private nursery.

I hope the house is restored shortly. I'll have to go over later today and see what's going on, she thought, when she gazed out of the window to see a car being driven up the drive. 'Mary, they're here,' she shouted as she rushed out of the bedroom and flew downstairs, to see Mary stood white-faced. 'Keep calm, take deep breaths,' she said as she hooked her arm around her shoulder and pulled her towards the window.

A sombre-faced woman dressed all in black from her hat to her shoes stepped out of the car. An equally sombre man with a trilby hat and overcoat got out of the car too. Then an olive-skinned, slim child stepped out and stood with a sullen look on his face as he swept his dark eyes around. Scowling at the woman, he turned and ran away up the gravelled path where he fell heavily, kicking and screaming.

Mildred stepped back from the window. Mary shrugged Mildred's arm away and rushed to the front entrance. She stood in the doorway with her hands clasped to her face watching the scene. He's too rough with that child, thought Mildred as he hauled the child up by the arm.

The child's face was creased and tears were streaming down his cheeks when he lifted his other arm and pointed his finger towards Mary. He lowered his head towards the child's ear. The child's tearful face turned to peer at Mary. His eyes widened with fear and his face twisted and he cast a look of revolt as he tugged at the man's arm, shaking his head.

The woman snatched him with a look of scorn on her face as she dragged him towards the house. His little face was soaked with tears and his expression twisted as he lifted his leg and kicked her shin. She glared at Dean. 'I'm sorry so sorry about this,' she said, facing Mary.

By now Dean was hysterical. 'I want to go home. I miss my daddy, why have I been brought here?' he wailed.

The woman hissed. 'Be quiet child, little boys shall be seen and not heard.' Mary glared at the woman as she lowered herself down to console her son, but he turned his face away and screeched.

This is going horribly wrong, thought Mildred as Dean was dragged into the house by the couple. The woman lowered herself down on the sofa while the man tussled with the boy. She turned her head and frowned. 'He is a ward of court. The outcome will be up to them,' she said, giving Mary a condescending and lingering look. 'You do understand what I am talking about, don't you? Because it is only through Miss McDine being well known with the social services that today's meeting has taken place here.'

'I might look ugly, but I am not a fool. You don't have to patronize me lady,' Mary said. The woman's eyebrows rose as she turned her head away and stuck her pointed nose in the air.

The atmosphere was tense and Dean was still snivelling and crying when Mildred held out her hand. 'Do you want to come with me and have some lemonade and chocolate cake?'

Dean stopped crying. He raised his tearful face at Mildred which made her want to wrap her arms around him and cuddle him tight. The woman's sharp manner reminded her of the matron in the mother and baby home, and no kid should have to deal with that.

Clenching her teeth, she imagined herself taking her hand right back and whacking the high and mighty look off that hatchet faced harridan. But then she reluctantly agreed and it made Mildred's anger for her melt away. Well, almost. She still wouldn't mind giving her a slap or ten.

'Well alright... Anything to calm him down, I suppose,' the woman said.

Mildred beckoned him to follow her. He ran towards her and clutched her outstretched hand. As she did, she glanced over her shoulder. Mary's face was rigid and the hardened look she cast towards her made the hairs on Mildred's arms rise. God, what the hell's wrong with her? Mildred thought as she turned her attention back to the child.

Dean raised his head. 'I wish I could stay with you. I don't like that man and woman,' he whispered. 'I miss my daddy too,' he said as he began crying again, with deep shuddering sobs.

Mildred put a comforting arm around his shoulder. She knew what it was like to feel sad after her grandmother died, but she was much older than Dean back then, and she wasn't sure if that was better or worse. 'Was your daddy nice and kind to you?' His little face was creased when he nodded his head. She handed him a soft toy to cuddle.

Dean stroked the toy then looked up at her. 'Who is the woman with the big staring eye?'

Mildred's lips compressed. 'She's a nice lady really, she was very pretty one time, but she was in an accident and now she looks the way she does,' she said, lying through her teeth. Smiling at the child, she thought, your thug of a father caused this and now he's brain damaged and your mother is scarred for life. What a mess the whole thing was.

Sighing heavily, she wondered what his future held, because if he was too scared of his mother and didn't want anything to do with her, what would happen then?

She couldn't apply to foster him as it would cause a rift between her and Mary. Already with his presence she could feel a void had formed between them. With her brow creased and face set, she took him into the kitchen for his lemonade and cake, while gently probing about his life in Spain, when a voice from the doorway made her jump.

'Dean will have to go now,' the woman said while raising her sharp eyes and casting Mildred a reproving look. 'Come along, you have been down here a long time.'

Dean scowled and stamped his feet, refusing to move. The woman stood with her arms on her hips. 'Do you want to go to the huff room, and spend the rest of the day alone?'

Dean looked under his eyelashes. 'No,' he replied, dropping his head to his chest.

'Well, stop creating a nuisance of yourself,' she said.

Mildred held the woman's gaze with a defiant lift of her chin. She was a hard-faced cow. It was no wonder Dean was unhappy. 'Is that the best way to treat children?' she snapped.

The woman looked her up and down. Curling her lip, she folded her arms beneath her flat chest. 'They have to know, we won't stand for bad behaviour,' she replied in a clipped manner.

'I wonder how you would behave if your life had been turned upside down,' she said.

The woman ignored the remark, grabbed Dean's hand and forced him out of the room towards the front door. She looked at her knees as she thanked Mildred, then turned abruptly around and snatched the child's arm, hauling him inside the car. Mildred stood in the doorway waving to the screwed up and reddened face that peered at her from the car back window.

'Well I never got a look in did I? You took charge as usual while I had to stay out of sight.' Mary said, as she approached from out of nowhere.

Mildred stopped in her tracks and lifting her arm, she pointed her finger at her. 'Now listen here, this isn't about you. Yes, it's terrible what happened to you, but Dean is a scared little boy and that bitch didn't help matters either, with her high and mighty attitude, so don't start on me Mary. I only tried to calm him down, that's all.'

Mary stepped towards her and thrust her face in hers, seeping her fingers through her hair with frustration. 'What is it with you? Everything you do just works out fine, but it doesn't for me does it?' she shouted at the top of her voice, while hot tears ran down her cheeks.

Mildred grabbed hold of her by the shoulders and pushed her towards the kitchen area. 'You better calm yourself down. I have a lot on my mind without you adding to it. I need this work completed on our new home and nursery, so that it's up and running as soon as the festive season is over.'

'Huh, you mean your new nursery, not mine,' she screeched, her eyes brimming with tears, face red with anger.

'Listen here, I'm in no mood for your frigging tantrums,' she snarled, as she stormed out of the room.

It's going to be a long day, thought Mildred as she stood in the passage with her fingers clenched and chest rising with anger, now beginning to regret having Mary living with her. But there had been nobody else for her, and since they had been so close, it seemed to be the only option.

Yanking the door open, she clashed it shut as she stormed towards her car. 'This was her own downfall,' she rasped as she drove towards the new building. 'Mary always blamed everyone but herself, well she's been warned.'

Cutting the car engine, she got out and stared intently at the completely-transformed structure that stood ahead of her. The roof had been stripped and now had red tiles, the rotten window frames were replaced and the front door was arched with bulls-eye glass in the centre. Just standing looking at her new home melted her harsh expression.

Entering the house, she swept her eyes around. The new plaster had dried and had been painted. The nursery was complete and the kitchen area was too. She ascended her living area and beamed. Now there was only the carpets and lighting to complete. The place looked as though they could be in by a few days.

She stood in the middle of the nursery. The worn floorboards had been replaced with varnished pine wood. She inhaled the scent of pine and fresh paint as she wrapped her arms around herself. Closing her eyes, she twirled around, feeling drunk with happiness. Clasping onto the windowsill, she steadied herself and blinked open her eyes. There was a lot to organise.

She picked the receiver out of the cradle and listened, there was a dialling tone. 'Wonderful, I can get organised now,' she said as she picked up the phone book and flicked through.

Glancing out of the window, she noticed a curtain twitch then saw it pulled aside. She smiled to see an elderly woman peering at her. She waved her hand and the curtain was quickly replaced. Locking up the house, she slid into her car, turned up the radio and sang along with the music as she drove back to her soon-to-be old home.

Mary was lying in front of the fire with a pitiful look on her face. Mildred breezed into the room. 'We're moving in a few days Mary. It'll be wonderful won't it?'

Mary looked up and gave a watery smile. 'I suppose so,' she said.

'Mary, you better snap out of this, I'm getting totally pissed off.'

'Do you blame me?' she shouted. 'After the way that paragon of virtue looked at me, as though I was a piece of shit under her shoe – and the look of disgust off Dean was too much to take,' she whimpered, her eyes brimming.

Mildred stepped towards her and slumped down on the sofa, just stopping herself from telling her that if she had looked after herself and him in the first place, then she wouldn't find herself in this gigantic mess. And more importantly, neither would Mildred.

Chapter Fifty-Two

Boxes of every size were stacked high in the passageway and every other space possible. Mildred was stood biting her lip as she waited for the removal men. Her hair was tied up in a headscarf and she wore a tabard. She kneeled onto the floor with a pen in her hand, writing on labels what each box contained.

A loud knock on the front door echoed along the passage and around the house. She pulled the door open and acknowledged a stocky man and a younger, beefy fellow. The men trooped inside. Lifting up the boxes, they stepped back and forth, and then skilfully handled the larger items of furniture through the front door. Pressing cash into the held out fleshy hand, Mildred faced them both. 'I'll meet you at the Beeches. You do know where it is?'

The man nodded as he stepped into his truck while swiping his brow.

'Mary, I need all hands on deck,' she shouted up the stairs. Mary's face appeared over the banister and she thudded down the stairs with her bottom lip jutting outwards. 'Never mind the petulant look, it's all hands on deck,' said Mildred, pointing towards the car.

Mary slunk towards it, slumped into the seat with her arms folded, and sat in silence, peering out of the window. Mildred ignored her, but as she drove the car she decided that after she had gotten the house and nursery put together, she would have to face telling Mary that she could no longer put up with her moods and that she would have to find a place of her own.

She pulled the car to a stop and headed towards the removal truck with the keys in her hand and didn't see the sullen look Mary cast behind her back.

'Will you help me to put everything in place?' asked Mildred. 'I'll pay you well, because I need to get this place up and running soon.'

The two men looked at each other and nodded. 'Of course dear, that's what you pay us for.' They lifted furniture and put it in place without a single break.

'I've still got a key for the old house, so I'll lock up and give this to the solicitor,' said Mildred. 'I'll not be long. When I get back, we'll go out and celebrate.' Clasping the removal man's hand she slipped a wad of money into his jacket and headed towards her car.

Mary stood at the window watching the vehicles drive away. She turned around and made her way downstairs to the nursery and swept her eyes around, wondering what she could do to stop the ball of fire in her chest that made her feel as though she was about to combust. Everything was neat and tidy. The books were placed on the shelves and chairs were stood next to the small wooden tables, while an assortment of toys had been put neatly into a large box.

In her mind's eye, she saw Dean sat smiling up at her and then running towards her as she walked inside the room, but remembering the look of disgust on his face, she screeched and gritted her teeth, while she headed for the shelves and began pulling the books out, scattering them onto the floor. Bending to pick some up, she tore pages out of them, then seeing the glitter and paints, she scattered the lot around the floor before kicking the chairs over.

Picking up the chairs one by one, she shrieked and screeched as they fell apart bouncing off the walls. Then the tables were turned over, but that wasn't enough, she kicked and threw them against the walls too. They lay broken. The paint on the walls was scuffed and indented with the force of Mary's fury. Toys were strewn around, scattered and broken everywhere.

Heaving and breathless with all the effort, she began laughing as she turned around to leave the room. 'Right, Miss Millie McDine, see what you think of that,' she rasped. 'I'll leave the door unlocked and pretend someone got in,' she said to herself as she swept upstairs cackling and laughing in a wild manner as she grabbed her bag and stumbled through the building, before standing inside the doorway with a menacing look on her face.

Clasping a hand to her face, her mouth dropped open. 'God, what have I done? What have I done?' she repeated, as she spun around to see what she had wrecked in her fury as she peered along the passage and through the open nursery door. The room had been demolished and was a shambles. Her face creased and her whole body shook.

Sobbing loudly, she ran out of the drive and along the road. Unable to see for tears, she bumped into a young man who was swaggering along the road. 'Hey, it can't be that bad can it,' he said, as he caught hold of her.

Pulling herself out of his grasp, she stood with her head lowered, pulling her hair over her false eye. 'Look, it's freezing out here, come into the pub with me and I'll buy you a drink, you're in right state,' he said, hooking an arm around her shaking shoulders.

They stepped into a smoky pub with a smell of stale beer in their nostrils. A festive song was heard from the juke box as the lad pushed open the door. He pointed to a seat near the stone-built, open fireplace where a welcome fire burned in the grate.

Mary's face was gaunt as she slumped down, avoiding the curious glances from the regulars sat all around her. Raising her head, she took a quick glance towards the bar and saw the young lad's reflection in the mirror. He was medium height, handsome in a rough kind of way, with long sideburns and a quiff. He turned around with the drinks in his hand and sauntered towards her with a wry smile on his face.

She pulled her hair over her eye and her cheek to cover the scars as he leaned over and put the drinks down on the table. Her lips pressed together to see him drop in the seat opposite with his eyebrows raised and quizzical look on his face. 'So, are you going to tell me what has upset you so much that you going tearing along the road and not looking where you're going?'

She shrugged her shoulders and with a shaking hand, she kept tugging her hair over the side of her face. 'I've done something bad,' she whispered.

He sat back in the seat with his arms folded. 'Like what?'

'My friend has just moved today and she is opening a private nursery. I've just trashed it in a fit of uncontrolled anger.'

Her frowned, holding her gaze as she raised her eye. 'What made you do something like that?' he asked.

She shrugged. 'I was jealous and angry. She has been a wonderful friend to me, seen me through thick and thin, and I've ruined everything,' she whimpered, as she sunk her head into her hands and began to weep.

He raised his head and gazed around to see they were being watched. 'Look, come with me. Everyone in this place is staring at you.'

He slid his chair back and she shot up, stumbling out of the place. He held his hand out and she clasped hold of it. 'I'm taking you to my place. It's a small cottage, and mother will be in bed. It's just around the next street.' Mary stopped in her tracks and shook her head. 'It's okay, we'll not be disturbed. You can start from the beginning, because it's obvious there's more to this,' he said as he pulled her towards him and began swaggering away.

Mary's tense face relaxed to see that his house was in darkness, as she followed him down a narrow path leading towards his front door. He took out a set of keys and unlocked the door. The small kitchen was warm and cosy, but was cluttered with units, chairs and a table. A small furry dog with chocolate brown eyes jumped up at her. She bent over to stroke it when he grabbed her arm and pulled her towards a closed door.

She stepped inside the door to see she was in his sweaty and stuffy bedroom. She looked at his eager face as he flung himself down on the bed, then watched him pat his hand on the bedcover while smirking. She moved slowly forward and he grabbed her, threw her down on the bed and covered her mouth with his.

But when he opened his eyes as he kissed her, he saw the glass eye peering lifelessly into his face. He stiffened and recoiled. Disentangling himself, he leapt up off the bed with his face twisted. 'This was a mistake, my mother might wake up,' he gasped, sweeping his fingers through his quiff.

She sat up and glowered at him. 'You look like you want to throw up. Well just think yourself lucky that you've never been attacked and left for dead like I was,' she yelled as she jumped off the bed.

He stood with his finger over his mouth. 'You'll wake mother up, shouting like that. You better get away,' he whispered, his eyes darting around nervously.

'Don't worry, I'm going. You were never interested as to why I was upset because you just wanted your leg over.' She swung around and strode out of the bedroom to face an old woman who was stood wearing a hairnet and a pink dressing gown.

'Boris, what have you been up to?' she croaked with eyes popping out her head as Mary stormed past her and flung the door open.

The cold air caught her breath as she stomped down the path. Worse still, it began to snow. Tears filled her eyes as the snow bleached down. She stepped along with hunched shoulders, wondering if Mildred had phoned for the police when she got back home. Snivelling, she peered around trying to remember where she had been.

She carried on with her toes nipping and hands frozen, all the while swiping hot tears from her cheeks. 'Best form of defence is attack,' she whispered to herself, as she eventually came across the large building. Sighing heavily, as she stepped into the drive, she was relieved there was no sign of a police car.

'Best form of defence is attack,' she repeated as she pulled open the door and stepped inside the house, sweeping her scared eyes around. The place was in total silence, only a faint light was visible beneath the nursery door. Forcing her legs to move, she tiptoed towards the door, lifted her hand and pushed it open.

Mildred was kneeling on the floor with her head in her hands, surrounded by the broken tables and chairs. The torn books, paint and glitter were scattered around the walls and floor. She lifted her head, her eyes brimming with tears.

Mary stood still with a look of horror on her face. 'What's happened here, who would want to ruin this lovely place?' she said stepping towards the paint-splattered walls, shaking her head with her jaw ajar.

'You tell me,' said Mildred, glaring up at her. 'When I got here the door was swinging open and you were nowhere to be seen. So, where have you been?'

'I just went out, you can't blame me for this.' she said, her voice shrill.

'Went out?' she repeated. 'You don't know the area.'

'Are you accusing me?' she yelled.

Mildred was too upset and furious to even argue. 'I'm ringing for the police,' she stated. 'I wish I hadn't told Jonty this new address now. I'm in no mood for company.'

'The police wont' be very happy to get called out, it's late,' said Mary, her face taut.

'It's not that late, I want them to check for fingerprints. The person responsible for this is going to wish they hadn't been born,' snarled Mildred.

Mary turned and ran upstairs. Even up there, she was sure that Mildred could hear her thudding heart.

Chapter Fifty-Three

The young constable dragged his foot up with a look of irritation, his skinny cheeks reddened as he tried to disengage his shoe from the glue spattered around the floor. Tables and chairs were still scattered, legs snapped off and lay where they had been flung. Torn books, broken toys and paint took up the rest of the space.

He peered around. 'You say the door was open when you got back?' he asked, his gaze meeting hers.

Mildred's face was sullen as she gave a nod of her head. 'Yes it was. Mary says she closed it on her way out – wherever that was,' she replied in a meaningful manner. 'I want fingerprints taken as soon as possible. I was supposed to have a photographer coming tomorrow. I was going to advertise the opening of this nursery in the Evening Standard. Now, thanks to some mindless bloody moron, it's going to be cancelled.'

The policeman's lips twitched. 'I'll get someone out tomorrow to check for fingerprints. In the meantime, I'll speak to the neighbours to see if they can shed some light on this.' His brow creased. 'It's strange, this is a quiet residential area and has not been known for a break-ins over the years.' Turning around, he glanced at Mary. She dropped her eyes and turned her head away.

Mildred shot a glance towards Mary as she walked to the front door with the policeman. Bracing herself, she turned around and stepped back inside the nursery.

Mary gave her a weak smile. 'You don't suspect me, do you?'

'What makes you say that?' snapped Mildred.

'I'm sensing a chilly atmosphere,' she remarked.

Mildred swung around with a thunderous look, brushing her hand across her face. 'Just leave me alone Mary,' she muttered.

Mary lifted her chin, stormed from the room and stomped up to the living quarters. Mildred sat down on the only chair that hadn't been obliterated. No matter what Mary said, the misgiving feeling loomed large like a slithering snake, lurking unseen. Her mind recalled the incident where her best dress was burned with the iron. Mary couldn't understand how it had happened as she put the dial on low. Funny how her eyes seemed to gleam, contradicting the solemn expression she had cast.

Then there was the time when the bath water had overflowed too. Luckily the ceiling didn't come down. Mary had apologised and said she had forgotten to turn the tap off.

Inhaling a deep shuddering breath, Mildred stood to her feet and pulled the blinds closed. She turned off the lights and climbed upstairs. She'll reap what she's sown if it was her, vowed Mildred, as she turned towards her bedroom.

'My goodness Millie, you have done well for yourself. This place is fantastic,' announced Jonty in his usual blasé manner, as he stepped inside the house. Following behind him was a pleasant looking chap with an open face. 'This is Archie – Archie let me introduce my very good friend Millie.'

She forced her face into a smile as she shook his hand. Jonty stood open-mouthed, gazing around. 'How many rooms are there?'

'Twelve, I've had an extension built, I wanted to keep this part private naturally.'

Jonty noticed that she had matured. Once she was attractive, now she was stunningly beautiful.

'Follow me, I will show you your room, and then we have lots to talk about,' Mildred said.

The two men followed her up the winding stairs that were covered in ivy and red berries, with the occasional gold bow. The place had a cosy feel. Mildred loved Christmas and wanted to make the place feel special. As they reached the top and headed into the sitting room, Mildred beckoned them to sit beside the roaring fire as she stepped over to the sideboard and held a decanter up. 'Drink?' she asked, and as she filled the glasses she became aware that there had been no sign of Mary.

She was in no mood for silences today. She wanted to relax and enjoy what time her and Jonty had together. Since they had last seen each other, there was so much to tell him. Especially about the nursery being trashed and whom she suspected.

'So, will you be going to the trial of Jonah and Jean then?' he asked, after she had told him what had happened in Spain.

'Well, they would have been charging Jean for abducting the child, but she's had a breakdown, and if the grandfather had lived, then he would have been jailed too. Jonah is blind with life changing disability; people have said he is a broken man. I really don't know or care. Can you remember one time I was terrified that he would catch up with me and get me back for what I did to him,' she said, then paused as if she was staring death in the eye.

'What's wrong? He can't get you now.'

She got to her feet and began pacing the floor. 'It's not that. It's what happened in the nursery two days ago. The place had just been renovated, I went to hand a key to the solicitor's and left Mary alone. When I got back, the front door was open and the whole nursery was trashed. I'll take you down and show you.'

They headed down the stairs and went inside the nursery. The two men stood wide-eyed, surveying the damage. 'Have you rang the police?' asked Jonty.

Mildred lowered her voice. 'Of course I have, I'm waiting for the fingerprint results. But, I can't help suspecting Mary.'

'Surely not, after you've gone above and beyond for her,' he said, as Mary stepped inside the room.

The silence was deafening. Mary swept her eye around at them Mildred forced a broad smile face and introduced her to the men. 'I've just been telling Jonty and Archie what happened in the nursery,' she said.

Mary's pale face flushed bright red as she dropped her gaze, grimaced and said, 'I know, it's awful isn't it? I can't get over what has happened.' Jonty's eyes screwed up as he gave her a long-lingering look. 'Anyway, I've got a terrible headache, so I'm going back to bed,' Mary said.

Once the door was closed, Jonty's face was stern. He turned his face to his friend. 'Well, do you think she looks guilty?' Archie's brow creased as he sat rubbing his forefinger over his chin. 'Come on,' he goaded. 'You're supposed to be able to read body language, it's your job.'

'Really?' Mildred's eyes shone with enthusiasm.

'From what I saw, she certainly seemed troubled. I know she only has one eye, but she averted that and her stature was rigid.'

Mildred's eyes clouded over as her eyebrows lowered. 'I knew it. How could she do that to me? But then again, I know she's screwed up with loads of issues.'

'Hey, Mildred, there's issues and issues. But why would she be so vindictive towards you if you have been so caring?' snapped Jonty, his eyes burning with anger.

Mildred shook her head and filled up their glasses. Swiftly knocking back hers, she filled it up again. 'Do you think she's jealous or something?'

'I don't know, but she must be pretty mixed up in the head to trash the place. What about the police? What have they said?' Archie asked.

'They're going to ask the neighbours if they saw anything, but I've not heard anything from them yet.'

'Well, why don't you go and ask them then? They won't bite,' Jonty said.

'I will when you and Archie leave,' she said in a flat tone. The jolly atmosphere was now sombre. 'This place is getting closed over the Christmas period and I'm going to Aldershot to stay with mother for a little while. I don't want Mary to stay with me, now that I suspect her,' Mildred said.

Archie got up and placed his hand on her arm. 'I may not be totally accurate. Don't go destroying your friendship through what I said. There is still a chance that she could be innocent.'

But Mildred was convinced that her intuition had been right. By now her eyes were glazed as she tipped her head back and emptied the glass. Standing to her feet, she swayed as she went towards the telephone. 'I'm ringing for these results from the fingerprint test, I've had enough waiting,' she snapped, when she halted in her tracks.

A policeman was stood with his hand clasped around the door knocker. He lifted it back once more, sending the sound of metal echoing throughout the cold night air. He peered through the bulls-eye glass panel, stamping the snow off his shoes at the same time.

Mildred held onto the handrail as she stepped down the stairs, wondering who it could be that was hammering on the door. She pulled the door aside and smiled broadly to see the young policeman. 'I was just going to ring the police station to see if the fingerprint results were ready,' she said, pressing her palm against the wall to steady herself.

She stood aside and swayed as she held her hand out to beckon him in. She closed the door, wishing now that she hadn't drunk so much, she needed a clear head. But, she was glassy-eyed as she beamed at the young policeman. 'Follow me,' she said as she stumbled up the stairs. 'I've had a bit to drink,' she said in a silly manner as he followed her up with his helmet tucked beneath his arm. He stepped inside the room and acknowledged the two men sat glassy- eyed too.

Mildred slumped down with her legs splayed out. 'So, what's the result from the fingerprints?' she asked.

'Whoever did this must have worn gloves, forensics found nothing I'm afraid,' he said.

Mildred remembered seeing a pair of rubber gloves, but thought nothing of it at the time. She thought that maybe one of the cleaners had left them behind. 'Well, what about the neighbours? Did anyone see anything suspicious?'

'We've asked everyone and they said they saw no one lurking around. It was dark, but you do have one nosy neighbour over the road. She said she saw a car leave the drive. Soon after that, the silhouette of a thin girl was seen behind the blinds in the front room. She seemed to be leaping about, throwing her arms in the air and kicking her legs, as though she was dancing. Then, shortly after that, the security light lit up as a small, skinny girl walked out of the lit-up passageway. She stepped outside and was wearing a red jumper and pair of jeans. She said she had a cream coat draped around her shoulders too. She left the door ajar and hurried away into the shadows.'

Mildred scowled. 'So did she notice anyone else step inside then?'

'She said she kept watching as she was concerned, but there was no one else. She saw a car pull into the drive, a young woman got out. She rushed towards the door and slammed it closed.'

'That was me,' Mildred rasped. 'Looks like you were right Archie, the offender is in her bedroom. You can go and ask her why she left the door ajar when the nursery was trashed and see what she has to say.'

'I would prefer it if you asked her to come here please,' replied the policeman.

Mildred's face was contorted with anger as she stood up and stumbled through to Mary's bedroom. 'Get up,' she barked. 'Headache or not, there's a policeman in the sitting room and he wants to ask you a few questions.'

The colour left Mary's face. 'I'm too ill,' she whimpered.'

Mildred lowered herself over her and yanked the clothes back. 'You will see him. There's been a witness who saw the silhouette of the person who trashed my nursery. There were only two people here that night, one of them was me and the other was you. She said she saw me leave in my car, and then behind the blinds she saw what she thought was a thin girl dancing – but she wasn't dancing, was she Mary? She was trashing the place.'

'I don't know,' she squeaked.

'I think you do lady,' she shouted, yanking the bed clothes back. 'Stop pissing about and get up now. You can explain yourself, he's sitting waiting and not going anywhere until you do.'

Mary's white face tinged with green as she slipped her legs over the bed and raised fearful eyes. Mildred simply stood with her arms folded.

Mary's shoulders were hunched and she was visibly shaking as she stepped inside the room with her head lowered.

'I wish to ask you a few questions about the night the nursery was damaged,' said the policeman, as Jonty and Archie got up and walked unsteadily out of the room. 'Please take a seat, you look fit to drop.'

Mary's face crumpled as she stepped towards a chair and sat on the edge of it, wringing her hands together. The policeman pulled out his notebook and removed a thick band from around it. 'There were two of you in the house at the time. Mildred left to go to the solicitors. Shortly afterwards, the silhouette of thin girl was seen to be dancing in the front room. That girl was you, wasn't it Mary?'

'No, it was not,' she cried.

'Then who was it, if there were only two of you?' he persisted.

'I don't know,' she squeaked.

'Now come on, don't insult my intelligence. You see, we have a witness who saw a young girl stood in the doorway with the light behind her. The woman has described what the person was wearing and what she looked like,' the policeman said, as he lowered his head and read his notes. 'The woman described a small, thin girl with fair hair. She also stated the colour and style of the coat that she had draped over her shoulders. So, do you mind if I go and check your wardrobe?'

'Yes, I do.' She snapped.

'What colour was it and what style?' asked Mildred.

'Cream with fur attached.'

'Same as yours Mary. What a coincidence, eh? Tell the man the truth because we all know it was you that left the door ajar and it was you who trashed my nursery, wasn't it?' Mildred yelled as she thrust her face into Mary's.

Mary gasped while her mind raced. Where will I go and where will I live if Mildred chucks me out? I've got no money or anything, she thought as her heart raced too. 'It wasn't me,' she screeched as she shot up and before anyone could stop her, flew down the stairs to bump into Jonty in the passageway. He reached for her as she pulled herself away. Before she could get out of the door, he dragged her back screeching and wailing. Mildred turned her face away, unable to look at her.

The policeman folded his notebook, placed it back inside his pocket and rose to his feet. 'Do you want to press charges for the broken furniture and everything else?'

Mildred sat with a dejected look on her face, her hands resting on her knees. 'The books can be replaced and the furniture too, but my broken heart won't mend. So no, pressing charges won't accomplish anything, please just leave.'

The young man's eyes met hers, now filling with tears. He cleared his throat, got to his feet and headed for the door. 'I'll see myself out. I wish you all a goodnight, and a very happy Christmas too,' he said in an undertone.

All the happiness was drained from the room, and was locked out eternally as the door was clicked shut.

Mildred's eyes were cold as ice as she lifted her arm and pointed her forefinger at Mary. 'Get your things together,' she snarled through her teeth. 'I never want to set eyes on you ever again. I bent backwards for you, took you under my wing when you were broken, paid a fortune to find your child, and you did this to me. Shame on you Mary Kelly, never darken my door again.'

Mary's stood speechless with her mouth gaping, before she ran out of the room and into her bedroom.

Mildred lowered her head into her hands to weep bitter tears. Jonty and Archie tried to cheer her but it was no good, she was inconsolable. The two men stood with faces set and sullen. Jonty went out of the room and headed for Mary's where he found her lying on the bed, also weeping. He slumped down onto the bed. 'You better collect your belongings. It's no good lying weeping and wailing, you've no one to blame but yourself. Millie has finished with you Mary. You have broken her heart; she doted on you, so why did you do it?'

Mary raised a reddened face. 'I was eaten up with jealousy when I saw how Dean looked at her. When he looked at me, he recoiled because I'm ugly with these facial injuries,' she screeched. 'How do you think that made me feel? My own son thinking I'm ugly,' she gulped, sobbing loudly.

Jonty peered at her and his annoyance towards her subsided as he realised that she was so broken. It was help she needed more than anything. He rose off the bed and went back to Mildred. 'Can't you give her a second chance? She's heartbroken, because her son found her repulsive and because he took to you, her jealousy boiled over.'

Mildred raised her hand in a dismissive manner with a look of affront on her face. 'I'm not interested Jonty. I'm too shocked and hurt, I want her gone.'

'But she has nowhere to live,' he said.

'That's her luck out. She had everything; I gave her a home, a job and anything she wanted, anything to make her feel better.'

'But you don't realise that it made her feel so inadequate. The girl is damaged, if you put her on the streets, she will just starve and die. Would you like that on your conscience?' Jonty asked.

Mildred stormed across to the drinks cabinet and poured another drink for them both. Archie left them alone to have a lie down. Drinking in the afternoon was never a good thing for him. Eventually, Mildred calmed down. 'I've thought things over and you're right, she wouldn't last two minutes on the street. It will be Christmas day in a week's time, so I'll contact the estate agents and get her a place to rent.'

Jonty's grave eyes met hers and he sighed. 'Well, that's good of you. Let's hope she manages to think over where she has gone wrong and vow to make something of her life.'

'That's entirely up to her Jonty. What plans have you got?' she asked.

'We're leaving in the morning. Archie has family in Dublin who he needs to visit.'

'Will you do me a favour first?' she asked, picking up her bag.

'Yes. Anything.'

'I'll write a cheque out to the estate agents. Take Mary there and drop her off with the cheque. There's enough for her to rent a place for a few months. After that – well it's up to her, she's no longer any concern of mine.' Seeing Jonty's wide-eyed, strained look, she held her hand up, smiled thinly and changed the subject. 'Jonty, I've never shown you the photographs in this locket that I wear around my neck, do you want to see them?' she asked

Jonty's eyebrows shot up. 'Yes, I would, who is it?'

Mildred lifted her arms back and untied the clasp in the chain. On opening the locket, she pointed her finger. 'That's Sadie when she was a teenage girl and opposite is my father Joseph Riley, the wondering gypsy boy. When my photo goes in the paper advertising the nursery, I wonder if he sees it and realises it's me. I would love to meet him. And the lad I fell in love with many years ago. He was a traveller too, he worked on the waltzer and visited many places. I've never forgotten him. We were torn apart when he had to leave. My grandmother was too ill and I had to stay with her. I wonder where my father is and also Danny, it would make my life complete if they were to come back into it,' she said.

'Well, that's easy. When you advertise the nursery, mention your past and how much you have come along since. You can only try,' Jonty said.

Mildred squeezed his hand. 'Go and tell her what we've discussed, but tell her to keep out of my way in the meantime.'

Jonty and Archie carried their cases to the car. Mary stood with her face downcast as she stood with her luggage. The two men leaned towards Mildred and gave her a hug before they got inside the car. Mary pulled the passenger door open, stood for a moment and cast Mildred a sorrowful look.

Mildred's lips pressed together. She swung around and went back inside the house, a sinking feeling threatened to consume her. Since she had reactive depression all those years ago, it would creep over her like a black cloak and consume her. Pushing all thoughts of Mary from her mind, she climbed upstairs and filled the bath. Sinking back, she closed her eyes and organised what she needed for the nursery. There was no time to dwell on pain-burdened hearts.

Driving into town, she accomplished what she set out to do in a matter of hours. She had only just got back home when a van pulled into the drive and man got out with a ladder and paint pots. He had just finished his job when a furniture van drove into the drive.

Sadie arrived in her car and between them they put the nursery back as it was. Books were back on the shelves, toys were replaced and broken furniture restored. A car drove into the drive and the photographer stepped out. Mildred stood beaming as the bulbs flashed.

'I'll send these straight to be printed with your advertisement and it will be in the evening edition,' he told her as he picked up his equipment and headed for the door.

The tumultuous chimes from the grandfather clock struck at six p.m. Mildred dashed to the door and hurried towards the local shop. With the paper tucked under her arm, she strode back home and laid it on the table. She leaned over, scrutinising the writing and liking what she read. The photo was good too. Now all she needed was the telephone to begin ringing and letters to start dropping through the door.

'I think it's time you had a night out Mildred,' said Sadie, breezing into the room and peering at the advert too. 'Forget all this and let your hair down for a day or two. We haven't seen Roxy or Crystal and Pandora for ages.'

Mildred's stern face melted into a broad smile. 'Yes, give them all a call and we'll meet them at the Ruby. It's been opened again under new management.'

The ringing sound of the telephone stopped her in her tracks on her way to her bedroom. She picked it up. 'Yes, that's me,' she answered with her eyes widening. 'Is this some kind of a joke?' she snapped, listening to the person on the other end. Her legs began to shake and she dropped the telephone and flopped down onto the nearest seat.

Sadie grabbed the phone and stood listening. 'Joseph! Is that really you? Oh my God, you don't know how much this means to Mildred,' she gushed. Then, covering the mouthpiece with her hand, she whispered hoarsely. 'Do you want to meet him? He says it's only a half hours drive away.'

Mildred could only nod her head and sit wide-eyed.

Sadie put the phone down and stood with her hands over her face. 'You're going to meet your father tomorrow after all this time? How do you feel?'

'Stunned,' replied Mildred.

'Well, get the champagne glasses out. This calls for a celebration,' she said, crossing the room. Putting a record on the radiogram she hummed a tune as she popped the cork and filled two glasses with champagne. Mildred was still sat with a blank expression, Sadie nudged her. 'Here get this down you, neck. Health, wealth and happiness Mildred,' she chuckled.

Mildred sipped her drink while her heart thudded in her chest. How will it be, she wondered, when she meets her father? Would she feel affection or would there be nothing? She gulped her drink back and filled another one. Her hand was clammy as she wrapped it around the stem.

Further down the country, a handsome young man also had clammy hands and a thudding heart. He was sat in his trailer unaware of the loud music, the carrousels whizzing around and the crowds stepping by his window. He was sat transfixed as he gazed at the photograph of Mildred with her sparkling brown eyes and crazy wild hair. She had always been in his heart and mind. He still loved her after all these years but thought she was lost from him forever.

Would she still be single or would there be someone else loving her like he did, like he used to? With his fingers of his left hand crossed, he leaned over the table, opened a notepad and began to write her a letter.

Lightning Source UK Ltd.
Milton Keynes UK
UKHW01f0634010618
323576UK00002B/88/P